Margaret Cavendish Duchess of Newcastle

The life of William Cavendish

Duke of Newcastle to which is added the true relation of my birth. Second Edition

Margaret Cavendish Duchess of Newcastle

The life of William Cavendish
Duke of Newcastle to which is added the true relation of my birth. Second Edition

ISBN/EAN: 9783744730426

Printed in Europe, USA, Canada, Australia, Japan

Cover: Foto ©Raphael Reischuk / pixelio.de

More available books at **www.hansebooks.com**

MEMOIRS OF

WILLIAM CAVENDISH

DUKE OF NEWCASTLE

AND MARGARET HIS WIFE

DUKE OF NEWCASTLE.

THE LIFE OF
WILLIAM CAVENDISH
DUKE OF NEWCASTLE

TO WHICH IS ADDED THE TRUE RELATION OF MY
BIRTH BREEDING AND LIFE

By

MARGARET, DUCHESS OF NEWCASTLE

Edited by C. H. FIRTH, M.A

Regius Professor of Modern History in the University of Oxford

SECOND EDITION, REVISED, WITH ADDITIONAL NOTES

With Twelve Appendices and an Index

LONDON
GEORGE ROUTLEDGE & SONS LIMITED
NEW YORK: E. P. DUTTON & CO

CONTENTS

EDITOR'S PREFACE

THE first edition of this *Life of the Duke of Newcastle* was published in 1667. It is a thin folio of about 200 pages. This was followed in 1668 by a Latin version, translated by Walter Charlton, well known in his later days as President of the College of Physicians. In 1675 was published the third edition, a quarto ; for the translation, like the original edition, is in folio. In 1872 a careful reprint of the first edition, edited by Mark Antony Lower, was included in Russell Smith's 'Library of Old Authors'. In the present edition, the spelling has been modernized, and the punctuation occasionally altered.

The three editions published during the lifetime of the subject testify to the popularity of the book at a time when the events recorded in it were still fresh in the memories of those who read it, and it still retains an enduring interest for later generations. Somewhat contradictory have been the judgments passed upon it. The volume of *Letters and Poems in Honour of the Incomparable Princess, Margaret, Duchess of Newcastle*, printed in 1676, preserves the opinions of the learned persons and learned bodies to whom the Duchess sent presentation copies. The response of the University of Cambridge was worthy of the gift and the giver. 'Hereafter, if generous and highborn men shall search our library for a model of a most accomplished general, they shall find it expressed to the life, not in Xenophon's Cyrus, but in the Duchess of Newcastle's William ! . . . In regard we could not be admitted to the favour of kissing your hand, we cease not to bestow ten thousand embraces upon every page of that book which hath so noble and immortal a subject as is his grace the Duke of Newcastle.' Whilst the heads of the University were expressing themselves with the mixture of gallantry and respect which becomes learned bodies on such occasions, Pepys was confiding to paper his contempt for the

vii

book and its writer : 'March 18, 1668—Thence home, and
there in favour to my eyes staid at home, reading the ridiculous history of my Lord Newcastle, wrote by his wife ; which
shows her to be a mad, conceited, ridiculous woman, and he
an ass to suffer her to write what she writes to him and of
him. So to bed, my eyes being very bad.' Without stopping
to inquire how far the state of the worthy Secretary's eyes
influenced his critical faculties, it may be taken for granted
that his recollections of the authoress influenced his judgment
of her book. Describing her visit to the Royal Society on
May 30, 1667, he had come to the conclusion that ' her dress
was so antick and her deportment so ordinary ' that he did
not like her at all, and expressed his terror lest her conduct
should make the Royal Society ridiculous. Perhaps it was
these very eccentricities and extravagances which had so
shocked Pepys which recommended the Duchess to Charles
Lamb. Certainly his larger sympathy, and keener insight,
enabled him to perceive in the style and in the writer those
finer qualities which the more conventional judgment of
Pepys had refused to recognize. Lamb never mentions without praise 'that princely woman, thrice noble Margaret of
Newcastle '. For a book such as the *Life of the Duke of Newcastle*, a book ' both good and rare ', he held no binding too
good. ' No casket is rich enough, no casing sufficiently durable
to honour and keep safe such a jewel.'

To decide between these conflicting sentences, and expound
the precise amount of truth contained in each, would be a
tedious and ungrateful task. This at least may be said, that
the ' generous and highborn men ' who follow the recommendation of the Cambridge Senate and study this Life as a contribution to military history will find little in it which they could
not learn more fully and accurately from the pages of Rushworth or Whitelock. An occasional incident or anecdote,
the name of a forgotten officer, or the locality of an obscure
skirmish, an account of the Duke's personal share in one or
two engagements, sum up the amount of its contributions to
the military history of the civil wars. The special interest of
the book lies rather in the picture of the exiled royalist, cheerfully sacrificing everything for the King's cause, struggling
with his debts, talking over his creditors, never losing confidence in the ultimate triumph of the right, and on his return

setting to work uncomplainingly to restore his ruined estate. It lies rather in the portrait drawn of a great English nobleman of the seventeenth century ; his manners and his habits, his occupations and amusements, his maxims and his opinions, his domestic policy and his alliances with neighbouring potentates, all are recorded and set down with the loving fidelity of a Boswell. For the account of her husband's exile and the description of his daily life the Duchess depended on her own observations and recollections. But for that part of the book which treats of his warlike exploits she relied on the information she received from his secretary, John Rolleston.

Rolleston had filled a position which must have enabled him to know the truth on many doubtful points, and to explain, had he thought fit, the causes which determined the strategy of his General. It is therefore much to be regretted that so meagre an account is given of many important incidents and resolutions during the Yorkshire campaigns. For these campaigns exercised a decisive influence on the course of the Civil War in the eastern and midland counties, and had Newcastle been a more capable general, the northern army might have forestalled the New-Model. The first and one of the most important services of Newcastle was the occupation of the town from which he took his title. The ports of the south and east of England, from Bristol to the towns of the Yorkshire coast, were all in the hands of the Parliament, and without communication with the Continent the King could hardly have conducted one campaign. The possession of Newcastle enabled him to receive the arms and ammunition which he urgently needed, and supplied, a landing-place for the old soldiers who flocked from Holland and Germany to officer his armies. In the next place, the great territorial influence of Lord Newcastle enabled him to raise an army in the four northern counties with unusual speed ; and, at a period when 2000 or 3000 men was a large army, to advance with double that number into Yorkshire, and occupy York just when it was on the point of falling into the hands of Lord Fairfax. Considering the great superiority of his forces, Newcastle's operations against Lord Fairfax, which commenced in December 1642, can hardly be considered very creditable to his military talents. It required three separate attacks to expel the Fairfaxes from the West Riding. The first commenced with the attack on Tadcaster (December 7, 1642); was followed by the repulse of Sir William Savile from Bradford (December 18, 1642); and was brought to an end by the brilliant recapture of Leeds by Sir Thomas Fairfax (January 23, 1643). The second began in April with an unsuccessful attack on Leeds, and was marked by the capture of Rotherham (May 4) and Sheffield (May 9). Again Sir Thomas Fairfax, by the surprise of Wakefield on May 21, 1643, forced the royalists to retreat. The third and successful attack began with the capture of Howley Hall and the battle of Adwalton Moor (June 30), and ended with the capture of Bradford and Leeds, and the flight of the Fairfaxes to Hull.

In the interval between the first and second of these attacks occurred the controversy between Newcastle and Lord Fairfax, recorded in the opposing proclamations printed by Rushworth. Newcastle sent Fairfax a characteristic challenge to come out and fight, to follow ' the exampes of our heroic ancestors, who used not to spend their time in scratching one another out of holes, but in pitched fields determined their doubts.' Lord Fairfax replied by a refusal ' to follow the rules of Amadis de Gaule, or the Knight of the Sun, which the language of the declaration seems to affect in offering pitched battles '; but withal protested his willingness to offer battle wheresoever he found an opportunity. With these taunts were combined legal arguments on the rights of kings and subjects, discussions on the lawfulness of employing Catholics and sectaries, and accusations of plunder and indiscipline against each other's armies.

The conquest of the West Riding left Hull the only important place in Yorkshire in the hands of the Parliament. Charles summoned Newcastle to move southwards, and ordered him to march through the eastern association on London [1]. He obeyed so far as to march into Lincolnshire, where he recaptured Gainsborough (July 30) and garrisoned Lincoln, but at the end of August he returned into Yorkshire to besiege Hull. The combined movement on London planned by the King might have changed the fortune of the war, for at the end of July the Parliament had no army capable of keeping

---

[1] ' He had orders to march into the associated counties, when, upon the taking of Bristol, his Majesty had a purpose to have marched towards London on the other side.' —Clarendon, *Rebellion*, viii, 86. See also vii, 177. Other statements are quoted in the note to p. 29.

the field. Waller's forces had been reduced to a few hundred horse, Essex's troops were diminished by disease and desertion, and disheartened by failure, and the army of the Eastern association was still in the process of formation. Even if the march on London had been unattempted, a vigorous invasion of the Eastern association might have made a breach in that stronghold of Puritanism, and would almost certainly have prevented the relief of Gloucester. The reasons which led Newcastle to disobey the King's order are differently stated. Warwick asserts that his desire to retain his independent command was the chief motive. To this was added the opposition of the gentlemen of Yorkshire to the proposed scheme, their objections to leaving their own county, and their urgent appeals to Newcastle to capture Hull and put a stop to Fairfax's inroads into Yorkshire. It was on this last ground that Newcastle based his refusal, but there is little doubt that it coincided with his own inclinations [1]. From the time that Newcastle turned back into Yorkshire his good fortune ended. One day (October 11, 1643) saw the defeat of his field army at Winceby, and the rout of the besieging army under the walls of Hull. November and December were spent in recruiting his shattered forces, and in January 1644 he was called northwards to oppose the entry of the Scots into England. Slowly the Scots forced their way south, Newcastle ever attempting to bring on a general action, and ever failing through Lesly's judicious choice of positions. Though he was able by means of his great superiority in cavalry to cut off their provisions, he could never absolutely reduce them to extremity, and his best horse were ruined by the severity of the season. At the same time, he had to contend against the criticisms of his own party, and even thought of laying down his commission to escape their complaints. 'I perceive', wrote the King to him, 'that the Scots are not the only, or the least enemies you contest with at this time ; wherefore I must tell you in a word you must as much contemn the impertinent or malicious tongues and pens of those that are or profess to be your friends, as well as you despise the sword of an equal enemy. The truth is, if either you or my Lord Ethyn leave my service, I am sure all the north is lost. Remember all courage is not in fighting, constancy in a good cause

[1] See Clarendon, vii, 177, and passages quoted on p. 29.

being the chief, and the despising of slanderous tongues and pens being not the least ingredient.'[1] This letter was written on April 6, 1644, and on the 11th of the same month New-castle's lieutenant, Bellasis, was defeated and taken prisoner, and the Marquis himself forced to make a hurried retreat to York, where the united armies of Fairfax, Lesly, and Man-chester closed in upon him, and made his surrender only a question of time. Prince Rupert raised the siege; but, not content with that, and misunderstanding the King's orders, pursued the retreating enemy, and, against the advice of the Marquis, forced on the battle of Marston Moor. In that battle the Marquis held no command, but fought as a private gentleman at the head of a company of volunteers. The day after, he, with his immediate friends, made his way to Scar-borough and embarked for the Continent. If he had been content to remain in England, and laboriously recommence the task of raising armies for the King, he might have con-siderably retarded the loss of the north. There were a hundred examples of men, less eminent in position and command, who struggled cheerfully, even though with little hope of success, until all further resistance was impossible. But Newcastle, loyal though he was, held no such troublesome and exacting a view of his duty. His wife represents him as leaving England because he saw there was nothing else to be done, and was 'loath to have aspersions cast upon him' for failing to do what was impossible. Another account makes him reply to Rupert's persuasions to recruit his forces for another effort, by saying 'I will not endure the laughter of the court.' Clarendon, whilst discussing the causes of this retirement, seizes the opportunity to draw one of those portraits which no biographer can leave unquoted:

'All that can be said for the Marquis is, that he was utterly tired with a condition and employment so contrary to his humour, nature, and education, that he did not at all con-sider the means or the way that would let him out of it, and free him for ever from having more to do with it. And it was a greater wonder, that he sustained the vexation and fatigue of it so long, than that he broke from it with so little circum-spection. He was a very fine gentleman, active and full of courage, and most accomplished in those qualities of horse-

[1] Ellis, *Original Letters*, I, iii. 298.

manship, dancing, and fencing which accompany a good breeding; in which his delight was. Besides that, he was amorous in poetry and music, to which he indulged the greatest part of his time; and nothing could have tempted him out of those paths of pleasure, which he enjoyed in a full and ample fortune, but honour and ambition to serve the King, when he saw him in distress, and abandoned by most of those who were in the highest degree obliged to him, and by him. He loved monarchy, as it was the foundation and support of his own greatness; and the Church, as it was well constituted for the splendour and security of the Crown; and religion, as it cherished and maintained that order and obedience that was necessary to both; without any other passion for the particular opinions which were grown up in it, and distinguished it into parties, than as he detested whatsoever was like to disturb the public peace. . . . He liked the pomp and absolute authority of a general well, and preserved the dignity of it to the full; and for the discharge of the outward state and circumstances of it, in acts of courtesy, affability, bounty, and generosity he abounded; which in the infancy of a war became him, and made him for some time very acceptable to men of all conditions. But the substantial part, and fatigue of a general, he did not in any degree understand (being utterly unacquainted with war) nor could submit to [1]; but referred all matters of that nature to his lieutenant-general, King . . . In all actions of the field he was still present, and never absent in any battle; in all which he gave instances of an invincible courage and fearlessness in danger; in which the exposing of himself notoriously did sometimes change the fortune of the day when his troops began to give ground. Such articles of action were no sooner over, than he retired to his delightful company, music, or his softer pleasures, to all which he was so indulgent, and to his ease, that he would not be interrupted upon what occasions soever; insomuch as he sometimes denied admission to the chiefest officers of the army, even to General King himself, for two days together; from whence many inconveniences fell out. . . The strange manner of the Prince's coming, and undeliberated throwing himself, and all the King's hopes, into that sudden and unnecessary engagement, by which all the force the

[1] Clarendon's private opinion is quoted in a note to p. 53, *post*.

Marquis had raised, and with so many difficulties preserved, was in a moment cast away and destroyed, so transported him with passion and despair, that he could not compose himself to think of beginning the work again, and involving himself in the same undelightful condition of life, from which he might now be free. He hoped his past meritorious actions might outweigh his present abandoning the thought of future action ; and so without further consideration, as hath been said, he transported himself out of the kingdom.'[1]

Very similar is the judgment passed on Newcastle by another contemporary, Sir Philip Warwick. 'He was a gentleman of grandeur, generosity, loyalty, and steady and forward courage ; but his edge had too much of the razor in it : for he had a tincture of a romantic spirit, and had the misfortune to have somewhat of the poet in him : so as he chose Sir William Davenant, an eminent good poet, and loyal gentleman, to be lieutenant-general of his ordnance. This inclination of his own and such kind of witty society (to be modest in the expression of it) diverted many counsels, and lost many opportunities, which the nature of that affair this great man had now entered into required.'[2]

The very defects which, according to these two authorities, prevented Newcastle from being a successful general, have given him an additional claim to the remembrance of posterity. His own writings, and his patronage of other writers, combine to secure him a niche in the literature of his age.

Newcastle's intimacy with Hobbes is attested by the stories which the Duchess tells in order to illustrate her husband's 'natural understanding and observation' (p. 106). Their acquaintance began long before they were fellow-exiles, as the letters from Hobbes to Newcastle, written between 1634 and 1637, sufficiently attest. These letters, now preserved at Welbeck, were published in 1893 in the *Report of the Historical Manuscripts Commission on the Duke of Portland's Papers* (vol ii, pp. 124–30). The intimacy owed its origin to Newcastle's interest in science and philosophy. Hobbes communicated to Newcastle his observations and experiments about light, motion, and other scientific questions, and his opinions about books. In one letter he mentions the publication of Lord Herbert of Cherbury's *De Veritate*, 'a

---

[1] *Rebellion*, viii, 82, 85, 87.   [2] *Memoirs*, p. 235.

booke concerning truth, which is a high point '. In a second, he relates his unsuccessful attempts to obtain for Newcastle a copy of Galileo's *Dialogues :* ' It is not possible to get it for money. There were but few brought over at first, and they that buy such bookes, are not such men as to part with them againe. I heare say it is called in, in Italy, as a booke that will do more hurt to their religion than all the bookes have done of Luther and Calvin, such opposition they thinke is between their religion and naturall reason.' In a third letter, after referring to Walter Warner, the mathematician and philosopher, whom Newcastle also patronised, Hobbes sets forth his own aims and hopes. Warner, he says, cannot fulfil Newcastle's expectations. ' For the soule I know he has nothing to give your Lordship any satisfaction. I would he could give good reasons for the facultyes and passions of the soule, such as may be expressed in playne English ; if he can, he is the first that I ever heard of could speake sense in that subject. If he cannot, I hope to be the first.'

With the generosity which he habitually showed to wits and men of learning Newcastle sent Hobbes a present of money, which Hobbes received with dignity. The gift, he said, was proportioned to Newcastle's goodness not to his service. ' If the world saw my little desert, so plainely as they see your great rewards, they might think me a mountebancke, and that all I do or would do were in the hope of what I receave. I hope your Lordship does not thinke so, at least let me tell your Lordship once for all, that though I honour you as my Lord, yet my love to you is just of the same nature that it is to Mr. Payne, bred out of private talke, without respect to your purse.' Then, referring to his friend Payne, Hobbes laid down the principle that patrons who wished to encourage the researches of learned men should reward the result rather than contribute to the undertaking. ' I hope your Lordship will not bestow much upon the hopes, but suffer the liberall sciences to be liberall, and after some worthy effort your Lordship then may be liberall also.'

What attracted Hobbes to Newcastle was Newcastle's sympathy with his ideas and his curiosity about questions for which most noblemen of the time cared nothing. In one of his letters he expresses to the Earl the hope that ' I may have the happiness which your Lordship partly promises me,

to conferre meditations for a good time together, which will
be not only honor to me, but that happiness which I and all
that are in love with knowledge, use to fancy to themselves
for the true happiness in this life.' Both men were 'in love
with knowledge' but with the one it was the passion of a lifetime, with the other little more than a passing fancy.

In October 1636 Newcastle apparently invited Hobbes
to leave the household of the Earl of Devonshire, and establish
himself permanently at Welbeck. Reluctant though he was to
part with the Earl and Countess, Hobbes was very nearly
accepting the invitation. 'Though my Lady and my Lord
do both accept so wel of my service as I could almost engage
myself to serve them as a domestique all my life, yet the
extreame pleasure I take in study overcomes in me all other
appetites. I am not willing to leave my Lord, so as not to
do him any service that he thinkes may not so well be done
by another; but I must not deny myselfe the content to
study in the way I have begun, and that I cannot conceave I
shall do any where so well as at Welbecke, and therefore I
mean if your lordship forbid me not, to come thither as
soone as I can, and stay as long as I can without inconvenience
to your Lordship.'

It is doubtful whether the long visit ever took place. One
year the plague prevented Hobbes from coming to Welbeck,
another year Newcastle's appointment as governor of Prince
Charles called him to London, and then came the Scottish
troubles and the Civil War. Doubtless the two met again in
London, but their next recorded meeting is that mentioned
by Waller when Gassendi, Descartes, Hobbes and himself
dined at Newcastle's table at Paris about 1648.

Newcastle's chief interest however was not in philosophy
but in the drama. He was not only a dramatic author
himself, but the friend and protector of most of the dramatic
authors of his time. 'Since the time of Augustus', says
Langbaine, 'no person better understood dramatic poetry,
nor more generously encouraged poets; so that we may truly
call him our English Mæcenas.'[1] Jonson dedicated to him
elegies on his riding and fencing, wrote the epitaphs of his
father, mother, and other members of his family, composed
an interlude for the christening of his son Charles, and the two

[1] *Dramatic Poets*, p. 386.

Masques entitled *Love's Welcome at Welbeck*, and *Love's Welcome at Bolsover*, for his entertainments to the King and Queen. Three of the poet's letters have been printed. In one he offers his patron ' the faith of a fast friend with the duties of an humble servant, and the hearty prayers of a religious bedesman '. In another, which probably accompanied *Love's Welcome at Welbeck*, he thanks the Earl for ' a timely gratuity, which fell like the dew of heaven on my necessities '. ' God sends you ', he continues, ' these chargeable and magnificent honours of making feasts, to mix with your charitable succours, dropt upon me your servant ; who have nothing to claim of merit but a cheerful undertaking whatsoever your lordship's judgment thinks me able to perform.' [1]

James Shirley also addressed a poem to Newcastle, and dedicated to him in 1638 his play of *The Traitor*. When the Civil War broke out, and Shirley was forced to leave London, ' he was invited ', says Wood, ' by his most noble patron, William, Earl of Newcastle, to take his fortune with him in the wars ; for that Count had engaged him so much by his generous liberality towards him, that he thought he could not do a worthier act than to serve him, and consequently his Prince '. According to the same author, ' Shirley did much assist the Duke in the composure of certain plays, which the Duke afterwards published.' On which Dyce remarks : ' The style of his Grace's dramas would certainly have induced me to suspect the truth of this statement, if I had not discovered that a drinking song which is inserted in the Duke's comedy called *The Country Captain* is printed amongst our author's poems.' [2]

Since Dyce published his edition of Shirley new evidence has come to light. In 1883 Mr. A. H. Bullen published in volume II of his ' Collection of Old English Plays ' an anonymous comedy called *Captain Underwit*. ' Gerard Langbaine ', he says in the introduction, ' tells us that Shirley left at his death some plays in manuscript : I have little doubt, or rather no doubt at all, that Captain Underwit is one of them. In the notes I have pointed out several parallelisms to passages

[1] Cunningham's Jonson, vol. iii, p. 459, Preface, pp. lvii–lix, and Underwood's *Epigrams*, 72 and 89. See also pp. 2, 4, 105, and 112 of these *Memoirs*.
[2] Wood, *Athenæ Oxonienses*, ed. Bliss, iii, 737. Dyce's Shirley, Preface, p. xliii. The song referred to is in act iv of *The Country Captain*, and commences *Come let us throw the dice.*

c

in Shirley's plays ; and occasionally we find actual repetitions word for word. But apart from these strong proofs, it would be plain from internal evidence that the present piece is a domestic comedy of Shirley's, written in close imitation of Ben Jonson. All the characters are old acquaintances. Sir Richard Huntlove, who longs to be among his own tenants, and eat his own beef in the country ; his lady who loves the pleasures of the town, balls in the Strand, and masques ; Device, the fantastic gallant,—these are well known figures in Shirley's plays. No other playwright of that day could have given us such exquisite poetry as we find in Captain Underwit. The briskness, too, and cleverness of the dialogue closely recall Shirley ; but it must be owned that there are few plays of Shirley's written with such freedom, not to say grossness.'

Now this anonymous play which Mr. Bullen, on internal evidence only, attributes to Shirley, is Newcastle's *Country Captain*. There are a few verbal differences between the version printed in 1649 and that printed in 1883, but that is all. Mr. Bullen's remarks on the style are very just, and it seems clear that much of the play was the work of Shirley. Some of the verses interspersed are undoubtedly Newcastle's, he wrote many passages, and doubtless conceived the plan of the play, but to fit it for the stage he had to call in the aid of an expert dramatist, and owed more to his assistant than he owned. As we shall see two other dramatists subsequently collaborated with him in a similar fashion.

Newcastle's relations with Davenant have already been mentioned. It is very likely that the poet owed his post in Newcastle's army to the recommendation of the Queen rather than to the merits of his verse [1]. It is somewhat remarkable that Davenant makes no mention of the Duke in his poems, and that, with the exception of a brief poem on the marriage of one of the Duke's daughters, there is no trace of this connection in his works. Dryden, who also shared the favours of Newcastle, takes the opportunity, in his florid dedication of *The Mock Astrologer* to the Duke, to refer to his kindnesses to former poets. 'The manes of Jonson and Davenant seem to require from me, that those favours which you placed on them, and which they wanted opportunity to own in public, yet

---

[1] *Letters of Queen Henrietta Maria*, ed. Green, p. 134.

might not be lost to the knowledge of posterity, with a forget-
fulness unbecoming of the Muses who are the daughters of
memory. . .   I am proud to be their remembrancer : for by
relating how gracious you have been to them, and are to me,
I, in some measure, join my name to theirs : and the continued descent of your favours to me is the best title which I
can plead for my succession.'   Dryden's enemy, Shadwell,
shared the Duke's bounty, and dedicated to him *The Virtuoso*
and *The Libertine*.   Flecknoe, another of the victims of
Dryden's satire, rhymes assiduously in praise of the Duke
and Duchess [1].   But Dryden's connection with Newcastle
was that of collaborateur as well as client.   The Duke translated or adapted Molière's *L'Étourdi*, which Dryden converted
into *Sir Martin Mar-all*.   It was performed under the name
of the Duke, and is entered on the books of the Stationers'
Company as his work [2].   Not till 1697 did it appear under
Dryden's name, but according to Pepys the secret of its
authorship was well known at the time.

Newcastle's own plays are four in number, viz. *The Country
Captain* and *The Variety*, published in 1649, and *The Humorous
Lovers* and *Triumphant Widow*, published in 1677.   Of the
first of these Pepys observes : ' so silly a play as in all my life
I never saw ' ; of the third, ' the most silly thing that ever
came upon a stage.' [3]   Shadwell, however, who knew what
was likely to succeed as well as most men, thought sufficiently
well of *The Triumphant Widow* to insert a large part of it into
his *Bury Fair*.   It is difficult to resist the conclusion that he
was the real author of this portion of the *Triumphant Widow*,
and that he was only reclaiming his own property.   But
whether original or not, the plays are certainly readable and
amusing.   There is less to be said in favour of the Duke's
poems.   They consist chiefly of songs in his own plays and
those of the Duchess, of adulatory verses prefixed to his wife's
publications, and some tales in verse in her *Nature's Pictures*.
They are as far inferior to her poems as his plays are superior
to those of the Duchess.

Walpole, who never loses an opportunity of sneering at

[1] See Walpole's *Royal and Noble Authors*, edited by Park, where specimens of Flecknoe's verses are given.   Richard Brome also prefixes to his play of *The Covent Garden
Weeded*, verses on the Duke's play entitled *The Variety*.

[2] Scott's *Dryden*, vol. iii.

[3] See the passages quoted from Pepys on p. 203.   Geneste, who describes the Duke's
plays (x. 73-75), sums up by saying that they ' ought not to have been forgotten '.

Newcastle, says, referring to his plays and poems : ' He would
soon have been forgotten in the walk of fame which he chose
for himself.   Yet as an author he is familiar to those who
scarce know any other author from his book of horsemanship.'[1]   Horsemanship was a study to which Newcastle had
devoted himself from his youth.   His father, Sir Charles
Cavendish, ' kept him several masters in the art of horsemanship, and sent him to the Mews to Mons. Antoine, who was
then accounted the best master in that art.'   As governor of
Prince Charles he also taught him to ride, and continually
celebrates the progress of his pupil (see the passages quoted
in the note to p. 121), to whom he afterwards dedicated his
Méthode Nouvelle de Dresser les Chevaux.   The same pursuit
filled the enforced leisure of his exile, and relieved its tedium.

Early in 1648, towards the end of his stay in France, Newcastle contrived to obtain credit, and promptly bought a
couple of Barbary horses, ' resolving for his own recreation
and divertisement to exercise the art of manage '.   After his
removal to Antwerp he increased his stable to eight horses,
' in which he took so much delight and pleasure that, though
he was then in distress for money, yet he would sooner have
tried all other ways than parted with any of them.'   No
stranger of note thought of passing through Antwerp without
coming to see Newcastle's riding-house.   ' It would fill a
volume ', he writes, ' to repeat all the commendations that
were given to horses and horsemanship, by several worthy
gentlemen of all nations, High and Low Dutch, Italians,
English, French, Spaniards, Polacks, and Swedes, in my own
private riding-house at Antwerp, which, though very large,
was often so full that my esquier, Captain Mazin, had hardly
room to ride.'   He relates in detail the compliments of some
of his more important visitors, tells us how he himself mounted
and performed before them, whilst Spaniards ' crossed themselves and cried Miraculo '.   And that, ' though the French
think that all the horsemanship in the world is in France ',
one said : ' Par Dieu, Monsieur, il est bien hardi qui monte
devant vous ', and another ' Il n'y a plus seigneur comme vous
en Angleterre.'[2]   The fruit of these experiences and studies
was published in 1658 at Antwerp under the title of *La*

---

[1] *Royal and Noble Authors*, iii. 175.
[2] Preface to the *New Method and Extraordinary Invention*, 1667.   Some extracts
are quoted in the notes to pp. 60, 62.

Méthode et Invention Nouvelle de Dresser les Chevaux. It is a
magnificent folio, with two title-pages and 42 fine plates. The
Marquis wrote in English, but had his work translated into
French for publication [1].

A letter which is printed in the Appendix shows that it was
owing to the help of his two friends, Sir Hugh Cartwright and
Mr. Loving, that Newcastle was able to produce so sumptuous
an edition of his book. In the numerous diagrams which
adorn it, we see the Duke and Captain Mazin alternately
exhibiting the various figures of their art in the riding-house.
Other plates represent Newcastle himself performing 'capri-
olles' and 'balottades' before the windows of Welbeck, or
under the towers of Bolsover. The frontispiece pictures
him mounted and upon a pedestal, crowned by flying Cupids,
with verses beneath stating that if he were to mount 'un
diable très robuste' it would become immediately as docile
as one of his own trained steeds. One emblematic design
displays the author driving a chariot drawn by centaurs
through a circle of kneeling horses ; in another he is seen
flying on a winged horse betwixt heaven and earth, below are
submissively adoring horses, whilst from above the gods look
down and admire. The verses attached to this last picture
are so much superior to most of those supplied by Mons. D. V.,
the poet employed by the Duke, that they deserve quotation :

> Il monte avec la main, les éperons et gaule,
> Le cheval de Pégase qui volle, en capriole ;
> Il monte si haut qu'il touche de sa tête les cieux,
> Et par ses merveilles ravit en extases les Dieux.
> Les chevaux corruptibles qui là bas sur terre sont,
> En courbettes demi-airs, terre à terre vont,
> Avec humilité soumission et bassesse,
> L'adorer comme Dieu auteur de leur addresse.

When the Duke returned from exile he continued to occupy
himself with his favourite pursuit. ' In his old age ', writes
his wife, ' though he doth not ride himself, as he hath done,
yet he takes delight in seeing his horses of manage rid by his
escuyers, whom he instructs in that art for his own pleasure.'
In 1667 he published a second book, under the following

---

[1] According to Lowndes (ed. Bohn) the book was published in 1657, and the printed
title is sometimes altered by hand to 1658. But the copies I have myself seen are dated
1658. The Duke's first draft of the book is preserved at Welbeck.

title : *A New Method and Extraordinary Invention to Dress Horses, and Work them, according to Nature* ; *as also to perfect Nature by the subtlety of Art* ; *which was never found out but by the thrice noble, high, and puissant Prince, William Cavendish,* etc. In the preface the Duke explains the relation of the later to the earlier work : ' I did (during my long exile) publish in French a book of Horsemanship ; and having again, since my return to my native country, had much leisure, in my solitary country life, to recollect my thoughts, and try new experiments about that art ; I now, for the more particular satisfaction of my countrymen, print this second book in English, which, being neither a translation of the first, nor an absolutely necessary addition to it, may be of use by itself without the other, as the other hath been hitherto, and is still, without this ; but both together will questionless do best.'

Another work of Newcastle's has come to light only lately. The Duchess tells us that during the exile her husband sent King Charles II ' a little book wherein he delivered his opinion concerning the goverment of his dominions, whensoever God should be pleased to restore him to his throne ' (p. 100). Two manuscript copies of this book are in existence, one in the Bodleian Library, which is probably the copy presented to the King, and the other in the possession of the Duke of Portland. The second was printed by Mr. S. A. Strong in 1903, in his *Catalogue of Letters and other historical Documents preserved in the Library at Welbeck.*

Newcastle's advice to the King in some respects resembles that which he gave the prince (Appendix p. 183). In both he insists on the maintenance of ceremony as a fence to monarchy, and the importance of externals as a means of impressing the mind of the people. But in the advice to the King Newcastle sets forth all his views on the arts of government in detail, and all his observations on the errors of policy committed by the king's father and grandfather. He passes in review the court, the country, the lawyers, the clergy, the city and the parliament, defining what the king's attitude should be to each class and profession in the nation. More than once in his reflections on the past and his recommendations as to the future Newcastle echoes the views of Hobbes, and there are many passages which might be paralleled from Leviathan or Behemoth.   Like Hobbes Newcastle traces the Rebellion to fanaticism.   ' The Bible in English under every weaver's and chambermaid's arm hath done us much hurt.'   Henceforth religious zeal must be systematically repressed, preachers controlled, and only permitted to deliver printed sermons licensed by the bishops, teachers rigidly supervised, the number of students in universities and schools limited, no books of controversy save in Latin allowed, and the press put under an effective censorship.   Newcastle regarded the Bishops as a sort of ecclesiastical policemen, intended to maintain order in their dioceses, and to keep the king informed about the movements of schismatics and papists.   Episcopacy was the only form of government compatible with monarchy, which Popery and Presbytery alike tended to destroy.   Therefore the king must begin by re-establishing the Church of England ' and thus shall your Majesty be not only an absolute king, but pope within your dominions ', and his subjects would have ' an easy and sweet government, in comparison of the other two most tyrannical governments either of Popery or Presbytery '.

The most important thing however for the peace of both Church and State was that the King should have complete and sole control of the military forces of the realm.   ' There is nothing can so well settle the Church, and keep it in order, as the power to be in your own hands, which is the drum and the trumpet, for disputes will never have an end, and make new and great disorders, but force quiets all things.'   To begin with therefore the London trained bands must be disarmed, and two forts must be built on each side the Thames below Greenwich to command the river and its trade, as the Spaniards had done at Antwerp.   There were to be good garrisons in the port towns, a troop of horse kept on foot in every county, and a militia commanded by trusty noblemen.

To provide money for the expenses of the army and navy the King must encourage trade by every means in his power. ' It is the merchant that brings honey to the hive.   Therefore keep up the merchant as high as possibly you can.'   Let there be no abuses in the farming of the customs, and no monopolies, but lower the rate of interest, and establish an excise.   Above all the King must be economical ; there must be no profuseness in unnecessary things such as jewels or pictures, for extravagance would make him dependent upon parliaments instead of their master. 'Riches, sir, in a king, is more advantageous both at home and abroad than I can express, therefore, Sir, put money in your purse and be rich.'

While however Newcastle thus warned Charles against extravagance he at the same time sketched a programme of 'divertisements' for the King throughout the year. In winter there were to be masques, and plays and balls at Whitehall. There were to be tiltings too, on coronation day, and riding 'horses of manége'. In the summer he was to make stately progresses through the country. In spring and autumn he was to recreate himself with hunting and hawking. Newmarket would be excellent for this, 'which is the sweetest place in the world and the best air, and no place like it for hunting, hawking and coursing, and horse races.' The people too were to have their amusements, and it was of great political importance that these should be encouraged when the King was restored. For 'the divertisements will amuse the people's thoughts and keep them in harmless action, which will free your majesty from faction and rebellion. Once more there must be bear-baiting at Paris Garden for 'the meaner people' and five or six playhouses for the pleasure of the better sort. 'Puppet plays there will be to please them besides, as also dancers on the ropes, with jugglers and tumblers, besides strange sights of beasts, birds, monsters, and many other things with several sorts of music and dancing, and all the old holidays with their mirth and rites set up again. Feasting daily will be in merry England, for England is so plentifull of all provisions, that if we do not eat them they will eat us, so we feast in our defence.' Still more enthusiastic is his enumeration of 'the country recreation'. There will be once more 'may games, morris dances, the Lords of the May and the Lady of the May ; the fool and the hobbyhorse must not be forgotten ; also the Whitsun Lord and Lady, threshing of hens at Shrovetide ; carols and wassails at Christmas, with goodly plum porridge and pies, which now are forbidden as profane, ungodly things ; wakes, fairs and markets (which maintain commerce and trade) ; and after evening prayer every Sunday and holiday, the country people with their fresher lasses to trip on the town green about the may-pole to the louder bagpipe and to be refreshed with their ale and cakes.'

So, forgetting statecraft for a moment, the mind of the exile reverted to the England he had known before the civil war began—to the country of which we catch a glimpse in Milton's *L'Allegro* and Herrick's *Hesperides*. The England to which Newcastle came back in 1660 was a different and a graver country, sobered by suffering as well as embittered by strife. He found his parks wasted, his woods cut down, and his houses dismantled. He had to set to work to restock his farms, rebuild his houses, and repay his debts, and to do all these with a diminished income. 'It may be concluded', says the Duchess, after computing his losses, 'that although my Lord's estate was very great before the wars, yet now it is shrunk into a very narrow compass, that it puts his prudence and wisdom to the proof to serve his necessities.' For this reason, and also no doubt on account of his advanced age, Newcastle after his return to England lived entirely in the country. He made no attempt to press his advice upon his royal pupil either in court or council. The *Advice* was his political testament.

Though the Duke of Newcastle's contribution to literature is by no means insignificant, his works are far surpassed in number by those of the Duchess. Poems and Plays, Letters, Orations, and Stories, combined with a whole series of works on Natural Philosophy, flowed from her facile pen. It was during her exile, more especially during her visit to England with Sir Charles Cavendish, that she published her earliest works. The volume of *Poems and Fancies* was first printed in 1653; a second edition followed in 1664, and a third in 1668; all three were published at London and in folio form. This volume contains some of her best work: *The Pastime and Recreation of the Queen of the Fairies in Fairyland*, and *The Dialogue between Melancholy and Mirth*, both of which will be found in the little volume of selections published by Mr. Jenkins. Other poems are scattered through the volume entitled *Nature's Pictures by Fancy's Pencil*. The first edition of the last-named book was published in 1656, and the second in 1671. It contains the autobiography of the Duchess, and several poems by the Duke, in addition to the tales in verse and prose which form the bulk of her volume. There should be a frontispiece representing the Duchess seated with her husband and his children telling them stories, but this is

d

generally missing. In one of the very numerous prefaces she prides herself on the tendency of her fictions, and condemns the romances of the day. ' As for those tales I name Roman-cicall, I would not have my readers think I writ them, either to please or to make foolish whining lovers, for it is a humour of all humours I have an aversion to ; but my endeavour is to express the sweetness of Virtue, and the Graces, and to dress and adorn them in the best expressions I can. . . Neither do I know the rule or method of Romancy writing ; for I never read a Romancy Book throughout in all my life, I mean such as I take to be Romances, wherein little is writ which ought to be practised, but rather shunned as foolish amorosities, and desperate follies, not noble love's discreet virtues, and true valour. The most I ever read of Romances was but part of three books, as the three parts of one, and the half of the two others. And if I thought those tales I call my Romancicall Tales, should or could neither benefit the life, nor delight the mind of my readers, no more than those pieces of Romances I read did me, I would never suffer them to be printed. . . Likewise if I could think that any of my writings should create amorous thoughts in idle brains, I would make blots instead of letters ; but I hope this work of mine will rather quench amorous passions than inflame them, and beget chaste thoughts, nourish love of Virtue, kindle humane Pity, warm Charity, increase Civility, strengthen fainting Patience, encourage noble Industry, crown Merit, instruct Life, and recreate Time.'

The book entitled *The World's Olio* is a collection of essays, observations, and aphorisms, published in 1655, with a second edition dated 1671 (London, folio). *The CCXI Sociable Letters*, published in 1664 (London, folio), consist of descriptions of imaginary scenes, persons, and conversations, with one or two letters to real persons intermixed, and one or two on critical subjects, such as the works of Shakespeare and Daven-ant. A still more curious proof of the versatility of the Duchess is the volume called *Orations of Divers Sorts accommo-dated to Divers Places* (first edition 1662, London, folio ; second 1668, do. do.). It contains orations for all times and places— for funerals, for weddings, for law courts and battlefields, speeches seditious and loyal, some to stir up mutiny, some to prevent civil war, some for and some against taxes, speeches to the King in council and to the citizens in market-place, and dying speeches for all conditions, from kings to courtesans. There is a collection of speeches for a convivial meeting of country gentlemen in a market town, ending with ' a speech of a quarter-drunk gentleman ' and ' a speech of a half-drunken gentleman '. Another little collection, headed *Female Orations*, reports the speeches delivered at a meeting of women on the great question of combining together to make themselves as ' free, happy, and famous as men ', and concludes with an oration persuading them to remain as they are and be content with their present position. It is hardly necessary to say that the orations are all singularly alike in style and expression, for the Duchess, with a considerable power of description, was entirely devoid of any dramatic instinct. In all her plays there is hardly a single character with any semblance of life ; her characters are mere abstractions, qualities, and humours, uttering the fantastic speeches and quaint conceits which she loved to write [1]. The plots are original enough, but there is no skill in the construction to redeem the weakness of the character-drawing. All that can be said for the dialogue is that it contains occasional passages of poetic beauty, and some amusing descriptions, but it is too strained and affected to be spoken on the stage. Nevertheless the Duchess was an indefatigable playwright : in 1662 she published a volume containing twenty-one plays (*Plays*, London, 1662, folio) ; this was followed in 1668 by a second containing five more (*Plays Never before Printed*, London, 1668, folio). They were not particularly well received by the world ; the Duchess complains that the critics condemned in them the very things she had admitted in her preface. ' My plays, they say, are not made up so exactly as they should be, having no plots, designs, catastrophes, and such like, I know not what, which I expressed in the Epistles prefixed before them ; acknowledging that I had neither skill nor art to form them as they should be ' (Preface to *Orations*). For this reason she boldly states, in the address to the readers in her second volume : ' When I call this new

[1] Some of the figures represent the authoress herself. ' In a scene in the second part of *Youth's Glory and Death's Banquet*, she appears under the character of Lady Sanspareile, and gives what may be supposed to be a picture of her own reception at Court. As the Lady Contemplation in the play of that name, as the Lady Chastity of the *Matrimonial Trouble*, and in a score of other characters, the Duchess is recognizable.'—*Dictionary of National Biography*.

one " Plays " I do not believe to have given it a very proper
title ; for it would be too great a fondness to my works to
think such plays as these suitable to ancient rules, in which
I pretend no skill ; or agreeable to the modern humour, to
which I dare acknowledge my aversion : but having pleased
my fancy in writing many dialogues upon several subjects,
and having afterwards ordered them into acts and scenes, I
will venture in spite of the critics to call them "Plays"; and
if you like them so, well and good ; if not, there is no harm
done ' [1].

But the philosophical, or rather scientific works of the
Duchess, were those of which she herself was most proud, and
those which were most famous in her time. The first of
these was the *Philosophical Fancies* (London, 1653), afterwards
developed into *Philosophical Opinions* (London, 1655), and
still further enlarged and amended in the second edition of
Philosophical Opinions in 1663. In some verses on this book,
quoted in the note to page 303, she terms it ' of all that I have
writ, my best beloved and greatest favourite'. Already,
in her Poems in 1653, and in *The World's Olio*, published in 1655,
she had set forth some of her views on natural philosophy.
One of the dozen prefaces to her Poems is specially addressed
' to natural philosophers '. She pleads her complete ignorance
of the works of former writers on the subject, and the fact
that she understands no language but her own, and only
colloquial English, as reasons for a kindly judgment of her
speculations. In the remarks attached to *Philosophical
Opinions* she prides herself that her views are all her own,
and all new. ' I desire all those that are friends to my book
to believe that whatsoever is new is my own, which I hope
all is ; for I never had any guide to direct me, nor intelligence
from any authors to advertise me, but writ according to my
own natural cogitations'. As might be expected from these
confessions, the ponderous tomes on science and philosophy
which the Duchess published are entirely valueless. This
was not only due to the ignorance of the writings of others,
which the Duchess admits, but to the method which she
adopted in reasoning on physical science. One of her cor-
respondents, Glanville, points this out to her. ' There are

1 There is a very fine portrait of the Duchess by Diepenbeck as frontispiece to the
Plays.

two sorts of reasoning ', he says ; ' those that the mind advanceth from its inbred store, such are all metaphysical contemplations ; and those natural researches which are raised from experiment and the objects of sense. Now, what I have said about these matters is to tie down the mind in physical things to consider nature as it is, to lay a foundation in sensible collections, and from thence to proceed to general propositions and discourses. So that my aim is that we may arise according to the order of nature, from the exercise of our senses to that of our reason ; which indeed is most noble and most perfect when it concludes aright, but not so when it is mistaken ; and that it may so conclude and arrive to that perfection it must begin in sense ; and the more experiments our reasons have to work on, by so much they are the more likely to be certain in their conclusions, and consequently more perfect in their actings '. Whilst the Royal Society and all those to whom the progress of physical science in England during the latter half of the seventeenth century was due were eagerly pursuing the experimental method, the Duchess continued to spin her ' metaphysical cogitations ' like a spider, as she says, from her own brain.[1]

It is not surprising that her husband praised them, for he held that nobody knew or could know the cause of anything, all were but guessers, and so his wife's opinions were as likely to be correct as any one else's. But it is rather a shock to find learned bodies and learned men lavishing unmeasured praise upon them. Dr. Walter Charlton gravely writes to her, bidding her not be discouraged, if her philosophy have not the fate to be publicly read in all the Universities of Europe, and discusses the question whether the jealousy of philosophical teachers, the dislike of dogmatism which had recently sprang up in England, or the influence of the opposing philosophy of Aquinas, was the cause of this delay[2]. Some such reward of her labours the Duchess seems to have expected, for she

---

[1] In addition to these works the Duchess published the following :

(1.) *Philosophical Letters, or Modest Reflections upon some Opinions in Natural Philosophy maintained by several learned authors of the age.* London, 1664, folio.

(2.) *Observations upon Experimental Philosophy, to which is added the Description of a New World.* London, 1666, folio ; second edition, 1668.

(3.) *Grounds of Natural Philosophy.* London, 1668, folio. This is a second edition, much altered, of *Philosophical and Physical Opinions.*

[2] *Letters and Poems in Honour of the incomparable Princess, Margaret, Duchess of Newcastle, written by several persons of honour and learning,* 1676, p. 111, and *The Bagford Ballads,* ii, 884.

liberally supplied the public libraries of Oxford and Cambridge,
and those of many of their Colleges, with copies of her works,
and dedicated her *Philosophical Opinions* to the Universities
of England, and her *Grounds of Natural Philosophy* to the
Universities of Europe.

Passing from the consideration of her works to the consideration of the Duchess herself, the task of the critic is
more delicate and more difficult.   She has been unduly praised
and unjustly depreciated.   Clever people have sneered at
her as a pedant, and dull people still term her 'the mad
Duchess'.   Her reputation has suffered something from the
pens of others, but more from her own.   She wrote a number
of excellent things, but carefully buried them in a vast heap
of rubbish.   No woman ever more frankly described herself
in her autobiography, or more carelessly displayed herself
in her writings.   Even those who admire and love her most
must admit that some of her defects are too highly developed
for the character of a perfect heroine.   Her love of singularity
amounted to a passion ; in her philosophy as in her clothes she
was determined above all things to be original.   Her vanity
was enormous and insatiable.   'Vanity,' she says somewhere,
' is so natural to our sex that it were unnatural not to be so ' ;
but her vanity was something superfeminine.

Yet her weaknesses were very largely the results of the
circumstances in which she grew up, and the position in which
Fortune placed her.   Her education was neglected, her youth
solitary and secluded.   She associated only with the members
of her own family, and shunned the company of even near
connections.   Her stay in the court of Henrietta Maria was
too brief to give her a taste for society, or to fit her for it.
After her marriage with the Marquis of Newcastle she continued
her secluded and contemplative way of living, immuring herself in a little world of speculations and fancies, out of sight
and out of sound of the real world outside.   She had no
children, and the management of an exile's household afforded
her little occupation ; writing became to her a resource, a
pleasure, and a necessity.   'Be not too severe in your censures ', she says in one of the prefaces to her first book, ' for
first, I have no children to employ my care and attendance
on.   Next, my Lord's estate being taken away in those times
when I writ this book, I had nothing for huswifery or thrifty

industry to employ myself in, having no stock to work on. Thirdly, you are desired to spare your severe censures, because I had not so many years of experience when I wrote this book, as could make me a garland to crown my head : only I had so much time, as to gather a little posy to stick upon my breast. Lastly, the time I have been writing them hath not been very long, but since I came into England, being eight years out and nine months in ; and of these nine months, only some hours in the day, or rather in the night ; for my rest being broken with discontented thoughts, because I was from my Lord and husband, knowing him to be in great wants, and myself in the same condition ; to divert them I strove to turn the stream, and, shunning the muddy and foul ways of vice, I went to the well of Helicon, and by the well's side I did sit, and wrote this work.' And again : ' Since all times must be spent either ill, or well, or indifferently, I thought this was the most harmless pastime : for sure this work is better than to sit still, and censure my neighbours' actions, which nothing concern me ; or to condemn their humours, because they do not sympathise with mine ; or their lawful recreations, because they are not agreeable to my delight ; or ridiculously to laugh at my neighbour's clothes, if they are not of the mode, colour, or cut, or the ribbons tied with a mode-knot ; or to busy myself out of the sphere of our sex, in politics of state, or to preach false doctrine in a tub ; or to entertain myself in hearkening to vain flatteries, or to the incitements of evil persuasions ; whereas all these follies, and many more, may be cut off by such innocent work as this.'

Another motive urged the Duchess to write, and she owns it with charming simplicity. ' I confess my ambition is restless, and not ordinary, because it would have an extraordinary fame : and since all heroic actions, public employments, powerful governments, and eloquent pleadings, are denied our sex in this age, or at least would be condemned for want of custom, is the cause I write so much ; for my ambition being restless, though rather busy than industrious, yet it hath made that little wit I have to run upon every subject I can think of, or is fit for me to write on ' (Epistle to the Reader, *Nature's Pictures*, 1656).

' It will satisfy me ', says she elsewhere, ' if my writing please the readers, though not the learned ; for I had rather be praised, in this, by the most, although not the best ; for all I desire is fame, and fame is nothing but a great noise, and noise lives most in a multitude'. By a curious reversal of her wishes, exactly the contrary of what she hoped for has happened. What fame she has is with the few, and not with the many, with the best and not with the most. To some she is still the 'incomparable Princess', as contemporary panegyrists termed her, and Lamb delighted to style her. But to most she is and will be merely the fantastic figure which flits for a moment across the pages of Pepys.

The last work written by the Duchess was the *Grounds of Natural Philosophy*, published in 1668. She died on December 15, 1673, leaving, it is said, three volumes of poems in manuscript. She was buried in Westminster Abbey, on January 7, 1674, near the chapel of St. Michael. Her husband survived her three years, dying on December 25, 1676 [1]. On their monument, erected by the Duke during his lifetime, is the following inscription :

Here lyes the Loyall Duke of Newcastle, and his Dutches, his second wife, by whom he had noe issue : Her name was Margarett Lucas, yongest sister to the Lord Lucas of Colchester, a noble familie ; for all the Brothers were Valiant, and all the Sisters virtuous. This Dutches was a wise, wittie, and Learned Lady, which her many Bookes do well testifie : she was a most Virtuous and a Loveing and carefull wife, and was with her Lord all the time of his banishment and miseries, and when he came home, never parted from him in his solitary retirements.

[1] The date of the death of the Duchess is given by Anthony Wood in his account of Walter Charlton, who translated her life of the Duke into Latin (Athenæ Oxonienses). The date of the Duke's death, and the epitaph, are from Collins, who gives an engraving of the monument (Collins, *Historical Collections*, p. 44).

THE LIFE

OF THE

Thrice noble, high and puissant PRINCE

WILLIAM CAVENDISH

Duke, Marquis, and Earl of Newcastle ; Earl of Ogle ; Viscount Mansfield ; and Baron of Bolsover, of Ogle, Bothal and Hepple : Gentleman of His Majesty's Bed-chamber ; one of His Majesty's most Honourable Privy Council ; Knight of the most noble Order of the Garter ; His Majesty's Lieutenant of the county and town of Nottingham ; and Justice in Eyre Trent-North : who had the honour to be Governor to our most glorious King and gracious Sovereign, in his youth, when he was Prince of Wales ; and soon after was made Captain-General of all the provinces beyond the river of Trent, and other parts of the kingdom of England, with power, by a special commission, to make Knights.

Written by the thrice noble, illustrious and excellent Princess, Margaret, Duchess of Newcastle, his Wife

LONDON,

Printed by *A. Maxwell*, in the Year 1667

TO HIS MOST SACRED MAJESTY

CHARLES THE SECOND,

By the Grace of God, of England, Scotland, France, and Ireland King, Defender of the Faith, &c.

MAY IT PLEASE YOUR MAJESTY,—I have, in confidence of your gracious acceptance, taken the boldness, or rather the presumption, to dedicate to your Majesty this short history (which is as full of truths, as words) of the actions and sufferings of your most loyal subject, my lord and husband (by your Majesty's late favour) Duke of Newcastle; who when your Majesty was Prince of Wales, was your most careful governor, and honest servant. Give me therefore leave to relate here, that I have heard him often say, he loves your royal person so dearly, that he would most willingly, upon all occasions, sacrifice his life and posterity for your Majesty: whom that Heaven will ever bless, is the prayer of your most obedient, loyal, humble subject and servant,

MARGARET NEWCASTLE.

THE DUKE OF NEWCASTLE,

MY NOBLE LORD,—It hath always been my hearty prayer to God, since I have been your wife, that first I might prove an honest and good wife, whereof your Grace must be the only judge : next, that God would be pleased to enable me to set forth and declare to after ages, the truth of your loyal actions and endeavours, for the service of your King and country ; for the accomplishing of which design, I have followed the best and truest observations of your secretary John Rolleston [1], and your Lordship's own relations, and have accordingly writ the history of your Lordship's life, which, although I have endeavoured to render as perspicuous as ever I could, yet one thing I find hath much darkened it ; which is, that your Grace commanded me not to mention any thing or passage to the prejudice or disgrace of any family or particular person (although they might be of great truth, and would illustrate much the actions of your life) which I have dutifully performed to satisfy your Lordship [2], whose nature is so generous, that you are as well pleased to obscure the faults of your enemies, as you are to divulge the virtues of your friends. And certainly, my Lord, you have had as many enemies, and as many friends, as ever any one particular person had ; and I pray God to forgive the one, and prosper the other. Nor do I so much wonder at it, since I, a woman, cannot be exempt from the malice and aspersions of spiteful tongues, which they cast upon my poor writings, some denying me to be the true authoress of them ; for your Grace remembers well, that those books I put out first to the judgment of this censorious age, were accounted not to be written by a woman, but that somebody else had writ and published

[1] Rolleston died in 1681. His epitaph is printed in Bailey's *Annals of Notts*, ii, 988.
[2] This is probably the reason for the obliteration of so many proper names in the first edition, which was done by hand after the book had been printed.

them in my name ; by which your Lordship was moved to
prefix an Epistle before one of them in my vindication, wherein
you assure the world upon your honour, that what was written
and printed in my name, was my own [1] ; and I have also
made known, that your Lordship was my only tutor, in
declaring to me what you had found and observed by your
own experience ; for I being young when your Lordship
married me, could not have much knowledge of the world ;
but it pleased God to command His servant Nature to indue
me with a poetical and philosophical genius, even from my
birth ; for I did write some books in that kind, before I was
twelve years of age, which for want of good method and
order, I would never divulge. But though the world would
not believe that those conceptions and fancies which I writ
were my own, but transcended my capacity, yet they found
fault that they were defective for want of learning ; and on
the other side, they said I had plucked feathers out of the
universities ; which was a very preposterous judgment. Truly,
my Lord, I confess that for want of scholarship, I could not
express myself so well as otherwise I might have done, in
those philosophical writings I published first ; but after I
was returned with your Lordship into my native country,
and led a retired country life, I applied myself to the reading
of philosophical authors, of purpose to learn those names and
words of art that are used in schools ; which at first were so
hard to me, that I could not understand them, but was fain
to guess at the sense of them by the whole context, and so
write them down as I found them in those authors, at which
my readers did wonder and thought it impossible that a
woman could have so much learning and understanding in
terms of art, and scholastical expressions ; so that I and my
books are like the old apologue, mentioned in Æsop, of a
father, and his son, who rid on an ass through a town when
his father went on foot, at which sight the people shouted and
cried shame, that a young boy should ride, and let his father,
an old man, go on foot : whereupon the old man got upon
the ass, and let his son go by. But when they came to the
next town, the people exclaimed against the father, that he,

---

[1] An Epistle to justify the Lady Newcastle, and truth against falsehood, laying those
false and malicious aspersions of her, that she was not author of her books, prefixed,
to *Philosophical and Physical Opinions*, 1655.

a lusty man, should ride, and have no more pity of his young
and tender child, but let him go on foot. Then both the
father and his son got upon the ass, and coming to the third
town, the people blamed them both for being so unconscionable as to overburden the poor ass with their heavy weight.
After this both father and son went on foot, and led the ass ;
and when they came to the fourth town, the people railed
as much at them as ever the former had done, and called
them both fools, for going on foot, when they had a beast
able to carry them.   The old man, seeing he could not please
mankind in any manner, and having received so many blemishes and aspersions, for the sake of his ass, was at last resolved
to drown him when he came to the next bridge.   But I am
not so passionate to burn my writings for the various humours
of mankind, and for their finding fault, since there is nothing
in this world, be it the noblest and most commendable action
whatsoever, that shall escape blameless.   As for my being the
true and only authoress of them, your Lordship knows best,
and my attending servants are witness that I have had none
but my own thoughts, fancies, and speculations to assist
me ;   and as soon as I have set them down, I send them to
those that are to transcribe them, and fit them for the press ;
whereof since there have been several, and amongst them
such as only could write a good hand, but neither understood
orthography, nor had any learning (I being then in banishment with your Lordship, and not able to maintain learned
secretaries), which hath been a great disadvantage to my poor
works, and the cause that they have been printed so false and
so full of errors ;   for besides that I want also the skill of
scholarship and true writing, I did many times not peruse
the copies that were transcribed, lest they should disturb
my following conceptions ; by which neglect, as I said, many
errors are slipt into my works, which yet I hope learned and
impartial readers will soon rectify, and look more upon the
sense than carp at words.   I have been a student even from
my childhood ; and since I have been your Lordship's wife,
I have lived for the most part a strict and retired life, as is
best known to your Lordship, and therefore my censurers
cannot know much of me, since they have little or no acquaintance with me.   'Tis true, I have been a traveller both before
and after I was married to your Lordship, and sometimes

show myself at your Lordship's command in public places or assemblies ; but yet I converse with few. Indeed, my Lord, I matter not the censures of this age, but am rather proud of them ; for it shows that my actions are more than ordinary, and according to the old proverb, it is better to be envied than pitied : for I know well, that it is merely out of spite and malice, whereof this present age is so full, that none can escape them, and they'll make no doubt to stain even your Lordship's loyal, noble, and heroic actions, as well as they do mine, though yours have been of war and fighting, mine of contemplating and writing: yours were performed publicly in the field, mine privately in my closet : yours had many thousand eye-witnesses, mine none but my waiting-maids. But the great God, that hath hitherto blessed both your Grace and me, will, I question not, preserve both our fames to after ages, for which we shall be bound most humbly to acknowledge His great mercy ; and I myself, as long as I live, be your Grace's honest wife, and humble servant,

M. NEWCASTLE.

THE PREFACE

WHEN I first intended to write this history, knowing myself to be no scholar, and as ignorant of the rules of writing histories, as I have in my other works acknowledged myself to be of the names and terms of art; I desired my Lord, that he would be pleased to let me have some elegant and learned historian to assist me; which request his Grace would not grant me; saying, that having never had any assistance in the writing of my former books, I should have no other in the writing of his life, but the informations from himself, and his secretary, of the chief transactions and fortunes occurring in it, to the time he married me. I humbly answered, that without a learned assistant, the history would be defective: but he replied, that truth could not be defective. I said again, that rhetoric did adorn truth: and he answered, that rhetoric was fitter for falsehoods than truths. Thus I was forced by his Grace's commands, to write this history in my own plain style, without elegant flourishings, or exquisite method, relying entirely upon truth, in the expressing whereof, I have been very circumspect; as knowing well, that his Grace's actions have so much glory of their own, that they need borrow none from anybody's industry.

Many learned men, I know, have published rules and directions concerning the method and style of histories, and do with great noise, to little purpose, make loud exclamations against those historians, that keeping close to the truth of their narrations, cannot think it necessary to follow slavishly such instructions; and there is some men of good understandings, as I have heard, that applaud very much several histories, merely for their elegant style, and well-observed method; setting a high value upon feigned orations, mystical designs, and fancied policies, which are, at the best, but pleasant romances. Others approve, in the relations of wars, and of military actions, such tedious descriptions, that the reader, tired with them, will imagine that there was more time spent

in assaulting, defending, and taking of a fort, or a petty garrison, than Alexander did employ in conquering the greatest
part of the world : which proves, that such historians regard
more their own eloquence, wit, and industry, and the knowledge they believe to have of the actions of war, and of all
manner of governments, than of the truth of the history,
which is the main thing, and wherein consists the hardest task,
very few historians knowing the transactions they write of,
and much less the counsels and secret designs of many different parties, which they confidently mention.

Although there be many sorts of histories, yet these three
are the chiefest : (1) a general history ; (2) a national history ;
(3) a particular history.   Which three sorts may, not unfitly,
be compared to the three sorts of governments, democracy,
aristocracy, and monarchy.   The first is the history of the
known parts and people of the world ; the second is the history of a particular nation, kingdom, or commonwealth.
The third is the history of the life and actions of some particular person.   The first is profitable for travellers, navigators,
and merchants ; the second is pernicious, by reason it teaches
subtle policies, begets factions, not only between particular
families and persons, but also between whole nations, and
great princes, rubbing old sores, and renewing old quarrels,
that would otherwise have been forgotten.   The last is the
most secure ; because it goes not out of its own circle, but
turns on its own axis, and for the most part keeps within the
circumference of truth.   The first is mechanical, the second
political, and the third heroical.   The first should only be
written by travellers and navigators ; the second by statesmen ; the third by the prime actors, or the spectators of those
affairs and actions of which they write, as Cæsar's Commen-
taries are, which no pen but of such an-author, who was also
actor in the particular occurrences, private intrigues, secret
counsels, close designs, and rare exploits of war he relates,
could ever have brought to so high perfection.

This history is of the third sort, as that is ; and being of
the life and actions of my noble lord and husband, who hath
informed me of all the particular passages I have recorded, I
cannot, though neither actor nor spectator, be thought ignor-
nant of the truth of what I write.   Nor is it inconsistent
with my being a woman, to write of wars, that was neither

between Medes and Persians, Greeks and Trojans, Christians and Turks, but among my own countrymen, whose customs and inclinations, and most of the persons that held any considerable place in the armies, was well known to me; and besides all that (which is above all) my noble and loyal Lord did act a chief part in that fatal tragedy, to have defended (if human power could have done it) his most gracious sovereign from the fury of his rebellious subjects.

This history being (as I have said) of a particular person, his actions and fortunes, it cannot be expected that I should here preach of the beginning of the world; nor seem to express understanding in the politics, by tedious moral discourses, with long observations upon the several sorts of government that have been in Greece and Rome, and upon others more modern. I will neither endeavour to make show of eloquence, making speeches that never were spoken, nor pretend to great skill in war, by making mountains of molehills, and telling romancical falsehoods for historical truths; and much less will I write to amuse my readers, in a mystical and allegorical style, of the disloyal actions of the opposite party, of the treacherous cowardice, envy, and malice of some persons, my Lord's enemies, and of the ingratitude of some of his seeming friends; wherein I cannot better obey his Lordship's commands to conceal those things, than in leaving them quite out, as I do, with submission to his Lordship's desire, from whom I have learned patience to overcome my passions, and discretion to yield to his prudence.

Thus am I resolved to write, in a natural plain style, without Latin sentences, moral instructions, politic designs, feigned orations, or envious and malicious exclamations, this short history of the loyal, heroic, and prudent actions of my noble Lord, as also of his sufferings, losses, and ill-fortunes, which in honour and conscience I could not suffer to be buried in silence; nor could I have undertaken so hard a task, had not my love to his person, and to truth, been my encourager and supporter.

I might have made this book larger, in transcribing (as is ordinary in histories) the several letters [1], full of affection,

---

[1] Seven of these letters of the King's have been published by Sir Henry Ellis, *Original Letters*, series I, vol. iii, pp. 291–303. Those of the Queen will be found in Mrs. M. E. Green's *Letters of Queen Henrietta Maria*.
The Declarations referred to below are reprinted in Rushworth's Collection: 'A

and kind promises he received from his Gracious Sovereign,
Charles the First, and from his royal consort, in the time he
was in the actions of war, as also since the war, from his dear
sovereign and master, Charles the Second: but many of
the former letters having been lost, when all was lost, I thought
it best, seeing I had not them all, to print none. As for
orations, which is another way of swelling the bulk of histories,
it is certain, that my Lord made not many; choosing rather
to fight than to talk; and his Declarations having been printed
already, it had been superfluous to insert them in these narrations.

This book would, however, have been a great volume, if
his Grace would have given me leave to publish his enemy's
actions. But being to write of his own only, I do it briefly
and truly; and not as many have done, who have written of
the late Civil War, with but few sprinklings of truth, like as
heat-drops upon a dry barren ground: knowing no more of
the transactions of those times, than what they learned in
the gazettes, which, for the most part (out of policy to amuse
and deceive the people), contain nothing but falsehoods and
chimeras; and were such parasites, that after the King's
party was overpowered, the government among the rebels
changing from one faction to another, they never missed to
exalt highly the merits of the chief commanders of the then
prevailing side, comparing some of them to Moses, and some
others to all the great and most famous heroes, both Greeks
and Romans [1]. Wherein, unawares, they exceedingly commended my noble Lord; for if those ringleaders of factions
were so great men as they are reported to be, by those time-
servers, how much greater must his Lordship be, who beat
most of them, except the Earl of Essex, whose employment
was never in the northern parts, where all the rest of the
greatest strength of the Parliament was sent, to oppose my
Lord's forces, which was the greatest the King's party had
anywhere

Declaration made by the Earl of Newcastle for his resolution of marching into Yorkshire, as also a just vindication of himself from that unjust aspersion laid upon him for
entertaining some Popish recusants in his service.'—Rushworth, III, i, 78–81. 'A
Declaration of his Excellency the Earl of Newcastle, in answer to the aspersions cast
upon him by the Lord Fairfax in his warrant bearing date February 2d.'—Rushworth
III, i, 133.
[1] This is evidently a hit at Thomas May's *History of the Long Parliament*.

Good fortune is such an idol of the world, and is so like the golden calf worshipped by the Israelites, that those arch-rebels never wanted astrologers to foretell them good success in all their enterprises, nor poets to sing their praises, nor orators for panegyrics ; nay, which is worse, nor historians neither, to record their valour in fighting, and wisdom in governing. But being, so much as I am, above base profit, or any preferment whatsoever, I cannot fear to be suspected of flattery, in declaring to the world the merits, wealth, power, loyalty, and fortunes of my noble Lord, who hath done great actions, suffered great losses, endured a long banishment, for his loyalty to his King and country ; and leads now, like another Scipio, a quiet country life. If, notwithstanding all this, any should say, that those who write histories of themselves, and their own actions, or of their own party, or instruct and inform those that write them, are partial to themselves ; I answer, that it is very improbable worthy persons, who having done great, noble, and heroic exploits, deserving to be recorded, should be so vain as to write false histories ; but if they do, it proves but their folly ; for truth can never be concealed, and so it will be more for their disgrace than for their honour and fame. I fear not any such blemishes in this present history, for I am not conscious of any such crime as partiality or falsehood, but write it whilst my noble Lord is yet alive, and at such a time where truth may be declared, and falsehood contradicted ; and I challenge any one (although I be a woman) to contradict anything that I have set down, or prove it to be otherwise than truth ; for be there never so many contradictions, truth will conquer all at last.

Concerning my Lord's actions in war, which are comprehended in the first Book, the relation of them I have chiefly from my Lord's secretary, Mr. Rolleston, a person that has been an eye-witness thereof, and accompanied my Lord as secretary in his army, and gave out all his commissions ; his honesty and worth is unquestionable by all that know him. And as for the second Book, which contains my Lord's actions and sufferings, during the time of his exile, I have set down so much as I could possibly call to mind, without any particular expression of time, only from the time of his banishment, or rather (what I can remember) from the time of my marriage, till our return into England. To the end of which I have joined a computation of my Lord's losses, which he hath suffered by those unfortunate wars. In the third Book I have set down some particular chapters concerning the description of his person, his natural faculties, and personal virtues, etc. And in the last, some essays and discourses of my Lord's, together with some notes and remarks of mine own ; which I thought most convenient to place by themselves at the end of this work, rather than to intermingle them with the body of the history.

It might be some prejudice to my Lord's glory, and the credit of this history, not to take notice of a very considerable thing I have heard, which is, that when his Lordship's army had got so much strength and reputation, that the rebellious Parliament finding themselves overpowered with it, rather than to be utterly ruined (as was unavoidable), did call the Scots to their assistance, with a promise to reward so great a service with the four northern counties of Northumberland, Cumberland, Westmoreland, and the bishopric of Durham, which I have not mentioned in the book.

And it is most certain, that the Parliament's forces were never powerful, nor their commanders or officers famous, until such time as my Lord was overpowered ; neither could loyalty have been overpowered by rebellion, had not treachery had better fortune than prudence.

When I speak of my Lord's pedigree, where Thomas, Earl of Arundel, grandfather to the now Duke of Norfolk, is mentioned, they have left out William, Viscount Stafford, one of his sons, who did marry the heir of the last Baron Stafford, descended from the Dukes of Buckingham ; which was set down in my original manuscript.

Some of those omissions, and very probably others, are happened, partly for want of timely information, and chiefly by the death of my secretary who did copy my writings for the press, and died in London, attending that service, afore the printing of the book was quite finished. And as I hope of your favour to be excused for omitting those things in the book ; so I expect of your justice to be approved in putting them here, though somewhat unseasonably.

Before I end this Preface, I do beseech my readers not to mistake me when I speak of my Lord's banishment, as if I would conceal that he went voluntarily out of his native country; for it is most true, that his Lordship prudently perceiving all the King's party lost, not only in England, but also in Scotland and Ireland; and that it was impossible to withstand the rebels, after the fatal overthrow of his army; his Lordship, in a poor and mean condition, quitted his own country, and went beyond sea; soon after which, the rebels having got an absolute power, and granted a general pardon to all those that would come in to them, upon composition, at the rates they had set down, his Lordship, with but few others, was excepted from it, both for life and estate, and did remain thus banished till his Majesty's happy restoration.

I must also acknowledge, that I have committed great errors in taking no notice of times as I should have done in many places of this history: I mention in one place the Queen Mother's being in France, when my Lord went thither, but do not say in what year that was; nor do I express when his Majesty (our now gracious Sovereign) came in, and went out again several times from that kingdom, which has happened for want of memory, and I desire my readers to excuse me for it

Nobody can certainly be more ready to find faults in this work, than I am to confess them; being very conscious that I have, as I told my Lord I should, committed many for want of learning, and chiefly of skill in writing histories. But having, according to his Lordship's commands, written his actions and fortunes truly and plainly, I have reason to expect, that whatsoever else shall be found amiss, will be favourably pardoned by the candid readers, to whom I wish all manner of happiness.

THE DUCHESS OF NEWCASTLE

MAY IT PLEASE YOUR GRACE,—I have been taught, and do believe, that obedience is better than sacrifice ; and know, that both are due from me to your Grace ; and since I have been so long in obeying your commands, I shall not presume to use any agruments for my excuse, but rather choose ingenuously to confess my fault, and beg your Grace's pardon. And because forgiveness is a glory to the supremest powers, I will hope that your Grace by that great example will make it yours. And now I humbly take leave to represent to your Grace, as faithfully and truly as my memory will serve me, all my observations of the most memorable actions, and honourable deportments of his Grace, my most noble lord and master, William, Duke of Newcastle, in the execution and performance of the trusts and high employments committed and commended to his care and charge by three kings of England ; that is to say, King James, King Charles the First, of ever blessed memory ; and our gracious King, Charles the Second ; under whom he hath had the happiness to live, and the honour to serve them in several capacities. And because I humbly conceive, that it is not within the intention of your Grace's commands, that I should give you a particular relation of his Grace's high birth, his noble and princely education and breeding, both at home and abroad ; his natural faculties, and personal virtues ; his justice, bounty, charity, friendship ; his right approved courage, and true valour, not grounded upon, or governed by passion, but reason ; his magnificent manner of living and supporting his dignity, testified by his great entertainments of their Majesties, and his private friends, upon all fit occasions, beside his ordinary and constant housekeeping and attendants, some for honour, and some for business, wherein he exceeded most of his quality ; and that he was and is, an incomparable master to his servants, is suffi-

ciently testified by all or most of the chiefest of them, living
and dying in his Grace's service, which is an argument that
they thought themselves as happy therein, as the world could
make them; nor of his well-chosen pleasures, which were
principally horses of all sorts, but more particularly horses
of manage; [1] his study and art of the true use of the sword;
his magnificent buildings. These are his chiefest delights,
wherein his Grace spared for no cost nor charge, which are sufficiently manifested to the world; for other delights, as those
of running horses, hawking, hunting, etc., his Grace used
them merely for society's sake, and out of a generous and
obliging nature to please others, though his knowledge in
them excelled, as well as in the other. And yet, notwithstanding these this large and vast expenses, before his Grace
was called to the court, he increased his revenue by way of
purchase to a great value; and when he was called to the
court, he was then free from debts, and, as I have heard,
some thousands of pounds in his purse. These particulars,
and as many more of this kind as would swell a volume,
I could enumerate to your Grace; but that they are so well
known to your Grace, it would be a presumption in me, rather
than a service, to give your Grace that trouble; and therefore
I humbly forbear, and proceed, according to my intention, to
give your Grace a faithful account of your Grace's commands,
as becomes, may it please your Grace, your Grace's most
humble and most obedient servant,

JOHN ROLLESTON.

---

1 Horses trained in the riding-school. Manage is from the French *manège*, the train-
ing of a horse in a riding-school; Italian *maneggiare*, to handle, train, from Latin *manus*.
In Book II of these *Memoirs* the Duchess speaks of her husband buying horses ' to
exercise the art of manage, which he is a great lover and master of '. ' They vault
from hunters to the managed steed ', says Young, and Scott even speaks of a ' managed
hawk '. Orlando, when complaining of his brother's neglect, says: ' His horses are
bred better; for, besides that they are fair with their feeding, they are taught their
manage, and to that end riders dearly hired.'—*As You Like It*, I, i, 11-3. Lady Hot-
spur also tells her husband that she has heard him in his sleep ' speak terms of manage
to thy bounding steed.'—1 Henry IV, II, iii, 52.

THE LIFE

OF

THE MOST ILLUSTRIOUS PRINCE,

WILLIAM, DUKE OF NEWCASTLE

THE FIRST BOOK

SINCE my chief intent in this present work is to describe the life and actions of my noble Lord and husband, William, Duke of Newcastle, I shall do it with as much brevity, perspicuity, and truth, as is required of an impartial historian. The history of his pedigree I shall refer to the Heralds, and partly give you an account thereof at the latter end of this work ; only thus much I shall now mention, as will be requisite for the better understanding of the following discourse.

His grandfather by his father's side was Sir William Cavendish, Privy Counsellor and Treasurer of the Chamber to King Henry the Eighth, Edward the Sixth, and Queen Mary. His grandfather by his mother was Cuthbert, Lord Ogle, an ancient Baron. His father, Sir Charles Cavendish, was the youngest son to Sir William, and had no other children but three sons, whereof my Lord was the second ; but his elder brother dying in his infancy, left both his title and birthright to my Lord, so that my Lord had then but one only brother left, whose name was Charles after his father, whereas my Lord had the name of his grandfather [1].

These two brothers were partly bred with Gilbert, Earl of Shrewsbury, their uncle-in-law, and their aunt Mary, Countess

---

[1] Sir William Cavendish died in 1557. His widow, Elizabeth Hardwick, married George Talbot, Earl of Shrewsbury, and thus began the connection between the Talbot and Cavendish families, which was strengthened and completed by the marriage of Mary Cavendish, youngest daughter of Sir William, to Gilbert Talbot, the eldest son of Earl George, whilst Henry Cavendish, eldest son of Sir William, married Grace Talbot, youngest daughter of the same Earl. William Cavendish, the hero of this Memoir,

of Shrewsbury, Gilbert's wife, and sister to their father ; for there interceded an entire and constant friendship between the said Gilbert, Earl of Shrewsbury, and my Lord's father, Sir Charles Cavendish, caused not only by the marriage of my Lord's aunt, his father's sister, to the aforesaid Gilbert. Earl of Shrewsbury, and by the marriage of George, Earl of Shrewsbury, Gilbert's father with my Lord's grandmother, by his father's side ; but Sir Charles Cavendish, my Lord's father, and Gilbert, Earl of Shrewsbury, being brought up and bred together in one family, and grown up as parts of one body, after they came to be beyond children, and travelled together into foreign countries, to observe the fashions, laws, and customs of other nations, contracted such an entire friendship which lasted to their death. Neither did they outlive each other long, for my Lord's father, Sir Charles Cavendish, lived but one year after Gilbert, Earl of Shrewsbury.

But both my Lord's parents, and his aunt and uncle-in-law, showed always a great and fond love to my Lord, endeavouring, when he was but a child, to please him with what he most delighted in. When he was grown to the age of fifteen or sixteen, he was made Knight of the Bath, an ancient and honourable order, at the time when Henry, King James, of blessed memory, his eldest son, was created Prince of Wales [1] : and soon after he went to travel with Sir Henry Wotton [2], who was sent as ambassador extraordinary to the then Duke of Savoy ; which Duke made very much of my Lord, and

was born in 1592. Gilbert, Earl of Shrewsbury, died May 8, 1616, and Sir Charles Cavendish died April 4, 1617. Ben Jonson wrote the following epitaph upon him :

Charles Cavendish to his Posterity.

Sons, seek me not amongst these polished stones,
These only hide part of my flesh and bones,
Which, did they ne'er so neat or proudly dwell,
Will all turn dust, and may not make me swell.

Let such as justly have outlived all praise,
Trust in the tombs their careful friends do raise ;
I made my life my monument and yours,
To which there's no material that endures.

Nor yet inscription like it. Write but that,
And teach your nephews it to emulate :
It will be matter loud enough to tell
Not when I died, but how I lived – farewell.

Collins' *Historical Collections*, p. 22, and Cunningham's Jonson, iii, 459.

[1] Prince Henry was created Prince of Wales, June 4, 1610. William Cavendish was made Knight of the Bath, June 3—Birch, *Life of Henry Prince of Wales*, p. 192.
[2] In 1612. See Nichols, *Progresses of King James I*, ii, 438.

when he would be free in feasting, placed him next to himself.
Before my Lord did return with the ambassador into England,
the said Duke proffered my Lord, that if he would stay with
him, he would not only confer upon him the best titles of
honour he could, but also give him an honourable command
in war, although my Lord was but young, for the Duke had
then some designs of war. But the ambassador, who had
taken the care of my Lord, would not leave him behind without his parents' consent.

At last, when my Lord took his leave of the Duke, the Duke
being a very generous person, presented him with a Spanish
horse, a saddle very richly embroidered, and with a rich jewel
of diamonds.

Some time after my Lord's return into England, Gilbert,
Earl of Shrewsbury, died, and left my Lord, though he was
then but young, and about twenty-two years of age, his
executor [1]; a year after, his father, Sir Charles Cavendish,
died also. His mother, being then a widow, was desirous
that my Lord should marry : in obedience to whose commands,
he chose a wife both to his own good liking, and his mother's
approving ; who was daughter and heir to William Basset of
Blore, Esq. ; a very honourable and ancient family in Staffordshire, by whom was added a great part to his estate, as hereafter shall be mentioned [2]. After my Lord was married, he
lived, for the most part, in the country, and pleased himself
and his neighbours with hospitality, and such delights as the
country afforded ; only now and then he would go up to
London for some short time to wait on the King.

About this time King James, of blessed memory, having a
purpose to confer some honour upon my Lord, made him
Viscount Mansfield, and Baron of Bolsover [3]; and after the
decease of King James, King Charles the First, of blessed
memory, constituted him Lord Warden of the Forest of Sherwood and Lieutenant of Nottinghamshire, and restored his

[1] The Earl of Shrewsbury died May 8, 1616. His will is printed in Hunter's *History of Hallamshire*, ed. Gatty p. 101.
[2] The rents of the Duke of Newcastle's Staffordshire estates amounted to £2349 17s. 4d. per annum. See the account of the Duke's estates given later. This lady was the widow of Henry Howard, third son of the Earl of Suffolk. The marriage probably took place in 1618.
[3] This took place after the King's visit to Welbeck in 1619. The patent creating Sir William Cavendish Lord Ogle of Bothal and Viscount Mansfield is dated November 3, 1620.—Collins, *Historical Collections of the Noble Families of Cavendish, Holles*, etc., p. 29.

mother, Catharine, the second daughter of Cuthbert, Lord
Ogle, to her father's dignity, after the death of her only sister
Jane, Countess of Shrewsbury, publicly declaring, that it
was her right [1]; which title, after the death of his mother,
descended also upon my Lord, and his heirs general, together
with a large inheritance of £3000 a year, in Northumberland.

About the same time, after the decease of William, late
Earl of Devonshire, his noble cousin-german, my Lord was
by his said Majesty made Lord Lieutenant of Derbyshire ;
which trust and honour, after he had enjoyed for several
years, and managed it, like as all other offices put to his trust,
with all possible care, faithfulness, and dexterity, during the
time of the said Earl's son, William, the now Earl of Devonshire, his minority, as soon as this same Earl was come to age,
and by law made capable of that trust, he willingly and freely
resigned it into his hands, he having hitherto kept it only for
him, that he and nobody else might succeed his father in that
dignity.

In these, and all other both public and private employments,
my Lord hath ever been careful to keep up the King's rights
to the uttermost of his power, to strengthen those mentioned

[1] Lady Jane Ogle died in 1625. Her epitaph was written by Jonson, *vide* Jonson's
works, ed. Cunningham, p. 460. Lady Catharine was created Baroness Ogle, December
4, 1628 (Collins, p. 24). She died about April 1629 (*Report on the Portland MSS.* ii, 120)
Jonson's epitaph on this lady is as follows :

> She was the light (without reflex
> Upon herself) of all her sex,
> The best of women !—Her whole life
> Was the example of a wife,
> Or of a parent, or a friend !
> All circles had their spring and end
> In her, and what could perfect be
> And without angles, *It was she*.
> All that was solid in the name
> Of virtue ; precious in the frame,
> Or else magnetic in the force,
> Or sweet, or various in the course ;
> What was proportion, or could be
> By warrant called just symmetry,
> In number, measure, or degree
> Of weight or fashion, *It was she*.
> Her soul possessed her flesh's state
> In freehold, not as an inmate,
> And when the flesh here shut up day,
> Fame's heat upon the grave did stay,
> And hourly brooding o'er the same,
> Keeps warm the spice of her good name,
> Until the ashes turned be
> Into a Phoenix—*Which is she*.

This is followed by two other pieces of verse on the same subject.—Jonson, ed. Cunningham, iii, 460.

counties with ammunition, and to adminster justice to every one ; for he refused no man's petition, but sent all that came to him, either for relief or justice, away from him fully satisfied [1].

Not long after his being made Lieutenant of Nottingham-shire, there was found so great a defect of arms and ammuni-tion in that county, that the Lords of the Council being adver-tised thereof, as the manner then was, his Majesty commanded a levy to be made upon the whole county for the supply thereof. Whereupon the sum of £500, or thereabout, was accordingly levied for that purpose, and three persons of quality, then Deputy Lieutenants, were desired by my Lord to receive the money, and see it disposed ; which being done accordingly, and a certain account rendered to my Lord, he voluntarily ordered the then Clerk of the Peace of that county, that the same account should be recorded amongst the sessions rolls, and be published in open sessions, to the end that the country might take notice how their monies were disposed of ; for which act of justice my Lord was highly commended.

Within some few years after, King Charles the First, of blessed memory, his gracious Sovereign, in regard of his true and faithful service to his King and country, was pleased to honour him with the title of Earl of Newcastle, and Baron of Bothal and Heple [2] ; which title he graced so much by his noble actions and deportments, that some seven years after, which was in the year 1638, his Majesty called him up to Court, and thought him the fittest person whom he might intrust with the government of his son Charles, then Prince of Wales, now our most gracious King, and made him withal a a member of the Lords of his Majesty's most honourable Privy Council ; which, as it was a great honour and trust, so he spared no care and industry to discharge his duty accord-ingly ; and to that end, left all the care of governing his own family and estate, with all fidelity attending his master, not without considerable charges, and vast expenses of his own [3].

---

[1] A letter from the Duke (as Viscount Mansfield) to Strafford is printed in the Strafford correspondence, vol. i, p. 43, vide Appendix.

[2] ' On the 7th day of March in the third year of King Charles I he was further advanced to the dignity of Baron Cavendish of Bolsover and Earl of Newcastle-upon-Tyne.'—Collins, *Historical Collections*, p. 26.

[3] Newcastle's letters to his wife show that he was seeking for this post as early as April 1636, and had good hopes of success. (*Portland MSS.*, ii, 127). The patent ap-pointing the Earl of Newcastle governor of the Prince is dated June 4, 1638, and has

In this present employment he continued for the space of three years, during which time there happened an insurrection and rebellion of his Majesty's discontented subjects in Scotland, which forced his Majesty to raise an army, to reduce them to their obedience, and his treasury being at that time exhausted he was necessitated to desire some supply and assistance of the noblest and richest of his loyal subjects. Amongst the rest, my Lord lent his Majesty £10,000 and raised himself a volunteer troop of horse, which consisted of 120 knights and gentlemen of quality [1], who marched to Berwick by his Majesty's command, where it pleased his Majesty to set this mark of honour upon that troop, that it should be independent, and not commanded by any general officer, but only by his Majesty himself. [2] The reason thereof was upon this following occasion.

His Majesty's whole body of horse, being commanded to march into Scotland against the rebels, a place was appointed for their rendezvous ; immediately upon their meeting, my Lord sent a gentleman of quality of his troop [3] to his Majesty's then General of the Horse, to know where his troop should march ; who returned this answer, That it was to march next after the troops of the General Officers of the Field. My Lord conceiving that his troop ought to march in the van, and not in the rear, sent the same messenger back again to the General, to inform him, that he had the honour to march with the Prince's colours, and therefore he thought it not fit to march

been printed by Collins (*Historical Collections*, p. 27). Windebanke's letter offering this post to the Earl, and the Earl's reply, are both contained in the Clarendon State Papers, and dated 19th and 21st March 1638. For these see the Appendix. ' It is certainly a mighty mark of his Majesty's estimation of you ', writes Strafford, ' that he intrusts you with the keeping of so precious a jewel '. The Lord Deputy sends at the same time a number of counsels for the Earl's guidance at court (*Strafford Papers*, ii, 174). The advice given by the Earl to his pupil, originally printed by Sir Henry Ellis, is also given in the Appendix. A letter in the Record Office, written by one Thomas Wiseman on Newcastle's retirement from this post, states that the Earl ran himself into debt to the amount of £40,000 during his employment.

1 Mrs. Hutchinson's testimony to the Earl's great popularity is worth quoting ; it will be observed that her account of the volunteer troop differs slightly from that given by the Duchess : ' The Earl of Newcastle . . . a lord once so much beloved in his country, that when the first expedition was against the Scots, the gentlemen of the country set him forth two troops, one all of gentlemen, the other of their men, who waited on him into the north at their own charges. He had, indeed, through his great estate, his liberal hospitality, and constant residence in his country, so endeared them to him, that no man was a greater prince than he was in all that northern quarter ; till a foolish ambition of glorious slavery carried him to court, where he ran himself much into debt, to purchase neglects of the King and Queen, and scorns of the proud courtiers.'—*Memoirs*, vol. i, p. 163.

2 On April 1, 1639 Newcastle was commissioned as captain of the troop of horse called Prince Charles's troop. (*Portland MSS.*, ii, 132).

3 Sir William Carnaby, Kt.

under any of the Officers of the Field ; yet nevertheless the General ordered that troop as he had formerly directed. Whereupon, my Lord thinking it unfit at that time to dispute the business, immediately commanded his Cornet[1] to take off the Prince's colours from his staff, and so marched in the place appointed, choosing rather to march without his colours flying, than to lessen his master's dignity by the command of any subject[2].

Immediately after the return from that expedition to his Majesty's leaguer, the General made a complaint thereof to his Majesty ; who being truly informed of the business, commended my Lord's discretion for it, and from that time ordered that troop to be commanded by none but himself. Thus they remained upon duty, *without receiving any payment or allowance from his Majesty*[3], until his Majesty had reduced his rebellious subjects, and then my Lord returned with honour to his charge, viz. the government of the Prince.

At last when the whole army was disbanded, then, and not before, my Lord thought it a fit time to exact an account from the said General for the affront he passed upon him, and sent him a challenge ; the place and hour being appointed by both their consents, where and when to meet, my Lord appeared there with his second[4], but found not his opposite. After some while his opposite's second came all alone, by whom my Lord perceived that their design had been discovered to the King by some of his opposite's friends, who presently caused them both to be confined until he had made their peace[5].

My Lord having hitherto attended the Prince, his master, with all faithfulness and duty befitting so great an employment, for the space of three years, in the beginning of that

---

[1] Mr. Gray, brother to the Lord Gray of the North.
[2] This incident took place on the march to Dunse, May 31, 1639. Accounts of the dispute confirming that given by the Duchess are printed in the *Report on the MSS.* of *the Duke of Rutland*, i, 512, 517, and in Warner's *Epistolary Curiosities*, i, 201.
[3] The words in italic have been carefully obliterated with ink.
[4] Francis Palmes.
[5] This General of the Horse was the Earl of Holland. Clarendon's account of this incident is very similar to that given in the text, and was very probably derived from the Duke himself. As soon as the army was disbanded, says Clarendon, Newcastle ' sent a challenge to the Earl of Holland, by a gentleman very punctual and well acquainted with those errands ; who took a proper season to mention it to him, without a possibility of suspicion. The Earl of Holland was never suspected to want courage, yet in this occasion he showed not that alacrity, but that the delay exposed it to notice ; and so by the King's authority the matter was composed.'—*History of the Rebellion*, ii, 23.

rebellious and unhappy Parliament, which was the cause of all the ruins and misfortunes that afterwards befell this kingdom, was privately advertised, that the Parliament's design was to take the government of the Prince from him, which he, apprehending as a disgrace to himself, wisely prevented, and obtained the consent of his late Majesty, with his favour, to deliver up the charge of being governor to the Prince, and retire into the country [1]. Which he did in the beginning of the year 1641, and settled himself, with his lady, children, and family, to his great satisfaction, with an intent to have continued there, and rested under his own vine, and managed his own estate. But he had not enjoyed himself long, but an express came to him from his Majesty, who was then unjustly and unmannerly treated by the said Parliament, to repair with all possible speed and privacy to Kingston-upon-Hull, where the greatest part of his Majesty's ammunition and arms then remained in that magazine, it being the most considerable place for strength in the northern parts of the kingdom.

Immediately upon the receipt of these his Majesty's orders and commands, my Lord prepared for their execution, and about twelve of the clock at night, hastened from his own house when his family were all at their rest, save two or three servants which he appointed to attend him. The next day

1 Newcastle resigned his post in May 1641, and was succeeded by the Marquis of Hertford, whose appointment is dated by Whitelock May 27 (vol. i, p. 44). Clarendon's account of the Earl's retirement is, that he, knowing the hostility of the Earls of Essex and Holland to himself, knowing also ' that they liked not his having the government of the Prince as one who would infuse such principles into him as would not be agreeable to their designs, and would not rest till they saw another man in that province ', therefore ' upon these considerations *and some other imaginations upon the prospect of affairs* he very wisely resolved to retire from the court ', and suggested the Marquis of Hertford to the King as his successor. (*Rebellion*, iv, 293.) The real cause of this retirement, however, seems to have been the *other imaginations* alluded to by Clarendon. The Earl was implicated in the Army plot, and his share in it became publicly known early in May. Suckling and Jermyn selected the Earl of Newcastle to be titular General of the Army in place of the Earl of Northumberland, and Goring was to be his Lieutenant-General. Though the King disapproved of the proposal and did not make the suggested appointment, the Queen encouraged the plot, and the plan for bringing the army up to London was persisted in. It was proposed to the officers, testifies Lieutenant-Colonel Ballard, ' that, if there were occasion, the army should remove their quarters into Nottinghamshire, where the Prince and the Earl of Newcastle should meet them with a thousand horse, and all the French that were in London should be mounted, and likewise meet them.' 'Sergeant-Major Willis said, moreover', according to Captain Chudleigh, that the army would be very well kept together, for that the Prince was to be brought thither, which would confirm their affections . . . and Willis told them also, that if my Lord of Newcastle was their General, he would feast them in Nottinghamshire, and would not use them roughly, but that they should be governed by a council of war.'— Husband's *Exact Collection*, quarto 1643, p. 222; *Portland MSS.* i, 20. Gardiner, *History of England*, ix, 313. With these facts before them it would have been impossible for the Parliament to trust the Prince longer in Newcastle's hands, and he therefore avoided an attack by retiring.

early in the morning he arrived at Hull, in the quality of a private gentleman, which place was distant from his house forty miles ; and none of his family that were at home knew what was become of him, till he sent an express to his lady to inform her where he was.

Thus being admitted into the town, he fell upon his intended design, and brought it to so hopeful an issue for his Majesty's service, that he wanted nothing but his Majesty's further commission and pleasure to have secured both the town and magazine for his Majesty's use : and to that end by a speedy express [1] gave his Majesty, who was then at Windsor, an account of all his transactions therein, together with his opinion of them, hoping his Majesty would have been pleased either to come thither in person, which he might have done with much security, or at least have sent him a commission and orders how he should do his Majesty further service.

But instead thereof he received orders from his Majesty to observe such directions as he should receive from the Parliament then-sitting : whereupon he was summoned personally to appear at the House of Lords, and a committee chosen to examine the grounds and reasons of his undertaking that design ; but my Lord showed them his commission, and that it was done in obedience to his Majesty's commands, and so was cleared of that action [2].

---

[1] Captain Mazine.

[2] The warrant to Newcastle is dated Hampton Court, January 11, 1642 (*Lords' Journals*, iv, 585). Captain Legg was despatched to Hull to prepare the citizens to receive Lord Newcastle as their governor. The Parliament obtained information of the King's purpose, and sent off Captain Hotham with orders to his father, Sir John Hotham, to secure Hull by means of the Yorkshire Trained Bands, and not to deliver it up till he was ordered to do so by ' the King's authority, signified unto him by the Lords and Commons now assembled in Parliament '. Newcastle was despatched by the King in person as soon as Captain Hotham's journey was known. The King's object was not only to secure the munitions stored up at Hull, but to obtain possession of a port where the Danish soldiers he was then purposing to hire might be safely landed. (Gardiner, *History of England*, vol. x, pp. 152, 159.) A letter from Legg to Sir E. Nicholas states that Newcastle arrived at Hull on January 14 ; Newcastle himself announced his arrival to the King in a letter dated January 15, which is given in the Appendix. (*Domestic State Papers, Charles I*, vol. 488, Nos. 55 and 62.) According to Rushworth (III, i, 564), the Earl ' desired to pass unknown, calling himself Sir John Savage, and at his first coming was brought before the Mayor under that name, till being known by some bystanders he was forced to own both his name and his errand.' The Mayor refused to admit either Hotham's or Newcastle's troops, and humbly desired the King and Parliament to join in appointing a garrison. ' A strong party bestirred themselves for the Earl with great expectations of the King's royal favour to the town thereby ', continues Rushworth, and he might possibly have secured the town if the King's ill success elsewhere had not obliged him to yield and recall Newcastle. On January 20, the House of Lords passed a resolution ordering him to attend the House. He made no haste to return upon the summons of the House, but sent to the King to know his pleasure ; who, not thinking matters yet ripe enough to make any such declaration, appointed him to come away (Clarendon, *Rebellion*, iv, 215). ' But the same day that

Not long after, my Lord obtained the freedom from his Majesty to retire again to his country life, which he did with much alacrity. He had not remained many months there, but his Majesty was forced, by the fury of the said Parliament, to repair in person to York, and to send the Queen beyond the seas for her safety.

No sooner was his Majesty arrived at York but he sent his commands to my Lord to come thither to him ; which, according to his wonted custom and loyalty, he readily obeyed, and after a few days spent there in consultation, his Majesty was pleased to command him to Newcastle-upon-Tyne, to take upon him the government of that town, and the four counties next adjoining [1] ; that is to say, Northumberland, Cumberland, Westmoreland, and the Bishopric of Durham. Which my Lord did accordingly, although he wanted men, money, and ammunition, for the performance of that design ; for when he came thither he neither found any military provision considerable for the undertaking that work, nor generally any great encouragement from the people in those parts, more than what his own interest created in them. Nevertheless, he thought it his duty rather to hazard all, than to neglect the commands of his Sovereign ; and resolved to show his fidelity, by nobly setting all at stake, as he did, though he well knew how to have secured himself, as too many others did, either by neutrality or adhering to the rebellious party ; but his honour and loyalty was too great to be stained with such foul adherences.

As soon as my Lord came to Newcastle, in the first place he sent for all his tenants and friends in those parts, and presently raised a troop of horse consisting of 120, and a regiment

---

the Earl departed, Mr. Hotham was freely received into the town, with three companies of Trained Bands, and the keys of the ports, and the magazine, were surrendered into his hands ' (Rushworth). This took place before the end of January. The Earl did not appear in the House of Lords till after the 9th February, and was finally, on the 14th February, after delivering up his commission, granted leave to go into the country for his health's sake. (*Lords' Journals*, February 14, 1642.) See also Sanford, *Studies and Illustrations of the Great Rebellion*, p. 474 ; and Buff, *Die Politik Karls des Ersten in den ersten Wochen nach seiner Flucht von London*, pp. 5-18.

1 The King's commission to the Earl is dated June 20, 1642 (Collins, *Historical Collections*, p. 30). Brand, referring to Rymer's *Fœdera*, tom. xx, p. 531, says June 29. The earlier date is most probable, for the Commons' Journals (June 30) mention the Earl having sent out his warrants from Newcastle into the county of Durham commanding 600 foot and 100 horse of the trained band of Durham to come into Newcastle. An abstract of some letters from Newcastle, dated 22 and 23 June, is printed in the *Lords' Journals*, v, 170. Moreover, a news letter in the Record Office, dated June 17, says that the Earl left York for Newcastle on the preceding Wednesday, i.e. June 15.

of foot, and put them under command, and upon duty and exercise in the town of Newcastle ; and with this small beginning took the government of that place upon him ; where with the assistance of the townsmen, particularly the Mayor [1] (whom, by the power of his forces, he continued Mayor for the year following, he being a person of much trust and fidelity, as he approved himself), and the rest of his brethren, within few days he fortified the town, and raised men daily, and put a garrison of soldiers into Tynmouth Castle, standing upon the river Tyne, betwixt Newcastle and the sea, to secure that port, and armed the soldiers as well as he could. And thus he stood upon his guard, and continued them upon duty ; playing his weak game with much prudence, and giving the town and country very great satisfaction by his noble and honourable deportment [2].

In the meantime, there happened a great mutiny of the train-band soldiers of the Bishopric at Durham, so that my Lord was forced to remove thither in person, attended with some forces to appease them ; where at his arrival (I mention it by the way, and as a merry passage) a jovial fellow used this expression, that he liked my Lord very well, but not his company (meaning his soldiers).

After my Lord had reduced them to their obedience and duty, he took great care of the Church government in the said bishopric (as he did no less in all other places committed to his care and protection, well knowing that schism and faction in religion is the mother of all or most rebellions, wars, and disturbances in a state or government) and constituted that learned and eminent divine the then Dean of Peterborough, now Lord Bishop of Durham [3], to view all sermons that were to be preached, and suffer nothing in them that in the least reflected against his Majesty's person and government, but to put forth and add whatsoever he thought convenient, and punish those that should trespass against it. In which that worthy person used so much care and industry, that never

---

[1] Sir John Marlay, Kt.

[2] Our information concerning the Earl's conduct at Newcastle is very scanty. Something, however, may be gathered from a paper amongst the Clarendon State Papers, attributed to Sir John Marlay, No. 2064 : ' An Account of the military proceedings in the North from 1641 to 1645 inclusive, chiefly those in which the Marquis of Newcastle was concerned, and which relate to the town of Newcastle.'

[3] Dr. Cosin ; unfortunately there occurs at this point a gap of five years in the letters of Cosin collected by Mr. Ornsby.

the Church could be more happily governed than it was at that present.

Some short time after, my Lord received from her Majesty the Queen [1], out of Holland, a small supply of money, viz. a little barrel of ducatoons, which amounted to about £500 sterling ; which my Lord distributed amongst the officers of his new-raised army, to encourage them the better in their service ; as also some arms, the most part whereof were consigned to his late Majesty ; and those that were ordered to be conveyed to his Majesty, were sent accordingly, conducted by that only troop of horse, which my Lord had newly raised, with orders to return again to him ; but it seems his Majesty liked the troop so well, that he was pleased to command their stay to recruit his own army.

About the same time the King of Denmark was likewise pleased to send his Majesty a ship, which arrived at Newcastle, laden with some ammunition, arms, regiment pieces, and Danish clubs [2] ; which my Lord kept for the furnishing of some forces which he intended to raise for his Majesty's service. For he perceiving the flames increase more and more in both the Houses of Parliament then sitting at Westminster, against his Majesty's person and government ; upon consultation with his friends and allies, and the interest he had in those northern parts, took a resolution to raise an army for his Majesty's service, and by an express acquainted his Majesty with his design ; who was so well pleased with it, that he sent him commissions for that purpose, to constitute him General

[1] The Queen's correspondence with Newcastle is contained in the *Letters of Queen Henrietta Maria*, edited by Mrs. M. E. Green. ' The Queen herself intended at first to land at Newcastle and join the Earl. She writes to the King on November 20, 1642 : " As I was ready to set out, and had fixed the day, the wind changed, which has made me change my resolution. I have received letters from the Earl of Newcastle, by which he begs me not to come yet, for he is constrained to march into Yorkshire. Hotham is playing the devil. So that I shall await the issue of his march, of which in a week I hope to hear tidings."—*Letters*, p. 145. Brand states that on October 13 a small vessel arrived at Newcastle with arms for a thousand men, and £10,000 in money. *History of Newcastle*, i, 461.

[2] Vicars mentions the capture in August 1643 of a Danish ship bringing arms to the King, including 1000 ' piked clubs or Roundheads ' (*God's Ark*, p. 22). One of the chief reasons which induced the King to attempt the seizure of Hull, in January 1642, was its convenience for landing Danish troops. The King was still seeking to obtain troops and munitions from Denmark, vide *Letters of Queen Henrietta Maria*, pp. 148, 153, and an intercepted letter from the Hague, dated November 26, 1642, addressed to Secretary Nicholas, and printed by order of the Parliament. ' From Denmark are likewise sent arms for 10,000 foot, and 1,500 horse, with a train of artillery and everything proportionable, to the very drums and halberds. Two good men of war come their convoy, and in them an ambassador to his Majesty, a person of great quality in Denmark.'—Rushworth, III, ii, 69.

of all the forces raised and to be raised in all the parts of the
kingdom, Trent-North, and moreover in the several counties
of Lincoln, Nottingham, Derby, Lancashire, Cheshire, Leicester, Rutland, Cambridge, Huntingdon, Norfolk, Suffolk,
and Essex, and Commander-in-Chief for the same ; as also
to empower and authorise him to confer the honour of knighthood upon such persons as he should conceive deserved it, and
to coin money and print whensoever he saw occasion for it.
Which as it was not only a great honour, but a great trust
and power ; so he used it with much discretion and wisdom,
only in such occurrences where he found it tending to the
advancement of his Majesty's service, and conferred the honour
of knighthood sparingly, and but on such persons whose
valiant and loyal actions did justly deserve it, so that he
knighted in all to the number of twelve [1].

Within a short time, my Lord formed an army of 8000 foot,
horse and dragoons, and put them into a condition to march
in the beginning of November 1642. No sooner was this
effected, but the insurrection grew high in Yorkshire, insomuch,
that most of his Majesty's good subjects of that country, as
well the nobility as gentry, were forced, for the preservation
of their persons, to retire to the city of York, a walled town,
but of no great strength ; and hearing that my Lord had not
only kept those counties in the northern parts generally faithful
to his Majesty, but raised an army for his Majesty's interest,
and the protection of his good subjects ; thought it convenient
to employ and authorise some persons of quality to attend
upon my Lord, and treat with him on their behalf, that he
would be pleased to give them the assistance of his army,
which my Lord granted them upon such terms as did highly
advance his Majesty's service, which was my Lord's chief
and only aim [2].

Thus my Lord being with his army invited into Yorkshire,
he prepared for it with all the speed that the nature of that

[1] The Earl of Essex in Queen Elizabeth's reign also enjoyed, and, according to the
Queen, too freely exercised, this power of making knights. Amongst his knights were
Sir John Harington (*Nugæ Antiquæ*, ed. Park, i, 318) and Sir Robert Cary (Lord Orrery's
preface to the *Memoirs of Sir Robert Cary*, p. xxiv, ed. 1808, where many similar cases
are cited).

[2] The letters relating to Newcastle's march into Yorkshire, and the terms finally
agreed upon, are printed in a pamphlet entitled, *A New Discovery of Hidden Secrets*,
1645. The first letter is dated September 26, three days before the treaty of neutrality
between the Yorkshire Cavaliers and Parliamentarians was signed at Rodwell. Part
of the correspondence is printed in Appendix iv., and other letters are to be found in
the *Portland MSS.*, i, 69.

business could possibly permit; and after he had fortified
the town of Newcastle, Tynmouth Castle, Hartlepool (a haven
town), and some other necessary garrisons in those parts, and
manned, victualled, and ordered their constant supply, he
thought it fit in the first place, before he did march, to manifest to the world, by a Declaration in print, the reasons and
grounds of his undertaking that design [1]; which were in
general, for the preservation of his Majesty's person and
government, and the defence of the orthodox Church of
England; where he also satisfied those that murmured for
my Lord's receiving into his army such as were of the Catholic
religion, and then he presently marched with his army into
Yorkshire to their assistance, and within the time agreed
upon, came to York, notwithstanding the enemy's forces gave
him all the interruption they possibly could, at several passes.
Whereof the chief was at Piercebridge, at the entering into
Yorkshire, where 1500 of the enemy's forces, commanded in
chief by Colonel Hotham, were ready to interrupt my Lord's
forces, sent thither to secure that pass, consisting of a regiment
of dragoons, commanded by Colonel Thomas Howard, and a
regiment of foot, commanded by Sir William Lambton, which
they performed with so much courage, that they routed the
enemy, and put them to flight, although the said Colonel
Howard in that charge lost his life by an unfortunate shot [2].

The enemy thus missing of their design, fled until they met
with a conjunction of their whole forces at Tadcaster, some
eight miles distant from York, and my Lord went on without
any other considerable interruption. Being come to York,
he drew up his whole army before the time, both horse and
foot, where the Commander-in-Chief, the then Earl of Cumberland, together with the gentry of the country, came to wait
on my Lord, and the then Governor of York, Sir Thomas
Glenham, presented him with the keys of the city [3].

---

[1] 'A Declaration made by the Earl of Newcastle for his resolution of marching into
Yorkshire, as also a just vindication of himself from that unjust aspersion laid upon him
for entertaining some Popish recusants in his service.'—Rushworth, III, ii, 78–81.
The Earl had been not merely permitted, but instructed by the King to employ Catholics who offered their services. See the King's letter to Newcastle (Ellis, Original Letters,
series I, vol. iii, p. 291, quoted also in the Memoirs of Col. Hutchinson, vol. i, p. 215):
'Therefore, I do not only permit, but command you to make use of all my loving subjects' services, without examining their consciences (more than their loyalty to me)
as you shall find most to conduce to the upholding of my just regal power.'
[2] A brief account of this action is contained in Rushworth, III, ii, 77. It is there
said to have taken place on December 1, 1642.
[3] According to Drake's Eboracum, Newcastle arrived at York on November 30. It
cannot be denied', says Clarendon, 'that the Earl of Newcastle, by his quick march

Thus my Lord marched into the town with great joy, and to the general satisfaction both of the nobility and gentry, and most of the citizens ; and immediately without any delay, in the later end of December 1642, fell upon consultations how he might best proceed to serve his King and country ; and particularly, how his army should be maintained and paid (as he did also afterwards in every country wheresoever he marched), well knowing, that no army can be governed without being constantly and regularly supported by provision and pay. Whereupon it was agreed, that the nobility and gentry of the several counties, should select a certain number of themselves to raise money by a regular tax, for the making provisions for the support and maintenance of the army, rather than to leave them to free-quarter, and to carve for themselves ; and if any of the soldiers were exorbitant and disorderly, and that it did appear so to those that were authorized to examine their deportment, that presently order should be given to repair those injuries out of the moneys levied for the soldiery ; by which means the country was preserved from many inconveniences, which otherwise would doubtless have followed.

And though the seasons of the year might well have invited my Lord to take up his winter quarters, it being about Christmas ; yet after he had put a good garrison into the city of York, and fortified it, upon intelligence that the enemy was still at Tadcaster, and had fortified that place, he resolved to march thither. The greatest part of the town stands on the west side of a river not fordable in any place near thereabout, nor allowing any passage into the town from York, but over a stone-bridge, which the enemy had made impassable by breaking down part of the bridge and planting their ordnance upon it, and by raising a very large and strong fort upon the top of a hill, leading eastward from that bridge towards York, upon design of commanding the bridge and all other places fit to draw up an army in, or to plant cannon against them [1].

with his troops, as soon as he had received his commission to be general, and in the depth of winter, redeemed or rescued the city of York from the rebels, when they looked upon it as their own, and had it even within their grasp.' -*Rebellion*, viii, 84.

[1] Lord Fairfax mentions merely ' some breastworks for our musketeers '. Sir Thomas, in his *Short Memorial*, says : ' In a council of war the town was judged untenable, and that we should draw out to an advantageous piece of ground by the town ; but, before we could all march out, the enemy advanced so fast that we were necessitated to leave some foot in a slight work above the bridge to secure our retreat ; but, the enemy pressing on us, forced us to draw back, to maintain that ground.'—*Short Memorial*, Maseres' *Tracts*, i, 417.

But notwithstanding all these discouragements, my Lord, after he had refreshed his army at York, and recruited his provisions, ordered a march before the said town in this manner : that the greatest part of his horse and dragoons should in the night march to a pass at Weatherby, five miles distant from Tadcaster, towards north-west, from thence under the command of his then Lieutenant-General of the army, to appear on the west side of Tadcaster early the next morning, by which time my Lord with the rest of his army resolved to appear at the east side of the said town. Which intention was well designed, but ill executed ; for though my Lord with that part of the army which he commanded in person, that is to say, his foot and cannon, attended by some troops of horse, did march that night, and early in the morning appeared before the town on the east side thereof, and there drew up his army, planted his cannon, and closely and orderly besieged that side of the town, and from ten in the morning till four o'clock in the afternoon, battered the enemy's forts and works, as being in continual expectation of the appearance of the troops on the other side, according to his order : yet (whether it was out of neglect or treachery that my Lord's orders were not obeyed) that day's work was rendered ineffectual as to the whole design [1].

However, the vigilancy of my Lord did put the enemy into such a terror, that they forsook that fort, and secretly fled away with all their train that very night to another stronghold not far distant from Tadcaster, called Cawood Castle, to which, by reason of its low and boggy situation, and foul and narrow lanes and passages, it was not possible for my Lord to pursue them without too great an hazard to his army [2]. Whereas

[1] The battle took place on Tuesday, December 6—at least Lord Fairfax, in his letter of December 10, mentions the preceding Tuesday as the day of the battle. Vicars, however (*Jehovah Jireh*, p. 230), fixes Wednesday, December 7, as the date. But December 7 was a Tuesday in 1642.

The Lieutenant-General of Newcastle's army was then the Earl of Newport. His delay is thus explained by Drake (Eboracum, 161) : 'Captain Hotham, at the beginning of the fight, wrote a letter to the Earl of Newport signed " Will. Newcastle ", and sent it by a running footboy to tell him that, though his commission was to come and assist him, yet he might now spare his pains, and stay till he sent him order the next morning.' Newport was deceived by this trick, delayed his march, and gave Lord Fairfax time to escape. Sir Henry Slingsby, however, says that Newport's march ' was so troublesome, having with him two drakes, that it grew too late, and a counter-order (was) sent him on Clifford Moor to march back to Wetherby and there quarter.'—*Memoirs*, p. 86.

[2] Fairfax thus explains his retreat : ' In this fight our men behaved themselves with very great resolution far beyond expectation, insomuch as I conceive we might have maintained the place still, if we had been furnished with powder and shot, but having

had the Lieutenant-General performed his duty, in all probability the greatest part of the principal rebels in Yorkshire would that day have been taken in their own trap, and their further mischief prevented. My Lord, the next morning, instead of storming the town (as he had intended), entered without interruption, and there stayed some few days to refresh his army, and order that part of the country.

In December 1642, my Lord thought it fit to march to Pomfret [1], and to quarter his army in that part of the country which was betwixt Cawood and some garrisons of the enemy, in the west part of Yorkshire, viz. Halifax, Bradford, Leeds, Wakefield, &c., where he remained some time to recruit and enlarge his army, which was much lessened by erecting of garrisons, and to keep those parts in order and obedience to his Majesty [2]. And after he had thus ordered his affairs, he was enabled to give protection to those parts of the country that were most willing to embrace it, and quartered his army for a time in such places which he had reduced. Tadcaster, which stood upon a pass, he made a garrison, or rather a strong quarter, and put also a garrison into Pomfret Castle, not above eight miles distant from Tadcaster, which commanded that town, and a great part of the country.

During the time that his army remained at Pomfret, my Lord settled a garrison at Newark in Nottinghamshire, standing upon the river Trent, a very considerable pass, which kept the greatest part of Nottinghamshire, and part of Lincolnshire, in obedience [3]; and after that he returned, in the beginning of January 1642, back to York, with an intention to supply himself with some ammunition, which he had

spent in a manner all our whole store of bullet, match, and powder, I advised with the commanders, and by general consent I was thought fit to rise with our forces and march to Cawood and Selby, to secure those places, and there receive supplies of ammunition and men; which was accordingly done: and now I am at Selby with part of the army, and the rest with Captain Hotham at Cawood.'—Letter of Lord Fairfax to the Speaker, December 10, 1642, Rushworth, III, ii, 92.

[1] Pontefract.

[2] The Duchess does not mention an important episode in the Yorkshire civil war which took place during this halt at Pomfret. Sir William Savile was detached by the Earl of Newcastle to subdue the manufacturing towns of the West Riding. Leeds and Wakefield submitted without fighting, and Sir William attacked Bradford on December 18, 1642. The men of Halifax came to the aid of the men of Bradford, and the royalists were beaten off with considerable loss. Sir Thomas Fairfax, with four or five hundred men, made his way to Bradford a few days later, and took command of the local levies. With these forces he attacked Sir William Savile at Leeds on January 23, 1643, and captured the town and about 500 prisoners.

[3] The garrisoning of Newark took place about Christmas 1642, under Sir John Henderson. Newcastle returned to York on January 27, 1643—Markham's *Fairfax*, p. 91.

ordered to be brought from Newcastle. A convoy of horse that were employed to conduct it from thence, under the command of the Lieutenant-General of the Army, the Lord Ethyn, was by the enemy at a pass, called Yarum Bridge, in Yorkshire, fiercely encountered; in which encounter my Lord's forces totally routed them, slew many, and took many prisoners, and most of their horse colours, consisting of seventeen cornets; and so marched on to York with their ammunition, without any other interruption [1].

My Lord, after he had received this ammunition, put his army into a condition to march, and having intelligence that the Queen was at sea, with intention to land in some part of the East Riding of Yorkshire, he directed his march, in February 1642, into those parts, to be ready to attend her Majesty's landing, who was then daily expected from Holland. Within a short time, after it had pleased God to protect her Majesty both from the fury of wind and waves, there being for several days such a tempest at sea that her Majesty, with all her attendance, was in danger to be cast away every minute, as also from the fury of the rebels, which had the whole naval power of the kingdom then in their hands, she arrived safely at a small port in the East Riding of Yorkshire called Burlington Key. Where her Majesty was no sooner landed, but the enemy at sea made continual shot against her ships in the port, which reached not only her Majesty's landing, but even the house where she lay (though without the least hurt to any), so that she herself, and her attendants, were forced to leave the same, and to seek protection from a hill near that place, under which they retired; and all that while it was observed that her Majesty showed as much courage as ever any person could do: for her undaunted and generous spirit was like her royal birth, deriving itself from that unparalleled king, her father, whose heroic actions will be in perpetual memory whilst the world hath a being [2].

[1] This fight at Yarum Bridge took place on February 1, 1643. Lord Ethyn (or Eythin) is better known as General King. He had served many years in the Swedish army in Germany and was created a peer of Scotland March 28, 1643. A life of King is given in vol. xxxi of the *Dictionary of National Biography* (p. 135).

[2] The Queen landed at Burlington on February 22nd. She gives the following account of her adventure (*Letters*, p. 166): 'God, who took care of me at sea, was pleased to continue his protection by land, for that night, four of the Parliament ships arrived at Burlington without our knowledge, and in the morning (February 24), about four o'clock, the alarm was given that we should send down to the harbour to secure our ammunition boats, which had not yet been able to be unloaded; but, about an hour

My Lord, finding her Majesty in this condition, drew his
army near the place where she was, ready to attend and
protect her Majesty's person, who was pleased to take a view
of the army as it was drawn up in order ; and immediately
after, which was in March 1643, took her journey towards
York, whither the whole army conducted her Majesty, and
brought her safe into the city. About this time, her Majesty
having some present occasion for money, my Lord presented
her with £3000 sterling, which she graciously accepted of,
and having spent some time there in consultation about the
present affairs, she was pleased to send some arms and ammunition to the King, who was then in Oxford. To which end,
my Lord ordered a party, consisting of 1500, well commanded,
to conduct the same, with whom the Lord Percy, who then
had waited upon her Majesty from the King, returned to
Oxford ; which party his Majesty was pleased to keep with
him for his own service [1].

Not long after, my Lord, who always endeavoured to win
any place or persons by fair means, rather than by using of
force, reduced to his Majesty's obedience a strong fort and
castle upon the sea, and a very good haven, called Scarborough
Castle, persuading the governor thereof, who heretofore had
opposed his forces at Yarum Bridge, with such rational and
convincible arguments, that he willingly rendered himself,
and all the garrison, unto his Majesty's devotion. By which
prudent action my Lord highly advanced his Majesty's interest ;
for by that means the enemy was much annoyed and preju-

after, these four ships began to fire so briskly, that we were all obliged to rise in haste,
and leave the village to them : at least the women, for the soldiers remained very reso-
lutely to defend the ammunition. One of these ships had done me the honour to flank
my house, which fronted the pier, and before I could get out of bed, the balls were whist-
ling upon me in such style that you may easily believe I loved not such music. Everybody came to force me to go out, the balls beating so on all the houses, that, dressed
just as it happened, I went on foot to some distance from the village, to the shelter of
a ditch, like those at Newmarket ; but before we could reach it, the balls were singing
round us in fine style, and a sergeant was killed twenty paces from me. We placed
ourselves then under this shelter, during two hours that they were firing upon us, and
the balls passing always over our heads, and sometimes covering us with dust. At
last, the Admiral of Holland sent to tell them, that if they did not cease, he would fire
upon them as enemies. . . . On this they stopped, and the tide went down, so that
there was not water enough for them to stay where they were. . . . I am told that
one of the captains of the Parliament ships had been beforehand to reconnoitre where
my lodging was, and I assure you that it was well marked, for they always shot upon
it.' The Queen arrived at York, March 7th, 1643—Rushworth.
[1] This convoy left Newark under the conduct of Col. Hastings on May 8 (Dugdale's
Diary), and arrived at Oxford on May 15. A note in *Mercurius Aulicus*, May 15, 1643,
says : ' The conductors were Col. Hastings, the Lord of Dover, and Mr. Percy ; they
brought with them twenty troops of horse and 2000 foot, and about two and fifty cart
loads of arms and ammunition.'

diced at sea, and a great part in the East Riding of Yorkshire kept in due obedience.[1]

After this, my Lord having received intelligence that the enemy's General of the Horse [2] had designed to march with a party from Cawood Castle, whither they were fled from Tadcaster, as before is mentioned, to some garrisons which they had in the west of Yorkshire, presently ordered a party of horse, commanded by the General of the Horse, the Lord George Goring, to attend the enemy in their march, who overtook them on a moor, called Seacroft Moor, and fell upon their rear, which caused the enemy to draw up their forces into a body ; to whom they gave a total route (although their number was much greater), and took about 800 prisoners, and 10 or 12 colours of horse, besides many that were slain in the charge ; which prisoners were brought to York, about 10 or 12 miles distant from that same place [3].

Immediately after, in pursuit of that victory, my Lord sent a considerable party into the west of Yorkshire, where they met with about 2000 of the enemy's forces, taken out of their several garrisons in those parts, to execute some design upon a moor called Tankerly Moor, and there fought them, and routed them ; many were slain, and some taken prisoners.

Not long after, the remainder of the army that were left at York marched to Leeds[4], in the west of Yorkshire, and from thence to Wakefield, being both the enemies' quarters,

[1] This governor was Sir Hugh Cholmley, who declared for the King on March 25.—Rushworth, III, ii, 264. See also Clarendon Rebellion, vi, 268.
[2] Sir Thomas Fairfax.
[3] The best account of the battle at Seacroft Moor is given in Sir Thomas Fairfax's Short Memorial, Maseres' Tracts, vol. i, p. 422 ; Markham's Life of the Great Lord Fairax, p. 95. The battle took place on March 30, 1643 (see Mercurius Aulicus, April 4).
[4] The Queen's Letters give an account of this second advance into the West Riding. Newcastle's army numbered, according to her, 7000 foot and 3500 horse. The Parliamentarians quitted Pontefract at their approach, and retired to Leeds, where they were besieged by Newcastle. General King and the officers of experience were against an assault, and thought an effectual siege impossible. Newcastle, after two or three days' ineffectual cannonading, thought best to follow their advice and raise the siege. This was done under colour of a cessation of arms for four days for the purpose of treating, and the army retired to Wakefield (see also Mercurius Aulicus, April 25). There Newcastle left them for a few days. ' I am still waiting the return of the Earl of Newcastle ' writes the Queen on April 23 ; ' he is gone to bury his wife, who has died, and is not yet returned. . . He is staying ', she adds, ' to treat with Hotham's son ; if he succeeds, our affairs will go well ' (Letters, p. 188). According to Dugdale's Diary, the Earl of Newcastle came privately to Welbeck on April 13. Four letters from young Hotham to Newcastle, written between April 20 and May 1, are printed by Sanford (Studies and Illustrations of the Great Rebellion, p. 553). Twelve are printed in Portland MSS., vol. i, which give a full history of this intrigue (pp. 81, 83, 87, 89, 99, 105, 109, 699, 701, 702, 704, 707).

to reduce and settle that part of the country. My Lord having possessed himself of the town of Wakefield, it being large and of great compass, and able to make a strong quarter, ordered it accordingly; and receiving intelligence that in two market towns south-west from Wakefield, viz. Rotherham and Sheffield, the enemy was very busy to raise forces against his Majesty, and had fortified them both about four miles distant from each other, hoping thereby to give protection and encouragement to all those parts of the country which were populous, rich, and rebellious, he thought it necessary to use his best endeavours to blast those their wicked designs in the bud; and thereupon took a resolution, in April 1643, to march with part of his army from Wakefield into the mentioned parts, attended with a convenient train of artillery and ammunition, leaving the greatest part of it at Wakefield, with the remainder of his army, under the care and conduct of his General of the Horse, and Major General of the Army [1]. which was so considerable, both in respect of their number and provision, that they did, as they might well, conceive themselves master of the field in those parts, and secure in that quarter, although in the end it proved not so, as shall hereafter be declared, which must necessarily be imputed to their invigilancy and carelessness.

My Lord first marched to Rotherham, and finding that the enemy had placed a garrison of soldiers in that town, and fortified it, he drew up his army in the morning against the town, and summoned it; but they refusing to yield, my Lord fell to work with his cannon and musket, and within a short time took it by storm, and entered the town that very night; some enemies of note that were found therein were taken prisoners: and as for the common soldiers, which were by the enemy forced from their allegiance, he showed such clemency to them, that very many willingly took up arms for his Majesty's service, and proved very faithful and loyal subjects and good soldiers [2].

---

[1] 'The Lord Goring and Sir Francis Mackworth, Knight'. These names were printed in a side note, and carefully obliterated by hand before publication.

[2] Lord Fairfax, in his letter of May 23rd to Lenthal, says: 'The forces in Rotherham held out two days' siege, and yielded up the town upon treaty: wherein it was agreed, that the town should not be plundered; and that all the gentlemen, commanders and soldiers (six only excepted that were especially named), leaving their arms, should have free liberty to go whither they pleased. But when the enemy entered, contrary to their articles, they have not only plundered the town, but have also made all the commanders and soldiers prisoners; and do endeavour to constrain them to take up

After my Lord had stayed two or three days there, and ordered those parts, he marched with his army to Sheffield, another market town of large extent, in which there was an ancient castle; which when the enemy's forces that kept the town came to hear of, being terrified with the fame of my Lord's hitherto victorious army, they fled away from thence into Derbyshire, and left both town and castle (without any blow) to my Lord's mercy. And though the people in the town were most of them rebelliously affected, yet my Lord so prudently ordered the business, that within a short time he reduced most of them to their allegiance by love, and the rest by fear, and recruited his army daily; he put a garrison of soldiers into the castle, and fortified it in all respects, and constituted a gentleman of quality [1] governor of both the castle, town, and country; and finding near that place some iron works, he gave present order for the casting of iron cannon for his garrisons, and for the making of other instruments and engines of war [2].

Within a short time after, my Lord receiving intelligence that the enemy in the garrisons near Wakefield had united themselves, and being drawn into a body in the night time, and surprised and entered the town of Wakefield, and taken all, or most of the officers and soldiers left there prisoners (amongst whom was also the General of the Horse, the Lord Goring, whom my Lord afterwards redeemed by exchange), and possessed themselves of the whole magazine, which was a very great loss and hindrance to my Lord's designs, it being

arms on their party.'—Rushworth, III, ii, 268. This statement as to the breach of the capitulation, is confirmed by the Rev. John Shaw, at that time the Vicar of Rotherham. See the dedication to his sermon, entitled *The Three Kingdoms Case*, 1646. Shaw states that the town was taken on Thursday, May 4.—*Yorkshire Diaries*, vol. i, pp. 136, 385 (Surtees Society).

[1] Sir William Savile, knight and baronet.

[2] The commanders at Sheffield, says Lord Fairfax in the letter before quoted, hearing of the loss of Rotherham, and seeing some of the enemy's forces advanced in view of the town, they all presently deserted the place, as not tenable with so few against so 'potent an army; and fled away with their arms, some to Chesterfield and some to Manchester'. The Earl of Newcastle appointed Sir William Savile governor of Sheffield on May 9, 1643.—Hunter's *Hallamshire*, ed. Gatty, p. 136. See also *Notes and Queries*, March 24, 1888. *Mercurius Aulicus* for May 9 thus notes the capture of these two places: 'News that Rotherham and Sheffield, two towns of principal note in the West Riding of Yorkshire, were yielded up to his Majesty: by getting which his Majesty had obtained two convenient passes, the one by Sheffield into Derbyshire, the other by Rotherham into those parts of Nottinghamshire which are most helpful unto Gell and his associates: and that besides the use his Majesty might have of the Sheffield cutlers (for which that town is very famous) in the employment of his armoury, there were found 1400 arms in Rotherham fit for present use, together with £5000 in ready money.'

the moiety of his army, and most of his ammunition [1], he fell upon new counsels, and resolved without any delay to march from thence back towards York, which was in May 1643, where after he had rested some time, her Majesty being resolved to take her journey towards the southern parts of the kingdom, where the king was, designed first to go from York to Pomfret, whither my Lord ordered the whole marching army to be in readiness to conduct her Majesty, which they did, he himself attending her Majesty in person. And after her Majesty had rested there some small time, she being desirous to proceed in her intended journey, no less than a formed army was able to secure her person : wherefore my Lord was resolved out of his fidelity and duty to supply her with an army of 7,000 horse and foot, beside a convenient train of artillery, for her safer conduct, choosing rather to leave himself in a weak condition (though he was even then very near the enemy's garrisons in that part of the country) than suffer her Majesty's person to be exposed to danger. Which army of 7,000 men, when her Majesty was safely arrived to the King, he was pleased to keep with him for his own service [2].

After her Majesty's departure out of Yorkshire, my Lord was forced to recruit again his army, and within a short time, viz. in June 1643, took a resolution to march into the enemy's quarters, in the western parts ; in which march he met with a strong stone house well fortified, called Howley House, wherein was a garrison of soldiers, which my Lord summoned ; but the governor disobeying the summons he battered it with his cannon, and so took it by force. The

---

[1] This victory took place on Sunday, May 21, 1643—Rushworth, III, ii, 269), where the despatches of Lord Fairfax and Sir Thomas are given, and the *Short Memorial* in Maseres' *Tracts*, p. 423. Sir Thomas says ' This appeared the greater mercy when we saw our mistake ; for we found 3000 men in the town and expected but half the number. We brought away 1400 prisoners, 80 officers, 28 colours, and great store of ammunition.' His own force numbered only 1100 men, and he concludes by observing ' This was more a miracle than a victory.'

[2] The Queen left York on June 4 (Drake's *Eboracum*) ; she arrived at Newark on June 16 (Dugdale's *Diary*), and left that place on July 3, reaching Oxford on July 14 (*ibid.*). The Queen at first thought of bringing with her merely her own two regiments of foot and horse, consisting of about two thousand men (*Letters*, pp. 180-91). On the 14th of May, the Queen speaks of bringing 4000 men ; the King desired at least 1000 foot and 1500 horse (*Letters*, pp. 200-5). Most of these troops were armed with the weapons brought by the Queen, but raised by the Earl of Newcastle. ' I carry with me ', writes Henrietta to the King from Newark, ' 3000 foot, thirty companies of horse and dragoons, six pieces of cannon and two mortars.'—*Letters of Queen Henrietta Maria*, ed. Green, p. 222. The number given in the text is certainly exaggerated ; 4500 or 5000 men probably represents the total strength of the Queen's army.

governor, having quarter given him contrary to my Lord's orders, was brought before my Lord by a person of quality, for which the officer that brought him received a check ; and though he resolved then to kill him, yet my Lord would not suffer him to do it, saying, it was inhuman to kill any man in cold blood. Hereupon the governor kissed the key of the house door, and presented it to my Lord ; to which my Lord returned this answer : ' I need it not ', said he, ' for I brought a key along with me, which yet I was unwilling to use, until you forced me to it.' [1]

At this house my Lord remained five or six days, till he had refreshed his soldiers ; and then a resolution was taken to march against a garrison of the enemy's called Bradford, a little but a strong town. In the way he met with a strong interruption by the enemy drawing forth a vast number of musketeers, which they had very privately gotten out of Lancashire, the next adjoining county to those parts of Yorkshire which had so easy an access to them at Bradford, by reason the whole country was of their party, that my Lord could not possibly have any constant intelligence of their designs and motions. For in their army there were near 5000 musketeers, and eighteen troops of horse, drawn up in a place full of hedges, called Atherton Moor, near to their garrison at Bradford, ready to encounter my Lord's forces, which then contained not above half so many musketeers as the enemy had ; their chiefest strength consisting in horse, and these made useless for a long time together by the enemy's horse possessing all the plain ground upon that field ; so that no place was left to draw up my Lord's horse, but amongst old coal-pits. Neither could they charge the enemy, by reason of a great ditch and high bank betwixt

---

[1] Howley House was garrisoned by the Parliamentarians on January 16, 1642 ; its owner, Lord Savile, had made a composition with young Hotham in the preceding October, and also received a similar promise of protection from Lord Fairfax, and had in consequence declined to receive a detachment sent by Newcastle to occupy the house. The suspicions raised by these transactions caused Newcastle to arrest Savile, and to send to the King a lengthy information against him. (*Information against the Lord Viscount Savile*, in *Papers relating to the Delinquency of Lord Savile, Camden Miscellany*, vol. viii). The King, however, decided that though Newcastle had very good cause for suspicion, and was justified in what he did, yet Savile's explanations were satisfactory. Howley House was about half way between Wakefield and Leeds. The capture mentioned above took place on June 22, 1643. (Rushworth III, ii, 279). The governor referred to was Sir John Savile of Lupset, cousin of Lord Savile. The House was retaken by the Parliament forces in February 1644 (*Scottish Dove*, 23rd February to 1st March).

my Lord's and the enemy's troops, but by two on a breast, and that within musket shot; the enemy being drawn up in hedges, and continually playing upon them, which rendered the service exceeding difficult and hazardous.

In the meanwhile the foot of both sides on the right and left wings encountered each other, who fought from hedge to hedge and for a long time together overpowered and got ground of my Lord's foot, almost to the environing of his cannon: my Lord's horse (wherein consisted his greatest strength) all this while being made, by reason of the ground, incapable of charging. At last the pikes of my Lord's army having had no employment all the day, were drawn against the enemy's left wing, and particularly those of my Lord's own regiment, which were all stout and valiant men, who fell so furiously upon the enemy, that they forsook their hedges, and fell to their heels. At which very instant my Lord caused a shot or two to be made by his cannon against the body of the enemy's horse, drawn up within cannon shot, which took so good effect, that it disordered the enemy's troops. Hereupon my Lord's horse got over the hedge, not in a body (for that they could not), but dispersedly two on a breast; and as soon as some considerable number was gotten over, and drawn up, they charged the enemy, and routed them. So that in an instant there was a strange change of fortune, and the field totally won by my Lord, notwithstanding he had quitted 7000 men, to conduct her Majesty, besides a good train of artillery, which in such a conjuncture would have weakened Cæsar's army. In this victory the enemy lost most of their foot, about 3000 were taken prisoners, and 700 horse and foot slain, and those that escaped fled into their garrison at Bradford, amongst whom was also their General of the Horse [1].

After this my Lord caused his army to be rallied, and

---

[1] Sir Thomas Fairfax. The battle of Atherton, or Adwalton Moor, took place on June 30th. Fairfax estimates the number of the Parliamentary troops at 3000. All accounts agree that the battle began favourably to the Parliamentarians. The enemy, says Fairfax, were thinking of retreating, and some had actually marched off the field. 'Whilst they were in this wavering condition, one Colonel Skirton desired his general to let him charge once with a stand of pikes, with which he broke in upon our men; and, they not being relieved by our reserves (which were commanded by some ill-affected officers, chiefly Major-General Gifford, who did not his part as he ought to do), our men lost ground, which the enemy seeing, pursued this advantage by bringing on fresh troops; ours being herewith discouraged began to fly, and were soon routed.'—*Short Memorial, Maseres' Tracts*, i, 426. A good account of the battle, in a letter from Thomas Stockdale to the Speaker, is printed in *Portland MSS.*, i, 717.

marched in order that night before Bradford, with an intention to storm it the next morning; but the enemy that were
in the town, it seems, were so discomfited, that the same night
they escaped all various ways, and amongst them the said
General of the Horse, whose Lady being behind a servant on
horseback, was taken by some of my Lord's soldiers, and
brought to his quarters, where she was treated and attended
with all civility and respect, and within a few days sent to
York in my Lord's own coach, and from thence very shortly
after to Kingston-upon-Hull, where she desired to be attended
by my Lord's coach and servants [1].

Thus my Lord, after the enemy was gone, entered the town
and garrison of Bradford, by which victory the enemy was
so daunted, that they forsook the rest of their garrisons, that
is to say, Halifax, Leeds, and Wakefield, and dispersed themselves severally, the chief officers retiring to Hull, a strong garrison of the enemy; and though my Lord, knowing they would
make their escape thither, as having no other place of refuge to
resort to, sent a letter to York to the Governor of that city, to
stop them in their passage; yet by neglect of the post, it coming not timely enough to his hands, his design was frustrated.

The whole county of York, save only Hull, being now
cleared and settled by my Lord's care and conduct, he marched
to the city of York, and having a competent number of horse
well armed and commanded, he quartered them in the East
Riding, near Hull, there being no visible enemy then to
oppose them. In the meanwhile my Lord, receiving news
that the enemy had made an invasion into the next adjoining
county of Lincoln, where he had some forces, he presently
despatched his Lieutenant-General of the Army [2] away with
some horse and dragoons, and soon after marched thither
himself with the body of the army, being earnestly desired
by his Majesty's party there. The forces which my Lord
had in the same county, commanded by the then Lieutenant-

1 Sir Thomas Fairfax had married, in 1637, Anne, daughter of Horace, Lord Vere
of Tilbury. ' My wife ', says Sir Thomas, ' ran the same hazard with us in this retreat,
and with as little expression of fear; not from any zeal or delight in the war, but through
a willing and patient suffering of this undesirable condition.' Lady Fairfax was captured during the passage from Bradford to Leeds, being mounted behind an officer
named Hill.—*Short Memorial*, p. 428. ' Not many days after the Earl of Newcastle
sent my wife back again in his coach, with some horse to guard her; which generous
act of his gained him more reputation than he could have got by detaining a lady prisoner
upon such terms.'—*ibid.*, p. 431.
2 The Lord Ethyn.

General of the Horse, Mr. Charles Cavendish, second brother to the now Earl of Devonshire, though they had timely notice, and orders from my Lord to make their retreat to the Lieutenant-General of the Army, and not to fight the enemy ; yet the said Lieutenant-General of the Horse being transported by his courage (he being a person of great valour and conduct) and having charged the enemy, unfortunately lost the field, and himself was slain in the charge, his horse lighting in a bog [1] ; which news being brought to my Lord when he was on his march, he made all the haste he could, and was no sooner joined with his Lieutenant-General, but fell upon the enemy, and put them to flight.

The first garrison my Lord took in Lincolnshire was Gainsborough, a town standing upon the river Trent, wherein (not long before) had been a garrison of soldiers for his Majesty under the command of the then Earl of Kingston, but surprised, and the town taken by the enemy's forces, who having an intention to convey the said Earl of Kingston from thence to Hull, in a little pinnace met with some of my Lord's forces by the way, commanded by the Lieutenant of the Army, who being desirous to rescue the Earl of Kingston, and making some shots with their regiment pieces, to stop the pinnace, unfortunately slew him and one of his servants [2].

---

[1] The Queen, in her letter to the King from Newark on 27th June, writes that she leaves behind her, for the protection of Nottinghamshire and Lincolnshire, 2000 foot and twenty companies of horse : ' all this to be under Charles Cavendish, whom the gentlemen of the county have desired me not to carry with me—against his will, for he desired extremely to go.' Cavendish, on the petition of the King's Commissioners for those two counties, had been appointed Commander-in-Chief of their forces, with the rank of Colonel-General. On April 11, he had defeated young Hotham and the Lincolnshire Parliamentarians at Ancaster, and on July 2, whilst convoying the Queen to Oxford, took Burton. Now, whilst attempting to prevent the raising of the siege of Gainsborough, he was defeated by Cromwell, and slain on July 28, 1643. The cavaliers were at one moment of the fight nearly gaining the victory. The main body of the Parliamentarians charged and routed the main body of the Royalists. Charles Cavendish, with their reserve, almost changed the fortune of the day ; but Cromwell, with three troops he had kept in hand, retrieved the battle. ' Whilst the enemy was following our flying troops, I charged him on the rear with my three troops ; drove him down the hill, brake him all to pieces : forced Lieutenant-General Cavendish into a bog, who fought in this reserve : one officer cut him on the head, and as he lay, my Captain-Lieutenant Berry thrust him into the short ribs, of which he died about two hours after in Gainsborough.'—Carlyle's *Cromwell*, Appendix 5, and also Letter xii. *Mercurius Aulicus* of August 1 contains the Royalist account of the battle. It is stated there that Cavendish, ' being cut most dangerously on the head, was struck off his horse, and so, unfortunately, shot with a trace of bullets after he was on the ground.' Lloyd, in his *Memoirs of Excellent Personages*, says ' He died magnanimously, refusing quarter and throwing the blood that ran from his wounds in their faces that shed it ' (p. 673).

[2] Gainsborough was taken by Lord Willoughby on the 16th of July.—Ricraft's *Champions*, p. 35. See also *The Kingdom's Weekly Intelligence*, 18–25 July ; Rushworth III, ii, 278.

' Lord Willoughby having sent away many of his carriages towards Lincoln, and

My Lord drawing near the mentioned town of Gainsborough, there appeared on the top of a hill, above the town, some of the enemy's horse drawn up in a body ; whereupon he immediately sent a party of his horse to view them ; who no sooner came within their sight, but they retreated fairly so long as they could well endure ; but the pursuit of my Lord's horse caused them presently to break their ranks, and fall to their heels, where most of them escaped, and fled to Lincoln, another of their garrisons.   Hereupon my Lord summoned the town of Gainsborough ; but the Governor thereof refusing to yield, caused my Lord to plant his cannon, and draw up his army on the mentioned hill ; and having played some little while upon the town, put the enemy into such a terror, that the Governor sent out and offered the surrender of the town upon fair terms, which my Lord thought fit rather to embrace than take it by force ; and though, according to the article of agreement made between them, both the enemy's arms and the keys of the town should have been fairly delivered to my Lord, yet it being not performed as it was expected, the arms being in a confused manner thrown down, and the gates set wide open, the prisoners that had been kept in the town began first to plunder ; which my Lord's forces seeing, did the same, although it was against my Lord's will and orders [1].

After my Lord had thus reduced the town, and put a good garrison of soldiers into it, and better fortified it, he marched

put his prisoners aboard a pinnace which was sent from Hull, did intend to quit the place, as not being able to defend it. But before those intents were put in execution he was surrounded by a part of the Earl of Newcastle's forces, who sat down before it.'— *Mercurius Aulicus*, July 30.

The death of the Earl of Kingston is also related by Mrs. Hutchinson.

[1] Gainsborough was surrendered on July 30. The breach of the capitulation is also mentioned by Mrs. Hutchinson. *Mercurius Aulicus* for August 3 gives the following account : ' It was advertised this day that Gainsborough was yielded to the Earl of Newcastle ; on whose first coming before the town, with the rest of his forces, the Lord Willoughby and other of the rebels in it did desire a parley, which being granted upon Saturday night last, July 29, the Commissioners for both parts did agree, in the next morning early (that is to say, about two of the clock), that the town should be delivered, by five of the clock that morning, to such as his Excellency the Earl of Newcastle should appoint to receive it for his Majesty ; the Lord Willoughby and other officers of the rebels to go away, with such arms as they brought into the town : no common soldier to go forth with any arms at all, nor with more baggage than he brought thither with him ; neither the officers nor soldiers to take with them any colours of horse or foot ; no ordnance, nor any kind of ammunition, to be carried out of the town, or destroyed in it, nor any part of the town or of the goods thereof to be burnt or hurt. All prisoners belonging to the army of the Earl of Newcastle, or which were there when the Lord Willoughby first entered, to be left behind ; and finally, no townsman to go out of the town under pretence of being soldiers.'

before Lincoln [1], and there he entered with his army without great difficulty, and placed also a garrison in it, and raised a considerable army, both horse, foot, and dragoons, for the preservation of that county, and put them under commanders, and constituted a person of honour [2] Commander-in-Chief with intention to march towards the South, which, if it had taken effect, would doubtless have made an end of that war [3]. But he being daily importuned by the nobility and gentry of Yorkshire, to return into that county, especially upon the persuasions of the Commander-in-Chief of the forces left there, who acquainted my Lord that the enemy grew so strong every day, being got together in Kingston-upon-Hull, and annoying that country, that his forces were not able to bear up against them ; alleging withal, that my Lord would

[1] Lord Willoughby on surrendering Gainsborough marched to Lincoln. ' But seeing an impossibility that Cromwell should time enough recruit his beaten and distracted forces, or that he could receive any seasonable supplies from London, on the first news that the Earl of Newcastle was coming towards him, he forsook the place, and made what haste he could to Boston.'—*Mercurius Aulicus*, August 10. Willoughby writes to Cromwell from Boston on August 5 : ' Since the business of Gainsborough, the hearts of our men have been so deaded that we have lost most of them by running away, so that we were forced to leave Lincoln upon a sudden ; and if I had not done it, then I should have been left alone in it.' –Carlyle's *Cromwell*, i, p. 140.

Lincoln was recaptured by Manchester on October 20, 1643, evacuated by the Parliamentary forces in March 1644, after the relief of Newark by Prince Rupert, and surrendered again to Manchester on May 6, 1644.

[2] The Lord Widdrington.

[3] The King repeatedly desired Newcastle to march southwards. The Queen writes to Newcastle, on the 18th June, that the King ' had sent me a letter to command you absolutely to march to him, but I do not send it you, since I have taken a resolution with you that you remain ' (*Letters*, p. 219) ; and again, on August 13 she writes : ' He had written me to send you word to go into Suffolk, Norfolk, or Huntingdonshire. I answered him that you were a better judge than he of that, and that I should not do it. The truth is, that they envy your army' (*Letters*, p. 225). Sir Philip Warwick was sent by the King to persuade Newcastle to march south, apparently about the end of July. ' But I found him very averse to this, and perceived, that he apprehended nothing more, than to be joined to the King's Army, or to serve under Prince Rupert ; for he designed himself to be the man that should turn the scale, and to be a self-subsisting and distinct army, wherever he was. Yet he told me that when he could quit Yorkshire, and leave it in a condition to defend itself against the before-mentioned enemies in it (which the Yorkshire men would not have been unwilling to have adventured, if he had left them in some measure their own forces, and marched with his own more northerly army ; for they knew the Parliament would command Fairfax after him), he would march through Lincolnshire, and recruit himself there, and so over the Washes into Norfolk, and Suffolk, and the associated counties ; which had been a noble design.' This march into Lincolnshire was Newcastle's first step towards carrying out this design. ' He took in Gainsborough and Lincoln ', says Sir T. Fairfax, ' and intended to take in Boston, which was the key of the associated counties ; for his orders (which I have seen) were to go into Essex, and block up London on that side. Having laid a great while still, and being now strong enough for those forces which remained in the country, we sent out a good party to make an attempt upon Stamford Bridge, near York. But the enemy upon the alarm fled thither, which put them also in such a fear, that they sent earnestly to my Lord of Newcastle to desire him to return, or the country would again be lost. Upon this he returned again into Yorkshire, and not long after came to besiege Hull.'—*Short Memorial*, Maseres' *Tracts*, i, 431. Mr. S. R. Gardiner discusses the question of Newcastle's motives in a criticism of the earlier edition of this book—*English Historical Review*, 1887, p. 172.

be suspected to betray the trust reposed in him, if he came not to succour and assist them; he went back with his army for the protection of that same country; and when he arrived there, which was in August 1643, he found the enemy of so small consequence, that they did all fly before him. About this time his Majesty was pleased to honour my Lord, for his true and faithful service, with the title of Marquis of Newcastle [1].

My Lord being returned into Yorkshire, forced the enemy first from a town called Beverley [2], wherein they had a garrison of soldiers; and from thence, upon the entreaty of the nobility and gentry of Yorkshire (as before is mentioned), who promised him ten thousand men for that purpose, though they came short of their performance, marched near the town of Kingston-upon-Hull, and besieged that part of the garrison that bordered on Yorkshire, for a certain time—in which time the enemy took the courage to sally out of the town with a strong party of horse and foot very early in the morning, with purpose to have forced the quarters of a regiment of my Lord's horse that were quartered next the town; but by the vigilancy of their commander, Sir Marmaduke Langdale, afterwards Lord Langdale, his forces being prepared for the reception, they received such a welcome as cost many of them their lives, most of their foot (but such as were slain) being taken prisoners; and those of their horse that escaped got into their hold at Hull [3].

The enemy, thus feeling that they could do my Lord's army no further damage on that side of the river in Yorkshire, endeavoured by all means (from Hull, and other con-

---

1 The patent is dated 27th October, 19 Charles I. It is quoted at length by Collins (*Historical Collections*, p. 13), and also by the Duchess in the third book of these *Memoirs*.
2 'The town (Hull) being little, I was sent to Beverley with the horse and 600 foot' says Sir T. Fairfax, who gives a detailed account of his retreat from Beverley to Hull (*Short Memorial*, Maseres' *Tracts*, i, 431). Newcastle occupied Beverley on August 25 (Dugdale's *Diary*). See also *Mercurius Britannicus*, 5–12 September.
3 The siege began on September 2, and ended on October 11 (Rushworth III, ii, 280). Warwick says the policy of besieging Hull was attributed to General King's advice. Warwick was sent on a second mission to Newcastle during September 1643, and found him before Hull. 'I went down', says Sir Philip, 'to see his trenches and works, and found (the season having been very wet) his men standing ankle deep in dirt a great distance from the town; so as I conceived those without were likelier to rot than those within to starve; and by assault there was not the least probability to carry it. Upon my return to him, relating but faintly and modestly my thoughts (for he knew I had not the least part of a soldier to warrant a discourse upon that subject) he merrily put it off, saying " You often hear us called the Popish Army; but you see we trust not in our good works." '—*Memoirs*, p. 265. An account of the sally mentioned in the text is given in *Mercurius Aulicus* for September 16, 1643. See also ' *The Sieges of Hull during the Great Civil War* ', by E. Broxap (*English Historical Review*, July 1905).

federate places in the eastern parts of the kingdom) to form a considerable party to annoy and disturb the forces raised by my Lord in Lincolnshire, and left there for the protection of that county ; where the enemy being drawn together in a body, fought my Lord's forces in his absence, and got the honour of the day near Hornby Castle in that county [1] ; which loss, caused partly by their own rashness, forced my Lord to leave his design upon Hull, and to march back with his army to York, which was in October 1643, where the remained but a few days to refresh his army ; and receiving intelligence that the enemy was got into Derbyshire, and did grow numerous there, and busy in seducing the people, that country being under my Lord's command, he resolved to direct his March thither in the beginning of November 1643, to suppress their further growth ; and to that end quartered his army at Chesterfield and in all the parts thereabout, for a certain time [2].

Immediately after his departure from York to Pomfret, in his said march into Derbyshire, the city of York sent to my Lord to inform him of their intention to choose another Mayor for the year following, desiring his pleasure about it. My Lord, who knew that the Mayor for the year before was

[1] The battle of Winceby, or Horncastle, fought on October 11 (Rushworth III, ii, 281 ; Vicar's *God's Ark*, pp. 43–8 ; and *Fairfax Correspondence*, *Memorials of the Civil War*, i, p. 62). When the siege of Hull commenced, the Earl of Manchester, with the army of the Eastern Association, was occupied in the siege of Lynn. Its surrender, on September 10, enabled him to despatch his horse under Cromwell into Lincolnshire, to join Sir Thomas Fairfax with the horse of the garrison of Hull, and Lord Willoughby with the local levies of Lincolnshire. The union of Fairfax and Cromwell took place on September 26. Manchester also sent 500 men, under Sir John Meldrum, into Hull, which they entered on October 5 ; and he himself, with his foot, joined Fairfax and Cromwell at Kirby in Lincolnshire on October 10. In the battle the Royalists lost 1000 prisoners and 35 colours. ' We have in a manner totally lost our foot and dragoons that were there, being near 800 horse, extremely dissevered but no great number cut off ' reports Sir William Widdington to Newcastle. The consequences of the battle were the evacuation of Gainsborough by the Royalists, the capture of Lincoln, and the blockade of Newark. The Duchess omits to mention the successful sally made by the garrison of Hull on October 11, in which many of Newcastle's guns were taken, and some of his works destroyed (*Portland MSS.*, i, 138). This defeat, not that at Winceby alone, obliged Newcastle to raise the siege of Hull.

[2] *Mercurius Aulicus* for Jan. 1, 1644 contains the following : ' The first day of this year brought us in good news from the Lord Marquis of Newcastle, who, as we are advertised lately, put in execution the commission of array at Chesterfield in Derbyshire ; where he was met with the greatest concourse of people that hath been seen in those parts these many years. And (as it was for certain advertised) his Excellency had then gathered up above 2300 stout Derbyshire volunteers, resolved to venture their lives for their King and country against this rebellion ; whereof Sir John Gell, by his meekness and humanity, hath made them very sensible. And as a further testimony of the people's loyalty, that noble knight, Sir John Harpur, had received very fair contributions of that county for the maintenance of those forces.' An account of the proceedings of Newcastle's forces in Derbyshire is given in a contemporary pamphlet, reprinted in Appendix vi.

a person of much loyalty and discretion, declared his mind to them, that he thought it fit to continue him Mayor also for the year following ; which it seems they did not like, but resolved to choose one which they pleased, contrary to my Lord's desire. My Lord perceiving their intentions, about the time of the election, sent orders to the Governor of the city of York to permit such forces to enter into the city as he should send ; which being done accordingly, they upon the day of the election repaired to the Town Hall, and with their arms stayed there until they had continued the said Mayor according to my Lord's desire.

During the time of my Lord's stay at Chesterfield in Derbyshire, he ordered some part of his army to march before a strong house and garrison of the enemy's, called Wingfield Manor, which in a short time they took by storm [1]. And when my Lord had raised in that county as many forces, horse and foot, as were supposed to be sufficient to preserve it from the fury of the enemy, he armed them, and constituted an honourable person [2] Commander-in-Chief of all the forces of that county and of Leicestershire ; and so leaving it in that condition, marched, in December 1643, from Chesterfield to Bolsover in the same county, and from thence to Welbeck in Nottinghamshire, to his own house and garrison, in which parts he stayed some time, both to refresh his army and to settle and reform some disorders he found there, leaving no visible enemy behind him in Derbyshire, save only an

---

[1] *Certain Informations*, 6–13 March 1643, gives the following account of the first garrisoning of Wingfield at Chesterfield. It says ' They are extremely pestered with the Earl of Newcastle's forces that lie in Bolsover, who, in the night, came out of that town and took thirty horses from the adjacent people ; whereupon the inhabitants of Chesterfield, to secure their town, have taken Wingfield Manor, and placed there thirty soldiers to guard it ; and they have also put forty musketeers into Chatsworth, under the command of Lieutenant Bagshaw, to defend it.' The capture mentioned in the text is thus related in *Mercurius Aulicus* : Letters came from my Lord Marquis of Newcastle, advertising as that yesterday was seven night, December 15, Sir Francis Mackworth, with five hundred horse and foot and some cannon, came before Wingfield Manor, a house of the late Earl of Shrewsbury, strengthened with a strong embattled wall of fifteen foot high and ten foot thick. The rebels refused to yield it up upon summons, whereupon Sir Francis played upon it with his cannon, but (through the great strength of the wall) did not much harm to the house. At length, upon exchange of the body of a gentleman slain by the King's forces for one killed near the walls who could not be brought off, some words passed, when Sir Francis told them, that if yet they would surrender they might find favour, which offer was soon embraced : and after a short treaty they were allowed to march away, leaving all their arms behind them, being about 160, with good store of ammunition and above three months' provision, all which was taken in the house, which through its strength and situation, standing in the middle way between Derby and Chesterfield, will be very advantageous to his Majesty's affairs.' Dugdale dates the surrender December 18.

[2] The Lord of Loughborough.

inconsiderable party in the town of Derby, which they had fortified, not worth the labour to reduce it.

About this time the report came, that a great army out of Scotland was upon their march towards the northern parts of England, to assist the enemy against his Majesty [1], which forced the nobility and gentry of Yorkshire to invite my Lord back again into those parts, with promise to raise for his service an army of 10,000 men. My Lord (not upon this proffer, which had already heretofore deceived him, but out of his loyalty and duty to preserve those parts which were committed to his care and protection) returned in the middle of January 1643. And when he came there, he found not one man raised to assist him against so powerful an army, nor an intention of raising any. Wherefore he was necessitated to raise himself, out of the country, what forces he could get ; and when he had settled the affairs in Yorkshire, as well as time and his present condition would permit, and consti- tuted an honourable person [2] Governor of York and Com- mander-in-Chief of a very considerable party of horse and foot for the defence of the county (for Sir Thomas Glemham was then made Colonel-General), and marched into the field with the army), he took his march to Newcastle in the begin- ning of February 1643, to give a stop to the Scots army [3].

Presently after his coming thither with some of his troops, before his whole army was come up, he received intelligence of the Scots army's near approach, whereupon he sent forth a party of horse to view them, who found them very strong, to the number of 22,000 horse and foot, well armed and com- manded. They marched up towards the town with such con- fidence, as if the gates had been opened for their reception ;

[1] According to Warwick, the Marquis had some time before received notice from the Marquis of Hamilton, that the Scots were at last going to march into England, with the recommendation to seize and garrison Carlisle and Berwick. He replied that this would be against the treaty, and waited for instructions from Oxford. Whilst he waited, Berwick was occupied for the Parliament (*Memoirs of Sir Philip Warwick*, p. 267). This statement is confirmed by Burnet, *Lives of the Hamiltons*, ed. 1852, p. 310. These events apparently took place in August and September 1643.

[2] Colonel John Bellasis (or Bellasyse), created Baron Belasyse of Worlaby Lines. on 22 Jan. 164⅟. There is a *Briefe Relation of the Life and Memories of John Lord Bela- syse*, written by his secretary Joshua Moone, which is printed in the *Report on the MSS. of the Marquis of Ormonde at Kilkenny*. It contains an account of his services as Governor of York (vol. ii, pp. 383–4).

[3] A full account of the progress of the Scotch army is given in Rushworth III, ii, 612 *et seq*. The Scots arrived before the town of Newcastle on February 3 ; the Mar- quis entered the town the day before. A good account of all this fighting round New- castle is contained in Professor C. S. Terry ; *Life of Alexander Leslie*, 1899, pp. 185– 214.

and the General of their army seemed to take no notice of my
Lord's being in it, for which afterwards he excused himself.
But as they drew near, they found not such entertainment
as they expected ; for though they assaulted a work that was
not finished, yet they were beaten off with much loss.

The enemy being thus stopped before the town, thought fit
to quarter near it, in that part of the country ; and so soon as
my Lord's army was come up, he designed one night to have
fallen into their quarter ; but by reason of some neglect of his
orders in not giving timely notice to the party designed for it,
it took not an effect answerable to his expectation.   In a word,
there were three designs taken against the enemy, whereof
if one had but hit, they would doubtless have been lost ; but
there was so much treachery, juggling, and falsehood in my
Lord's own army, that it was impossible for him to be successful in his designs and undertakings.   However, though it failed
in the enemy's foot-quarters, which lay nearest the town, yet
it took good effect in their horse-quarters, which were more
remote ; for my Lord's horse, commanded by a very gallant
and worthy gentleman [1], falling upon them, gave them such
an alarm, that all they could do was to draw into the field,
where my Lord's forces charged them, and in a little time
routed them totally, and killed and took many prisoners,
to the 'number of 1500 [2].

Upon this the enemy was forced to draw their whole army
together, and to quarter them a little more remote from the
town, and to seek out inaccessible places for their security, as
afterwards appeared more plainly ; for so soon as my Lord
had prepared his army for a march, he drew them forth against
the Scots, which he found quartered upon high hills close by
the river Tyne, where they could not be encountered but upon
very disadvantageous terms ; besides, that day proved very
stormy and tempestuous, so that my Lord was necessitated
to withdraw his forces, and retire into his own quarters [3].

---

[1] The Lord Langdale.

[2] This skirmish took place on Monday, February 5 (Rushworth III, ii, 614). The loss
of the Scots appears to be exaggerated by the Duchess. See also the letter of the
Marquis and General King, quoted in Appendix vii.

[3] The Scots marched from before Newcastle on February 22, leaving a detachment
to blockade the town ; they passed the Tyne on February 28, and entered Sunderland on March 4. See the letter of the Marquis in Appendix vii.   During the latter
part of the campaign the great aim of the Marquis was to cut off the supplies of the
Scots by means of his great superiority in cavalry. This he partially effected, ' so that
sometimes their whole army had neither meat nor drink, and never had above twenty-

The next day after, the Scots army, finding ill harbour in those quarters, marched from hill to hill into another part of the bishopric of Durham, near the sea coast, to a town called Sunderland; and thereupon my Lord thought fit to march to Durham to stop their further progress, where he had contrived the business so, that they were either forced to fight or starve within a little time. The first was offered to them twice, that is to say, at Pensher hills one day, and at Bowden hills another day, in the bishopric of Durham. But my Lord found them at both times drawn up in such places, as he could not possibly charge them [1]; wherefore he retired again to Durham, with an intention to straiten their quarters, and to wait upon them, if ever they left their holds and inaccessible places. In the meantime it happened that the Earl of Montrose came to the same place, and having some design for his Majesty's service in Scotland, desired my Lord to give him the assistance of some of his forces; and although my Lord stood then in present need of them, and could not conveniently spare any, having so great an army to oppose, yet out of a desire to advance his Majesty's service as much as lay in his power, he was willing to part with 200 horse and dragoons to the said earl [2].

The Scots perceiving my Lord's vigilancy and care, contented themselves with their own quarters, which could not have served them long, but that a great misfortune befell my Lord's forces in Yorkshire; for the Governor whom he had left behind with sufficient forces for the defence of that country, although he had orders not to encounter the enemy, but to keep himself in a defensive posture; yet he being a man of

four hours' provision beforehand' (Rushworth, p. 615.) Nevertheless, owing to the severity of the season, Newcastle's army, and especially his cavalry, was greatly diminished in numbers and efficiency.

[1] The Marquis offered battle on the 7th and 8th of March at Bowden hills, near Sunderland, and again on the 23rd, 24th, and 25th of the same month at Hilton. An account of the proceedings of these days from *Mercurius Aulicus* is given in the Appendix. The Marquis began his march back to York on April 13.

[2] Montrose writes to Sir R. Spottiswood from York on March 13, 1644: 'At our arrival here, being uncertain of all business, I directed Cornet Cochrane to my Lord Newcastle to learn the condition of affairs, and inform him particularly of what we had to expect; which necessarily occasioned our stay here for some days. His return to us was, that for supplies he would dispense none for the present; for monies he had none, neither was he owing to the Lord Jermyn any; for arms and ammunition he had not to the two parts of his own, but had been so long expecting them beyond sea, as he was now out of hopes.' Finally, Montrose followed Newcastle to Durham, and obtained from him, according to Wishart, ' an hundred horse, and those very lean and ill appointed, and two small brass field-pieces.'—Napier's *Memorials of Montrose*, ii, 124.

great valour and courage, it transported him so much, that he resolved to face the enemy, and offering to keep a town that was not tenable [1], was utterly routed, and himself taken prisoner, although he fought most gallantly [2].

So soon as my Lord received this sad intelligence, he upon consultation, and upon very good grounds of reason, took a resolution not to stay between the two armies of the enemy's, viz. the Scots and the English, that had prevailed in Yorkshire ; but immediately to march into Yorkshire with his army, to preserve (if possible) the city of York out of the enemy's hands : which retreat was ordered so well, and with such excellent conduct, that though the army of the Scots marched close upon their rear, and fought them every day of their retreat, yet they gained several passes for their security and entered safe and well into the city of York, in April 1643 [3].

My Lord being now at York, and finding three armies against him, viz. the army of the Scots, the army of the English that gave the defeat to the Governor of York, and an army that was raised out of associate counties, and but little ammunition and provision in the town, was forced to send his horse away to quarter in several counties, viz. Derbyshire, Nottinghamshire, Leicestershire, for their subsistence, under the conduct of his Lieutenant-General of the Horse, my dear brother Sir Charles Lucas, himself remaining at York, with his foot and train for the defence of that city [4].

---

1 Selby in Yorkshire.

2 This defeat took place at Selby on April 11, 1644. Lord Fairfax's despatch is given in Rushworth III, ii, 618. Sir Thomas gives an account of the battle in his *Short Memorial*, Maseres' *Tracts*, ii. Bellasis himself was taken prisoner with 1,600 men, and his artillery and baggage.

3 Newcastle started on April 13, and arrived at York on April 19. Next day Fairfax and Leven joined at Tadcaster, and beleaguered the city, and on June 3 they were joined by Manchester (Rushworth III, ii, 620). There is a good letter from Lord Fairfax to the committee of both kingdoms on these occurrences, printed from the Duke of Manchester's papers in the *Eighth Report of the Royal Commission on Historical Manuscripts*, part ii, p. 60. See also Newcastle's letter of 18th April ; Warburton's *Prince Rupert*, ii, 434. In the *Report on the Eglinton MSS.*, p. 53, is a letter from a Scotch officer describing the pursuit.

4 Sir Charles Lucas had only recently received a command in Newcastle's army. He writes to Rupert from Doncaster on February 2, 1644, beginning ' Your Highness having been pleased to dispense with my service to be employed for a time in these parts, where I know not at first coming almost where I am ' etc. He continues : ' Here I live and move by the warmth of your liberal recommendations of me to my Lord Marquis of Newcastle ' ; and ends by saying, that the Marquis has gone north, leaving him behind with 2,000 horse to protect the country, whilst Doncaster is being fortified (Warburton's *Prince Rupert*, vol. ii, p. 370). Lucas joined Newcastle, with twelve troops of horse, near Sunderland, some time before March 6 (Rushworth III, ii, 615). After parting from the Marquis, as described in the text, the body of horse Lucas commanded passed under the command of Goring, and joined Rupert on his march to York.

In the meantime, the enemy, having closely besieged the city on all sides, came to the very gates thereof, and pulled out the earth at one end, as those in the city put it in at the other end ; they planted their great cannons against it, and threw in granadoes at pleasure : but those in the city made several sallies upon them with good success. At last, the General of the Associate army of the enemy, having closely beleaguered the north side of the town, sprung a mine under the wall of the Manor Yard, and blew part of it up ; and having beaten back the town forces (although they behaved themselves very gallantly), entered the Manor House with a great number of their men, which as soon as my Lord perceived, he went away in all haste—even to the amazement of all that were by, not knowing what he intended to do—and drew 80 of his own regiment of foot, called the White Coats, all stout and valiant men, to that post, who fought the enemy with that courage, that within a little time they killed and took 1,500 of them ; and my Lord gave present order to make up the breach which they had made in the wall [1]. Whereupon the enemy remained without any other attempt in that kind, so long, till almost all provision for the support of the soldiery in the city was spent, which nevertheless was so well ordered by my Lord's prudence, that no famine or great extremity of want ensued.

My Lord having held out in that manner above two months, and withstood the strength of three armies ; and seeing that his Lieutenant-General of the Horse whom he had sent for relief to his Majesty, could not so soon obtain it (although he used his best endeavour), for to gain yet some little time, began to treat with the enemy ; ordering in the meanwhile, and upon the treaty, to double and treble his guards [2]. At last after

---

[1] The breach was made by the blowing up of St. Mary's Tower, whence the Manor House was easily reached (Markham's *Fairfax*, p. 148). The assault was made prematurely, and in insufficient force, by General Crawford, who was eager to monopolise the honour of the expected success. The Duchess greatly exaggerates the loss of the besiegers, which Rushworth puts at a total of 300 (Rushworth III, ii, 631). Baillie blames ' the foolish rashness of Major Crawford, and his great vanity to assault alone the breach made by his mine, without the acquainting Lesley or Fairfax with it ' (*Letters*, ii, 195). Slingsby, who was there, speaks only of 200 prisoners, and estimates the strength of the storming party at 500 (*Memoirs*, p. 109, ed. 2).

[2] The Marquis made overtures for a treaty on June 8, and the negotiations were carried on till the 15th. The correspondence is printed in Rushworth III, ii, 624-631. Newcastle demanded that the garrison should be allowed to march out with arms, ammunition, and baggage, to join the King or Prince Rupert. These terms were of course refused by the besiegers, who sent counter-propositions, to which Newcastle replied :

' My Lords,—I have perused the conditions and demands your Lordships sent ; but when I considered the many professions made to avoid the effusion of Christian

three months time from the beginning of the siege, his Majesty
was pleased to send an army, which, joining with my Lord's
horse that were sent to quarter in the aforesaid countries, came
to relieve the city under the conduct of the most gallant and
heroic Prince Rupert, his nephew ; upon whose approach near
York, the enemy drew from before the city into an entire body,
and marched away on the west side of the river Ouse, that runs
through the city, his Majesty's forces being then of the east
side of that river [1].

My Lord immediately sent some persons of quality to attend
his Highness, and to invite him into the city to consult with
him about that important affair, and to gain so much time
as to open a port to march forth with his cannon and foot
which were in the town, to join with his Highness' forces ;
and went himself the next day in person to wait on his Highness ; where, after some conferences, he declared his mind
to the Prince, desiring his Highness not to attempt anything
as yet upon the enemy ; for he had intelligence that there was
some discontent between them, and that they were resolved
to divide themselves, and so to raise the siege without fighting :
besides my Lord expected within two days Colonel Cleavering,
with above three thousand men out of the North, and two
thousand drawn out of several garrisons (who also came at the
same time, though it was then too late).   But his Highness
answered my Lord, that he had a letter from his Majesty (then
at Oxford), with a positive and absolute command to fight
the enemy ; which in obedience, and according to his duty he
was bound to perform [2].   Whereupon my Lord replied, That

blood, I did admire to see such propositions from your Lordships, conceiving this not
the way to it ; for I cannot suppose that your Lordships do imagine, that persons of
honour can possibly condescend to any of these propositions, and so remain, my Lords,
your Lordships' most humble servant,

' WILL NEWCASTLE.

' YORK, 15th June 1644.'

[1] The siege was raised on July 1. The allied army were retreating towards Tadcaster on July 2, when Rupert's pursuit forced them to halt and give battle. A letter
from Newcastle to Rupert on the raising of the siege is printed in the *Pythouse Papers*, p. 19.
Rupert and Newcastle did not meet till the morning of the fight. A detailed account
of the preliminaries of the battle is given in Sir Hugh Cholmley's *Memorials* touching
the battle of York, which is printed in *The English Historical Review* for April 1890,
p. 345.
[2] The King's letter is printed in the Nicholas correspondence at the end of Evelyn's
Diary, iv, 152, and in Warburton's *Prince Rupert and the Cavaliers*, ii, 437. The King's
words are : ' If York be lost I shall esteem my crown little less ; unless supported by
your sudden march to me ; and a miraculous conquest in the south, before the effects
of their northern power can be found here. But if York be relieved, and you beat the
rebel's army of both kingdoms, which are before it ; then (but otherwise not) I may

he was ready and willing, for his part, to obey his Highness in all things, no otherwise than if his Majesty was there in person himself ; and though several of my Lord's friends advised him not to engage in battle, because the command (as they said) was taken from him : yet my Lord answered them, that happen what would, he would not shun to fight, for he had no other ambition but to live and die a loyal subject to his Majesty.

Then the Prince and my Lord conferred with several of their officers, amongst whom there were several disputes concerning the advantages which the enemy had of sun, wind, and ground. The horse of his Majesty's forces was drawn up in both wings upon that fatal moor called Hessom Moor ; and my Lord asked his Highness what service he would be pleased to command him ; who returned this answer, that he would begin no action upon the enemy till early in the morning ; desiring my Lord to repose himself till then. Which my Lord did, and went to rest in his own coach that was close by in the field, until the time appointed [1].

Not long had my Lord been there, but he heard a great noise and thunder of shooting, which gave him notice of the armies being engaged. Where upon he immediately put on

possibly make a shift (upon the defensive) to spin out time until you come to assist me. Wherefore, I command and conjure you, by the duty and affection which I know you bear me, that all new enterprises laid aside, you immediately march, according to your first intention, with all your force to the relief of York. But if that be either lost, or have freed themselves from the besiegers, or that for want of powder you cannot undertake that work, that you immediately march with your whole strength directly to Worcester, to assist me and my army ; without which, or your having relieved York by beating the Scots, all the successes you can afterwards have must infallibly be useless unto me.' The letter is dated ' Ticknell, June 14, 1644 '.

[1] There is an interesting account of this discussion amongst the *Clarendon State Papers* (No. 1805), which Dr. Gardiner was kind enough to point out to me. It is a paper of rough notes on the northern campaign, drawn up by Clarendon himself, and based, no doubt, on the information of some of the persons concerned in it.

' The next morning the Marquis went out of the city to attend the Prince, and found him upon his march and the enemy having placed themselves upon a hill ; and when the Marquis overtook the Prince they both alighted, and after salutations went again to horse, and the Prince said " My Lord, I hope we shall have a glorious day. So the Earl asked whether he meant to put it to a day, and urged many reasons against it ; the Prince replied " Nothing venture, nothing have " etc. Several persons had that morning reported that the Prince had an absolute commission to command those parts, and that the Marquis's power was at an end. When Major-General King came up Prince Rupert showed the Marquis and the Earl a paper, which he said was the draught of the battle as he meant to fight it, and asked them what they thought of it. King answered " By God, sir, it is very fine in the paper, but there is no such thing in the fields." The Prince replied " Not so " etc. The Marquis asked the Prince what he would do ? His Highness answered " We will charge them to-morrow morning." My Lord asked him, whether he were sure the enemy would not fall on them sooner ; he answered No ; and the Marquis goes to his coach hard by, and calling for a pipe of tobacco, before he could take it the enemy charged, and instantly all the Prince's horse were routed. Goring beat the other wing, etc.'

his arms, and was no sooner got on horseback, but he beheld
a dismal sight of the horse of his Majesty's right wing, which
out of a panic fear had left the field, and run away with all the
speed they could; and though my Lord made them stand once
yet they immediately betook themselves to their heels again,
and killed even those of their own party that endeavoured
to stop them.   The left wing in the meantime, commanded
by those two valiant persons, the Lord Goring and Sir Charles
Lucas, having the better of the enemy's right wing, which they
beat back most valiantly three times, and made their general
retreat, insomuch that they sounded victory.

In this confusion my Lord (accompanied only with his
brother Sir Charles Cavendish, Major Scot, Captain Mazine [1],
and his page), hastening to see in what posture his own regiment was, met with a troop of gentlemen volunteers, who
formerly had chosen him their captain, notwithstanding he was
general of an army ; to whom my Lord spake after this manner.
'Gentlemen', said he, 'you have done me the honour to choose
me your captain, and now is the fittest time that I may do you
service ; wherefore if you will follow me, I shall lead you on the
best I can, and show you the way to your own honour.'   They
being as glad of my Lord's proffer as my Lord was of their
readiness, went on with the greatest courage ; and passing
through two bodies of foot, engaged with each other not at
forty yards' distance, received not the least hurt, although
they fired quick upon each other ; but marched towards a
Scots regiment of foot, which they charged and routed ; in
which encounter my Lord himself killed three with his page's
half-leaden sword, for he had no other left him ; and though
all the gentlemen in particular offered him their swords, yet
my Lord refused to take a sword of any of them.   At last, after
they had passed through this regiment of foot, a pikeman
made a stand to the whole troop ; and though my Lord
charged him twice or thrice, yet he could not enter [2] him ; but
the troop despatched him soon.

In all these encounters my Lord got not the least hurt,
though several were slain about him ; and his White Coats
showed such an extraordinary valour and courage in that
action, that they were killed in rank and file.   And here I can-

---

[1] Captain Mazine,' the old great horseman,' died in 1677. *Savile Correspondence*, p. 63.
[2] Enter, i.e. get within his guard.

not but mention by the way, that it is remarkable, that in all
actions and undertakings where my Lord was in person himself, he was always victorious, and prospered in the execution
of his designs; but whatsoever was lost or succeeded ill, happened in his absence, and was caused either by the treachery
or negligence and carelessness of his officers.

My Lord being last in the field, and seeing that all was lost,
and that every one of his Majesty's party made their escapes
in the best manner they could; he being, moreover, inquired
after by several of his friends, who had all a great love and
respect for my Lord, especially by the then Earl of Crawford
(who loved my Lord so well that he gave 20s. to one that
assured him of his being alive and safe, telling him, that that
was all he had), went towards York late at night, accompanied
only with his brother and one or two of his servants; and
coming near the town, met his Highness Prince Rupert, with
the Lieutenant-General of the Army, the Lord Ethyn. His
Highness asked my Lord how the business went? To whom
he answered, that all was lost and gone on their side [1].

That night my Lord remained in York; and having nothing
left in his power to do his Majesty any further service in that
kind; for he had neither ammunition, nor money to raise more
forces, to keep either York, or any other towns that were yet
in his Majesty's devotion, well knowing that those which
were left could not hold out long, and being also loath to have
aspersions cast upon him, that he did sell them to the enemy,
in case he could not keep them, he took a resolution, and that
justly and honourably, to forsake the kingdom; and to that
end, went the next morning to the Prince, and acquainted him
with his design, desiring his Highness would be pleased to give
this true and just report of him to his Majesty, that he had
behaved himself like an honest man, a gentleman, and a loyal
subject. Which request the Prince having granted, my Lord
took his leave; and being conducted by a troop of horse and
a troop of dragoons to Scarborough, went to sea, and took

---

[1] Warburton quotes from Rupert's *Diary* the following notes of this conversation:
Says General King ' What will you do ? ' Says the Prince ' I will rally my men.' Says
General King ' Now you what Lord Newcastle will do ? ' (' Now what will you, Lord
Newcastle, do ? ') Says Lord Newcastle ' I will go to Holland ', looking upon all as
lost. The Prince would have him endeavour to recruit his forces. ' No ', says he,
' I will not endure the laughter of the court ', and King said he would go with him.—
Warburton's *Prince Rupert*, vol. ii, p. 468.

shipping for Hamburgh! the gentry of the country, who also came to take their leaves of my Lord, being much troubled at his departure, and speaking very honourably of him, as surely they had no reason to the contrary [1].

---

[1] Clarendon severely blames both Rupert and Newcastle. 'This may be said of it, that the like was never done or heard or read of before; that two great generals, whereof one had still a good army left, his horse, by their not having performed their duty, remaining upon the matter entire, and much the greater part of his foot having retired into the town, the great execution having fallen upon the northern foot; and the other having the absolute commission over the northern counties, and very many considerable places in them still remaining under his obedience, should both agree in nothing else but in leaving that good ally and the whole country as a prey to the enemy. . . All that can be said for the Marquis is, that he was utterly tired with a condition and employment so contrary to his humour, nature, and education; that he did not at all consider the means or the way that would let him out of it, and free him for ever from having more to do with it. . . The strange manner of the Prince's coming, and undeliberated throwing himself and all the King's hopes into that sudden and unnecessary engagement, by which all the force the Marquis had raised, and with so many difficulties preserved, was in a moment cast away and destroyed, so transported him with passion and despair that he could not compose himself to think of beginning the work again, and involving himself in the same undelightful condition of life, from which he might now be free.'—Clarendon, *Rebellion*, viii, 76–87.

Sir Hugh Cholmley, in his Memorials touching the battle of York, says: 'General King, considering the King's affairs absolutely destroyed by loss of this battle, persuaded the Marquis, against all the power of his other friends, to quit the kingdom.'

A discussion of the different questions connected with the history of the battle, and a critical examination of the various contemporary accounts, are to be found in a paper on Marston Moor in the *Transactions of the Royal Historical Society* for 1898 (New Series, vol. xii).

HAVING hitherto faithfully related the life of my noble Lord and husband, and the chief actions which he performed during the time of his being employed in his Majesty's service for the good and interest of his King and country, until the time of his going out of England, I shall now give you a just account of all that passed during the time of his banishment till the return into his native country.

My Lord being a wise man, and foreseeing well what the loss of that fatal battle upon Hessam Moor, near York, would produce, by which not only those of his Majesty's party in the northern parts of the kingdom, but in all other parts of his Majesty's dominions, both in England, Scotland, and Ireland, were lost and undone, and that there was no other way but either to quit the kingdom or submit to the enemy, or die, he resolved upon the former, and preparing for his journey, asked his steward how much money he had left; who answered that he had but £90. My Lord, not being at all startled at so small a sum, although his present design required much more, was resolved to seek his fortune, even with that little; and thereupon, having taken leave of his Highness Prince Rupert and the rest that were present, went to Scarborough (as before is mentioned), where two ships were prepared for Hamburgh to set sail within twenty-four hours, in which he embarked with his company, and arrived in four days' time to the said city, which was on the 8th of July 1644.

In one of these ships was my Lord, with his two sons, Charles Viscount Mansfield and Lord Henry Cavendish now Earl of Ogle; as also Sir Charles Cavendish, my Lord's brother; the then Lord Bishop of Londonderry, Dr. Bramhall; the Lord Falconbridge; the Lord Widdrington; Sir William Carnaby, who after died at Paris, and his brother Mr. Francis Carnaby, who went presently in the same ship back again for England, and soon after was slain by the enemy near Sherborne, in Yorkshire ; besides many of my Lord's and their servants. In the other ship was the Earl of Ethyn, Lieutenant General of my Lord's Army, and the Lord Cornworth [1]. But before my Lord landed at Hamburgh, his eldest son Charles, Lord Mansfield, fell sick of the smallpox ; and not long after his younger son, Henry, now Earl of Ogle, fell likewise dangerously ill of the measles ; but it pleased God that they both happily recovered.

My Lord, finding his company and charge very great, although he sent several of his servants back again into England, and having no means left to maintain him, was forced to seek for credit ; where at last he got so much as would in part relieve his necessities ; and whereas heretofore he had been contented, for want of a coach, to make use of a waggon, when his occasions drew him abroad, he was now able (with the credit he had got) to buy a coach and nine horses of an Holsatian breed ; for which horses he paid £160, and was afterwards offered for one of them an hundred pistoles at Paris, but he refused the money, and presented seven of them to her Majesty the Queen-Mother of England, and kept two for his own use.

After my Lord had stayed in Hamburgh from July 1644, till February 1645 [2], he being resolved to go into France, went by sea from Hamburgh to Amsterdam, and from thence to Rotterdam, where he sent one of his servants with a compliment and tender of his humble service to her Highness the then Princess Royal, the Queen of Bohemia, the Princess

[1] At Sherborne, on October 15, 1645, Colonel Copley defeated Lord Digby and Sir Marmaduke Langdale on their way from Newark to join Montrose in Scotland. Colonel Sir Francis Carnaby is in the list of slain given by Vicars (*Burning Bush*, 299). Lord Widdrington, before mentioned in this Memoir, p. 29, was slain in Lord Derby's defeat at Bolton in 1651. Clarendon speaks of him thus : ' The Lord Widdrington was one of the most goodly persons of that age, being near the head higher than most tall men, and a gentleman of the best and most ancient extraction of the county of Northumberland, and of a very fair fortune, and one of the four which the last king made choice of to be about the person of his son the prince, as gentleman of his privy-chamber, when he first erected his family. . . . As soon as the war broke out, he was of the first who raised both horse and foot at his own charge, and served eminently with them under the Marquis of Newcastle, from whom he had a very particular and entire friendship, as he was very nearly allied to him ; and by his testimony that he had performed many signal services, he was, about the middle of the war, made a peer of the realm.'—*Rebellion*, xiii, 68. Clarendon concludes by saying ' He was a man of great courage and choler '.

Lord Cornworth, or rather Robert Dalzell, second Earl of Carnwath, was the Scottish peer who seized the King's bridle rein at Naseby, and prevented him heading a last charge.—Clarendon, *Rebellion*, ix, 40.

[2] While at Hamburg Newcastle wrote to his old pupil Prince Charles, then nominally commanding the royal army in the west of England, congratulating him on being made a general. ' It is no small comfort,' he said, ' to me and mine, that we have lived to see you a man ; and could I see but peace in our Israel, truly then I care not how soon death closes my eyes '—*Portland MSS.*, ii, 134.

Dowager of Orange, and the Prince of Orange, which was received with much kindness and civility.

From Rotterdam he directed his journey to Antwerp, and from thence, with one coach, one chariot, and two waggons, he went to Mechlin and Brussels, where he received a visit from the Governor, the Marquis of Castle Rodrigo, the Duke of Lorraine, and Count Piccolomini.

From thence he set forth for Valenciennes and Cambray, where the Governor of the town used my Lord with great respect and civility, and desired him to give the word that night. Thence he went to Peronne, a frontier town in France (where the Vice-Governor, in absence of the Governor of that place, did likewise entertain my Lord with all respect, and desired him to give the word that night), and so to Paris without any further stay.

My Lord being arrived at Paris, which was in April 1645, immediately went to tender his humble duty to her Majesty, the Queen-Mother of England, where it was my fortune to see him the first time, I being then one of the Maids of Honour to her Majesty; and after he had stayed there some time, he was pleased to take some particular notice of me, and express more than an ordinary affection for me; insomuch that he resolved to choose me for his second wife [1]. For he, having but two sons, purposed to marry me, a young woman that might prove fruitful to him and increase his posterity by a masculine offspring. Nay, he was so desirous of male issue that I have heard him say he cared not (so God would be pleased to give him many sons) although they came to be persons of the meanest fortunes; but God (it seems) had ordered it otherwise, and frustrated his designs by making me barren, which yet did never lessen his love and affection for me.

After my Lord was married, having no estate or means left him to maintain himself and his family, he was necessitated to seek for credit, and live upon the courtesy of those that were pleased to trust him; which, although they did for some while, and showed themselves very civil to my Lord, yet they grew weary at length, insomuch that his steward was forced one time to tell him that he was not able to provide a dinner

---

[1] They were married in Sir Richard Browne's chapel at Paris (Evelyn's *Diary*, vol. ii, p. 217, ed. Wheatley). The marriage took place about December 1645 (*Portland MSS.*, ii, 137).

for him, for his creditors were resolved to trust him no longer.
My Lord, being always a great master of his passions, was—
at least showed himself—not in any manner troubled at it,
but in a pleasant humour told me that I must of necessity pawn
my clothes to make so much money as would procure a dinner.
I answered that my clothes would be but of small value, and
therefore desired my waiting-maid [1] to pawn some small toys
which I had formerly given her, which she willingly did.   The
same day, in the afternoon, my Lord spake himself to his
creditors, and both by his civil deportment and persuasive
arguments, obtained so much that they did not only trust him
for more necessaries, but lent him money besides to redeem
those toys that were pawned.   Hereupon I sent my waiting-
maid into England to my brother, the Lord Lucas, for that
small portion which was left me, and my Lord also immediately
after despatched one of his servants [2], who was then governor
to his sons, to some of his friends, to try what means he could
procure for his subsistence.   But though he used all the
industry and endeavour he could, yet he effected but little, by
reason everybody was so afraid of the Parliament that they
durst not relieve him who was counted a traitor for his honest
and loyal service to his King and country.

   Not long after, my Lord had proffers made him of some rich
matches in England for his two sons, whom, therefore, he sent
thither with one Mr. Loving, hoping by that means to provide
both for them and himself ; but they, being arrived there,
out of some reasons best known to them, declared their unwil-
lingness to marry as yet, continuing, nevertheless, in England
and living as well as they could [3].

   Some two years after my Lord's marriage, when he had prevailed so far with his creditors that they began to trust him
anew, the first thing he did was, that he removed out of those
lodgings in Paris where he had been necessitated to live hitherto, to a house which he hired for himself and his family, and
furnished it as well as his new-gotten credit would permit ;
and withal, resolving for his own recreation and divertisement,
in his banished condition, to exercise the art of manage, which

---

[1] Mrs. Chaplain, now Mrs. Top.   [2] Mr. Benoist.
[3] Charles Viscount Mansfield married the eldest daughter and heir of Mr. Richard
Rogers ; Henry, afterwards Earl of Ogle, married a daughter of Mr. William Pierrepont, who is so frequently mentioned by Mrs. Hutchinson.   But see Section 16, in Book
III, of this *Memoir*, which treats of the Duke's pedigree.

he is a great lover and master of, bought a Barbary horse for that purpose, which cost him 200 pistoles, and, soon after another Barbary horse from the Lord Crofts for which he was to pay him £100 when he returned into England.

About this time there was a council called at St. Germain, in which were present, besides my Lord, her Majesty the now Queen-Mother of England ; his Highness the Prince, our now gracious King ; his cousin Prince Rupert ; the Marquis of Worcester ; the then Marquis, now Duke of Ormond ; the Lord Jermyn, now Earl of St. Albans, and several others ; where, after several debates concerning the then present condition of his Majesty King Charles the First, my Lord delivered his sentiment, that he could perceive no other probability of procuring forces for his Majesty but an assistance of the Scots. But her Majesty was pleased to answer my Lord that he was too quick.

Not long after, when my Lord had begun to settle himself in his mentioned new house, his gracious master the Prince having taken a resolution to go into Holland upon some designs, her Majesty the Queen-Mother desired my Lord to follow him, promising to engage for his debts which hitherto he had contracted at Paris, and commanding her Controller [1] and Treasurer [2] to be bound for them in her behalf ; which they did, although the creditors would not content themselves until my Lord had joined his word to theirs. So great and generous was the bounty and favour of her Majesty to my Lord !—considering she had already given him heretofore near upon £2000 sterling, even at the time when her Majesty stood most in need of it.

My Lord, after his Highness the Prince was gone, being ready to execute her Majesty's commands in following him and preparing for his journey, wanted the chief thing, which was money ; and having much endeavoured for it, at last had the good fortune to obtain upon credit three or four hundred pounds sterling ; with which sum he set out of Paris in the same equipage he entered, viz. one coach, which he had newly caused to be made (wherein were the Lord Widdrington, my Lord's brother, Sir Charles Cavendish, Mr. Loving, my waiting-maid, and some others, whereof the two latter were then returned out of England), one little chariot that would only

[1] Sir Henry Wood.   [2] Sir Richard Foster.

hold my Lord and myself ; and three waggons, besides an indifferent number of servants on horseback.

That day, when we left Paris, the creditors, coming to take their farewell of my Lord, expressed so great a love and kindness for him, accompanied with so many hearty prayers and wishes, that he could not but prosper on his journey.

Being come into the King of Spain's dominions, my Lord found a very noble reception.   At Cambray the Governor was so civil that my Lord coming to that place somewhat late, and when it was dark, he commanded some lights and torches to meet my Lord and conduct him to his lodgings.   He offered my Lord the keys of the city, and desired him to give the word that night, and, moreover, invited him to an entertainment which he had made for him of purpose ; but it being late, my Lord (tired with his journey) excused himself as civilly as he could ; the Governor notwithstanding being pleased to send all manner of provisions to my Lord's lodgings, and charging our landlord to take no pay for anything we had : which extraordinary civilities showed that he was a right noble Spaniard.

The next morning early my Lord went on his journey, and was very civilly used in every place of his Majesty of Spain's dominions where he arrived.   At last coming to Antwerp, he took water to Rotterdam (which town he chose for his residing-place during the time of his stay in Holland), and sent thither to a friend of his [1], a gentleman of quality, to provide him some lodgings ; which he did, and procured them at the house of one Mrs. Beynham, widow to an English merchant who had always been very loyal to his Majesty the King of England, and serviceable to his Majesty's faithful subjects in whatsoever lay in his power [2].

My Lord, being come to Rotterdam, was informed that his Highness the Prince (now our gracious King) was gone to sea. Wherefore he resolved to follow him, and for that purpose hired a boat, and victualled it ; but since nobody knew whither his Highness was gone, and I being unwilling that my Lord should venture upon so uncertain a voyage, and (as the proverb is) seek a needle in a bottle of hay, he desisted from that design. The Lord Widdrington, nevertheless, and Sir William Throck-

---

[1] Sir William Throckmorton, Knight.
[2] Probably the widow of Theophilus Baynham, concerning whom see the *Journals of the House of Lords*, July 6, 1644.

morton, being resolved to find out the Prince, but having by a storm been driven towards the coast of Scotland, and endangered their lives, they returned without obtaining their aim [1].

After some little time, my Lord having notice that the Prince was arrived at the Hague, he went to wait on his Highness (which he also did afterwards at several times, so long as his Highness continued there), expecting some opportunity where he might be able to show his readiness to serve his King and country, as certainly there was no little hopes for it ; for, first it was believed that the English fleet would come and render itself into the obedience of the Prince ; next, it was reported that the Duke of Hamilton was going out of Scotland with a great army, into England, to the assistance of his Majesty, and that his Majesty had then some party at Colchester. But it pleased God that none of these proved effectual ; for the fleet did not come in, the Duke of Hamilton's army was destroyed, and Colchester was taken by the enemy, where my dear brother, Sir Charles Lucas, and his dear friend, Sir George Lisle, were most inhumanly murdered and shot to death, they being both valiant and heroic persons, good soldiers, and most loyal subjects to his Majesty ; the one an excellent commander of horse, the other of foot [2].

My Lord having now lived in Rotterdam almost six months, at a great charge, keeping an open and noble table for all comers, and being pleased especially to entertain such as were excellent soldiers and noted commanders of war, whose kindness he took as a great obligation, still hoping that some occasion would happen to invite those worthy persons into

[1] Sir William Throckmorton afterwards succeeded in reaching Scotland, when the King went thither in 1650, took part in the expedition to England, and was dangerously wounded in Lord Derby's defeat at Wigan. ' He received so many wounds that he was looked upon as dead, and not fit to be carried away with the prisoners ; and so fell into such charitable and generous hands in the town, that, being believed to be dead, he was afterwards so well recovered though with great maims and loss of limbs, that he at last got himself transported into Holland, where he was at first appearance taken for a ghost, all men having believed him to be buried long before.'—Clarendon, *Rebellion*, xiii, 67.

[2] Sir Charles Lucas and Sir George Lisle were shot on August 28, 1648, by sentence of a court-martial after the surrender of Colchester. This can hardly be termed a murder. By the fourth article of the capitulation the Lords, Captains, superior officers, and gentlemen of quality were ' to render themselves to the mercy of My Lord General ' which, in answer to a question from the Commissioners of the besieged, was defined to mean ' without certain assurance of quarter ; so as the Lord General may be free to put some immediately to the sword, if he see cause ' (Rushworth IV, ii, 1247). The executions therefore involved no breach of the terms of the treaty. Lives of Lucas and Lisle are contained in the *Dictionary of National Biography*. For a discussion of the question of their execution see Appendix x.

England to serve his Majesty ; but seeing no probability of
either returning into England or doing his Majesty any service
in that kind, he resolved to retire to some place where he
might live privately ; and having chosen the city of Antwerp
for that purpose, went to the Hague to take his leave of his
Highness the Prince, our now gracious Sovereign. My Lord
had then but a small stock of money left ; for though the then
Marquis of Hertford (after Duke of Somerset) and his cousin-
german, once removed, the now Earl of Devonshire had lent
him £2000 between them ; yet all that was spent, and above
£1000 more, which my Lord borrowed during the time he lived
in Rotterdam, his expense being the more, by reason (as I
mentioned) he lived freely and nobly.

However my Lord, notwithstanding that little provision
of money he had, set forth from Rotterdam to Antwerp, where
for some time he lay in a public inn, until one of his friends
that had a great love and respect for my Lord, Mr. Endymion
Porter, who was Groom of the Bed-chamber to his Majesty
King Charles the First (a place not only honourable, but very
profitable) being not willing that a person of such quality as
my Lord should lie in a public-house, proffered him lodgings
at the house where he was, and would not let my Lord be at
quiet, until he had accepted of them [1].

My Lord, after he had stayed some while there, endeavouring
to find out a house for himself which might fit him and his
small family (for at that time he had put off most of his train),
and also be for his own content, lighted on one that belonged
to the widow of a famous picture-drawer, Van Ruben,[2] which
he took.

About this time my Lord was much necessitated for money,
which forced him to try several ways for to obtain so much
as would relieve his present wants. At last Mr. Aylesbury,
the only son to Sir Thomas Aylesbury, Knight and Baronet,
and brother to the now Countess of Clarendon, a very worthy
gentleman [3], and great friend to my Lord, having some moneys
that belonged to the now Duke of Buckingham, and seeing

1 See The Life and Letters of Endymion Porter, by Dorothea Townshend, 1897, p. 231.
2 This ' picture-drawer ' was Rubens. Mr. Lower says that he ' had a magnificent
museum, which the Duke afterwards purchased for £1000 '.
3 William Aylesbury, the translator of Davila's History of the Civil Wars of France,
born 1615, died 1656. Hyde married his sister Frances. See his life in the Dictionary
of National Biography, vol. ii.

my Lord in so great distress, did him the favour to lend him £200 (which money my Lord since his return hath honestly and justly repaid). This relief came so seasonably, that it got my Lord credit in the city of Antwerp, whereas otherwise he would have lost himself to his great disadvantage ; for my Lord having hired the house afore-mentioned, and wanting furniture for it, was credited by the citizens for as many goods as he was pleased to have, as also for meat and drink, and all kind of necessaries and provisions, which certainly was a special blessing of God, he being not only a stranger in that nation, but, to all appearance, a ruined man.

After my Lord had been in Antwerp some time, where he lived as retiredly as it was possible for him to do, he gained much love and respect of all that knew or had any business with him. At the beginning of our coming thither, we found but few English (except those that were merchants) but afterwards their number increased much, especially of persons of quality ; and whereas at first there were no more but four coaches that went the Tour [1], viz. the Governor's of the Castle, my Lord's, and two more, they amounted to the number of above a hundred, before we went from thence ; for all those that had sufficient means, and could go to the price, kept coaches, and went the Tour for their own pleasure. And certainly I cannot in duty and conscience but give this public testimony to that place. That whereas I have observed, that most commonly such towns or cities where the prince of that country does not reside himself, or where there is no great resort of the chief nobility and gentry, are but little civilised ; certainly, the inhabitants of the said city of Antwerp are the civilest and best-behaved people that ever I saw. So that my Lord lived there with as much content as a man of his condition could do, and his chief pastime and divertisement consisted in the manage of the two afore-mentioned horses ; which he had not enjoyed long, but the Barbary horse, for which he paid 200 pistoles in Paris, died, and soon after the horse which he had from the Lord Crofts ; and though he wanted present means to repair these his losses, yet he endeavoured and obtained so much credit at

---

1 The Duchess, in her *Life*, explains this to signify driving about the town and the principal streets in a coach, ' which we call here a Tour, where all the chief of the town go to see and be seen, likewise all strangers, of what quality soever '.

last that he was able to buy two others, and by degrees so
many as amounted in all to the number of eight.   In which
he took so much delight and pleasure, that though he was
then in distress for money, yet he would sooner have tried all
other ways, than parted with any of them ; for I have heard
him say, that good horses are so rare, as not to be valued for
money, and that he who would buy him out of his pleasure
(meaning his horses), must pay dear for it.   For instance I
shall mention some passages which happened when my Lord
was in Antwerp.

First, a stranger coming thither, and seeing my Lord's horses,
had a great mind to buy one of them, which my Lord loved
above the rest, and called him his favourite, a fine Spanish
horse ;   entreating my Lord's escuyer to acquaint him with
his desire, and ask the price of the said horse.   My Lord,
when he heard of it, commanded his servant, that if the chapman returned, he should be brought before him ;   which being
done accordingly, my Lord asked him, whether he was resolved to buy his Spanish horse ?   Yes, answered he, my
Lord, and I'll give your Lordship a good price for him.   I
make no doubt of it, replied my Lord, or else you shall not
have him :   but you must know, said he, that the price of
that horse is £1000 to-day, to-morrow it will be £2000, next
day £3000, and so forth.   By which the chapman perceiving
that my Lord was unwilling to part with the said horse for
any money, took his leave, and so went his ways.

The next was, that the Duke de Guise, who was also a
great lover of good horses, hearing much commendation of a
grey leaping horse, which my Lord then had, told the gentleman that praised and commended him, that if my Lord was
willing to sell the said horse, he would give 600 pistoles for
him.   The gentleman knowing my Lord's humour, answered
again, that he was confident my Lord would never part with
him for any money, and to that purpose sent a letter to my
Lord from Paris ;   but my Lord was so far from selling that
horse, that he was displeased to hear that any price should be
offered for him :   so great a love hath my Lord for good horses !
And certainly I have observed, and do verily believe, that
some of them had also a particular love to my Lord ;   for they
seemed to rejoice whensoever he came into the stables, by
their trampling action, and the noise they made ;   nay, they

would go much better in the manage [1] when my Lord was by, than when he was absent ; and when he rid them himself, they seemed to take much pleasure and pride in it. But of all sorts of horses, my Lord loved Spanish horses and barbs best ; saying, that Spanish horses were like princes, and barbs like gentlemen, in their kind.   And this was the chief recreation and pastime my Lord had in Antwerp.

I will now return to my former discourse, and the relation of some important affairs and actions which happened about this time. His Majesty (our now gracious King, Charles the Second) some time after he was gone out of Holland, and returned into France, took his journey from thence to Breda (if I remember well) to treat there with his subjects of Scotland, who had then made some offers of agreement [2]. My Lord, according to his duty, went thither to wait on his Majesty, and was there in council with his Majesty, his Highness the then Prince of Orange, his Majesty's brother-in-law, and some other privy-counsellors ; in which, after several debates concerning that important affair, his Highness the Prince of Orange, and my Lord, agreed in one opinion, viz. that they could perceive no other and better way at that present for his Majesty, but to make an agreement with his subjects of Scotland, upon any condition, and to go into Scotland in person himself, that he might but be sure of an army, there being no probability or appearance then of getting an army anywhere else.   Which counsel, either out of the then alleged

---

1 Manage=*manège*, riding-school.

2 These negotiations took place at Breda, in the spring of 1650. Charles sailed for Scotland on June 2. In his letter from Jersey to the Estates of Scotland Charles had fixed March 15 for the opening of the negotiations (Carte, *Original Letters*, i, 356). Nicholas writes to Ormonde on April 3, 1650 : ' The King hath lately sworn of his Privy Council here, the Dukes of Buckingham and Hamilton and the Marquis of Newcastle ' (p. 376). According to Doyle's *Official Baronage*, Newcastle entered the Council on April 6, 1650. Hopton and Nicholas were excluded from the Council for opposing the concessions made by the King to the Scots. Hyde, referring to this, writes to Nicholas : ' You have a very precious junto to determine concerning three kingdoms ; you will find the Marquis of Newcastle a very lamentable man, and as fit to be a general as a bishop, but I doubt though you choose officers you are not in the way of raising armies.' —Clarendon *State Papers*, iii, 20.

Hyde was at Madrid during this treaty, but his letters show that he was thoroughly opposed to the policy which dictated it.   ' What secret spirit possesses the hearts of all the King's party, that from all parts they cry out " Agree with the Scots upon any terms '.   It were as possible for me to rebel as to govern myself by those senseless sayings ; and yet people of all kinds sing that tune.' If any agreement was to be made with the Scots, it ought to be straightforward and sincere. The Scots required the acceptance of the Covenant. Hopton and Nicholas urged the King to refuse ; others urged that the King should take it and break it afterwards, which Clarendon characterised as ' such folly and atheism that we should be ashamed to avow it or think it.'—*Clarendon State Papers*, iii, 15.

reasons, or some others best known to his Majesty, was embraced ; his Majesty agreeing with the Scots so far (notwithstanding they were so unreasonable in their treaty, that his
Majesty had hardly patience to hear them), that he resolved
to go into Scotland in person ; and though my Lord had an
earnest desire to wait on his Majesty thither, yet the Scots
would not suffer him to come, or be in any part of that kingdom.
Wherefore, out of his loyalty and duty, he gave his Majesty
the best advice he could, viz. that he conceived it most safe
for his Majesty to adhere to the Earl of Argyle's party, which
he supposed to be the strongest ; but especially, to reconcile
Hamilton's and Argyle's party, and compose the differences
between them ; for then his Majesty would be sure of two
parties, whereas otherwise he would leave an enemy behind
him, which might cause his overthrow, and endanger his
Majesty's person ; and if his Majesty could but get the power
into his own hands, he might do hereafter what he pleased.

His Majesty being arrived in Scotland, ordered his affairs
so wisely, that soon after he got an army to march with him
into England ; but whether they were all loyal, is not for me
to dispute. However, Argyle was discontented, as it appeared
by two complaining letters he sent to my Lord, which my
Lord gave his Majesty notice of [1] ; so that only the Duke of
Hamilton went with his Majesty, who fought and died like a
valiant man, and a loyal subject. In this fight between the
English and Scots, his Majesty expressed an extraordinary
courage ; and though his army was in a manner destroyed,
yet the glory of an heroic prince remained with our gracious
sovereign.

In the meantime, whilst his Majesty was yet in Scotland,
and before he marched with his army into England, it happened that the Elector of Brandenburg, and Duke of Neuburg,
upon some differences, having raised forces against each
other, but afterwards concluded a peace between them, were
pleased to proffer those forces to my Lord for his Majesty's
use and service, which (as the Lord Chancellor, who was then
in France, sent word to my Lord) was the only foreign proffer
that had been made to his Majesty. My Lord immediately

---

[1] Four letters written to Newcastle in Dec. 1650 and Jan. 1651 by noblemen then
with the King in Scotland are printed in *Portland MSS*. ii, 136–9. One is from Argyle,
but it does not refer to the march into England.

gave his Majesty notice of it ; but whether it was for want of convenient transportation, or money, or that the Scots did not like the assistance, that proffer was not accepted [1].

Concerning the affairs and intrigues that passed in Scotland and England, during the time of his Majesty's stay there, I am ignorant of them ; neither doth it belong to me now to write, or give an account of anything else but what concerns the history of my noble Lord and husband's life, and his own actions ; who, so soon as he had intelligence that the Scottish army, which went with his Majesty into England, was defeated and that nobody knew what was become of his Majesty, fell into so violent a passion, that I verily believed it would have endangered his life ; but when afterwards the happy news came of his Majesty's safe arrival in France, never any subject could rejoice more than my Lord did.

About this time it chanced, that my Lord's brother, Sir Charles Cavendish, and myself, took a journey into England, occasioned both by my Lord's extreme want and necessity, and his brother's estate ; which having been under sequestration from the time (or soon after) he went out of England, was then, in case he did not return and compound for it, to be sold outright. Sir Charles was unwilling to receive his estate upon such conditions, and would rather have lost it, than compounded for it. But my Lord, considering it was better to recover something, than lose all, entreated the Lord Chancellor, who was then in Antwerp, to persuade his brother to a composition, which his Lordship did very effectually,

1 Nicholas writes to Ormond on June 20, 1651, that he hears from the Hague ' that the Marquess of Brandenburgh and his lady arrived there Friday last, and on Sunday following he and his lady (when the Princess Royal was at sermon) went to see the young Prince of Orange, and on Tuesday following intended to leave the Hague, without making one visit to her Highness Royal. The Marquess resolves to make war against the Duke of Neuburg, who will be assisted by the King of Spain and the Duke of Lorraine, as the Marquess hopes to be by the Swede.'—Carte, *Original Letters*, ii, 38. On August 8, however, the Elector of Brandenburgh wrote to the Marquess of Newcastle that his being obliged to take up arms against the Duke of Neuburg hindered his helping Charles at present, but that as soon as matters were settled he would not fail to let his soldiers put themselves at the service of the King. On September 11 he wrote further congratulating him on the success of the King of Great Britain, and saying that as he hoped soon to have no further need of his troops he would willingly enter into a treaty for their employment in the King's service. A letter from one of the Elector's Ministers stated that his sovereign would provide 6000 infantry and 4000 cavalry, adding that he had been employed to proceed to Denmark to solicit ships, and asking in what British harbour the troops were to land. The Marquess replied saying that he was about to send a messenger to make arrangements with the King of Denmark. *Calendar of the Clarendon State Papers*, vol. ii, pp. 105–7. But the battle of Worcester put an end to all these hopes. Nevertheless the Elector of Brandenburgh continued to exercise his good offices on behalf of Charles in the Diet of the Empire, and in January 1654 the King sent him the Order of the Garter (p. 303).

and proved himself a noble and true friend in it [1].   We had
so small a provision of money when we set forth our journey
for England, that it was hardly able to carry us to London,
but were forced to stay at Southwark ; where Sir Charles sent
into London for one that had formerly been his steward, and
having declared to him his wants and necessities, desired him
to try his credit.   He seemed ready to do his master what
service he could in that kind ;   but pretending withal, that
his credit was but small, Sir Charles gave him his watch to
pawn, and with that money paid those small scores we had
made in our lodging there.   From thence we went to some
other lodgings that were prepared for us in Covent Garden ;
and having rested ourselves some time, I desired my brother,
the Lord Lucas, to claim in my behalf some subsistence for
myself out of my Lord's estate (for it was declared by the
Parliament, that the lands of those that were banished, should
be sold to any that would buy them, only their wives and
children were allowed to put in their claims) :   but he received
this answer, that I could not expect the least allowance, by
reason my Lord and husband had been the greatest traitor of
England (that is to say, the honestest man, because he had
been most against them) [2].

Then Sir Charles entrusted some persons to compound for
his estate ;   but it being a good while before they agreed in
their composition, and then before the rents could be received,
we having in the meantime nothing to live on, must of necessity

[1] See Clarendon's letter to Nicholas, November 1, 1657.   Newcastle had placed
most of his lands in the hands of trustees ;   nevertheless the Commonwealth laid hands
on them.   'Where any clauses of revocation are', writes Hyde, 'the Commonwealth
takes the advantage to do that which the persons dead in law might do ;   and so they
disappoint all those engagements, as they have done or declare they will do in the case
of my Lord Newcastle, who before these times conveyed his lands for the payment of
debts and raising younger children's portions, with a power of revocation, which the
sovereign power will now execute, and so defraud the creditors and all other intentions.   In very good earnest the whole business of proceeding with them is so intricate
and perplexed and ridiculous, that I do not intend to trouble myself at all about it ;
and I fear whosoever does, except he resolves to do that which he is to be damned for
doing, will get nothing by it ;   and yet my Lady Marquis of Newcastle ventures thither
this week ;   and no question it is wisely done, and with her Sir Charles Cavendish, as
well to urge some deeds of trust, which he hath long been in for his brother, as to endeavour to enjoy the benefit of a composition which was made long since for his own
estate.'—Clarendon State Papers, iii, 34.   The papers relating to the case of Sir Charles
Cavendish are to be found in the Calendar of the Proceedings of the Committee for Compounding, p. 2091.   Dring's Catalogue, ed. 1733, p. 27.   The arguments by which Clarendon converted Sir Charles Cavendish are given in his Life, Book vi,   30–4.
[2] Her petition is dated Dec. 10 1651.   It was refused, as she says in her life of herself (p. 167 post), not because of the reason given above, but because her marriage had
taken place since her husband's delinquency—Calendar of the Proceedings of the Committee for Compounding, p. 1733.

have been starved, had not Sir Charles got some credit of several persons, and that not without great difficulty; for all those that had estates, were afraid to come near him, much less to assist him, until he was sure of his own estate. So much is misery and poverty shunned!

But though our condition was hard, yet my dear Lord and husband, whom we left in Antwerp, was then in a far greater distress than ourselves; for at our departure he had nothing but what his credit was able to procure him; and having run upon the score so long without paying any the least part thereof, his creditors began to grow impatient, and resolved to trust him no longer. Wherefore he sent me word, that if his brother did not presently relieve him, he was forced to starve. Which doleful news caused great sadness and melancholy in us both, and withal made his brother try his utmost endeavour to procure what moneys he could for his subsistence, who at last got £200 sterling upon credit, which he immediately made over to my Lord.

But in the meantime, before the said money could come to his hands, my Lord had been forced to send for all his creditors, and declare to them his great wants and necessities; where his speech was so effectual, and made such an impression in them, that they had all a deep sense of my Lord's misfortunes: and instead of urging the payment of his debts, promised him, that he should not want anything in whatsoever they were able to assist him; which they also very nobly and civilly performed, furnishing him with all manner of provisions and necessaries for his further subsistence; so that my Lord was then in a much better condition amongst strangers, than we in our native country.

At last when Sir Charles Cavendish had compounded for his estate, and agreed to pay £4500 for it, the Parliament caused it again to be surveyed, and made him pay £500 more, which was more than many others had paid for much greater estates; so that Sir Charles, to pay this composition, and discharge some debts, was necessitated to sell some land of his at an under-rate. My Lord's two sons (who were also in England at that time) were no less in want and necessity than we, having nothing but bare credit to live on; [1] and my Lord's

---

[1] The petitions of Charles Viscount Mansfield and his brother Henry for leave to compound are given in the *Proceedings of the Committee for Compounding with Delinquents*,

I

estate being then to be sold outright, Sir Charles, his brother, endeavoured, if possible, to save the two chief houses, viz. Welbeck and Bolsover, being resolved rather to part with some more of his land, which he had lately compounded for, than to let them fall into the enemy's hands. But before such time as he could compass the money, somebody had bought Bolsover, with an intention to pull it down, and make money of the materials; of whom Sir Charles was forced to buy it again at a far greater rate then he might have had it at first, notwithstanding a great part of it was pulled down already; and though my Lord's eldest son Charles, Lord Mansfield, had those mentioned houses some time in possession after the death of his uncle, yet for want of means he was not able to repair them.

I having now been in England a year and a half, some intelligence which I received of my Lord's being not very well, and the small hopes I had of getting some relief out of his estate, put me upon design of returning to Antwerp to my Lord, and Sir Charles, his brother, took the same resolution, but was prevented by an ague that seized upon him. Not long had I been with my Lord, but we received the sad news of his brother's death, which was an extreme affliction both to my Lord and myself, for they loved each other entirely. In truth, he was a person of so great worth, such extraordinary civility, so obliging a nature, so full of generosity, justice and charity, besides all manner of learning, especially in the mathematics, that not only his friends, but even his enemies, did much lament his loss [1].

p. 1799. Three letters from Newcastle to his son Charles about the means to be adopted to preserve the pictures and furniture at Welbeck and Bolsover are to be found in *Port-land MSS.*, ii, 143.
[1] The death of Sir Charles Cavendish took place on the 4th of February, 1654. Claren-don announces it to Nicholas in a letter dated March 6, 1654 (*Clarendon State Papers*, iii, 223).   In his *Life* (vi, 29) he draws the following portrait:
   'The conversation the Chancellor took most delight in was that of Sir Charles Caven-dish, brother to the Marquis, who was one of the most extraordinary persons of that age, in all the noble endowments of the mind. He had all the disadvantages imaginable in his person, which was not only of so small a size that it drew the eyes of men upon him, but with such deformity in his little person, and an aspect in his countenance, that was apter to raise contempt than application; but in this unhandsome or homely habitation, there was a mind and a soul lodged, that was very lovely and beautiful; cultivated and polished by all the knowledge and wisdom that arts and sciences could supply it with. He was a great philosopher, in the extent of it, and an excellent mathe-matician; whose correspondence was very dear to Gassendus and Descartes, the last of which dedicated some of his works to him. He had very notable courage, and the vigour of his mind so adorned his body, that being with his brother the Marquis in all the war, he usually went out in all parties, and was present and charged the enemy in all battles, with as keen a courage as could dwell in the heart of man. But then

After my return out of England, to my Lord, the creditors supposing I had brought great store of money along with me, came all to my Lord to solicit the payment of their debts ; but when my Lord had informed them of the truth of the business and desired their patience somewhat longer, with assurance that so soon as he received any money, he would honestly and justly satisfy them, they were not only willing to forbear the payment of those debts he had contracted hitherto, but to credit him for the future, and supply him with such necessaries as he should desire of them.   And this was the only happiness which my Lord had in his distressed condition, and the chief blessing of the eternal and merciful God, in whose power are all things, who ruled the hearts and minds of men, and filled them with charity and compassion.   For certainly it was a work of Divine Providence, that they showed so much love, respect, and honour to my Lord, a stranger to their nation ; and notwithstanding his ruined condition, and the small appearance of recovering his own, credited him wheresoever he lived, both in France, Holland, Brabant, and Germany ; that although my Lord was banished his native country, and dispossessed from his own estate, could nevertheless live in so much splendour and grandeur as he did.

In this condition (and how little soever the appearance was) my Lord was never without hopes of seeing yet (before his death) a happy issue of all his misfortunes and sufferings, especially of the restoration of his most gracious King and master, to his throne and kingly rights, whereof he always had assured hopes, well knowing, that it was impossible for the kingdom to subsist long under so many changes of government ; and whensoever I expressed how little faith I had in it, he would gently reprove me, saying, I believed least, what I desired most ; and could never be happy if I endeavoured to exclude all hopes, and entertained nothing but doubts and fears.

the gentleness of his disposition, the humility and meekness of his nature, and the vivacity of his wit, was admirable.   He was so modest that he could hardly be prevailed with to enlarge himself on subjects he understood better than other men, except he were pressed by his very familiar friends, as if he thought it presumption to know more than handsomer men use to do.   Above all, his virtue and piety was such that no temptation could work upon him to consent to anything that swerved in the least degree from the precise rules of honour, or the most severe rules of conscience.'

Several letters from Sir Charles Cavendish to Pell are printed in the second volume of Robert Vaughan's *Protectorate of Cromwell*, others have been printed by Halliwell, *Letters on Scientific Subjects* (1841).

The city of Antwerp, in which we lived, being a place of great resort for strangers and travellers, his Majesty (our now gracious King, Charles the Second) passed through it, when he went his journey towards Germany; and after my Lord had done his humble duty, and waited on his Majesty, he was pleased to honour him with his presence at his house. The same did almost all strangers that were persons of quality; if they made any stay in the town, they would come and visit my Lord, and see the manage of his horses: and, amongst the rest, the Duke of Oldenburg, and the Prince of East Friesland, did my Lord the honour, and presented him with horses of their own breed.

One time it happened, that his Highness Dom John d'Austria (who was then governor of those provinces) came to Antwerp, and stayed there some few days; and then almost all his court waited on my Lord, so that one day I reckoned about seventeen coaches, in which were all persons of quality, who came in the morning of purpose to see my Lord's manage. My Lord receiving so great an honour thought it fit to show his respect and civility to them, and to ride some of his horses himself, which otherwise he never did but for his own exercise and delight [1]. Amongst the rest of those great and noble persons, there were two of our nation, viz. the then Marquis, now Duke of Ormond, and the Earl of Bristol; but Dom John was not there in person, excusing himself afterwards to my Lord (when my Lord waited on him) that the multiplicity of his weighty affairs had hindered his coming thither, which my Lord accounted as a very high honour and favour from so great a Prince; and conceiving it his duty to wait on his Highness, but being unknown to him, the Earl of Bristol, who

[1] In the introduction to the Duke's second book on horsemanship (*A New Method and Extraordinary Invention to Dress Horses*), the Duke tells the following story: ' When I had the honour to wait on Don John of Austria, at Antwerp, brought to him by my Lord of Bristol, his Highness was pleased to use me extreme civilly; and to ask both then, and at several other times, for my book of horsemanship, before it was printed; and to receive it with great satisfaction, when I presented his Highness with one. But he did not see my horses, which, in above twenty coaches, all the Spaniards of his court went to my manage to see; with many noblemen of Flanders, as the Duke of Ascot, and others, before whom I rid myself three horses, and my esquire, five. Being returned to Don John, he asked them, whether my horses were as rare, as their reputation was great; to which they answered, that my horses were such that they wanted nothing of reasonable creatures but speaking. And the Marquess of Seralvo, Master of the Horse to his Highness, and Governor of the Castle of Antwerp, told his Highness, that he had asked me, what horses I liked best? and that I had answered, there were good and bad of all nations; but that the Barbs were the gentlemen of horse-kind, and Spanish horses the princes. Which answer did infinitely please the Spaniards; and it is very true, that horses are so as I said.'

had acquaintance with him, did my Lord the favour, and upon his request, presented him to his Highness ; which favour of the said Earl my Lord highly resented [1].

Dom John received my Lord with all kindness and respect ; for although there were many great and noble persons that waited on him in an out-room, yet so soon as his Highness heard of my Lord's and the Earl of Bristol's being there, he was pleased to admit them before all the rest. My Lord, after he had passed his compliments, told his Highness, that he found himself bound in all duty to make his humble acknowledgments for the favour he received from his Catholic Majesty for permitting and suffering him (a banished man) to live in his dominions, and under the government of his Highness. Whereupon Dom John asked my Lord whether he wanted anything, and whether he lived peaceably without any molestation or disturbance ? My Lord answered, that he lived as much to his own content as a banished man could do ; and received more respect and civility from that city than he could have expected, for which he returned his most humble thanks to his Catholic Majesty, and his Highness. After some short discourse, my Lord took his leave of Dom John, several of the Spaniards advising him to go into Spain, and assuring him of his Catholic Majesty's kindness and favour ; but my Lord being engaged in the city of Antwerp, and besides in years, and wanting means for so long and chargeable a voyage, was not able to embrace their motions. And surely he was so well pleased with the great civilities he received from that city, that then he was resolved to choose no other residing place all the time of his banishment but that ; he being not only credited there for all manner of provisions and necessaries for his subsistence, but also free both from ordinary and extraordinary taxes, and from paying excise, which was a great favour and obligation to my Lord [2].

After his Highness Dom John had left the government of those provinces the Marquis of Caracena succeeded in his place, who having a great desire to see my Lord ride in the manage,

[1] Resented, felt.

[2] This indulgence was granted to most of the exiles. On August 7, 1656, Hyde writes to Talbot : 'In consequence of being incognito, the King is the only gentleman who has lived in this country without being exempt from paying excise and other similar impositions', an exemption enjoyed by Lord Newcastle at Antwerp, Hyde himself while at Antwerp, and Lord Hopton and many others at Bruges. *Calendar of Clarendon State Papers*, iii, 154.

entreated a gentleman of the city, that was acquainted with my Lord, to beg that favour of him. My Lord having not been at that exercise six weeks, or two months, by reason of some sickness that made him unfit for it, civilly begged his excuse ; but he was so much importuned by the said gentleman that at last he granted his request, and rid one or two horses in presence of the said Marquis of Caracena, and the then Marquis, now Duke of Ormond, who often used to honour my Lord with his company. The said Marquis of Caracena seemed to take much pleasure and satisfaction in it, and highly complimented my Lord ; and certainly I have observed, that noble and meritorious persons take great delight in honouring each other [1].

But not only strangers, but his Majesty himself (our now gracious Sovereign) was pleased to see my Lord ride, and one time did ride himself, he being an excellent master of that art, and instructed by my Lord, who had the honour to set him first on a horse of manage, when he was his governor ; where his Majesty's capacity was such, that being but ten years of age, he would ride leaping horses, and such as would overthrow others, and manage them with the greatest skill and dexterity, to the admiration of all that beheld him. [2]

[1] In the preface to the book before mentioned the Duke thus relates this incident : ' The Marquess of Caracena was so civilly earnest to see me ride, that he was pleased to say, it would be a great satisfaction to him to see me on horseback, though the horse should but walk. And seeing that no excuses would serve (though I did use many) I was contented to satisfy his so obliging a curiosity ; and told him, I would obey his commands, though I thought I should hardly be able to sit in the saddle. Two days after he came to my manage, and I rid first a Spanish horse, called "Le Superbe," of a light bay, a beautiful horse, and though hard to be rid, yet when he was hit right, he was the readiest horse in the world. He went in corvets forward, backward, sideways, on both hands ; made the cross perfectly upon his voltoes ; and did change upon his voltoes so just, without breaking time, that a musician could not keep time better ; and went terra a terra perfectly. The second horse I rid, was another Spanish, called Le Genty ; and was rightly named so, for he was the finest-shaped horse that ever I saw, and the neatest ; a brown bay with a white star in his forehead ; no horse ever went terra a terra like him, so just, and so easy ; and for the piroyte in his length, so just and so swift that the standers-by could hardly see the rider's face when he went and truly when he had done, I was so dizzy, that I could hardly sit in the saddle. The third and last horse I rid then was a Barb, that went a metz-ayre very high, both forward and upon his voltoes, and terra a terra. And when I had done riding the Marquess of Caracena seemed to be very well satisfied ; and some Spaniards that were with him, crossed themselves, and cried Miraculo ! '
For an explanation of the terms of horsemanship used I must refer readers to the Duke's two books on the subject.
[2] The Duke himself says, in the preface before quoted : ' Having had the honour, when I was his governor, to be the first that set him on horseback, and did instruct him in the art of horsemanship, it is a great satisfaction to me, to make mention here of the joy I had then, to see that his Majesty made my horses go better than any Italian or French riders (who had often rid them) could do.' And again at p. 7 of the Dublin edition of the same book : ' Our gracious and most excellent King is not only the handsomest, and most comely horseman in the world, but as knowing and understanding

Nor was this the only honour my Lord received from his Majesty—but his Majesty and all the royal race, that is to say, her Highness the then Princess-Royal, his Highness the Duke of York, with his brother the Duke of Gloucester (except the Princess Henrietta, now Duchess of Orleans), being met one time in Antwerp, were pleased to honour my Lord with their presence, and accept of a small entertainment at his house, such as his present condition was able to afford them.[1]. And some other time his Majesty passing through the city was pleased to accept of a private dinner at my Lord's house; after which I receiving that gracious favour from his Majesty, that he was pleased to see me, he did merrily, and in jest, tell me that he perceived my Lord's credit could procure better meat than his own. Again, some other time, upon a merry challenge playing a game at butts with my Lord (when my Lord had the better of him), What (said he) my Lord, have you invited me to play the rook with me?[2] although their stakes were not at all considerable, but only for pastime.

These passages I mention only to declare my Lord's happiness in his miseries, which he received by the honour and kindness not only of foreign princes, but of his own master and gracious sovereign. I will not speak now of the good esteem and repute he had by his late Majesty King Charles the First, and her Majesty the now Queen-mother, who always held and found him a very loyal and faithful subject, although fortune was pleased to oppose him in the height of his endeavours; for his only and chief intention was to hinder his

---

in the art as any man; and no man makes a horse go better than I have seen some go under his Majesty the first time that ever he came upon their backs, which is the height and quintessence of the art.'

[1] This entertainment is probably the one mentioned as taking place in February 1658. Sir Charles Cotterell writes to Nicholas: 'At the ball at Lord Newcastle's was the Duchess of Lorraine and her son and daughter, with the King and his brothers and sister, several French people, and some of the town. The King was brought in with music, and all being placed, Major Mohun, the player, in a black satin robe and garland of bays, made a speech in verse of his lordship's own poetry, complimenting the King in his highest hyperbole. Then there was dancing for two hours, and then my Lady's Moor, dressed in feathers, came in and sang a song of the same author's, set and taught him by Nich. Lanier. Then was the banquet brought in in eight great chargers, each borne by two gentlemen of the court, and others bringing wines, drinks, etc. Then they danced again two hours more, and Major Mohun ended all with another speech, prophesying his Majesty's re-establishment.'— *Calendar of State Papers*, 1657-8, pp. 296, 311.

[2] Rook, a sharper. Cotton, describing an ordinary at night, says: 'This is the time (when ravenous beasts naturally seek their prey) wherein comes shoals of Huffs, Hectors, Setters, Gills, Pads, Biters, Divers, Listers, Filers, Budgies, Droppers, Crossbiters, etc., and these may all pass under the general and common appellation of Rooks.'—*The Complete Gamester.*

Majesty's enemies from executing that cruel design which they had upon their gracious and merciful King. In which he tried his uttermost power, insomuch that I have heard him say out of a passionate zeal and loyalty, that he would willingly sacrifice himself and all his posterity, for the sake of his Majesty and the royal race. Nor did he ever repine either at his losses or sufferings, but rejoiced rather that he was able to suffer for his King and country. His army was the only army that was able to uphold his Majesty's power ; which, so long as it was victorious, it preserved both his Majesty's person and crown. But so soon as it fell, that fell too ; and my Lord was then in a manner forced to seek his own preservation in foreign countries, where God was pleased to make strangers his friends, who received and protected him when he was banished his native country, and relieved him when his own countrymen sought to starve him, by withholding from him what was justly his own, only for his honesty and loyalty ; which relief he received more from the commons of those parts where he lived, than from princes, he being unwilling to trouble any foreign prince with his wants and miseries, well knowing, that gifts of great princes came slowly, and not without much difficulty ; neither loves he to petition any one but his own Sovereign.

But though my Lord by the civility of strangers, and the assistance of some few friends of his native country, lived in an indifferent condition, yet (as it hath been declared heretofore) he was put to great plunges and difficulties, insomuch that his dear brother Sir Charles Cavendish would often say, that though he could not truly complain of want, yet his meat never did him good by reason my Lord, his brother, was always so near wanting, that he was never sure after one meal to have another : and though I was not afraid of starving or begging, yet my chief fear was, that my Lord for his debts would suffer imprisonment, where sadness of mind, and want of exercise and air, would have wrought his destruction, which yet by the mercy of God he happily avoided.

Some time before the restoration of his Majesty to his royal throne, my Lord, partly with the remainder of his brother's estate (which was but little, it being wasted by selling of land for compounding with the Parliament, paying of several debts, and buying out the two houses aforementioned, viz. Welbeck and Bolsover), and the credit which his sons had got, which amounted in all to £2400 a year, sprinkled something amongst his creditors, and borrowed so much of Mr. Top and Mr. Smith (though without assurance) that he could pay such scores as were most pressing, contracted from the poorer sort of tradesmen, and send ready money to market, to avoid cozenage (for small scores run up most unreasonably, especially if no strict accounts be kept, and the rate be left to the creditor's pleasure) by which means there was in a short time so much saved, as it could not have been imagined.

About this time, a report came of a great number of sectaries, and of several disturbances in England, which heightened my Lord's former hopes into a firm belief of a sudden change in that kingdom, and a happy restoration of his Majesty, which it also pleased God to send according to his expectation [1]; for his Majesty was invited by his subjects, who were not able longer to endure those great confusions and encumbrances they had sustained hitherto, to take possession of his hereditary rights, and the power of all his dominions : and being then at the Hague in Holland, to take shipping in those parts for England, my Lord went thither to wait on his Majesty, who used my Lord very graciously ; and his Highness the Duke of York was pleased to offer him one of those ships that were ordered to transport his Majesty ; for which he returned his most humble thanks to his Highness, and begged leave of his Highness that he might hire a vessel for himself and his company.

In the meantime, whilst my Lord was at the Hague, his Majesty was pleased to tell him, that General Monk, now Duke of Albemarle, had desired the place of being Master of the Horse : to which my Lord answered, that that gallant person was worthy of any favour that his Majesty could confer upon him : and having taken his leave of his Majesty, and his Highness the Duke of York, went towards the ship that was to transport him for England (I might better call it a boat, than a ship ; for those that were intrusted by my Lord to hire a ship for that purpose, had hired an old rotten frigate that was lost the next voyage after ; insomuch, that when some of the company that had promised to go over with my Lord, saw it, they turned back, and would not endanger

[1] See the Duke's letters to Nicholas in Appendix viii.

K

their lives in it, except the now Lord Widdrington, who was resolved not to forsake my Lord).

My Lord (who was so transported with the joy of returning into his native country, that he regarded not the vessel) having set sail from Rotterdam, was so becalmed, that he was six days and six nights upon the water, during which time he pleased himself with mirth, and passed his time away as well as he could ; provisions he wanted not, having them in great store and plenty. At last, being come so far that he was able to discern the smoke of London, which he had not seen in a long time, he merrily was pleased to desire one that was near him, to jog and awake him out of his dream, for surely, said he, I have been sixteen years asleep, and am not thoroughly awake yet. My Lord lay that night at Greenwich, where his supper seemed more savoury to him, than any meat he had hitherto tasted ; and the noise of some scraping fiddlers he thought the pleasantest harmony that ever he had heard.

In the meantime my Lord's son, Henry, Lord Mansfield, now Earl of Ogle, was gone to Dover with intention to wait on his Majesty, and receive my Lord his father, with all joy and duty, thinking he had been with his Majesty ; but when he missed of his design, he was very much troubled, and more, when his Majesty was pleased to tell him that my Lord had set to sea, before his Majesty himself was gone out of Holland, fearing my Lord had met with some misfortune in his journey, because he had not heard of his landing. Wherefore he immediately parted from Dover, to seek my Lord, whom at last he found at Greenwich. With what joy they embraced and saluted each other, my pen is too weak to express.

But all this while, and after my Lord was gone from Antwerp, I was left alone there with some of my servants ; for my Lord being in Holland with his Majesty, declared in a letter to me his intention of going for England, withal commanding me to stay in that city, as a pawn for his debts, until he could compass money to discharge them ; and to excuse him to the magistrates of the said city for not taking his leave of them, and paying his due thanks for their great civilities, which he desired me to do in his behalf. And certainly my Lord's affection to me was such, that it made him very industrious in providing those means ; for it being uncertain what or whether he should have anything of his estate, made it a difficult business for him to borrow money. At last he received some of one Mr. Ash, now Sir Joseph Ash, a merchant of Antwerp, which he returned to me ; but what with the expense I had made in the meanwhile, and what was required for my transporting into England, besides the debts formerly contracted, the said money fell too short by £400, and although I could have upon my own word taken up much more, yet I was unwilling to leave an engagement amongst strangers. Wherefore I sent for one Mr. Shaw, now Sir John Shaw, a near kinsman to the said Mr. Ash, entreating him to lend me £400, which he did most readily, and so discharged my debts.

My departure being now divulged in Antwerp, the magistrates of the city came to take their leaves of me, where I desired one Mr. Duart [1], a very worthy gentleman, and one of the chief of the city, though he derives his race from the Portuguese (to whom and his sisters, all very skilful in the art of music, though for their own pastime and recreation, both my Lord and myself were much bound for their great civilities) to be my interpreter. They were pleased to express that they were sorry for our departure out of their city, but withal rejoiced at our happy returning into our native country, and wished me soon and well to the place where I most desired to be. Whereupon I having excused my Lord's hasty going away without taking his leave of them, returned them mine and my Lord's hearty thanks for their great civilities, declaring how sorry I was that it lay not in my power to make an acknowledgment answerable to them. But after their departure from me, they were pleased to send their under-officers (as the custom there is) with a present of wine, which I received with all respect and thankfulness.

I being thus prepared for my voyage, went with my servants to Flushing, and finding no English man-of-war there, being loath to trust myself with a less vessel, was at last informed that a Dutch man-of-war lay there ready to convoy some merchants. I forthwith sent for the captain thereof, whose name was Bankert, and asked him whether it was possible to obtain the favour of having the use of his ship to transport me into England ? To which he answered,

---

[1] Letters cvii and ccvi in the Duchess of Newcastle's *Sociable Letters* are addressed to Eleanora Duarte, and in the *Letters and Poems in honour of the Duchess*, p. 131, is a letter from J. Duarte in 1671, thanking her for some of her books.

that he questioned not but I might; for the merchants which he was to convey, were not ready yet, desiring me to send one of my servants to the State, to request that favour of them; with whom he would go himself, and assist him the best he could; which he also did. My suit being granted, myself and my chief servants embarked in the said ship; the rest, together with the goods, being conveyed in another good strong vessel, hired for that purpose.

After I was safely arrived at London, I found my Lord in lodgings; I cannot call them unhandsome; but yet they were not fit for a person of his rank and quality, nor of the capacity to contain all his family. Neither did I find my Lord's condition such as I expected: wherefore out of some passion I desired him to leave the town, and retire into the country; but my Lord gently reproved me for my rashness and impatience, and soon after removed into Dorset House; which, though it was better than the former, yet not altogether to my satisfaction, we having but a part of the said house in possession. By this removal I judged my Lord would not hastily depart from London; but not long after, he was pleased to tell me, that he had despatched his business, and was now resolved to remove into the country, having already given order for waggons to transport our goods, which was no unpleasant news to me, who had a great desire for a country life [1].

My Lord, before he began his journey, went to his gracious Sovereign, and begged leave that he might retire into the country, to reduce and settle, if possible, his confused, entangled, and almost ruined estate. ' Sir ', said he to his Majesty, ' I am not ignorant, that many believe I am discontented; and 'tis probable they'll say, I retire through discontent: but I take God to witness, that I am in no kind or ways displeased; for I am so joyed at your Majesty's happy restoration, that I cannot be sad or troubled for any concern to my own particular; but whatsoever your Majesty is pleased to

---

[1] Clement Ellis, Newcastle's chaplain, thus comments on his retirement in the prefatory epistle to a sermon preached on May 29, 1661: ' With much pleasure I have hearkened to you discoursing of that satisfaction you reaped from that sweet privacy and retirement his Majesty is pleased to grant your Lordship here in the country. Indeed, the greatest reward his Majesty can possibly recompense your services withal, is thus to bestow yourself upon yourself, and I know you think it greater happiness to enjoy my Lord Marquis of Newcastle at Welbeck, than all the offices and honours which your exemplary loyalty has merited.'—Kennet's *Ecclesiastical and Civil Register*, 455.

command me, were it to sacrifice my life, I shall most obedi-
ently perform it ; for I have no other will, but your Majesty's
pleasure.'

Thus he kissed his Majesty's hand, and went the next day
into Nottinghamshire, to his manor-house called Welbeck ;
but when he came there, and began to examine his estate, and
how it had been ordered in the time of his banishment, he
knew not whether he had left anything of it for himself or
not, till by his prudence and wisdom he informed himself the
best he could, examining those that had most knowledge
therein. Some lands, he found, could be recovered no further
than for his life, and some not at all ; some had been in the
rebels' hands, which he could not recover, but by his Highness
the Duke of York's favour, to whom his Majesty had given
all the estates of those that were condemned and executed
for murdering his Royal Father of blessed memory, which by
the law were forfeited to his Majesty ; whereof his Highness
graciously restored my Lord so much of the land that formerly
had been his, as amounted to £730 a year [1]. And though my
Lord's children had their claims granted, and bought out the
life of my Lord, their father, which came near upon the third
part, yet my Lord received nothing for himself out of his
own estate, for the space of eighteen years, viz. during the
time from the first entering into war, which was June 11,
1642, till his return out of banishment, May 28, 1660. For
though his son Henry, now Earl of Ogle, and his eldest daughter, the now Lady Cheiny, did all what lay in their power to
relieve my Lord their father, and sent him some supplies of
moneys at several times when he was in banishment, yet that
was of their own, rather than out of my Lord's estate ; for
the Lady Cheiny sold some few jewels which my Lord, her
father, had left her, and some chamber-plate which she had
from her grandmother, and sent over the money to my Lord,
besides £1000 of her portion ; and the now Earl of Ogle did

[1] The grant restoring these lands is amongst the Egerton MSS. in the British Museum
(No. 2551). The King grants to Newcastle three manors sold under the Common-
wealth and bought by regicides, viz. Sibthorpe in Nottinghamshire, purchased by
Edward Whalley ; certain lands in the said county in Carcolston, purchased by Colonel
Hacker ; and the Granges of Kirby Woodhouse and Annesley Woodhouse, purchased
by Gilbert Millington. The grant is dated September 5, 1660.
  The Duchess omits to mention that on Sept. 13, 1660, Charles II gave his assent to
a private Act ' for restoring to Wiliam, Marquis of Newcastle, all his Honours, Manors,
Lands, and Tenements in England, whereof he was in possession on the 20th day
of May 1640, or at any time since '. This Act, however, would not touch lands sold
or mortgaged by Newcastle himself.

at several times supply my Lord, his father, with such moneys as he had partly obtained upon credit, and partly made by his marriage.

After my Lord had begun to view those ruins that were nearest, and tried the law to keep or recover what formerly was his (which certainly showed no favour to him, besides that the Act of Oblivion proved a great hindrance and obstruction to those his designs, as it did no less to all the royal party), and had settled so much of his estate as possibly he could, he cast up the sum of his debts, and set out several parts of land for the payment of them, or of some of them (for some of his lands could not be easily sold, being entailed) and some he sold in Derbyshire to buy the Castle of Nottingham, which, although it is quite ruined and demolished, yet, it being a seat which had pleased his father very much, he would not leave it since it was offered to be sold [1].

His two houses Welbeck and Bolsover he found much out of repair, and this later half pulled down ; [2] no furniture or any necessary goods were left in them, but some few hangings and pictures, which had been saved by the care and industry of his eldest daughter the Lady Cheiny, and were bought over again after the death of his eldest son Charles, Lord Mansfield. For they being given to him, and he leaving some debts to be paid after his death, my Lord sent to his other son Henry, now Earl of Ogle, to endeavour for so much credit, that the said hangings and pictures (which my Lord esteemed very much, the pictures being drawn by Van Dyke) might be saved [3] ; which he also did, and my Lord hath paid the debt since his return.

Of eight parks, which my Lord had before the wars, there was but one left that was not quite destroyed, viz. Welbeck

[1] After the restoration, George Villiers, second Duke of Buckingham, having claimed the Castle of Nottingham in right of his mother, the sole daughter and heiress of Francis Earl of Rutland, to whom it had been granted by James I, sold it to the Duke of Newcastle in 1674. Bailey, *Annals of Nottinghamshire*, vol. ii, p. 971.

[2] On June 23 the Council of State ordered Bolsover to be made untenable. On July 2, 1649, the Council of State wrote to the Committee of Derbyshire : ' To avoid the charge of a garrison in Bolsover Castle, and yet to prevent danger if it should be surprised and kept by an enemy, we refer it to your care to do it so as the house itself, as it relates to private habitation, may be as little prejudiced as may be ; but let the outworks abroad, and garden walls, with the turrets and walls of the frontier court that are of strength be demolished, and all the doors of the house be taken away, and slight ones set in their place ; as also the iron bars of the windows, and the materials of the walls that are taken down be improved to the best, and the charge of demolishing defrayed out of the revenue thereof.'—*Calendar of Domestic State Papers*, 1649, p. 217.

[3] A letter written by Newcastle to Van Dyke in February 1637 shows that he was on very friendly terms with the painter.—*Portland MSS.*, ii, 131, 143.

Park, of about four miles' compass; for my Lord's brother, Sir Charles Cavendish, who bought out the life of my Lord in that lordship, saved most part of it from being cut down; and in Blore Park there were some few deer left. The rest of the parks were totally defaced and destroyed, both wood, pales, and deer [1]; amongst which was also Clipston Park, of seven miles' compass, wherein my Lord had taken much delight formerly, it being rich of wood, and containing the greatest and tallest timber-trees of all the woods he had; insomuch, that only the pale-row was valued at £2000. It was watered by a pleasant river that runs through it, full of fish and otters; was well-stocked with deer, full of hares, and had great store of partridges, poots [2], pheasants, &c., besides all sorts of water-fowl; so that this park afforded all manner of sports, for hunting, hawking, coursing, fishing, etc., for which my Lord esteemed it very much. And although his patience and wisdom is such, that I never perceived him sad or discontented for his own losses and misfortunes, yet when he beheld the ruins of that park, I observed him troubled, though he did little express it, only saying, he had been in hopes it would not have been so much defaced as he found it, there being not one timber-tree in it left for shelter. However, he patiently bore what could not be helped, and gave present order for the cutting down of some wood that was left him in a place near adjoining, to repale it, and got from several friends deer to stock it.

Thus, though his lawsuits and other unavoidable expenses were very chargeable to him, yet he ordered his affairs so prudently, that by degrees he stocked and manured those lands he keeps for his own use, and in part repaired his manor-houses, Welbeck [3] and Bolsover, to which latter he made some additional building; and though he has not yet built

[1] On the destruction of these woods see the *Calendar of Domestic State Papers* for 1655, p. 137. The verderers of Sherwood Forest complained to Lord Clare, who had been made Warden in Newcastle's place: ' The forest is ruined, especially Clipston Woods, where the inhabitants have right of estovers, by Mr. Clark, on pretence of a grant from the Committee for Sale of Traitors' Estates. He has felled 1000 trees, and daily fells more. He fells in the heart of the forest, where the deer have their greatest relief. There is much good ship-timber in the forest.'

[2] According to Mr. Lower's note on this passage in the edition of 1872, poot means either blackcock or red grouse, probably the former. Poot or pout means a young bird of any kind.—Halliwell.

[3] See the paper entitled *A Note . . . about my Building at Welbeck*, printed in Mr. Strong's *Catalogue of Letters, etc., preserved in the Library at Welbeck*, p. 56.

the seat at Nottingham, yet he hath stocked and paled a little park belonging to it [1].

Nor is it possible for him to repair all the ruins of the estate that is left him, in so short a time, they being so great, and his losses so considerable, that I cannot without grief and trouble remember them ; for before the wars my Lord had as great an estate as any subject in the kingdom, descended upon him most by women, viz. by his grandmother of his father's side, his own mother, and his first wife.

What estate his grandfather left to his father Sir Charles Cavendish, I know not ; nor can I exactly tell what he had from his grandmother, but she was very rich ; for her third husband, Sir William Saint Loo, gave her a good estate in the west, which afterwards descended upon my Lord, my Lord's mother being the younger daughter of the Lord Ogle, and sole heir, after the death of her eldest sister Jane, Countess of Shrewsbury, whom King Charles the First restored to her father's dignity, viz. Baroness of Ogle. This title descended upon my Lord and his heirs general, together with £3000 a year in Northumberland ; and besides the estate left to my Lord, she gave him £20,000 in money, and kept him and his family at her own charge for several years.

My Lord's first wife, who was daughter and heir to William Basset, of Blore, Esq. ; widow to Henry Howard, younger son to Thomas, Earl of Suffolk, brought my Lord £2400 a year inheritance, between six and seven thousand pounds in money, and a jointure for her life of £800 a year. Besides, my Lord increased his own estate, before the wars, to the value of £100,000, and had increased it more, had not the unhappy wars prevented him ; for though he had some disadvantages in his estate, even before the wars, yet they are not considerable to those he suffered afterwards for the service of his King and country. For example, his father Sir Charles Cavendish had lent his brother-in-law Gilbert, Earl of Shrewsbury, £16,000, for which, although afterward before his death he settled £2000 a year upon him, yet he having enjoyed the

---

[1] Not yet, i.e. in 1667. Bailey, in the passage previously quoted from his *History of Nottinghamshire*, is evidently wrong in saying that the castle was not acquired by the Duke till 1674. It was in that year that the Duke commenced rebuilding, as stated in the ' inscription on an oblong square white marble tablet in the wall over the back door ': ' This house was begun by William, Duke of Newcastle, in the year 1674 (who died in the year 1676), and according to his appointment by his last will, and by the model he left, was finished in the year 1679.'—Bailey, *Annals of Nottinghamshire*, p. 971.

said money for many years without paying any use for it, it might have been improved to my Lord's better advantage, had it been in his father's own hands, he being a person of great prudence in managing his estate ; and though the said Earl of Shrewsbury made my Lord his executor, yet my Lord was so far from making any advantage by that trust, even in what the law allowed him, that he lost £17,000 by it ; and afterwards delivered up his trust to William, Earl of Pembroke, and Thomas, Earl of Arundel, who both married two daughters of the said Earl of Shrewsbury ; and since his return into England, upon the desire of Henry Howard, second son to the late Earl of Arundel, and heir-apparent (by reason of his eldest brother's distemper), he resigned his trust and interest to him, which certainly is a very difficult business, and yet questionable whether it may lawfully be done or not ? But such was my Lord's love to the family of the Shrewsburys, that he would rather wrong himself than it.

To mention some lawful advantages which my Lord might have made by the said trust, it may be noted in the first place, that the Earl of Shrewsbury's estate was let in long leases, which, by the law, fell to the executor. Next, that after some debts and legacies were paid out of those lands, which were set out for that purpose, they were settled so, that they fell to my Lord. Thirdly, seven hundred pounds a year was left as a gift to my Lord's brother, Sir Charles Cavendish, in case the Countess of Kent, second daughter to the said Earl of Shrewsbury, had no children. But my Lord never made any advantage for himself, of all these ; neither was he inquisitive whether the said Countess of Kent cut off the entail of that land, although she never had a child ; for my Lord's nature is so generous, that he hates to be mercenary, and never minds his own profit or interest in any trust or employment, more than the good and benefit of him that entrusts or employs him.

But, as I said heretofore, these are but petty losses in comparison of those he sustained by the late Civil Wars, whereof I shall partly give you an account [1]. I say partly ; for though

---

[1] Newcastle was too great a 'delinquent' to be allowed to compound, even if he had wished to do so. His whole estate was confiscated and sold. The proceedings in the case of persons having claims on his estate are given in the *Calendar of the Committee for Compounding*, which also contains a list of the purchasers of his lands, and many other particulars about the disposal of his property (pp. 1732–7).

it may be computed what the loss of the annual rents of his lands amounts to, of which he never received the least worth for himself and his own profit, during the time both of his being employed in the service of war, and his sufferings in banishment ; as also the loss of those lands that are alienated from him, both in present possession, and in reversion ; and of his parks and woods that were cut down ; yet it is impossible to render an exact account of his personal estate.

As for his rents during the time he acted in the wars ; though he suffered others to gather theirs for their own use, yet his own either went for the use of the army, or fell into the hands of the enemy, or were suppressed and withheld from him by the cozenage of his tenants and officers, my Lord being then not able to look after them himself.

About the time when his late Majesty undertook the expedition into Scotland for the suppressing of some insurrection that happened there ; my Lord, as afore is mentioned, amongst the rest, lent his Majesty £10,000 sterling ; but having newly married a daughter to the then Lord Brackly, now Earl of Bridgwater, whose portion was £12,000, the moiety whereof was paid in gold on the day of her marriage, and the rest soon after (although she was too young to be bedded)—this, together with some other expenses, caused him to take up the said £10,000 at interest, the use whereof he paid many years after [1].

Also, when, after his sixteen years' banishment, he returned into England, before he knew what estate was left him, and was able to receive any rents of his own, he was necessitated to take £5000 upon use for the maintenance of himself and his family ; whereof the now Earl of Devonshire, his cousin-german, once removed, lent him £1000, for which and the former £1000 mentioned heretofore, he never desired nor received any use from my Lord, which I mention, to declare the favour and bounty of that noble Lord.

But though it is impossible to render an exact account of all the losses which my Lord has sustained by the said wars, yet as far as they are accountable, I shall endeavour to represent them in these following particulars :

In the first place, I shall give you a just particular of my Lord's estate in lands, as it was before the wars, partly accord-

---

[1] Use—i.e. interest.

ing to the value of his own surveyors, and partly according to the rate it is let at this present.

Next, I shall accompt the woods cut down by the rebellious party, in several places of my Lord's estate.

Thirdly, I shall compute the value of those lands which my Lord hath lost, both in present possession, and in reversion ; that is to say, those which he has lost altogether, both for himself and his posterity ; and those he has recovered only during the time of his life, and which his only son and heir, the now Earl of Ogle, must lose after his father's decease.

Fourthly, I shall make mention, how much of land my Lord hath been forced to sell for the payment of some of his debts, contracted during the time of the late Civil Wars, and when his estate was sequestered ; I say some, for there are a great many to pay yet.

To which I shall, fifthly, add the composition of his brother's estate ; and the loss of it for eight years.

A particular of my Lord's estate in plain rents, as it was partly surveyed in the year 1641, and partly is let at this present [1].

NOTTINGHAMSHIRE	£	s.	d.
The Manor of Welbeck	600	0	0
The Manor of Norton, Carburton and the Granges	454	19	1
Warsop	51	6	8
The Manor-house of Sookholm	308	10	3
The Manor of Clipston and Edwinstowe	334	9	8
Drayton	8	16	6
Dunham	99	17	8
Sutton	185	0	5
The Manor of Kirby, etc.	1075	7	2
The Manor of Cotham	833	18	8
The Manor of Sibthorpe	704	1	0
Carcolston	450	3	0
Hawksworth, etc.	139	4	2
Flawborough	512	11	8
Mearing and Holm Meadow	471	2	0
	£6229	7	11

LINCOLNSHIRE			
Wellingore and Ingham Meales [2]	£100	0	0

[1] When the places mentioned could be identified the modern spelling of their names has been adopted.

[2] Camden, in his map of Lincolnshire, places Ingold-meles just above Skegness, and elsewhere explains ' meales ' or ' meles ' to mean sand-hills.

DERBYSHIRE [1]

	£	s.	d.
The Barony of Bolsover and Woodthorp .	846	8	11
The Manor of Chesterfield .	378	0	0
The Manor of Barlow	796	17	6
Tissington	159	11	0
Dronfield	486	15	10
The Manor of Brampton	142	4	8
Little Longston	87	2	0
The Manor of Stoke	212	3	0
Beard Hall, and Peak Forest	131	8	0
The Manor of Grindlow	156	8	0
The Manor of Hucklow	162	10	8
The Manor of Blackwall	306	0	4
Buxton and Tideswell	153	2	0
Mansfield Park	100	0	0
Mapleton and Thorpe	207	5	0
The Manor of Win Hill	238	18	0
The Manor of Litchurch and Mackworth .	713	15	1
Church and Meynel Langly Manor	850	1	0
	£6128	11	10

STAFFORDSHIRE

	£	s.	d.
The Manor of Blore with Caulton	£573	13	4
The Manor of Grindon, Cauldon, with Water-fall	822	3	0
The Manor of Cheadle with Kingsley	259	18	0
The Manor of Barlaston, etc.	694	3	0
	£2349	17	4

GLOUCESTERSHIRE

	£	s.	d.
The Manor of Tormorton with Litleton .	£1193	16	0
The Manor of Acton Turvil	388	3	2
	£1581	19	2

SOMERSETSHIRE

	£	s.	d.
The Manor of Chewstoke	£816	15	6
Knighton Sutton	300	14	4
Stroud and Kingsham (Keynsham ?) Park .	186	4	0
	£1303	13	10

[1] Birth Hall, Tids Hall, and Windly Hill are the names given by the Duchess to three of these manors.

YORKSHIRE

The Manors of Slingsby, Hoverngham (Hov-
    ingham) and Friton, Northinges and
    Pomfret £1700 0 0

NORTHUMBERLAND

The Barony of Bothal, Ogle and Hepple, etc. £3000 0 0

                            Total . £22,393 10 1

    That this particular of my Lord's estate was no less than
is mentioned, may partly appear by the rate, as it was surveyed, and sold by the rebellious Parliament ; for they raised,
towards the later end of their power, which was in the year
1652, out of my Lord's estate, the sum of £111,593, 10s. 11d.,
at five years' and a half purchase, which was at above the rate
of £18,000 a year, besides woods ; and his brother Sir Charles
Cavendish's estate, which estate was £2000 a year, which falls
not much short of the mentioned account ; and certainly
had they not sold such lands at easy rates, few would have
bought them, by reason the purchasers were uncertain how
long they should enjoy their purchase : besides, under-officers
do not usually refuse bribes ; and it is well known that the
surveyors did underrate estates according as they were fee'd
by the purchasers.

    Again, many of the estates of banished persons were given
to soldiers for the payment of their arrears, who again sold
them to others which would buy them at easier rates. But
chiefly, it appears by the rate as my Lord's estate is let at
present, there being several of the mentioned lands that are
let at a higher rate now than they were surveyed ; nor are
they all valued in the mentioned particular according to the
survey, but many of them which were not surveyed, are
accounted according to the rate they are let at this present.

    The loss of my Lord's estate, in plain rents, as also upon
ordinary use, and use upon use, is as followeth [1] :

    The annual rent of my Lord's lands, viz. £22,393 10s. 1d.,
being lost for the space of eighteen years, which was the time
of his acting in the wars, and of his banishment, without any
benefit to him, reckoned without any interest, amounts to
£403,083. But being accounted with the ordinary use at six

---

[1] ' Use ', interest ; ' use upon use ', compound interest.

in the hundred, and use upon use for the mentioned space of eighteen years, it amounts to £733,579.

But some perhaps will say, that if my Lord had enjoyed his estate, he would have spent it, at least so much as to maintain himself according to his degree and quality.

I answer, that it is very improbable my Lord should have spent all his estate, if he had enjoyed it, he being a man of great wisdom and prudence, knowing well how to spend, and how to manage ; for though he lived nobly before the time of the wars, yet not beyond the compass of his estate. Nay, so far he would have been from spending his estate, that no doubt but he would have increased it to a vast value, as he did before the wars ; where, notwithstanding his hospitality and noble housekeeping, his charges of building came to about £31,000 : the portion of his second daughter, which was £12,000 ; the noble entertainments he gave King Charles the First, one whereof came to almost £15,000, another to above £4000, and a third to £1700, as hereafter shall be mentioned ; and his great expenses during the time of his being governor to his Majesty that now is, he yet increased his estate to the value of £100,000, which is £5000 per annum, when it was by so much less.

But if any one will reckon the charges of his housekeeping during the time of his exile, and when he had not the enjoyment of his estate, he may substract [1] the sum accounted for the payment of his debts, contracted in the time of his banishment, which went to the maintenance of himself and his family ; or in lieu thereof, considering that I do not account all my Lord's losses, but only those that are certainly known, he may compare it with the loss of his personal estate, whereof I shall make some mention anon, and he'll find that I do not heighten my Lord's losses, but rather diminish them.   For surely the losses of his personal estate, and those I account not, will counterbalance the charges of his housekeeping, if not exceed them.

Again, others will say, that there was much land sold in the time of my Lord's banishment by his sons, and feoffees in trust.

I answer, first, that whatsoever was sold, was first bought of the rebellious power : next, although they sold some lands, yet my Lord knew nothing of it, neither did he receive a

---

[1] Substract = subtract.

pennyworth for himself, neither of what they purchased, nor sold, all the time of his banishment till his return [1].

And thus much of the loss of my Lord's estate in rents. Concerning the loss of his parks and woods, as much as is generally known (for I do not reckon particular trees cut down in several of his woods yet standing), 'tis as follows :

1. Clipston Park and woods, cut down to the value of £20,000.
2. Kirkby Woods, for which my Lord was formerly proffered £10,000.
3. Woods cut down in Derbyshire, £8000.
4. Red Lodge Wood, Rome Wood, and others near Welbeck, £4000.
5. Woods cut down in Staffordshire, £1000.
6. Woods cut down in Yorkshire, £1000.
7. Woods cut down in Northumberland, £1500.

The total, £45,000.

The lands which my Lord hath lost in present possession are £2015 per annum, which at twenty years' purchase come to £40,300 : and those which he hath lost in reversion are £3214 per annum, which at sixteen years' purchase amount to the value of £51,424.

The lands which my Lord since his return has sold for the payment of some of his debts, occasioned by the wars (for I do not reckon those he sold to buy others), come to the value of £56,000, to which out of his yearly revenue he has added £10,000 more, which is in all £66,000.

Lastly, the composition of his brother's estate was £5000, and the loss of it for eight years comes to £16,000.

All which, if summed up together, amounts to £941,303 [2].

These are the accountable losses, which my dear Lord and husband has suffered by the late Civil Wars, and his loyalty to his King and country. Concerning the loss of his personal

---

[1] See the Duke's letter to Secretary Nicholas on this subject, written during his exile, in Appendix viii.

[2] The amount of the losses incurred by the Duke on behalf of the royal cause finds a parallel only in the somewhat similar statement drawn up by the Marquis of Worcester, and presented by him to Charles II. His total 'spent, lent, etc., for my King and country, £918,000 '. Warburton's *Prince Rupert*, iii, 515.

estate, since (as I often mentioned) it cannot be exactly known ; I shall not endeavour to set down the particulars thereof, only in general give you a note of what partly they are:

1. The pulling down of several of his dwelling or manor-houses.

2. The disfurnishing of them, of which the furniture at Bolsover and Welbeck was very noble and rich.   Out of his London house at Clerkenwell, there were taken, amongst other goods, suits of linen, viz. table-cloths, sideboard-cloths, napkins, &c., whereof one suit cost £160 ; they being bought for an entertainment which my Lord made for their Majesties, King Charles the First, and the Queen, at Bolsover Castle ; and of 150 suits of hangings of all sorts in all his houses, there were not above ten or twelve saved.

Of silver plate, my Lord had so much as came to the value of £3800, besides several curiosities of cabinets, cups, and other things, which after my Lord was gone out of England, were taken out of his manor-house, Welbeck, by a garrison of the King's party that lay therein [1]. whereof he recovered only £1100, which money was sent him beyond the seas ; the rest was lost.

As for pewter, brass, bedding, linen, and other household stuff, there was nothing else left but some few old feather-beds, and those all spoiled, and fit for no use.

3. My Lord's stock of corn, cattle, &c., was very great before the wars, by reason of the largeness and capacity of those grounds, and the great number of granges he kept for his own use ; as, for example, Barlow, Carcolston, Gleadthorp, Welbeck, and several more, which were all well manured and stocked.   But all this stock was lost, besides his race of horses

---

[1] Welbeck was captured by the Earl of Manchester about August 2, 1644 (Rush-worth, III, ii, 64 : Manchester's letter of August 6, in a volume published by the Camden Society under the title *Manchester's Quarrel with Cromwell*, p. 5). An account of some of the spoils found there is given in Mrs. Hutchinson's *Memoirs*, vol. ii, p. 24. Welbeck was retaken by the Royalists on July 16, 1645 (*Mercurius Belgicus*).   Symonds gives the following account of its capture : 'Welbeck was surprised by Newark horse under the command of Sir Richard Willis, about three weeks since.   In a wood near the port stood his horse in ambush, and when the trevall was beat, and they let down their bridge for their scouts, our horse, under the command of Major Jarnot, a French-man, rid hard, and though they pulled up the bridge a foot high yet they got in and took it.   They disputed every yard, and our men alighted and with their pistols scaled and got in.'—Symonds, p. 224.   Major Jarnot, more properly (as in the *Life of Colonel Hutchinson*) Jammot, was a Walloon.   Welbeck was finally disgarrisoned, by arrange-ment between the two parties, in November 1645.

in his grounds, grange horses, hackney-horses, manage-horses, coach-horses, and others he kept for his use.

To these losses I may well and justly join the charges which my Lord hath been put to since his return into England, by reason they were caused by the ruins of the said wars ; whereof I reckon :

1. His law-suits, which have been very chargeable to him, more than advantageous.

2. The stocking, manuring, paling, stubbing,[1] hedging, etc., of his grounds and parks ; where it is to be noted, that no advantage or benefit can be made of grounds, under the space of three years, and of cattle not under five or six.

3. The repairing and furnishing of some of his dwelling-houses.

4. The setting up a race or breed of horses, as he had before the wars ; for which purpose he hath bought the best mares he could get for money.

In short, I can reckon £12,000 laid out barely for the repair of some ruins, which my Lord could not be without, there being many of them to repair yet ; neither is this all that is laid out, but much more which I cannot well remember ; nor is there more but one grange stocked, amongst several that were kept for furnishing his house with provisions. As for other charges and losses, which my Lord hath sustained since his return, I will not reckon them, because my design is only to account such losses as were caused by the wars.

By which, as they have been mentioned, it may easily be concluded, that although my Lord's estate was very great before the wars, yet now it is shrunk into a very narrow compass, that it puts his prudence and wisdom to the proof, to make it serve his necessities, he having no other assistance to bear him up ; and yet notwithstanding all this, he hath since his return paid both for himself and his son, all manner of taxes, loans, levies, assessments, etc., equally with the rest of his Majesty's subjects, according to that estate that is left him, which he has been forced to take upon interest.

---

1 'Stub', to grub up stumps or roots.—Halliwell, *Dictionary of Archaic and Provincial Words*.

Thus having given you a faithful account of all my Lord's actions, both before, in, and after the Civil Wars, and of his losses, I shall now conclude with some particular heads concerning the description of his own person, his natural humour, disposition, qualities, virtues ; his pedigree, habit, diet, exercises, etc., together with some other remarks and particulars which I thought requisite to be inserted, both to illustrate the former books, and to render the history of his life more perfect and complete.

1. *Of his Power*

After his Majesty King Charles the First had entrusted my Lord with the power of raising forces for his Majesty's service, he effected that which never any subject did, nor was (in all probability) able to do ; for though many great and noble persons did also raise forces for his Majesty, yet they were brigades, rather than well-formed armies, in comparison to my Lord's. The reason was, that my Lord, by his mother, the daughter of Cuthbert, Lord Ogle, being allied to most of the most ancient families in Northumberland, and other the northern parts, could pretend a greater interest in them, than a stranger ; for they, through a natural affection to my Lord as their own kinsman, would sooner follow him, and under his conduct sacrifice their lives for his Majesty's service, than anybody else, well knowing, that by deserting my Lord, they deserted themselves. And by this means my Lord raised first a troop of horse, consisting of a hundred and twenty, and a regiment of foot ; and then an army of eight thousand horse, foot and dragoons, in those parts ; and afterwards upon this ground, at several times, and in several places, so many several troops, regiments and armies, that in all, from the first to the last, they amounted to above 100,000 men, and those most

upon his own interest, and without any other considerable
help or assistance ; which was much for a particular subject,
and in such a conjuncture of time ; for since armies are soonest
raised by covetousness, fear, and faction ; that is to say,
upon a constant and settled pay, upon the ground of terror,
and upon the ground of rebellion ; but very seldom or never
upon uncertainty of pay ; and when it is as hazardous to be
of such a party, as to be in the heat of a battle ; also when
there is no other design but honest duty. It may easily be
conceived that my Lord could have no little love and affection
when he raised his army upon such grounds as could promise
them but little advantage at that time.

Amongst the rest of his army, my Lord had chosen for his
own regiment of foot, 3000 of such valiant, stout, and faithful
men (whereof many were bred in the moorish grounds of the
northern parts) that they were ready to die at my Lord's
feet, and never gave over, whensoever they were engaged in
action, until they had either conquered the enemy, or lost
their lives. They were called White-coats, for this following
reason : my Lord being resolved to give them new liveries,
and there being not red cloth enough to be had, took up so
much of white as would serve to clothe them, desiring withal,
their patience until he had got it dyed ; but they, impatient
of stay, requested my Lord, that he would be pleased to let
them have it un-dyed as it was, promising they themselves
would dye it in the enemy's blood. Which request my Lord
granted them, and from that time they were called White-
coats.

To give you some instances of their valour and courage, I
must beg leave to repeat some passages mentioned in the first
book. The enemy having closely besieged the city of York,
and made a passage into the manor-yard, by springing a mine
under the wall thereof, was got into the manor-house with a
great number of their forces ; which my Lord perceiving, he
immediately went and drew eighty of the said White-coats
thither, who with the greatest courage went close up to the
enemy, and having charged them, fell pell-mell with the butt-
ends of their muskets upon them, and with the assistance of
the rest that renewed their courage by their example, killed
and took 1500, and by that means saved the town [1].

1 See p. 40.

How valiantly they behaved themselves in the last fatal battle upon Hessom Moor near York, has been also declared heretofore ; insomuch, that although most of the army were fled, yet they would not stir, until by the enemy's power they were overcome, and most of them slain in rank and file [1].

Their love and affection to my Lord was such, that it lasted even when he was deprived of all his power, and could do them little good ; to which purpose I shall mention this following passage :

My Lord being in Antwerp, received a visit from a gentleman, who came out of England, and rendered my Lord thanks for his safe escape at sea ; my Lord being in amaze, not knowing what the gentleman meant, he was pleased to acquaint him, that in his coming over sea out of England, he was set upon by pickaroons [2], who having examined him, and the rest of his company, at last some asked him, whether he knew the Marquess of Newcastle ? To whom he answered, that he knew him very well, and was going over into the same city where my Lord lived. Whereupon they did not only take nothing from him, but used him with all civility, and desired him to remember their humble duty to their Lord-General, for they were some of his White-coats that had escaped death ; and if my Lord had any service for them, they were ready to assist him upon what designs soever, and to obey him in whatsoever he should be pleased to command them.

This I mention for the eternal fame and memory of those valiant and faithful men. But to return to the power my Lord had in the late wars : as he was the head of his own army, and had raised it most upon his own interest for the service of his Majesty ; so he was never ordered by his Majesty's privy council (except that some forces of his were kept by

---

[1] 'A most memorable action happened on that day. There was one entire regiment of foot belonging to Newcastle, called the Lambs, because they were all new clothed in white woollen cloth, two or three days before the fight. This sole regiment, after the day was lost, having got into a small parcel of ground ditched in, and not of easy access of horse, would take no quarter ; and by mere valour, for one whole hour, kept the troops of horse from entering amongst them at near push of pike : when the horse did enter, they would have no quarter, but fought it out till there was not thirty of them living ; those whose hap it was to be beaten down upon the ground as the troopers came near them, though they could not rise for their wounds, yet were so desperate as to get either a pike or sword, or piece of them, and to gore the troopers' horses, as they came over them, or passed by them. Captain Camby, then a trooper under Cromwell, and an actor, who was the third or fourth man that entered amongst them, protested he never, in all the fights he was in, met with such resolute brave fellows, or whom he pitied so much, and said " He saved two or three against their wills ".'—*Diary of William Lilly*, p. 178, ed. 1822.

[2] Rogues, from the Spanish *Picaro*.

his late Majesty (which he sent to him), together with some arms and ammunition heretofore mentioned) until his Highness Prince Rupert came from his Majesty, to join with him at the siege of York.   He had, moreover, the power of coining, printing, knighting, etc., which never any subject had before, when his sovereign himself was in the kingdom ; as also the command of so many counties, as is mentioned in the first book, and the power of placing and displacing what governors and commanders he pleased, and of constituting what garrisons he thought fit ; of the chief whereof I shall give you this following list :

A Particular of the Principal Garrisons and the Governors of them, constituted by my Lord [1]

IN NORTHUMBERLAND [2]

Newcastle-upon-Tyne, Sir John Marley, Knight.
Tynmouth Castle and Shields, Sir Thomas Riddal, Knight.

IN THE BISHOPRIC OF DURHAM [3]

Hartlepool, Lieutenant-Colonel Henry Lambton.
Raby Castle, Sir William Savile, Knight and Baronet.

IN YORKSHIRE [4]

The city of York, Sir Thomas Glenham, Knight and Baronet ; and afterwards, when he took the field, the Lord John Bellasis.
Pomfret Castle, Colonel Mynn, and after him Sir John Redman.
Sheffield Castle, Major Beaumont.

---

[1] I have endeavoured to give as far as possible the dates of the capture of these garrisons, as they show the fate of the royalist cause in the North after Newcastle's departure.
[2] Newcastle-upon-Tyne. The town captured by the Scots, October 20, 1644 ; the Castle, October 27.   Vicars' *Burning Bush*, pp. 46–61.
Tynmouth Castle, October 27, 1644.   *Burning Bush*, p. 63.
[3] Hartlepool, July 24, 1644.   Thurloe, State Papers, i, 41.
Raby Castle.   The date of its first capture I have not been able to find.   Whitelock notes on July 7, 1645 : ' the King's forces from Bolton surprised Raby Castle, belonging to Sir Henry Vane, but were again close blocked up by forces raised by Sir George Vane ', and notes its surrender to the Parliament on July 28.   Whitelock, vol. i, pp. 465, 487, ed. 1853.
[4] York.   Articles signed July 16, 1644.   Rushworth, III, ii, 640
Pomfret Castle, July 21, 1645.   *Burning Bush*, p. 202.   See also the Surtees Society's Volume of *Miscellanies* containing the history of the siege of Pontefract.
Sheffield Castle, 11th August 1644.   Hunter's *Hallamshire*, ed. Gatty. p. 142.
Wortley Hall.   Possibly Walton Hall is meant, captured with Sir Francis Wortley in it on 3rd June 1644.   Rushworth, III, ii, 622.
Tickhill Castle, July 26, 1644.   Vicars' *God's Ark*, p. 293.
Doncaster, fortified in January 1644.   Rushworth, III, ii, 305.   In *The Kingdom's*

Wortley Hall, Sir Francis Wortley.

Tickhill Castle, Major Mounteney.

Doncaster, Sir Francis Fane, Knight of the Bath, afterwards Governor of Lincoln.

Sandal Castle, Captain Bonivant.

Skipton Castle, Sir John Mallary, Baronet.

Bolton Castle, Mr. Scroope.

Hemsley Castle, Sir Jordan Crosland.

Scarborough Castle and town, Sir Hugh Cholmley.

Stamford Bridge, Colonel Galbraith.

Halifax, Sir Francis Mackworth.

Tadcaster, Sir Gamaliel Dudley.

Eyrmouth, Major Kaughton.

IN CUMBERLAND [1]

The city of Carlisle, Sir Philip Musgrave, Knight and Baronet.

Cockermouth, Colonel Kirby.

IN NOTTINGHAMSHIRE [2]

Newark-upon-Trent, Sir John Henderson, Knight; and afterwards Sir Richard Byron, Knight, now Lord Byron.

Wyrton House, Colonel Rowland Hacker.

Welbeck, Colonel Van Peire; and after Colonel Beeton.

Shelford House, Colonel Philip Stanhop.

IN LINCOLNSHIRE [3]

The city of Lincoln, first Sir Francis Fane, Knight of the Bath; secondly Sir Peregrine Bartu.

Weekly Intelligencer for April 2–10, 1644, it is stated that the royalists had abandoned Doncaster.

Sandal Castle, October 2, 1645.

Skipton Castle, December 21, 1645. *Burning Bush*, 337.

Bolton Castle, beginning of November 1645. Vicars' *Burning Bush*, p. 318.

Helmsley Castle, November 22, 1644. The Articles are printed in the *Fairfax Correspondence*, vol. iii, p. 121.

Scarborough, the town taken 17th February 1645; the castle, July 22, 1645.

Stamford Bridge. On the history of this garrison see Slingsby's *Memoirs*, p. 93. It was captured about the same time as Tadcaster.

Tadcaster, March 3, 1644. Ricraft's *Champions*.

Eyrmouth, 24th May 1644, taken by Sir John Meldrum. *Mercurius Civicus*, May 23–30, 1644. He had also captured Cawood Castle on May 19.

[1] Carlisle, July 1645. Vicars' *Burning Bush*, p. 186. Whitelock notes its surrender under July 2.

[2] Newark. The articles for the surrender of Newark are signed 6th May, the garrison marched out May 8, 1646. Rushworth, IV, i, 269.

Wyrton, or Wiverton, before November 6, 1645. Vicars' *Burning Bush*, p. 316.

Welbeck, August 2, 1644. Rushworth, III, ii, 644. *Manchester's Quarrel with Cromwell*, p. 6.

Shelford, November 3, 1645. *Memoirs of Col. Hutchinson*, vol. ii, pp. 82, 376, ed. 1885.

[3] Lincoln taken by Manchester's forces after the battle of Winceby, about October 24, 1643. Vicars' *God's Ark*, p. 51. Abandoned in March 1644, after Prince Rupert's

Gainsborough, Colonel St. George.
Bullingbrook Castle, Lieutenant-Colonel Chester.
Belvoir Castle, Sir Gervas Lucas.

In Derbyshire [1]

Bolsover Castle, Colonel Muschamp.
Wingfield Manor, Colonel Roger Molyneux.
Staveley House, the now Lord Fretchvile.

A List of the General Officers of the Army

1. The Lord-General, the now Duke of Newcastle, the noble subject of this book.
2. The Lieutenant-General of the Army ; first the Earl of Newport, afterwards the Lord Eythin.
3. The General of the Ordnance, Charles, Viscount Mansfield.
4. The General of the Horse, Lord Goring.
5. The Colonel-General of the Army, Sir Thomas Glenham.
6. The Major-General of the Army, Sir Francis Mackworth.
7. The Lieutenant-General of the Horse, first Mr. Charles Cavendish, after him Sir Charles Lucas.
8. Commissary-General of Horse, first Colonel Windham, after him Sir William Throckmorton, and after him Mr. George Porter.
9. Lieutenant-General of the Ordnance, Sir William Davenant.
10. Treasurer of the Army, Sir William Carnaby.
11. Advocate-General of the Army, Dr. Liddal.
12. Quartermaster-General of the Army, Mr. Ralph Errington.
13. Providore-General [2] of the Army, Mr. Gervas Nevil, and after Mr. Smith.
14. Scout-Master-General of the Army, Mr. Hudson [3].
15. Wagon-Master General of the Army, Baptist Johnson.

---

relief of Newark ; reoccupied by the Cavaliers, and taken again by Manchester, May 6, 1644. Rushworth, III, ii, 621. Gainsborough was taken the same October 1643.
    Bullingbrook Castle is mentioned as captured in *The Scottish Dove*, October 27 to November 3, 1643.
    Belvoir, surrendered January 31, 1646. Peck's *Desiderata Curiosa*, p. 345.
    [1] Bolsover Castle, August 12, 1644.
    Wingfield Manor, August 14, 1644.
    Staveley House, August 21, 1644. These three houses were all taken by Major-General Crawford with a detachment of Manchester's army, after the battle of Marston Moor. Rushworth, III, ii, 644.
    [2] The precise duties of these officers can best be gathered from Markham's *Five Decades of Epistles of War*. Providore-General is what he calls Victual Master, Provant-Master, or Purveyor.
    [3] Michael Hudson, D.D., of Queen's College, Oxford, the King's guide and companion in his flight from Oxford. He was killed at the capture of Woolcroft House in Northamptonshire, June 6, 1648. See the numerous documents relating to him in Peck's *Desiderata Curiosa*, pp. 347, 379 ; and also *Portland MSS.*, i, 368-84.

William, Lord Widdrington, was President of the Council of War, and Commander-in-Chief of the three counties of Lincoln, Rutland, and Nottingham, and the forces there.

When my Lord marched with his army to Newcastle against the Scots, then the Lord John Bellasis was constituted Governor of York, and Commander-in-Chief, or Lieutenant-General of Yorkshire.

As for the rest of the officers and commanders of every particular regiment and company, they being too numerous, cannot well be remembered, and therefore I shall give you no particular account of them.

2. *Of his Misfortunes and Obstructions*

Although Nature had favoured my Lord, and endued him with the best qualities and perfections she could inspire into his soul; yet Fortune hath ever been such an inveterate enemy to him, that she invented all the spite and malice against him that lay in her power; and notwithstanding his prudent counsels and designs, cast such obstructions in his way, that he seldom proved successful, but where he acted in person. And since I am not ignorant that this unjust and partial age is apt to suppress the worth of meritorious persons, and that many will endeavour to obscure my Lord's noble actions and fame, by casting unjust aspersions upon him, and laying (either out of ignorance or malice) Fortune's envy to his charge, I have purposed to represent these obstructions which conspired to render his good intentions and endeavours ineffectual, and at last did work his ruin and destruction, in these following particulars.

1. At the time when the kingdom became so infatuated, as to oppose and pull down their gracious King and Sovereign, the treasury was exhausted, and no sufficient means to raise and maintain armies to reduce his Majesty's rebellious subjects; so that my Lord had little to begin withal but what his own estate would allow, and his interest procure him.

2. When his late Majesty, in the beginning of the unhappy wars, sent my Lord to Hull, the strongest place in the kingdom, where the magazine of arms and ammunition was kept, and he by his prudence had gained it to his Majesty's service; my Lord was left to the mercy of the Parliament, where he had surely suffered for it (though he acted not without his Majesty's

commission), if some of the contrary party had not quitted him, in hopes to gain him on their side.

3. After his Majesty had sent my Lord to Newcastle-upon-Tyne, to take upon him the government of that place, and he had raised there, of friends and tenants, a troop of horse and regiment of foot, which he ordered to convey some arms and ammunition to his Majesty, sent by the Queen out of Holland; his Majesty was pleased to keep the same convoy with him to increase his own forces, which, although it was but of a small number, yet at that present time it would have been very serviceable to my Lord, he having then but begun to raise forces,

4. When her Majesty, the now Queen Mother, after her arrival out of Holland to York, had a purpose to convey some arms to his Majesty, my Lord ordered a party of 1500 to conduct the same, which his Majesty was pleased to keep with him for his own service.

5. After her Majesty had taken a resolution to go from York to Oxford, where the King then was, my Lord for her safer conduct quitted 7,000 men of his army, with a convenient train of artillery, which likewise never returned to my Lord.

6. When the Earl of Montrose was going into Scotland, he went to my Lord at Durham, and desired of him a supply of some forces for his Majesty's service; when my Lord gave him 200 horse and dragoons, even at such a time when he stood most in need of a supply himself, and thought every day to encounter the Scottish army [1].

7. When my Lord out of the northern parts went into Lincoln- and Derby- shires with his army, to order and reduce them to their allegiance and duty to his Majesty, and from thence resolved to march into the Associate Counties (where in all probability he would have made an happy end of the war), he was so importuned by those he left behind him, and particularly the Commander-in-Chief, to return into Yorkshire (alleging the enemy grew strong and would ruin them all if he came not speedily to succour and assist them), that in honour and duty he could do no otherwise but grant their requests; when as yet being returned into those parts, he found them secure and safe enough from the enemy's attempts.

[1] See p. 35.
[2] See p. 30. Slingsby says Lord Newcastle marched in Lincolnshire, took Gainsborough, 'and had done greater matters in that county had he not been too hastily

8. My Lord (as heretofore mentioned) had as great private enemies about his Majesty, as he had public enemies in the field, who used all the endeavour they could to pull him down.

9. There was such juggling, treachery, and falsehood in his own army, and amongst some of his own officers, that it was impossible for my Lord to be prosperous and successful in his designs and undertakings.

10. My Lord's army being the chief and greatest army which his Majesty had, and in which consisted his prime strength and power, the Parliament resolved, at last, to join all their forces with the army of the Scots (which when it came out of Scotland, was above 20,000 men), to oppose, and if possible, to ruin it; well knowing, that if they did pull down my Lord, they should be masters of all the three kingdoms; so that there were three armies against one. But although my Lord suffered much by the negligence (and sometimes treachery) of his officers, and was unfortunately called back into Yorkshire, from his march he designed for the Associate Counties, and was forced to part with a great number of his forces and ammunition, as afore-mentioned; yet he would hardly have been overcome, and his army ruined by the enemy, had he but had some timely supply and assistance at the siege of York, or that his counsel had been taken in not fighting the enemy then, or that the battle had been deferred some two or three days longer, until those forces were arrived which he expected, namely, 3,000 men out of Northumberland, and 2,000 drawn out of several garrisons. But the chief misfortune was that the enemy fell upon the King's forces, before they were all put into a battallia, and took them at their great disadvantage; which caused such a panic fear amongst them, that most of the horse of the right wing of his Majesty's forces betook themselves to their heels; insomuch, that although the left wing (commanded by the Lord Goring and my brother Sir Charles Lucas) did their best endeavour, and beat back the

called away by the gentlemen of Yorkshire, who began again to fear my Lord Fairfax's power; for after he was once got to Hull, his shattered troops began to drop in one after another, and what he wanted in foot he made the country supply him with out of the East Riding. He begins to enlarge his quarters, and held Beverley too, and doubted not within a while to be able to visit his dearly beloved the West Riding again. This I say was the cause that moved the gentlemen to send to his Excellency to desire him to come back; and being come gave their opinions that his only way would be to besiege him in Hull; and of that opinion was Lieutenant-General King, and that it might be won if the gentlemen would undertake to raise an addition of force to those out of the country. They go about it and in several parts of the country sits in commission, makes great levies if they could be kept together.'—Slingsby, *Memoirs*, p. 99.

enemy three times, and my Lord's own regiment of foot charged them so courageously, that they never broke, but died most of them in their ranks and files; yet the power of the enemy being too strong, put them at last to a total rout and confusion. Which unlucky disaster put an end to all future hopes of his Majesty's party; so that my Lord, seeing he had nothing left in his power to do his Majesty any further service in that kind (for had he stayed, he would have been forced to surrender all those towns and garrisons in those parts, that were yet in his Majesty's devotion, as afterwards it also happened), resolved to quit the kingdom, as formerly is mentioned.

And these are chiefly the obstructions to the good success of my Lord's designs in the late Civil Wars; which being rightly considered, will save him blameless from what otherwise would be laid to his charge. For, as according to the old saying, ' 'Tis easy for men to swim when they are held up by the chin '; so, on the other side, it is very dangerous and difficult for them to endeavour it, when they are pulled down by the heels, and beaten upon their heads.

3. *Of his Loyalty and Sufferings*

I dare boldly and justly say, that there never was, nor is a more loyal and faithful subject than my Lord, not to mention the trust he discharged in all those employments, which either King James, or King Charles the First, or his now gracious master King Charles the Second, were pleased to bestow upon him, which he performed with such care and fidelity, that he never disobeyed their commands in the least; I will only note—

1. That he was the first that appeared in arms for his Majesty, and engaged himself and all his friends he could for his Majesty's service; and though he had but two sons which were young, and one only brother yet they all were with him in the wars. His two sons had commands, but his brother, though he had no command, by reason of the weakness of his body, yet he was never from my Lord when he was in action, even to the last; for he was the last with my Lord in the field in that fatal battle upon Hessom Moor, near York; and though my brother, Sir Charles Lucas, desired my Lord to send his sons away, when the said battle was fought, yet he would not,

saying, his sons should show their loyalty and duty to his Majesty, in venturing their lives, as well as himself.

2. My Lord was the chief and only person, that kept up the power of his late Majesty ; for when his army was lost, all the King's party was ruined in all three of his Majesty's kingdoms ; because in his army lay the chief strength of all the royal forces ; it being the greatest and best formed army which his Majesty had, and the only support both of his Majesty's person and power, and of the hopes of all his loyal subjects in all his dominions.

3. My Lord was sixteen years in banishment, and hath lost and suffered most of any subject, that suffered either by war, or other ways, except those that lost their lives, and even that he valued not, but exposed it to so imminent dangers that nothing but Heaven's decree had ordained to save it.

4. He never minded his own interest more than his loyalty and duty, and upon that account never desired nor received anything from the Crown to enrich himself, but spent great sums in his Majesty's service ; so that after his long banishment and return into England, I observed his ruined estate was like an earthquake, and his debts like thunderbolts, by which he was in danger of being utterly undone, had not patience and prudence, together with Heaven's blessings, saved him from that threatening ruin.

5. He never repined at his losses and sufferings, because he lost and suffered for his King and country ; nay, so far was he from that, that I have heard him say, if the same wars should happen again, and he was sure to lose both his life and all he had left him, yet he would most willingly sacrifice it for his Majesty's service.

6. He never connived or conspired with the enemy, neither directly nor indirectly ; for though some person of quality being sent in the late wars to him into the north [1], from his late Majesty, who was then at Oxford, with some message, did withal in private acquaint him, that some of the nobility that were with the King, desired him to side with them against his Majesty, alleging that if his Majesty should become an abso-

---

[1] Sir Philip Warwick was twice employed on errands from Oxford to the northern army, and may possibly be the person referred to, but there is no hint of any such intrigue in his Memoirs. Wilmot may have been concerned in it, for, as Sir Philip remarks, ' he that marks Wilmot's whole progress through the war shall find him much affected to be an arbiter of peace '.

lute conqueror, both himself and the rest of the nobility would lose all their rights and privileges ; yet he was so far from consenting to it, that he returned him this answer, namely, that he entered into actions of war, for no other end, but for the service of his king and master, and to keep up his Majesty's rights and prerogatives, for which he was resolved to venture both his life, posterity, and estate ; for certainly, said he, the nobility cannot fall if the King be victorious, nor can they keep up their dignities if the King be overcome.

This message was delivered by word of mouth, but none of their names mentioned ; so that it is not certainly known whether it was a real truth or not ; more probable it was, that they intended to sound my Lord, or to make, if possible, more division. For certainly not all that pretended to be for the King, were his friends ; and I myself remember very well, when I was with her Majesty, the now Queen Mother, in Oxford (although I was too young to perceive their intrigues, yet I was old enough to observe), that there were great factions both amongst the courtiers and soldiers. But my Lord's loyalty was such, that he kept always faithful and true to his Majesty, and could by no means be brought to side with the rebellious party, or to juggle and mind his own interest more than his Majesty's service ; and this was the cause that he had as great private enemies at court, as he had public enemies in the field, who sought as much his ruin and destruction privately, and would cast aspersions upon his loyalty and duty, as these did publicly oppose him.

In short, that it may appear the better what loyal and faithful services my Lord has done both for his late Majesty King Charles the First and his now gracious master King Charles the Second, I have thought fit to subjoin both their Majesty's commendations which they were pleased to give him, when for his great and loyal services they conferred upon him the titles and dignities of Marquess, and Duke of Newcastle [1].

A Copy of the Preamble of my Lord's Patent for Marquess, Englished

' REX, ETC., SALUTEM.—Whereas it appears to us, that William, Earl of Newcastle-upon-Tyne, besides his most emi-

---

[1] Given also by Collins, *Historical Collections*, p. 31, and there dated Oxford, 27th October 1643.

nent birth and splendid alliances, hath equalled all those titles
with which he is adorned by desert, and hath also won them
by virtue, industry, prudence, and a steadfast faith : whilst
with dangers and expenses gathering together soldiers, arms,
and all other warlike habiliments ; and applying them as well
in our affairs, as most plentifully sending them to us (having
forethought of our dignity and security), he was ready with
us in all actions in Yorkshire, and governed the town of Newcastle and castle, in the mouth of Tyne, at the time of that
fatal revolt of the people who were got together ; and with a
band of his friends did opportunely seize that port, and settled
it a garrison ; bringing arms to us (then our only relief) :
in which service so strongly going on (which was of grand
moment to our affairs) we do gratefully remember him still
to have stood to : afterwards, having mustered together a
good army (ourself being gone elsewhere), the rebels now
enjoying almost all Yorkshire, and the chiefest fortress of all
the country now appearing to have scarce refuge or safety for
him against the swelling rebels (the whole country then desiring
and praying for his coming, that he might timely relieve them
in their desperate condition) : and leading his said army
in the midst of winter gave the rebels battle in his passage,
vanquished them, and put them to flight, and took from them
several garrisons and places of refuge, and restored health
to the subjects, and, by his many victories, peace and security
to the countries : witness those places, made noble by the death
and flight of the rebels : in Lincolnshire, Gainsborough and
Lincoln ; in Derbyshire, Chesterfield ; but in Yorkshire,
Peircebridge, Seacroft, Tankerly, Tadcaster, Sheffield, Rotherham, Yarum, Beverley, Cawood, Selby, Halifax, Leeds, and,
above all, Bradford ; where, when the Yorkshire and Lancashire rebels were united, and battle joined with them ; when
our army, as well by the great numbers of the rebels, as much
more the badness of our ground, was so prest upon, that the
soldiers now seemed to think of flying ; he, their General, with
a full career, commanding two troops to follow him, broke into
the very rage of the battle, and with so much violence fell upon
the right wing of those rebels, that those who were but now
certain of victory, turned their backs, and fled from the conqueror, who by his wisdom, virtue, and his own hand, brought
death and flight to the rebels, victory and glory to himself,

plunder to the soldiery, and twenty-two great guns, and many ensigns to us. Nor was there before this, wanting to so much virtue, equal felicity, for our most beloved Consort, after a dismal tempest coming from Holland, being drove ashore at Burlington, and undergoing a more grievous danger, by the excursions of the rebels, than the tossing and tumbling of the sea ; he having heard of it, speedily goes to her with his army, and dutifully receiveth her, in safety brings her, and with all security conducts her to us at Oxford. Whereas therefore the aforesaid Earl hath raised so many monuments of his virtue and fidelity towards us, our Queen, children, and our kingdom ; when also he doth at this time establish with safety, and with his power defend, the northern parts of our kingdom against the rebels ; when, lastly, nothing more concerns mankind and princes, and nothing can be more just, than that he may receive for his deeds a reward suitable to his name, which requires that he who defends the Borders should be created by us, Governor or Marquess of the Borderers. Know therefore ', etc.

A Copy of the Preamble of my Lord's Patent for Duke, Englished [1]

' REX, ETC., SALUTEM.—Whereas our most beloved and faithful cousin and counsellor, William, Earl and Marquess of Newcastle-upon-Tyne, etc., worthy by his famous name, blood, and office, of large honours, has been eminent in so many, and so great services performed to us and our father (of ever-blessed memory) that his merits are still producing new effects, we have decreed likewise to add more honour to his former. And though these his such eminent actions, which he hath faithfully and valiantly performed to us, our father, and our kingdom, speak loud enough in themselves ; yet since the valiant services of a good subject are always pleasant to remember, we have thought fit to have them in part related for a good example and encouragement to virtue.

' The great proofs of his wisdom and piety are sufficiently known to us from our younger years, and we shall always

---

[1] Collins' *Historical Collections*, p. 43, dated 16th March 166¾. Newcastle asked for a dukedom. ' I have received yours by your son ', replied Charles II, on June 7, 1664, ' and am resolved to grant your request. Send me therefore word what title you desire to have, or whether you will keep your old, and leave the rest to me.'—*Portland MSS.*, ii, 145.

retain a sense of those good principles he instilled into us; the care of our youth which he happily undertook for our good, he as faithfully and well discharged. Our years growing up amidst bad times, and the harsh necessities of war, a new charge and care of loyalty, the kingdom and religion, called him off to make use of his further diligence and valour. Rebellion spread abroad, he levied loyal forces in great numbers, opposed the enemy, won so many and so great victories in the field, took in so many towns, castles, and garrisons, as well in our northern parts, as elsewhere; and behaved himself with so great courage and valour in the defending also what he had got, especially at the siege of York, which he maintained against three potent armies, of Scots and English, closely beleaguering, and with emulation assaulting it for three months (till relief was brought), to the wonder and envy of the enemy; that, if loyal and human force could have prevailed, he had soon restored fidelity, peace, and his KING to the nation, which was then hurrying to ruin by an unhappy fate; so that rebellion getting the upper hand, and no place being left for him to act further valiantly in, for his King and country, he still retained the same loyalty and valour in suffering, being an inseparable follower of our exile; during which sad catastrophe, his whole estate was sequestered and sold from him, and his person always one of the first of those few who were excepted, both for life and estate (which was offered to all others). Besides, his virtues are accompanied with a noble blood, being of a family by each stock equally adorned and endowed with great honours and riches. For which reasons we have resolved to grace the said Marquess with a new mark of our favour, he being every way deserving of it, as one who loved virtue equal to his noble birth, and possessed patrimonies suitable to both, as long as loyalty had any place to show itself in our realm; which possessions he so well employed, and at last for us and our father's service lost, till he was with us restored. Know therefore ', etc.

4. *Of his Prudence and Wisdom*

My Lord's prudence and wisdom hath been sufficiently apparent both in his public and private actions and employments; for he hath such a natural inspection, and judicious observation of things, that he sees beforehand what will come to pass, and orders his affairs accordingly. To which purpose I cannot but mention, that Laud, the then Archbishop of Canterbury (between whom and my Lord interceded a great and entire friendship, which he confirmed by a legacy of a diamond, to the value of £200, left to my Lord when he died, which was much for him to bequeath ; for though he was a great statesman, and in favour with his late Majesty, yet he was not covetous to hoard up wealth, but bestowed it rather upon the public, repairing the Cathedral of St. Paul's in London, which, had God granted him life, he would certainly have beautified, and rendered as famous and glorious as any in Christendom): this said Archbishop was pleased to tell his late Majesty, that my Lord was one of the wisest and prudentest persons that ever he was acquainted with.

For further proof, I cannot pass by that my Lord told his late Majesty, King Charles the First, and her Majesty the now Queen Mother, some time before the wars, that he observed, by the humours of the people, the approaching of a civil war, and that his Majesty's person would be in danger of being deposed, if timely care was not taken to prevent it.

Also when my Lord was at Antwerp, the Marquess of Montrose, before he went into Scotland, gave my Lord a visit, and acquainted him with his intended journey, asking my Lord whether he was not also going for England ? My Lord answered, he was ready to do his Majesty what service he could, and would shun no opportunity, where he perceived he could effect something to his Majesty's advantage ; nay, said he, if his Majesty should be pleased to command my single person to go against the whole army of the enemy, although I was sure to lose my life, yet out of a loyal duty to his Majesty, and in obedience to his commands, I should never refuse it. But to venture (said he) the life of my friends, and to betray them in a desperate action, without any probability of doing the least good to his Majesty, would be a very unjust and unconscionable act ; for my friends might perhaps venture with me upon an implicit faith, that I was so honest as not to engage them without a firm and solid foundation ; but I wanting that, as having no ships, arms, ammunition, provision, forts, and places of rendezvous, and what is the chief thing, money ; to what purpose would it be to draw them into so hazardous an action, but to seek their ruin and destruction, without the least benefit to his Majesty ? Then the Marquess of Montrose asked my Lord's advice, and what he should do in such a case ? My Lord answered, that he, knowing best his own country, power, and strength, and what probability he had of forces, and other necessaries for war, when he came into Scotland, could give himself the best advice ; but withal told him, that if he had no provision nor ammunition, arms and places of rendezvous for his men to meet and join, he would likely be forced to hide his head, and suffer for his rash undertaking : which unlucky fate did also accordingly befall that worthy person.

These passages I mention to no other end, but to declare my Lord's judgment and prudence in worldly affairs ; whereof there are so many, that if I should set them all down, it would swell this history to a big volume. They may in some sort be gathered from his actions mentioned heretofore, especially the ordering of his affairs in the time of war, with such conduct, prudence, and wisdom, that, notwithstanding at the beginning of his undertaking that great trust and honourable employment which his late Majesty was pleased to confer upon him, he saw so little appearance of performing his designs with good success, his Majesty's revenues being then much weakened, and the magazines and public purse in the enemy's power, besides several other obstructions and hindrances ; yet as he undertook it cheerfully, and out of pure loyalty and obedience to his Majesty ; so he ordered it so wisely, that so long as he acted by his own counsels and was personally present at the execution of his designs, he was always prosperous in his success. And although he had so great an army, as afore-mentioned, yet by his wise and prudent conduct, there appeared no visible sign of devastation in any of the countries where he marched ; for first, he settled a constant rule for the regular levy of money for the convenient maintenance of the soldiery. Next, he constituted such officers of his army, that most of them were known to be gentlemen of large and fair estates, which drew a good part of their private revenues, to serve and support them in their public employments ; wherein my Lord did lead them the way by his own good example.

To which may be added his wisdom in ordering the government of the Church, for the advancement of the orthodox religion, and suppression of factions; as also in coining, printing, knighting, and the like, which he used with great discretion and prudence, only for the interest of his Majesty, and the benefit of the kingdom, as formerly has been mentioned.

The prudent manage of his private and domestic affairs appears sufficiently. (1) In his marriage; (2) in the ordering and increasing his estate before the wars, which, notwithstanding his noble housekeeping and hospitality, and his generous bounty and charity, he increased to the value of £100,000; (3) in the ordering his affairs in the time of banishment, where, although he received not the least of his own estate, during all the time of his exile, until his return: yet maintained himself handsomely and nobly, according to his quality, as much as his condition at that time would permit; (4) in reducing his torn and ruined estate after his return, which, beyond all probability, himself hath settled and ordered so, that his posterity will have reason gratefully to remember it.

In short, although my Lord naturally loves not business, especially those of state (though he understands them as well as anybody), yet what business or affairs he cannot avoid, none will do them better than himself. His private affairs he orders without any noise or trouble, not over-hastily, but wisely. Neither is he passionate in acting of business, but hears patiently, and orders soberly, and pierces into the heart or bottom of a business at the first encounter; but before all things, he considers well before he undertakes a business, whether he be able to go through it or no, for he never ventures upon either public or private business, beyond his strength.

And here I cannot forbear to mention, that my noble Lord, when he was in banishment, presumed out of his duty and love to his gracious master, our now sovereign King, Charles the Second, to write and send him a little book, or rather a letter wherein he delivered his opinion concerning the government of his dominions, whensoever God should be pleased to restore him to his throne, together with some other notes and observations of foreign states and kingdoms; but it being a private offer to his sacred Majesty, I dare not presume to publish it [1].

---

[1] Two copies of this little book have survived. One is in the Bodleian Library amongst the Clarendon MSS. It is described in Mr. Madan's *Summary Catalogue of the Western MSS.*, vol. iii, number 16,195. It is bound in white parchment, with fine gold tool-

5. *Of his Blessings*

Although my Lord hath been one of the most unfortunate persons of his rank and quality, which this later age did produce ; yet Heaven hath been so propitious to him, that it bestowed some blessings upon him even in the midst of his misfortunes, and supported him against Fortune's malice, which otherwise, as it seems, had designed his total ruin and destruction. Of these blessings I may name in the first place.

1. The royal favours of his gracious sovereigns, and the good esteem they had of his fidelity and loyalty ; which, as it was the chief of his endeavours, so he esteemed it above all the rest. To repeat them particularly would be too tedious, and they are sufficiently apparent out of the precedent history ; only this I may add, that King Charles the First, out of a singular favour to my Lord, was pleased, upon his most humble request, to create several noblemen ; the names of them, lest I commit an offence, I shall not mention, by reason most men usually pretend such claims upon the ground of their own merit.

2. That God was pleased to bless him with wealth and power, to enable him the better for the service of his King and country.

3. That He made him happy in his marriage ; (for his first wife was a very kind, loving, and virtuous lady) and blessed him with dutiful and obedient children, free from vices, noble and generous both in their natures and actions ; who did all that lay in their power to support and relieve my Lord their father in his banishment, as before is mentioned.

4. The kindness and civility which my Lord received from strangers, and the inhabitants of those places, where he lived during the time of his banishment ; for had it not been for them, he would have perished in his extreme wants ; but it pleased God so to provide for him, that although he wanted an estate, yet he wanted not credit ; and although he was banished and forsaken by his own friends and countrymen, yet he was civilly received and relieved by strangers, until God blessed him.

Lastly, with a happy return to his native country, his dear children, and his own estate ; which, although he found much ruined and broke, yet by his prudence and wisdom, hath ordered as well as he could ; and I hope, and pray God to add this blessing to all the rest, that he may live long to increase it for the benefit of his posterity.

6. *Of his Honours and Dignities*

The honours, titles, and dignities which were conferred upon my Lord, by King James, King Charles the First, and King Charles the Second, partly as an encouragement for future service, and a reward for past, are following :

1. He was made Knight of the Bath, when he was but fifteen or sixteen years of age, at the creation of Henry, Prince of Wales, King James's eldest son [1].

2. King James created him Viscount Mansfield, and Baron of Bolsover.

3. King Charles the First constituted him Lord Lieutenant of Nottinghamshire, and

4. Lord Warden of the Forest of Sherwood ; as also,

5. Lord Lieutenant of Derbyshire.

6. He chose him Governor to his son Charles, our now gracious King ; and

7. Made him one of his honourable Privy Council.

8. He constituted him Governor of the town and county of Newcastle, and General of all his Majesty's forces raised, and to be raised, in the northern parts of England ; as also of the several counties of Nottingham, Lincoln, Rutland, Derby, Stafford, Leicester, Warwick, Northampton, Huntingdon, Cambridge, Norfolk, Sussex, Essex, and Hertford, together with all the appurtenances belonging to so great a power, as is formerly declared.

9. He conferred upon him the honour and title of Earl of Newcastle, and Baron of Bothal and Hepple.

10. He created him Marquess of Newcastle.

11. His Majesty King Charles the Second was pleased, when my Lord was in banishment, to make him Knight of the most noble Order of the Garter [2] ; and

---

[1] These honours have already been mentioned in their proper places. Newcastle was made one of the Privy Council of Charles I, November 29, 1639. Doyle, *Official Baronage.*

[2] He was appointed Knight of the Garter 12th January 1650, but not solemnly installed in that dignity till April 15, 1661. Collins' *Historical Collections*, pp. 38-42.

12. After his return into England, Chief-Justice in Eyre Trent-North [1].

13. He created him Duke of Newcastle and Earl of Ogle.

7. Of the Entertainments he made for King Charles the First

Though my Lord hath always been free and noble in his entertainments and feastings, yet he was pleased to show his great affection and duty to his gracious King, Charles the First, and her Majesty the Queen in some particular entertainments which he made of purpose for them before the late wars.

When his Majesty was going into Scotland to be crowned, he took his way through Nottinghamshire ; and lying at Work-sop Manor, hardly two miles distant from Welbeck, where my Lord then was, my Lord invited his Majesty thither to a dinner, which he was graciously pleased to accept of [2]. This entertainment cost my Lord between four and five thousand pounds ; which his Majesty liked so well, that a year after his return out of Scotland, he was pleased to send my Lord word, that her Majesty the Queen was resolved to make a progress into the northern parts, desiring him to prepare the like entertainment for her, as he had formerly done for him. Which my Lord did, and endeavoured for it with all possible care and industry, sparing nothing that might add splendour to that feast, which both their Majesties were pleased to honour with their presence : Ben Jonson he employed in fitting such scenes and speeches as he could best devise ; and sent for all the gentry of the country to come and wait on their Majesties ; and, in short, did all that ever he could imagine, to render it great, and worthy of their royal acceptance.

This entertainment he made at Bolsover Castle in Derbyshire, some five miles distant from Welbeck, and resigned Welbeck for their Majesties' lodging ; it cost him in all between fourteen and fifteen thousand pounds.

---

[1] July 10, 1661. Doyle, *Official Baronage.*

[2] Clarendon thus describes these entertainments (*Rebellion*, i, 167): 'Both King and court were received and entertained by the Earl of Newcastle, and at his own proper expense, in such a wonderful manner, and in such an excess of feasting, as had never before been known in England ; and would still be thought very prodigious, if the same noble person had not, within a year or two afterwards, made the King and Queen a more stupendous entertainment ; which (God be thanked), though possibly it might too much whet the appetite of others to excess, no man ever after imitated.'

Jonson's two Masques are entitled *The King's Entertainment at Welbeck in Nottinghamshire*, etc., and *Love's Welcome—The King's and Queen's entertainment at Bolsover, the 30th of July* 1634.

Besides these two, there was another small entertainment which my Lord prepared for his late Majesty, in his own park at Welbeck, when his Majesty came down, with his two nephews, the now Prince Elector Palatine, and his brother Prince Rupert, into the Forest of Sherwood ; which cost him fifteen hundred pounds.

And this I mention not out of a vain glory, but to declare the great love and duty my Lord had for his gracious King and Queen, and to correct the mistakes committed by some historians, who, not being rightly informed of those entertainments, make the world believe falsehood for truth. But, as I said, they were made before the wars, when my Lord had the possession of a great estate ; and wanted nothing to express his love and duty to his sovereign in that manner ; whereas now he should be much to seek to do the like, his estate being so much ruined by the late Civil Wars, that neither himself nor his posterity will be able so soon to recover it.

8. *His Education*

His education was according to his birth ; for as he was born a gentleman, so he was bred like a gentleman [1]. To school learning he never showed a great inclination ; for though he was sent to the University, and was a student of St. John's College in Cambridge, and had his tutors to instruct him ; yet they could not persuade him to read or study much, he taking more delight in sports, than in learning ; so that

---

[1] In *Nature's Pictures*, by *Fancy's Pencil* the Duchess describes the education of her day (pp. 273, 333, ed. 1656). In *The Tale of a Traveller* she thus sketches a boy's bringing up : ' His education, in the first place, was to learn the horn-book, from that his primer, and so the Bible, by his mother's chambermaid or the like. But after he came to ten years old or thereabouts, he was sent to a free school, where the noise of each scholar's reading aloud did drown the sense of what they read, burying the knowledge and understanding in the confusion of many words, and several languages ; yet was whipt for not learning by their tutors, for their ill teaching them, which broke and weakened their memories with the over heavy burthens, striving to thrust in more learning than could be digested or kept in the brain. . . . After some time he was sent to the University, there continuing from the years of fourteen to the years of eighteen ; at last considering with himself that he was buried to the world and the delights therein, conversing more with the dead than the living, in reading old authors, and that little company he had, was only at prayers, and meat ; wherein the time of the one was taken up in devotion, the other in eating, or rather fasting ; for their prayers were so long, and their commons so short, that it seemed rather an humiliation and fasting, than an eating and thanksgiving. But their conversation was a greater penance than their spare diet ; for their disputations, which are fed by contradictions, did more wrack the brain, than the other did gripe the belly, the one filling the head with vain opinions and false imaginations, for want of the light of truth, as the other with wind and rude humours, for want of a sufficient nourishment. Where upon these considerations he left the University.'

his father being a wise man, and seeing that his son had a good natural wit, and was of a very good disposition, suffered him to follow his own genius ; whereas his other son Charles, in whom he found a greater love and inclination to learning, he encouraged as much that way as possibly he could.

One time it happened that a young gentleman, one of my Lord's relations, had bought some land, at the same time when my Lord had bought a singing-boy for £50, a horse for £50, and a dog for £2 ; which humour his father Sir Charles liked so well, that he was pleased to say, that if he should find his son to be so covetous, that he would buy land before he was twenty years of age, he would disinherit him. But above all the rest, my Lord had a great inclination to the art of horsemanship and weapons, in which later his father Sir Charles, being a most ingenious and unparalleled master of that age, was his only tutor [1], and kept him also several masters in the art of horsemanship, and sent him to the Mews to Mons. Antoine, who was then accounted the best master in that art [2]. But my Lord's delight in those heroic exercises was such, that he soon became master thereof himself, which increased much his father's hopes of his future perfections, who being himself a person of a noble and heroic nature, was extremely well pleased to observe his son take delight

---

[1] Jonson, in his *Underwoods*, has an epigram on the Duke's fencing (No. LXXXIX) :

> They talk of Fencing and the use of arms,
> The art of urging and avoiding harms,
> The noble science, and the mastering skill
> Of making just approaches how to kill ;
> To hit in angles, and to clash with time :
> As all defence or offence were a chime !
> I hate such measured—give me mettled fire,
> That trembles in the blaze, but then mounts higher
> A quick and dazzling motion ; when a pair
> Of bodies meet like rarefied air !
> Their weapons darted with that flame and force
> As they outdid the lightning in the course ;
> This were a spectacle, a sight to draw
> Wonder to valour ! No, it is the law
> Of daring not to do a wrong ; 'tis true
> Valour to slight it, being done to you,
> To know the heads of danger, where 'tis fit
> To bend, to break, provoke, or suffer it ;
> All this, my Lord, is valour, this is yours,
> And was your father's, all your ancestors !
> Who durst live great 'mongst all the colds and heats
> Of human life ; as all the frosts and sweats
> Of fortune, when or death appeared, or bands ;
> And valiant were, with or without their hands.

[2] St. Antoine was the riding master of Prince Henry.—Dalton, *Life of Sir Edward Cecil*, i, 210.

in such arts and exercises as were proper and fit for a person of quality.

9. *His Natural Wit and Understanding*

Although my Lord has not so much of scholarship and learning as his brother Sir Charles Cavendish had, yet he hath an excellent natural wit and judgment, and dives into the bottom of everything ; as it is evidently apparent in the forementioned art of horsemanship and weapons, which by his own ingenuity he has reformed and brought to such perfection, as never any one has done heretofore. And though he is no mathematician by art, yet he hath a very good mathematical brain, to demonstrate truth by natural reason, and is both a good natural and moral philosopher, not by reading philosophical books, but by his own natural understanding and observation, by which he hath found out many truths.

To pass by several other instances, I'll but mention, that when my Lord was at Paris, in his exile, it happened one time, that he discoursing with some of his friends, amongst whom was also that learned philosopher Hobbes [1], they began, amongst the rest, to argue upon this subject, namely, Whether it were possible to make man by art fly as birds do ; and when some of the company had delivered their opinion, viz. That they thought it probable to be done by the help of artificial wings ; my Lord declared, that he deemed it altogether impossible, and demonstrated it by this following reason. Man's arms, said he, are not set on his shoulders in the same manner as bird's wings are : for that part of the arm which joins to the shoulder is in man placed inward, as towards the breast, but in birds outward, as toward the back ; which difference and contrary position or shape hinders that man cannot have the same flying action with his arms, as birds

---

[1] ' I have heard Mr. Edmund Waller say that W. Lord Marquis of Newcastle was a great patron to Dr. Gassendi, and M. Des Cartes, as well as to Mr. Hobbes, and that he hath dined with them all three at the Marquis's table, at Paris.'—*Aubrey's Letters*, iii, 602. I have not succeeded in finding these arguments which the Duchess mentions in the following pages, in the *Leviathan*. Hobbes, however, acknowledges Newcastle's patronage by several dedications to him, viz. the dedication of his *Liberty and Necessity* and that of his *Elements of Law*. He also wrote for Newcastle's benefit a paper of ' Considerations touching the Facility or Difficulty of the Motions of a Horse on straight lines and circular,' which is printed in Mr. Strong's *Catalogue of the Letters and other Historical Documents exhibited in the Library at Welbeck*, p. 237.

have with their wings. Which argument Mr. Hobbes liked
so well, that he was pleased to make use of it in one of his
books called Leviathan, if I remember well.

Some other time they falling into a discourse concerning
witches, Mr. Hobbes said, that though he could not rationally
believe there were witches, yet he could not be fully satisfied
to believe there were none, by reason they would themselves
confess it, if strictly examined.

To which my Lord answered, that though for his part he
cared not whether there were witches or no : yet his opinion
was, that the confession of witches, and their suffering for it,
proceeded from an erroneous belief, viz. that they had made
a contract with the devil to serve him for such rewards as
were in his power to give them ; and that it was their religion
to worship and adore him ; in which religion they had such
a firm and constant belief, that if anything came to pass
according to their desire, they believed the devil had heard
their prayers, and granted their requests, for which they gave
him thanks ; but if things fell out contrary to their prayers
and desires, then they were troubled at it, fearing they had
offended him, or not served him as they ought, and asked
him forgiveness for their offences. Also (said my Lord)
they imagine that their dreams are real exterior actions ;
for example, if they dream they fly in the air, or out of the
chimney top, or that they are turned into several shapes,
they believe no otherwise, but that it is really so. And this
wicked opinion makes them industrious to perform such cere-
monies to the devil, that they adore and worship him as their
god, and choose to live and die for him.

Thus my Lord declared himself concerning witches, which
Mr. Hobbes was also pleased to insert in his fore-mentioned
book. But yet my Lord doth not count this opinion of his
so universal, as if there were none but imaginary witches ;
for he doth not speak but of such a sort of witches as make
it their religion to worship the devil in the manner aforesaid.
Nor doth he think it a crime to entertain what opinion seems
most probable to him, in things indifferent ; for in such cases
men may discourse and argue as they please, to exercise
their wit, and may change and alter their opinions upon more
probable grounds and reasons ; whereas in fundamental
matters, both of Church and State, he is so strict an adherent

to them, that he will never maintain or defend such opinions which are in the least prejudicial to either [1].

One proof more I'll add to confirm his natural understanding and judgment, which was upon some discourse I held with him one time, concerning that famous chemist Van Helmont, who in his writings is very invective against the schoolmen, and, amongst the rest, accuses them for taking the radical moisture for the fat of animal bodies. Whereupon my Lord answered, that surely the schoolmen were too wise to commit such an error; for, said he, the radical moisture is not the fat or tallow of an animal, but an oily and balsamous substance; for the fat and tallow, as also the watery parts, are cold; whereas the oily and balsamous parts have at all times a lively heat, which makes that those creatures which have much of that oil or balsam are long lived, and appear young; and not only animals, but also vegetables, which have much of that oil of balsam, as ivy, bays, laurel, holly, and the like, live long, and appear fresh and green, not only in winter, but when they are old. Then I asked my Lord's opinion concerning the radical heat: to which he answered, that the radical heat lived in the radical moisture; and when the one decayed, the other decayed also; and then was produced either an unnatural heat, which caused an unnatural dryness, or an unnatural moisture, which caused dropsies, and these, an unnatural coldness.

Lastly, his natural wit appears by his delight in poetry; for I may justly call him the best lyric and dramatic poet

---

[1] The Duke, like most of his contemporaries, made occasional scientific experiments and held views of his own about natural science. In a preface written by him to the *Philosophical and Physical Opinions* of his wife he says: 'Since it is now *à la mode* to write of natural philosophy, and I know nobody knows what is the cause of anything, and since they are all but guessers, not knowing, it gives every man room to think what he lists, and so I mean to set up for myself, and play at this philosophical game as follows, without patching or stealing from anybody.' He then proceeds to deliver his opinion concerning the grounds of natural philosophy: 'Salt is the life that giveth motion to all things in the world', which he proves, amongst other reasons, by the following experiment: 'The sun, no doubt, is a great fire, and must have something to maintain it; but before I deliver my opinion to you, I desire leave to make you a little relation, and it is this: Dr. Payn, a divine, and my chaplain, who hath a very witty searching brain of his own, being at my house at Bolsover, locked up with me in a chamber to make Lapis Prunellæ, which is saltpetre and brimstone inflamed, looking at it a while, I said, Mark it, Mr. Payn, the flame is pale, like the Sun, and hath a violent motion in it, like the Sun; saith he, It hath so, and the more to confirm you, says he, look what abundance of little suns, round like a globe, appear to us everywhere, just the same motion as the Sun makes in every one's eyes. So we concluded the Sun could be nothing else but a very solid body of salt and sulphur, inflamed by his own violent motions upon his own axis. . . .
'This', he concludes, 'is my opinion, which I think can as hardly be disproved as proved; since any opinion may be right or wrong, for anything that anybody knows, for certainly there is none can make a mathematical demonstration of natural philosophy'.

of this age [1]. His Comedies do sufficiently show his great observation and judgment, for they are composed of these three ingredients, viz. wit, humour, and satire; and his chief design in them is to divulge and laugh at the follies of mankind; to persecute vice, and to encourage virtue. [2]

10. *Of his Natural Humour and Disposition*

My Lord may justly be compared to Titus the deliciæ of mankind, by reason of his sweet, gentle, and obliging nature; for though his wisdom and experience found it impossible to please all men, because of their different humours and dispositions; yet his nature is such, that he will be sorry when he seeth that men are displeased with him out of their own ill natures, without any cause; for he loves all that are his friends, and hates none that are his enemies [3]. He is a

---

[1] The Duke's poems are represented by songs in his own plays and in those of the Duchess, by dedicatory verses to her different books, and by several pieces in her *Nature's Pictures* (pp. 65, 79, 94, 97). A book containing songs and sketches of plays in the handwriting of the Duke is preserved at Welbeck. (Strong, *Catalogue of the Letters, etc. exhibited in the Library at Welbeck*, p. 57). At the end of her volume of Poems the Duchess says:

> A Poet I am neither born nor bred,
> But to a witty poet married,
> Whose brain is fresh, and pleasant, as the Spring,
> Where fancies grow, and where the Muses sing;
> There oft I lean my head, and listening hark,
> T' observe his words, and all his fancies mark;
> And from that garden flowers of fancies take,
> Whereof a posy up in verse I make:
> Thus I that have no garden of my own
> There gather flowers, that are newly blown.

[2] The Duke was the author of four Comedies: (1) *The Country Captain*, 12mo, 1649, said to have been acted with applause at Black Friars and printed at the Hague and at London. On October 26, 1661, Pepys notes seeing this play: 'the first time it hath been acted this twenty-five years . . . but so silly a play as in all my life I never saw.'
(2) *The Variety*, printed with *The Country Captain*, 12mo, 1649, London and the Hague. A droll called *The French-Dancing Master*, was made out of this play, and is printed in *The Wits, or Sport upon Sport*, 1671.
(3) *The Humorous Lovers*, acted at the Duke's Theatre. 4to, 1677. Pepys, who attributes it to the Duchess, saw it on March 30, 1667, and calls it 'the most silly thing that ever came upon a stage.'
(4) *The Triumphant Widow, or the Medley of Humours*, acted at the Duke's Theatre. 4to, 1677. Shadwell incorporated the greater part of this play in *Bury Fair*.
The Duke also wrote five scenes of *The Lady Contemplation*, a play by the Duchess. He also translated Molière's *L'Etourdi*, which Dryden converted into *Sir Martin Mar-All*. Though printed in 1668, this play did not appear with Dryden's name till 1697, and was entered in the Stationers' Register under the Duke's name. Pepys saw it on August 16, 1667, and calls it 'a play made by my Lord Duke of Newcastle, but, as everybody says, corrected by Dryden. It is the most entire piece of mirth, a complete farce from one end to the other, that was ever writ. I never laughed so in all my life, and at very good wit therein, not fooling.'
[3] The Duke's generosity to his political opponents was shown in his treatment of those accused of sharing in the Yorkshire plot of 1663. He treated Colonel Hutchinson 'very honourably', and 'dismissed him without a guard to his own house, only engaging him to stay there one week, till he gave account to the Council'—*Memoirs*, ii, 290. Mr. John Cromwell, another sufferer on the same occasion, found a powerful protector in the Duke, who finally secured his release. Kennet's *Register*, p. 890.

loyal subject, a kind husband, a loving father, a generous master, and a constant friend.

His natural love to his parents has been so great, that I have heard him say, he would most willingly, and without the least repining, have begged for his daily relief, so God would but have let his parents live.

He is true and just both in his words and actions, and has no mean or petty designs, but they are all just and honest.

He condemns not upon report, but upon proof ; nor judges by words, but actions ; he forgets not past service, for present advantage ; but gives a present reward to a present desert.

He hath a great power over his passions, and hath had the greatest trials thereof ; for certainly he must of necessity have a great share of patience, that can forgive so many false treacherous, malicious, and ungrateful persons as he hath done ; but he is so wise, that his passion never outruns his patience, nor his extravagances his prudence ; and although his private enemies have been numerous, yet I verily believe, there is never a subject more generally beloved than he is.

He hates pride and loves humility ; is civil to strangers, kind to his acquaintance, and respectful to all persons, according to their quality ; he never regards place, except it be for ceremony : to the meanest person he'll put off his hat, and suffer everybody to speak to him.

He never refuses any petition, but accepts them ; and being informed of the business, will give a just, and as much as lies in him, a favourable answer to the petitioning party.

He easily pardons, and bountifully rewards ; and always praises particular men's virtues, but covers their faults with silence.

He is full of charity and compassion to persons that are in misery, and full of clemency and mercy ; insomuch, that when he was general of a great army, he would never sit in council himself upon causes of life and death, but granted pardon to many delinquents that were condemned by his council of war ; so that some were forced to petition him not to do it, by reason it was an ill precedent for others. To which my Lord merrily answered, that if they did hang all, they would leave him none to fight.

His courage he always showed in action, more than in words, for he would fight, but not rant.

He is not vain-glorious to heighten or brag of his heroic actions ; witness that great victory upon Atherton Moor, after which he would not suffer his trumpets to sound, but came quietly and silently into the city of York ; for which he would certainly have been blamed by those that make a great noise upon small causes, and love to be applauded, though their actions little deserve it.

His noble bounty and generosity is so manifest to all the world, that I should light a candle to the sun, if I should strive to illustrate it ; for he has no self-designs or self-interest, but will rather wrong and injure himself than others.   To give you but one proof of this noble virtue, it is known, that where he hath a legal right to felons' goods, as he hath in a great part of his estate, yet he never took or exacted more than some inconsiderable share for acknowledgement of his right ; saying, that he was resolved never to grow rich by other men's misfortunes.

In short, I know him not addicted to any manner of vice except that he has been a great lover and admirer of the female sex ; which, whether it be so great a crime as to condemn him for it, I'll leave to the judgment of young gallants and beautiful ladies.

11. *Of his outward Shape and Behaviour*

His shape is neat, and exactly proportioned ; his stature of a middle size, and his complexion sanguine.

His behaviour is such, that it might be a pattern for all gentlemen : for it is courtly, civil, easy and free, without formality or constraint ; and yet hath something in it of grandeur, that causes an awful respect towards him.

12. *Of his Discourse*

His discourse is as free and unconcerned as his behaviour, pleasant, witty, and instructive ; he is quick in repartees or sudden answers, and hates dubious disputes, and premeditated speeches. He loves also to intermingle his discourse with some short pleasant stories, and witty sayings, and always names the author from whom he hath them ; for he hates to make another man's wit his own [1].

---

[1] Shadwell, in his dedication of *The Libertine* to Lord Newcastle, says : ' By the great honour I had to be daily admitted unto your Grace's public and private conversation

13. *Of his Habit*

He accoutres his person according to the fashion, if it be one that is not troublesome and uneasy for men of heroic exercises and actions.   He is neat and cleanly ; which makes him to be somewhat long in dressing, though not so long as many effeminate persons are.   He shifts ordinarily once a day, and every time when he uses exercise, or his temper is more hot than ordinary.

14. *Of his Diet*

In his diet he is so sparing and temperate, that he never eats nor drinks beyond his set proportion, so as to satisfy only his natural appetite.   He makes but one meal a day, at which he drinks two good glasses of small-beer, one about the beginning, the other at the end thereof, and a little glass of sack in the middle of his dinner ; which glass of sack he also uses in the morning for his breakfast, with a morsel of bread.   His supper consists of an egg, and a draught of small-beer.   And by this temperance he finds himself very healthful, and may yet live many years, he being now of the age of seventy-three, which I pray God from my soul to grant him.

15. *His Recreation and Exercise*

His prime pastime and recreation hath always been the exercise of manage and weapons ; which heroic arts he used to practise every day ; but I observing that when he had overheated himself, he would be apt to take cold, prevailed so far, that at last he left the frequent use of the manage, using nevertheless still the exercise of weapons ; and though he doth not ride himself so frequently as he hath done, yet he takes delight in seeing his horses of manage rid by his escuyers[1], whom he instructs in that art for his own pleasure[2].   But

I observed that admirable experience and judgment surmounting all the old, and that vigorousness of wit, and smartness of expression, exceeding all the young, I ever saw ; and not only in sharp and apt replies, but, which is much more difficult, by giving easy and unforced occasions, the most admirable way of beginning one, and all this adapted to men of all circumstances and conditions.'

[1] Escuyer, groom ; *écuyer*, Fr., the English esquire.

[2] Jonson dedicates the following epigram to Newcastle (*Underwoods*, lxxii.) :

> When first, my Lord, I saw you back your horse,
> Provoke his mettle, and command his force
> To all the uses of the field and race,
> Methought I read the ancient art of Thrace,
> And saw a Centaur past those tales of Greece,
> So seemed your horse and you both of a piece !

in the art of weapons (in which he has a method beyond all that ever were famous in it, found out by his own ingenuity and practice) he never taught anybody but now the Duke of Buckingham, whose guardian he hath been, and his own two sons.

The rest of his time he spends in music, poetry, architecture, and the like.

16. *Of his Pedigree*

Having made promise in the beginning of the first Book that I would join a more large description of the pedigree of my noble Lord and husband to the end of the history of his life, I shall now discharge myself ; and though I could derive it from a longer time, and reckon up a great many of his ancestors, even from the time of William the Conqueror, he being descended from the most ancient family of the Gernouns, as Camden relates in his Britannia, in the description of Derbyshire [1] ; yet it being a work fitter for heralds, I shall proceed no further than his grandfather, and show you only those noble families which my Lord is allied to by his birth.

My Lord's grandfather, by his father (as is formerly mentioned), was Sir William Cavendish, Privy-Counsellor and Treasurer of the Chamber to King Henry the Eighth, Edward the Sixth, and Queen Mary ; who married two wives [2]. By the first he had only two daughters ; but by the second, Elzabeth, who was my Lord's grandmother, he had three

> You showed like Perseus upon Pegasus,
> Or Castor mounted on his Cyllarus :
> Or what we hear our home-born legends tell,
> Of bold Sir Bevis and his Arundel :
> Nay, so your seat his beauties did endorse,
> As I began to wish myself a horse ;
> And surely, had I but your stable seen
> Before, I think my wish absolved had been,
> For never saw I yet the Muses dwell,
> Nor any of their household, half so well.
> So well ! as when I saw the floor and room,
> I looked for Hercules to be the groom ;
> And cried, Away with the Cæsarian bread !
> At these immortal mangers Virgil fed.

[1] Camden's *Britannia*, p. 491, ed. 1695. See also Collins' *Peerage*, ed. Brydges, i 303.

[2] Sir William Cavendish married (1) Margaret, daughter of Edmund Bostock, of Cheshire, who died in 1540 ; (2) Elizabeth, daughter of Thomas Parker, of Poslingford, Suffolk ; (3) Elizabeth Hardwick, August 20, 1547. See Sir William Cavendish's biographical notes in Collins' *Historical Collections*, p. 10. Elizabeth Hardwick married Robert Barley, of Barley in Derbyshire ; she was then fourteen, and her first husband died in 1532. She herself died on the 13th of February 1607, about the age of eighty-seven. Her will and epitaph are both printed by Collins.

sons and four daughters, wherof one daughter died young. She was daughter to John Hardwick, of Hardwick, in the county of Derby, Esq. ; and had four husbands : the first was — Barlow, Esq., who died before they were bedded together, they being both very young ; the second was Sir William Cavendish, my Lord's grandfather, who being somewhat in years, married her chiefly for her beauty. She had so much power in his affection, that she persuaded him to sell his estate which he had in the southern parts of England (for he was very rich) and buy an estate in the northern parts, viz. in Derbyshire, and thereabout, where her own friends and kindred lived, which he did ; and having there settled himself, upon her further persuasion built a manor-house in the same county, called Chatsworth, which, as I have heard, cost first and last above £80,000 sterling. But before this house was finished, he died, and left six children, viz. three sons and three daughters, which before they came to be marriageable, she married a third husband, Sir William St. Loo, Captain of the Guard to Queen Elizabeth, and Grand Butler of England [1] ; who dying without issue, she married a fourth husband, George, Earl of Shrewsbury, by whom she left no issue.

The children which she had by her second husband, Sir William Cavendish, being grown marriageable ; the eldest son, Henry, married Grace, the youngest daughter of his father-in-law, the said George, Earl of Shrewsbury, which he had by his former wife Gertrude, daughter of Thomas Manners, Earl of Rutland, but died without issue.

The second son William, after Earl of Devonshire, had two wives. The first was an heiress, by whom he had children, but all died save one son, whose name was also William, Earl of Devonshire. His second wife was widow to Sir Edward Wortley, who had several children by her first husband, and but one son by the said William Cavendish, after Earl of Devonshire, who died young.

His son by his first wife (William, Earl of Devonshire) married Christian, daughter of Edward, Lord Bruce, a Scotsman, by whom he had two sons and one daughter. The eldest son William, now Earl of Devonshire, married Elizabeth, the second daughter of William, Earl of Salisbury, by whom

1 A life of Sir William St. Loe, by Joseph Hunter, is printed in *The Retrospective Review*, 2nd series, vol. ii, p. 314

he has three children, viz. two sons and one daughter, whereof
the eldest son William is married to the second daughter of
James, now Duke of Ormond[1]. The second son Charles
is yet a youth. The daughter Anne married the Lord Rich,
the only son and child to Charles now Earl of Warwick ; but
he died without issue.

The second son of William, Earl of Devonshire, and brother
to the now Earl of Devonshire, was unfortunately slain in
the late Civil Wars, as is before mentioned.

The daughter of the said William, Earl of Devonshire,
sister to the now Earl of Devonshire, married Robert, Lord
Rich, eldest son to Robert, Earl of Warwick, by whom
she had but one son, who married, but died without issue.

The third and youngest son of Sir William Cavendish,
Charles Cavendish (my Lord's father), had two wives. The
first was daughter and co-heir to Sir Thomas Kidson, who
died a year after her marriage without issue. The second
was the younger daughter of Cuthbert, Lord Ogle, and after
her elder and only sister Jane, wife to Edward, Earl of Shrewsbury, who died without issue, became heir to her father's
estate and title ; by whom he had three sons, whereof the
eldest died in his infancy ; the second was William, my dear
Lord and husband ; the third Charles, who died a bachelor
about the age of sixty-three.

My Lord hath had two wives ; the first was Elizabeth,
daughter and heir to William Basset of Blore, in the county
of Stafford, Esq. ; and widow to Henry Howard, younger
son to Thomas, Earl of Suffolk ; by whom he had ten
children, viz. six sons and four daughters ; whereof five, viz.
four sons and one daughter, died young ; the rest, viz. two
sons and three daughters, came to be married.[2]

---

[1] Henry Cavendish died October 12, 1616 (Collins, p. 13). William Cavendish, first
Earl of Devonshire, died on March 3, 1625 ; he married (1) Anne, daughter of Henry
Kighley, of Kighley, Yorkshire ; (2) Elizabeth, daughter of Edward Boughton of,
Causton, Warwickshire, and widow of Sir Richard (?) Wortley (Collins' *Peerage*, ed.
Brydges, i, 323). William Cavendish, second Earl, died on June 20, 1628. Pomfret's
Life of Christian, Countess of Devonshire, which is largely quoted by Collins and Ken-
net, well deserves perusal. Some account of the circumstances of her marriage is given
in Lodge's *Illustrations of English History*, vol. iii, p. 232. ' The wench is a pretty red-
headed wench, and her portion is £7,000 ' write the Earl and Countess of Arundel to
the Earl of Shrewsbury.
  William, third Earl of Devonshire, died in 1684 ; his son of the same name, who married the Duke of Ormond's daughter, was the first Duke of Devonshire. Collins, ed.
Brydges, vol. i.
[2] The statement originally printed in the text was ' five sons and five daughters, whereof five, viz. three sons and two daughters, died young '. It was corrected by hand
before publication.

His elder son Charles, Viscount of Mansfield, married the eldest daughter and heir of Mr. Richard Rogers, by whom he had but one daughter, who died soon after her birth ; and he died also without any other issue.[1]

His second son Henry, now Earl of Ogle, married Francis the eldest daughter of Mr. William Pierrepont, by whom he hath had three sons and four daughters. Two sons were born before their natural time ; the third, Henry, Lord Mansfield, is alive ; the four daughters are, the Lady Elizabeth, Lady Frances, Lady Margaret, and Lady Catherine.[2]

My Lord's three daughters were thus married. The eldest, Lady Jane, married Charles Cheiney, Esq., descended of a very noble and ancient family ; by whom she hath one son and two daughters. The second, Lady Elizabeth, married John, now Earl of Bridgwater, then Lord Brackley, and eldest son to John, then Earl of Bridgwater ; who died in childbed, and left five sons and one daughter, whereof the eldest son John, Lord Brackley, married the Lady Elizabeth, only daughter and child to James, then Earl of Middlesex.

My Lord's third daughter, the Lady Frances, married Oliver, Earl of Bullingbrook, and hath had no child yet.[3]

After the death of my Lord's first wife, who died the 17th of April in the year 1643, he married me, Margaret, daughter to Thomas Lucas of St. John's, near Colchester, in Essex, Esq., but hath no issue by me.

And this is the posterity of the three sons of Sir William Cavendish, my Lord's grandfather by his father's side. The three daughters were disposed of as followeth :

1 Charles, Viscount Mansfield, died in 1659. On June 15, 1659, Nicholas writes to Newcastle condoling with him on his recent loss (*Calendar of Domestic State Papers*, 1659, p. 374). His widow married Charles Stuart, Duke of Richmond. On the Rogers family, see Clarendon, *Rebellion*, vii, 95, and Christie's *Life of Shaftesbury*, vol. i, Appendix, pp. xiii, xxi.

2 This Henry, Earl of Ogle, succeeded to the title of Duke of Newcastle on his father's death in 1676, and died on July 26, 1691. The *Second Report of the Royal Commission on Historical MSS.* gives abstracts of some of his letters now in the possession of Earl Spencer (p. 17). Others are printed in vol. ii of the *Portland MSS*. His son Henry, Lord Mansfield, died in 1680. The Duke by his will settled all his real estate on his third daughter Margaret and her heirs, who married John Holles, Earl of Clare, created Duke of Newcastle in 1694. Collins' *Historical Collections*, pp. 47–179.

3 These ladies were left in England when their father retired to the Continent after the battle of Marston Moor ; they were in Welbeck when it surrendered to the Earl of Manchester. (*Manchester's Quarrel with Cromwell*, Camden Society, p. 6). Lady Jane and Lady Frances wrote to Lord Fairfax on April 17, 1645, thanking him for his favour and protection (*Fairfax Correspondence*, iii, 194). There is in Davenant's works (p. 291) a short poem on the marriage of Lady Jane. Lady Elizabeth's marriage, which has been before referred to (p. 74), took place in 1639. Lord Brackley performed the elder brother in Milton's *Comus*.

The eldest, Frances Cavendish, married Sir Henry Pierrepont of Holm Pierrepont, in the county of Nottingham, by whom she had two sons, whereof the first died young ; the second, Robert, after Earl of Kingston-upon-Hull, married Gertrude, the eldest daughter and co-heir to Henry Talbot, fourth son to George, Earl of Shrewsbury, by whom he had five sons and three daughters, whereof the eldest son, Henry, now Marquess of Dorchester, hath had two wives ; the first Cecilia, eldest daughter to the Lord Viscount Bayning, by whom he had several children, of which there are living only two daughters ; the eldest Anne, who married John Ross, only son to John now Earl of Rutland ; the second, Grace, who is unmarried. His second wife was Catherine, second daughter to James, Earl of Derby, by whom he has no issue living.[1]

The second son of the Earl of Kingston, William, married the sole daughter and heir of Sir Thomas Harries, by whom he had issue five sons and five daughters, whereof two sons and two daughters died unmarried. The other six are : [2]

Robert, the eldest, who married Elizabeth, daughter and co-heir to Sir John Evelyn, by whom he has three sons, and one daughter. The second son George, and the third Gervase, are yet unmarried.

The eldest daughter of William Pierrepont, Frances, is married to my Lord's now only son and heir, Henry, Earl of Ogle, as before is mentioned.

The second, Grace, is married to Gilbert, now Earl of Clare, by whom he hath issue two sons and three daughters.[3]

The third, Gertrude, is unmarried.

The third son of the Earl of Kingston, Francis Pierrepont,

---

[1] Robert, Earl of Kingston, died on July 30, 1643, in the manner described on page 27 of this *Life*. Henry, Marquis of Dorchester, is frequently mentioned in the *Memoirs of Mrs. Hutchinson*, see vol. i, 164 ; vol. ii, 168. Lady Roos was divorced by Act of Parliament in 1668 : Vide Collins' *Peerage*, ed. Brydges, i, 480, and Clarendon's *Life : Continuation*, 999-1008.

[2] William Pierrepont, whose character is sketched in the *Memoirs of Colonel Hutchinson*. The three sons of Robert Pierrepont, mentioned above, grandsons of William Pierrepont, became in succession Earls of Kingston, and the third, Evelyn, was the first Duke of that name and the father of Lady Mary Wortley Montague. Gervase, third son of William Pierrepont, became in 1703 Lord Pierrepont, but died without issue.

[3] Gilbert, third Earl of Clare, 1633-1689. His son, John Holles, married Margaret, daughter of Henry Cavendish, second Duke of Newcastle ; inherited the estates of his father-in-law, and in 1694 obtained the title of Duke of Newcastle. Grace, fourth and youngest daughter of this Gilbert, Earl of Clare, was the mother of Henry Pelham the statesman, and Thomas Pelham, heir of his uncle, John Holles, created Duke of Newcastle in 1715.

married Elizabeth the eldest daughter of Mr. Bray, by whom
he had issue one son and one daughter.[1]   The son, Robert,
married Anne, the daughter of Henry Murray.   The daughter,
Frances, married William Paget, eldest son to William, Lord
Paget.

The fourth son of the Earl of Kingston, Gervase, is unmarried.

The fifth son, George Pierrepont, married the daughter
of Mr. Jonas, by whom he had two sons unmarried, Henry
and Samuel.

The three daughters of the said Earl of Kingston are, Frances
the eldest who was married to Philip Rolleston ; the second,
Mary, died young ; the third, Elizabeth, is unmarried.

The second daughter of Sir William Cavendish, Elizabeth,
married the Earl of Lennox, uncle to King James ; by whom
she had only one daughter, the Lady Arabella, who against
King James' commands (she being, after him and his children,
the next heir to the Crown) married William, the second son
to the Earl of Hertford ; for which she was put into the
Tower, where not long after she died.[2]

The youngest daughter, Mary Cavendish, married Gilbert
Talbot, second son to George, Earl of Shrewsbury ; who
after the decease of his father, and his elder brother Francis,
who died without issue, became Earl of Shrewsbury ; by
whom she had issue four sons and three daughters ; the
sons all died in their infancy, but the daughters were married [3].

The eldest, Mary Talbot, married William Herbert, Earl
of Pembroke, by whom (some eighteen years after her marriage)
she had one son, who died young [4].

The second daughter, Elizabeth, married Sir Henry Gray,
after Earl of Kent (the fourth Earl of England) by whom she
had no issue [5].

---

1 For some account of Francis Pierrepont see the *Memoirs of Colonel Hutchinson*,
i, 194 ; ii, 177. His widow Alisamon married Sir John Read in 1662, and was badly
treated by him. See her petition in the *Eighth Report of the Historical Manuscripts
Commission*, p. 136.

2 Margaret, sister of Henry VIII, married Matthew, Earl of Lennox, and became
the mother of Henry Stuart, Lord, and Charles Stuart, Earl of Lennox. The latter
married Elizabeth Cavendish in 1574, against the commands of Queen Elizabeth. Arabella Stuart, born in 1575, married William Seymour in 1610, and died in 1615. Cooper's
Life of Arabella Stuart.

3 Gilbert, seventh Earl of Shrewsbury, died in 1616.

4 This marriage took place in 1606. Clarendon in his character of the Earl (*Rebellion*, i, 120) says ' He paid much too dear for his wife's fortune by taking her person
into the bargain '.

5 The Earl of Kent died in 1639, the Countess on December 7, 1651. After the Earl's
death, John Selden, according to Aubrey, married the Countess, but ' never owned the

The third and youngest daughter, Aletheia, married Thomas Howard, Earl of Arundel, the first earl, and Earl Marshal of England ; by whom she left two sons, James, who died beyond the seas without issue ; and Henry, who married Elizabeth, daughter of Esmé Stuart, Duke of Lennox ; by whom he had issue several sons and one daughter ; whereof the eldest son Thomas (since the restoration of King Charles the Second) was restored to the dignity of his ancestors, viz. Duke of Norfolk, next to the royal family, the first Duke of England[1]

And this is briefly the pedigree of my dear Lord and husband, from his grandfather by his father's side. Concerning his kindred and alliances by his mother, who was Katherine daughter to Cuthbert, Lord Ogle, they are so many, that it is impossible for me to enumerate them all, my Lord being by his mother related to the chief of the most ancient families of Northumberland, and other the northern parts ; only this I may mention, that my Lord is a peer of the realm, from the first year of King Edward the Fourth his reign[2].

marriage till after her death upon some law account '. Aubrey terms her an ' ingeniose lady ', and there is in *Mercurius Politicus* for May 10–17, 1655, a curious advertisement to prove it : ' That excellent Cordial, called the Countess of Kent's powder, approved by long experience of the nobility. gentry, and best physicians of this nation, in any malign disease, Plague, Small Pox, Burning Fevers, Wind, Colic, Women in Labour, Children newly born, etc. It is now made by one Mistress Williamson, living in Whitefriars, near the late Countess's house, who was a servant to her, and for many years compounded it by her Lady's direction. The whole stock of powder, and of the ingredients left by the Countess, was, after her death, given to the said Mistress Williamson by Mr. Selden, her Ladyship's executor. This notice is ʃpublished because of the many counterfeit powders uttered up and down by apothecaries and others, under the same name, to the intent that it may be known where the right powder is to be had.'

[1] Thomas, Earl of Arundel, was born in 1592, and died in 1646. He collected the Arundel Marbles, and was commander of the King's army in the campaign of 1639 against the Scots. His character is described by Clarendon (*Rebellion*, i, 118) and by Sir Edward Walker (*Historical Collections*, p. 209). His son Henry married Elizabeth Stuart in 1626, became Earl of Arundel on his father's death, and died in 1652. Thomas was restored to the title of Duke of Norfolk in 1664.

[2] Some account of the Ogle family is given by Collins in his *Historical Collections of the Noble Families of Cavendish, Holles, Vere, Harley, and Ogle*.

Containing several Essays and Discourses Gathered
from the Mouth of my noble Lord and Husband.

With some few notes of mine own.
I have heard my Lord say :

I

That those which command the wealth of a kingdom, command the hearts and hands of the people.

II

That he is a great monarch, who hath a sovereign command over Church, laws, and arms ; and he a wise monarch, that employs his subjects for their own profit (for their profit is his), encourages tradesmen, and assists and defends merchants.

III

That it is a part of prudence in a commonwealth or kingdom to encourage drainers ; for drowned lands are only fit to maintain and increase some wild ducks, whereas being drained, they are able to afford nourishment and food to cattle, besides the producing of several sorts of fruit and corn.

IV

That, without a well-ordered force, a prince doth but reign upon the courtesy of others.

V

That great princes should not suffer their chief cities to be stronger than themselves.

R

VI

That great princes are half-armed, when their subjects are unarmed, unless it be in time of foreign wars.

VII

That the prince is richest, who is master of the purse ; and he strongest that is master of the arms ; and he wisest that can tell how to save the one, and use the other.

VIII

That great princes should be the only paymasters of their soldiers, and pay them out of their own treasuries ; for all men follow the purse ; and so they'll have both the civil and martial power in their hands.

IX

That great monarchs should rather study men, than books ; for all affairs or business are amongst men.

X

That a prince should advance foreign trade or traffic to the utmost of his power, because no state or kingdom can be rich without it ; and where subjects are poor, the sovereign can have but little.

XI

That trade and traffic brings honey to the hive ; that is to say, riches to the commonwealth ; whereas other professions are so far from that, that they rather rob the commonwealth, instead of enriching it.

XII

That it is not so much unseasonable weather that makes the country complain of scarcity, but want of commerce ; for whensoever commodities are cheap, it is a sign that com-

merce is decayed ; because the cheapness of them shows a
scarcity of money. For example, put the case five men came
to market to buy a horse, and each of them had no more but
ten pounds, the seller can receive no more than what the
buyer has, but must content himself with those ten pounds,
if he be necessitated to sell his horse : but if each one of the
buyers had an hundred pounds to lay out for a horse, the
seller might receive as much. Thus commodities are cheap
or dear, according to the plenty or scarcity of money ; and
though we had mines of gold and silver at home, and no traffic
into foreign parts, yet we should want necessaries from other
nations, which proves that no nation can live or subsist well,
without foreign trade and commerce ; for God and nature
have ordered it so, that no particular nation is provided with
all things.

XIII

That merchants by carrying out more commodities than
they bring in, that is to say, by selling more than they buy,
do enrich a state or kingdom with money, that hath none in
its own bowels ; but what kingdom or state soever hath mines
of gold and silver, there merchants buy more than they sell,
to furnish and accommodate it with necessary provisions.

XIV

That debasing, and setting a higher value upon money, is
but a present shift of poor and needy princes ; and doth more
hurt for the future, than good for the present.

XV

That foreign commerce causes frequent voyages, and
frequent voyages make skilful and experienced seamen, and
skilful seamen are a brazen wall to an island.

XVI

That he is the powerfullest monarch that hath the best
shipping ; and that a prince should hinder his neighbours as
much as he can, from being strong at sea.

XVII

That wise statesmen ought to understand the laws, customs, and trade of the commonwealth, and have good intelligence both of foreign transactions and designs, and of domestic factions ; also they ought to have a treasury, and well-furnished magazine.

XVIII

That it is a great matter in a state or kingdom, to take care of the education of youth, to breed them so, that they may know first how to obey, and then how to command and order affairs wisely.

XIX

That it is great wisdom in a state, to breed and train up good statesmen : as, first, to let them be some time at the Universities : next, to put them to the Inns of Court, that they may have some knowledge of the laws of the land ; then to send them to travel with some ambassador, in the quality of secretary ; and let them be agents or residents in foreign countries. Fourthly, to make them Clerks of the Signet, or Council : and lastly, to make them Secretaries of State, or give them some other employment in state affairs.

XX

That there should be more praying, and less preaching ; for much preaching breeds faction, but much praying causes devotion [1].

XXI

That young people should be frequently catechised, and that wise men, rather than learned, should be chosen heads of schools and colleges.

---

[1] A similar opinion about preaching inspired the Royal Declaration against controversial preaching issued in 1628, and the King's instructions in 1629, imposing restrictions on all lecturers and preachers, and substituting catechizing of children for afternoon sermons. See Heylin's remarks on the feeling of the Puritans with respect to these measures (*Cyprianus Anglicus*, 202).

XXII

That the more divisions there are in Church and State, the more trouble and confusion is apt to ensue ; wherefore too many controversies and disputes in the one, and too many law cases and pleadings in the other, ought to be avoided and suppressed.

XXIII

That disputes and factions amongst statesmen are fore-runners of future disorders, if not total ruins.

XXIV

That all books of controversies should be writ in Latin, that none but the learned may read them, and that there should be no disputations but in schools, lest it breed factions amongst the vulgar, for disputations and controversies are a kind of civil war, maintained by the pen, and often draw out the sword soon after. Also that all prayer-books should be writ in the native language ; that excommunications should not be too frequent for every little and petty trespass ; that every clergyman should be kind and loving to his parishioners, not proud and quarrelsome.

XXV

That ceremony is nothing in itself, and yet doth everything ; for without ceremony there would be no distinction, neither in Church nor State.

XXVI

That orders and professions ought not to entrench upon each other, lest in time they make a confusion amongst themselves [1].

XXVII

That in a well-ordered state or government, care should be

[1] Compare Clarendon's remarks (Book iv, sect. 38) on the encroachments of the common lawyers on the Church.

taken lest any degree or profession whatsoever swell too big, or grow too numerous, it being not only a hindrance to those of the same profession, but a burden to the commonwealth, which cannot be well if it exceeds in extremes.

XXVIII

That the taxes should not be above the riches of the commonwealth, for that must upon necessity breed factions and civil wars, by reason a general poverty united, is far more dangerous than a private purse ; for though their wealth be small, yet their unity and combination makes them strong, so that, being armed with necessity, they become outrageous with despair.

XXIX

That heavy taxes upon farms ruin the nobility and gentry ; for if the tenant be poor, the landlord cannot be rich, he having nothing but his rents to live on.

XXX

That it is not so much laws and religion, nor rhetoric, that keeps a state or kingdom in order, but arms ; which if they be not employed to an evil use, keep up the right and privileges both of Crown, Church, and State.

XXXI

That no equivocation should be used either in Church or Law ; for the one causes several opinions, to the disturbance of men's consciences ; the other long and tedious suits, to the disturbance of men's private affairs : and both do oftentimes ruin and impoverish the state.

XXXII

That in cases of robberies and murders, it is better to be severe than merciful ; for the hanging of a few will save the lives and purses of many.

XXXIII

That many laws do rather entrap than help the subject.

XXXIV

That no martial law should be executed, but in an army.

XXXV

That the sheriffs in this kingdom of England have been so expensive in liveries and entertainments in the time of their sheriffalty, as it hath ruined many families that had but indifferent estates [1].

XXXVI

That the cutting down of timber in the time of rebellion has been an inestimable loss to this kingdom, by reason of shipping; for though timber might be had out of foreign countries that would serve for the building of ships, yet there is none of such a temper as our English oak; it being not only strong and large, but not apt to splint, which renders the ships of other nations much inferior to ours: and that therefore it would be very beneficial for the kingdom, to set out some lands for the bearing of such oaks, by sowing of acorns, and then transplanting them: which would be like a storehouse for shipping, and bring an incomparable benefit to the kingdom, since in shipping consists our greatest strength they being the only walls that defend an island [2].

[1] In 1647 Sir Anthony Ashley Cooper was Sheriff of Wiltshire. He says, in his *Diary*, that, when the judges came to Salisbury during his term of office, ' I had sixty men in livery and kept an ordinary for all gentlemen, four shillings, and two shillings for blue men. I paid for all.' Sir Hugh Cholmley also, in his Memoirs, states, that being Sheriff of Yorkshire in 1625 cost Sir Richard Cholmley £1000. Cromwell endeavoured to put a stop to this expenditure. It was ordered by the Council of State on February 13, 1656, ' that, as for many years complaints have been made of the excessive charges burdening the office of sheriff, through the example of some, which discourage those employed, the Major-Generals appoint in their respective counties a troop of horse to attend the sheriff at the assizes, to wait on the judge, and perform the services that have been required of the sheriff's men, and to demean themselves with all respect and diligence. That no gratuity be given by any sheriff to the judge's clerks or officers, nor any table or entertainment kept for them or for the justices of the peace at the assizes, at the sheriff's charge.'—*Calendar of Domestic State Papers*, 1655-6, p. 175. Heath says that it was pretended indeed that this substitution of troopers for men in livery was to lessen the charge of the place, ' but in truth, the Protector, knowing he could not be served faithfully by the gentry, would name such, no matter whom, as he could confide in, and the expense of retinue and treating the judges being taken off, a yeoman or tradesman of the well-affected might serve the turn and make profit of his place, as in all other offices of the Commonwealth.'—Heath, *Chronicle*, p. 730, ed. 1663.

[2] ' This ', says Mr. Lower, ' is the first allusion I have met with to the " Wooden Walls of Old England ".'

XXXVII

That the nobility and gentry in this kingdom have done themselves a great injury, by giving away (out of a petty pride) to the commonalty, the power of being juries and justices of peace : for certainly they cannot but understand that that must of necessity be an act of great consequence and power, which concerns men's lives, lands, and estates.

XXXVIII

That it is no act of prudence to make poor and mean persons governors or commanders, either by land or sea ; by reason their poverty causes them to take bribes, and so betray their trust : at best, they are apt to extort, which is a great grievance to the people. Besides, it breeds envy in the nobility and gentry, who by that means rise into factions, and cause disturbances in a state or commonwealth ; wherefore the best way is to choose rich and honourable persons (or, at least, gentlemen) for such employments, who esteem fame and honourable actions above their lives ; and if they want skill, they must get such under-officers as have more than themselves, to instruct them.

XXXIX

That great princes should consider, before they make war against foreign nations, whether they be able to maintain it : for if they be not able, then it is better to submit to an honourable peace, than to make war to their great disadvantage : but if they be able to maintain war, then they'll force (in time) their enemies to submit and yield to what terms and conditions they please.

XL

That, when a state or government is ensnarled [1] and troubled, it is more easy to raise the common people to a factious mutiny, than to draw them to a loyal duty.

---

[1] Ensnarle, i.e. ensnare or entangle—Halliwell.

XLI

That in a kingdom where subjects are apt to rebel, no offices or commands should be sold ; for those that buy, will not only use extortion, and practise unjust ways to make out their purchase, but be ablest to rebel, by reason they are more for private gain than the public good ; for it is probable their principles are like their purchases.

But, that all magistrates, officers, commanders, heads and rulers, in what profession soever, both in Church and State, should be chosen according to their abilities, wisdom, courage, piety, justice, honesty, and loyalty ; and then they'll mind the public good more than their particular interest.

XLII

That those which have politic designs are for the most part dishonest, by reason their designs tend more to interest than justice.

XLIII

That great princes should only have great, noble, and rich persons to attend them, whose purses and power may always be ready to assist them.

XLIV

That a poor nobility is apt to be factious ; and a numerous nobility is a burden to a commonwealth [1].

XLV

That in a monarchical government, to be for the king is to be for the commonwealth ; for when head and body are divided, the life of happiness dies, and the soul of peace is departed.

XLVI

That, as it is a great error in a state to have all affairs put

[1] Compare Sir Edward Walker's *Observations upon the Inconveniences that have attended the frequent Promotions to Titles of Honour, since King James came to the Crown of England* (*Historical Discourses*, p. 291).

into gazettes (for it over-heats the people's brains, and makes them neglect their private affairs, by over-busying themselves with state business) ; so it is great wisdom for a Council of State to have good intelligences (although they be bought with great cost and charges) as well of domestic, as foreign affairs and transactions, and to keep them in private for the benefit of the commonwealth [1].

XLVII

That there is no better policy for a prince to please his people, than to have many holidays for their ease, and order several sports and pastimes for their recreation, and to be himself sometime spectator thereof ; by which means he'll not only gain love and respect from the people, but busy their minds in harmless actions, sweeten their natures, and hinder them from factious signs [2].

XLVII

That it is more difficult and dangerous for a prince or commander to raise an army in such a time when the country is embroiled in a civil war, than to lead out an army to fight a battle ; for when an army is raised, he hath strength ; but in raising it hath none.

[1] Burnet praises Cromwell for his excellent intelligence. 'He laid it down for a maxim to spare no cost or charge in order to procure intelligence. . . . He had on all occasions very good intelligence : he knew everything that passed in the King's little court, and yet none of his spies were discovered but one only.'

[2] The same idea inspired James I and his son when they published in 1618 and 1633 respectively their *Declarations concerning Lawful Sports* to be used. The prohibition of lawful sports, says the *Declaration*, 'barreth the common and meaner sort of people from using such exercises, as may make their bodies more able for war when we or our successor shall have occasion to use them ; and in place thereof, sets up filthy tipplings and drunkenness, and breeds a number of idle and discontented speeches in their ale-houses.' When the Long Parliament abolished the observation of Christmas and other holy-days, it was obliged to ordain days of recreation, 'that all scholars, apprentices, and other servants shall, with the leave and approbation of their masters respectively first had and obtained, have such convenient relaxation and recreation from their constant and ordinary labours on every second Tuesday in the month, throughout the year, as formerly they have used to have on such aforesaid festivals, commonly called Holy-days. And that masters of all scholars, apprentices, and servants shall grant unto them respectively such time for their recreations on the aforesaid second Tuesdays in every month, as they may conveniently spare from their extraordinary and necessary services and occasions.' This ordinance was passed on June 8, 1647, and on the renewed petition of the apprentices, followed by another on June 28, which made its observance compulsory by ordaining that the windows of all shops and warehouses should be shut from eight in the morning till eight in the evening, and by adding the clause 'That no master shall wilfully detain or withhold his apprentice or other servant within doors, or from his recreation, in his usual duty or service on the said day of recreation, unless market-days, fair days, or other extraordinary occasion ; yet so as such master shall allow unto such apprentice or other servant, one other day instead', etc. Provisions were also added against the abuse of such days by riots or other misconduct.

XLIX

That good commanders, and experienced soldiers, are like skilful fencers, who defend with prudence, and assault with courage, and kill their enemies by art, not trusting their lives to chance or fortune ; for as a little man with skill may easily kill an ignorant giant, so a small army that hath experienced commanders may easily overcome a great army that hath none.

L

That gallant men having no employment for heroic actions become lazy, as hating any other business ; whereas cowards and base persons are only active and stirring in times of peace, working ill designs to breed factions, and cause disturbances in a commonwealth.

LI

That there have been many questions and disputes concerning the governments of princes ; as, whether they ought to govern by love, or fear ?   But the best way of government is, and has always been, by just rewards and punishments ; for that state which cannot tell how and when to punish and reward, does not know how to govern, by reason all the world is governed that way.

LII

That if the ancient Britons had had skill according to their courage, they might have conquered all the world, as the Romans did.

LIII

That it would be very beneficial for great princes to be sometimes present in courts of judicature, to examine the causes of their poor subjects, and find out the extortions and corruptions of magistrates and officers ; by which glorious act they would gain much love and fame from the people.

LIV

That it would be very advantageous for subjects, and not in the least prejudicial to the sovereign, to have a general register in every county, for the entry of all manner of deeds, and conveyance of land between party and party, and offices of record ; for by this means, whosoever buys, would see clearly what interest and title there is in any land he intends to purchase, whereby he shall be assured that the sale made to him is good and firm, and prevent many lawsuits touching the title of his purchase [1].

LV

That there should be a limitation for lawsuits ; and that the longest suits should not last above two terms, at length not above a year ; which would certainly be a great benefit to the subjects in general, though not to lawyers ; and though some politicians object, that the more the people is busy about their private affairs, the less time have they to make disturbance in the public ; yet this is but a weak argument, since lawsuits are as apt to breed factions, as anything else ; for they bring people into poverty, that they know not how to live, which must of necessity breed discontent, and put them upon ill designs.

LVI

That power, for the most part, does more than wisdom ; for fools, with power, seem wise ; whereas wise men, without power, seem fools ; and this is the reason that the world takes power for wisdom, and the want of power for foolishness.

LVII

That a valiant man will not refuse an honourable duel ; nor a wise man fight upon a fool's quarrel.

---

1 This idea of the desirability of a public register for the transfer of land was very frequently put forward in the seventeenth century. *The Harleian Miscellany* contains *Reasons and Proposals for a Registry of all Deeds or Encumbrances to be had in every County*, etc., by Nicholas Philpot, 1671. There is also a tract in the same collection against such registers by William Pierrepont. It is one of the proposals made in the pamphlet entitled *The Grand Concern of England Explained*, 1673. Yarranton brings forward the same plan in *England's Improvement by Sea and Land*, 1677. Sir William Petty, in his *Political Arithmetic*, and Sir Robert Moray, also argued in favour of a system of registers.

LVIII

That men are apt to find fault with each other's actions ; believing they prove themselves wise in finding fault with their neighbours.

LIX

That a wise man will draw several occasions to the point of his design, as a burning glass doth the several beams of the sun.

LX

That although actions may be prudently designed, and valiantly performed ; yet none can warrant the issue ; for Fortune is more powerful than prudence, and had Cæsar not been fortunate, his valour and prudence would never have gained him so much applause.

LXI

That ill fortune makes wise and honest men seem fools and knaves ; but good fortune makes fools and knaves seem wise and honest men.

LXII

That ill fortune doth oftener succeed good, than good fortune succeeds ill ; for those that have ill fortune do not so easily recover it, as those that have good fortune are apt to lose it.

LXIII

That he had observed, that seldom any person did laugh, but it was at the follies or misfortunes of other men ; by which we may judge of their good natures.

LXIV

I have heard my Lord say, that when he was in banishment, he had nothing left him but a clear conscience, by which he had and did still conquer all the armies of misfortunes that ever seized upon him.

LXV

Also I have heard him say, that he was never beholding to Lady Fortune; for he had suffered on both sides, although he never was but on one side.

LXVI

I have heard him say, that his father one time, upon some discourse of expenses, should tell him, it was but just that every man should have his time.

LXVII

I have heard my Lord say, that bold soliciting and intruding men shall gain more by their importunate petitions, than modest honest men shall get by silence (as being loath to offend or be too troublesome) both in the manner and matter of their requests. The reason is, said he, that great princes will rather grant sometimes an unreasonable suit, than be tired with frequent petitions, and hindered from their ordinary pleasures. And when I asked my Lord, whether the grants of such importunate suits were fitly and properly placed ? he answered, not so well as those that are placed upon due consideration, and upon trial and proof.

LXVIII

I have heard my Lord say, that it is a great error and weak policy in a state to advance their enemies, and endeavour to make them friends, by bribing them with honours and offices, saying 'they are shrewd men, and may do the state much hurt': and on the other side, to neglect their friends, and those that have done them great service, saying 'they are honest men, and mean the state no harm'. For this kind of policy comes from the heathen, who prayed to the devil, and not to God, by reason they supposed God was good, and would hurt no creature ; but the devil they flattered and

worshipped out of fear, lest he should hurt them. But by
this foolish policy, said he, they most commonly increase their
enemies, and lose their friends. For, first, it teaches men to
observe, that the only way to preferment, is to be against the
state or government. Next, since all that are factious cannot
be rewarded or preferred (by reason a state hath more subjects,
than rewards or preferments) there must of necessity be numerous enemies ; for when their hopes of reward fail them, they
grow more factious and inveterate than ever they were at
first. Wherefore the best policy in a state or government,
said my Lord, is to reward friends, and punish enemies, and
prefer the honest before the factious ; and then all will be
real friends, and proffer their honest service, either out of pure
love and loyalty, or in hopes of advancement, seeing there
is none but by serving the state.

LXIX

I have heard him say several times, that his love to his
gracious master King Charles the Second was above the love
he bore to his wife, children, and all his posterity, nay, to his
own life : and when, since his return into England, I answered
him that I observed his gracious master did not love him so
well as he loved him ; he replied, that he cared not whether
his Majesty loved him again or not ; for he was resolved to
love him [1].

LXX

I asking my Lord one time, what kind of fate it was that
restored our gracious King, Charles the Second, to his throne,
he answered, it was a blessed kind of fate. I replied, that I
had observed a perfect contrariety between the fortunes of his
royal father, of blessed memory, and him. For as there was
a division amongst the generality of the people, in the reign
of King Charles the First, tending to his destruction ; so
there was a general combination and agreement between them
in King Charles the Second his restoration ; and as there

---

[1] In the spirit of Butler's lines :

Loyalty is still the same,
Whether it win or lose the game,
True as the dial to the sun,
Although it be not shined upon.

was a general malice amongst the people against the father to depose him ; so there was a general love for the son to enthrone him. My Lord answered, I had observed something, but not all ; for, said he, there was a necessity for the people to desire and restore King Charles the Second ; but there was no necessity to murder King Charles the First. For the kingdom being through so many alterations and changes of government, divided into several factions and parties, was at last hurried into such a confusion, that it was impossible in that manner to subsist, or hold out any longer. Which confusion having opened the people's eyes, the generality being tired with the evil effects and consequences of their unsettled governments under unjust usurpers, and frightened with the apprehension of future dangers, began to call to mind the happy times, when in an uninterrupted peace they enjoyed their own, under the happy reign of their lawful sovereigns ; and hereupon with an unanimous consent recalled and restored our now gracious King ; which, although it was opposed by some factious parties, yet the generality of the people outweighed the rest ; neither was the royal party wanting in their endeavours.

LXXI

Asking my Lord one time, whether it was easy or difficult to govern a state or kingdom ? he answered me, that most states were governed by secret policy and so with difficulty ; for those that govern, are (at least should be) wiser than the state or commonwealth they govern. I replied, that in my opinion, a state was easily governed, if their government was like unto God's ; that is to say, if governors did reward and punish according to the desert. My Lord answered, I said well ; but he added, the follies of the people are many times too hard for the prudence of the governor ; like as the sins of men work more evil effects in them, than the grace of God works good ; for if this were not, there would be more good than bad, which, alas, experience proves otherwise.

LXXII

Some gentlemen making a complaint to my Lord, that some he employed in his Majesty's affairs were too hasty and over-busy, my Lord told them, that he would rather choose such persons for his Majesty's service as were over-active, than such that would be fuller of questions than actions. The same he would do for his own particular affairs.

LXXIII

Some condemning my Lord for having Roman Catholics and Scots in his army ; he answered them, that he did not examine their opinions in religion, but looked more upon their honesty and duty ; for certainly there were honest men and loyal subjects amongst Roman Catholics,as well as Protestants; and amongst Scots as well as English. Nevertheless, my Lord, as he was for the King, so he was also for the orthodox Church of England, as sufficiently appears by the care he took in ordering the Church government, mentioned in the history. To which purpose, when my Lord was walking one time with some of his officers in the church at Durham, and wondered at the greatness and strength of the pillars that supported that structure, my brother, Sir Charles Lucas, who was then with him, told my Lord, that he must confess those pillars` were very great, and of a vast strength ; but, said he, your Lordship is a far greater pillar of the Church than all these. Which certainly was also a real truth, and would have more evidently appeared, had Fortune favoured my Lord more than she did.

LXXIV

My Lord being in banishment, I told him, that he was happy in his misfortunes, for he was not subject to any state or prince. To which he jestingly answered, that as he was subject to no prince, so he was a prince of no subjects.

LXXV

In some discourse which I had with my Lord concerning princes and their subjects, I declared that I had observed great princes were not like the sun, which sends forth out of itself rays of light, and beams of heat, effects that did both glorify the sun, and nourish and comfort sublunary creatures ;

T

but their glory and splendour proceeded rather from the ceremony which they received from their subjects. To which my Lord answered, that subjects were so far from giving splendour to their princes, that all the honours and titles, in which consists the chief splendour of a subject, were principally derived from them ; for, said he, were there no princes, there would be none to confer honours and titles upon them.

LXXVI

My Lord entertaining one time some gentlemen with a merry discourse, told them, that he would not keep them company except they had done and suffered as much for their King and country as he had. They answered, that they had not a power answerable to my Lord's. My Lord replied, they should do their endeavour according to their abilities. No, said they, if we did, we should be like yourself, lose all, and get but little for our pains.

LXXVII

I being much grieved that my Lord, for his loyalty and honest service, had so many enemies, used sometimes to speak somewhat sharply of them ; but he gently reproving me, said, I should do like experienced seamen, and as they either turn their sails with the wind, or take them down, so should I either comply with time, or abate my passion.

LXXVIII

A soldier's wife, whose husband had been slain in my Lord's army, came one time to beg some relief of my Lord ; who told her, that he was not able to relieve all that had been loyal to his Majesty ; for, said he, my losses are so many, that if I should give away the remainder of my estate, my wife and children would have nothing to live on. She answered, that his Majesty's enemies were preferred to great honours, and had much wealth. Then it is a sign (replied my Lord) that your husband and I were honest men.

LXXIX

A friend of my Lord's complaining that he had done the state much service, but received little reward for it ; my Lord answered him, that states did not usually reward past services : but if he could do some present service, he might perhaps get something ; but, said he, those men are wisest that will be paid beforehand.

LXXX

I observing that in the late Civil Wars, many were desirous to be employed in state's affairs, and at the noise of war endeavoured to be commanders, though but of small parties, asked my Lord the reason thereof, and what advantage they could make by their employments ? My Lord smilingly answered, that for the generality, he knew not what they could get, but danger, loss, and labour for their pains. Then I asked him, whether generals of great armies were ever enriched by their heroic exploits, and great victories ? My Lord answered, that ordinary commanders gained more, and were better rewarded than great generals. To which I added, that I had observed the same in histories, namely, that men of great merit and power had not only no rewards, but were either found fault withal, or laid aside when they had no more business or employment for them, and that I could not conceive any reason for it, but that states were afraid of their power. My Lord answered, the reason was, that it was far more easy to reward under-officers than great commanders.

LXXXI

My Lord having, since the return from his banishment, set up a race of horses, instead of those he lost by the wars, uses often to ride through his park to see his breed. One time it chanced when he went through it, that he espied some labouring men sawing of woods that were blown down by the wind, for some particular uses ; at which my Lord, turning to his attendants, said, that he had been at that work a great part of his life. They not knowing what my Lord meant, but thinking he jested ; I speak very seriously, added he, and not in jest ; for you see that this tree which is blown down by the wind, although it was sound and strong, yet it could not withstand its force ; and now it is down, it must be cut in pieces, and made serviceable for several uses ; whereof some will serve for building, some for paling, some for firing, etc. In the like manner, said he, have I been cut down by the Lady Fortune ; and being not able to resist so powerful a princess, I have been forced to make the best use of my misfortunes, as the chips of my estate.

LXXXII

My Lord discoursing one time with some of his friends, of judging of other men's natures, dispositions, and actions ; and some observing that men could not possibly know or judge of them, the events of men's actions falling out often-times contrary to their intentions ; so that where they hit once, they failed twenty times in their judgments : my Lord answered, that his judgment in that point seldom did miss, although he thought it weaker than theirs. The reason is, said he, because I judge most men to be like myself, that is to say, fools ; when as you do judge them all according to yourself, that is, wise men ; and since there are more fools in the world than wise men, I may sooner guess right than you : for though my judgment roves at random, yet it can never miss of errors ; which yours will never do, except you can dive into other men's follies by the length of your own line, and sound their bottom by the weight of your own plummet, for the depth of folly is beyond the line of wisdom.

Besides, said he, you believe that other men would do as you would have them, or as you would do to them ; wherein you are mistaken, for most men do the contrary. In short, folly is bottomless, and hath no end ; but wisdom hath bounds to all her designs, otherwise she would never compass them :

LXXXIII

My Lord discoursing some time with a learned doctor of divinity concerning faith, said, that in his opinion, the wisest way for a man was to have as little faith as he could for this world, and as much as he could for the next world.

LXXXIV

In some discourse with my Lord, I told him that I did speak sharpest to those I loved best.   To which he jestingly answered, that if so, then he would not have me love him best.

LXXXV

After my Lord's return from a long banishment, when he had been in the country some time, and endeavoured to pick up some gleanings of his ruined estate ; it chanced that the widow of Charles, Lord Mansfield, my Lord's eldest son, afterwards Duchess of Richmond, to whom the said Lord of Mansfield had made a jointure of £2000 a year, died not long after her second marriage.   For whose death, though my Lord was heartily sorry, and would willingly have lost the said money, had it been able to save her life ; yet discoursing one time merrily with his friends, was pleased to say, that though his earthly king and master seemed to have forgot him, yet the King of Heaven had remembered him, for he had given him £2000 a year.

SOME FEW NOTES OF THE AUTHORESS

I

It was far more difficult in the late Civil Wars, for my Lord to raise an army for his Majesty's service, than it was for the Parliament to raise an army against his Majesty. Not only because the Parliament were many, and my Lord but one single person ; but by reason a kingly or monarchical government was then generally disliked, and most part of the kingdom proved rebellious, and assisted the Parliament either with their purses or persons, or both ; when as the army which my Lord raised for the defence and maintenance of the King, and his rights, was raised most upon his own and his friends' interest. For it is frequently seen and known, by woful experience, that rebellious and factious parties do more suddenly and numerously flock together to act a mischievous design, than loyal and honest men to assist or maintain a just cause : and certainly 'tis much to be lamented, that evil men should be more industrious and prosperous than good, and that the wicked should have a more desperate courage, than the virtuous an active valour.

II

I have observed, that many, by flattering poets, have been compared to Cæsar, without desert ; but this I dare freely and without flattery say of my Lord, that though he had not Cæsar's fortune, yet he wanted not Cæsar's courage, nor his prudence, nor his good nature, nor his wit. Nay, in some particulars he did more than Cæsar ever did ; for though Cæsar had a great army, yet he was first set out by the state or senators of Rome, who were masters almost of all the world ; when as my Lord raised his army (as before is mentioned) most upon his own interest (he having many friends and kindred in the northern parts) at such a time when his

gracious King and sovereign was then not master of his own
kingdoms, he being overpowered by his rebellious subjects.

III

I have observed that my noble Lord has always had an
aversion to that kind of policy that now is commonly practised
in the world, which in plain terms is dissembling, flattery,
and cheating, under the cover of honesty, love, and kindness.
But I have heard him say that the best policy is to act justly,
honestly, and wisely, and to speak truly ; and that the old
proverb is true, ' To be wise is to be honest ' ; for, said he,
that man of what condition, quality, or profession soever,
that is once found out to deceive either in words or actions,
shall never be trusted again by wise and honest men.   But,
said he, a wise man is not bound to take notice of all dissem-
blers and their cheating actions, if they do not concern him ;
nay, even of those he would not always take notice, but
choose his time ; for the chief part of a wise man is to time
business well, and to do it without partiality and passion.
But, said he, the folly of the world is so great that one honest
and wise man may be overpowered by many knaves and
fools ; and if so, then the only benefit of a wise man consists
in the satisfaction he finds by his honest and wise actions,
and that he has done what in conscience, honour, and duty,
he ought to do ; and all successors of such worthy persons
ought to be more satisfied in the worth and merit of their
predecessors, than in their title and riches.

IV

I have heard that some noble gentleman (who was servant
to his Highness, then Prince of Wales, our now gracious
sovereign, when my Lord was Governor) should relate, that
whensoever my Lord by his prudent inspection and foresight
did foretell what would come to pass hereafter, it seemed so
improbable to him, that both himself and some others believed
my Lord spoke extravagantly ; but some few years after,
his predictions proved true, and the event did confirm what
his prudence had observed.

V

I have heard that in our late Civil Wars there were many petty skirmishes and fortifications of weak and inconsiderable houses, where some small parties would be shooting and pottering [1] at each other ; an action more proper for bandits or thieves than stout and valiant soldiers ; for I have heard my Lord say, that such small parties divide the body of an army, and by that means weaken it ; whereas the business might be much easier decided in one or two battles, with less ruin both to the country and army. For I have heard my Lord say, that as it is dangerous to divide a limb from the body, so it is also dangerous to divide armies or navies in time of war ; and there are often more men lost in such petty skirmishes than in set battles, by reason those happen almost every day, nay, every hour in several places.

VI

Many in our late Civil Wars had more title than power ; for though they were generals or chief commanders, yet their forces were more like a brigade than a well-formed army ; and their actions were accordingly, not set battles, but petty skirmishes between small parties ; for there were no great battles fought, but by my Lord's army, his being the greatest and best-formed army which his Majesty had.

VII

Although I have observed that it is a usual custom of the world to glorify the present power and good fortune, and vilify ill fortune and low conditions, yet I never heard that my noble Lord was ever neglected by the generality, but was, on the contrary, always esteemed and praised by all ; for he is truly an honest and honourable man, and one that may be relied upon both for trust and truth.

VIII

I have observed that many instead of great actions make only a great noise, and like shallow fords, or empty bladders,

---

[1] ' Pottering ' seems to be used as a synonym for shooting, as we should say ' potting ', and not in the sense of sauntering, or working inefficiently.

sound most when there is least in them, which expresses a flattering partiality, rather than honesty and truth ; for truth and honesty lie at the bottom, and have more action than show.

IX

I have observed, that good fortune adds fame to mean actions, when as ill fortune darkens the splendour of the most meritorious ; for mean persons, plied with good fortune, are more famous than noble persons that are shadowed or darkened with ill fortune ; so that Fortune, for the most part, is Fame's champion.

X

I observe, that as it would be a grief to covetous and miserable persons to be rewarded with honour rather than with wealth, because they love wealth before honour and fame ; so, on the other side, noble, heroic, and meritorious persons prefer honour and fame before wealth ; well knowing, that as infamy is the greatest punishment of unworthiness, so fame and honour is the best reward of worth and merit.

XI

I observe, that spleen and malice, especially in this age, is grown to that height, that none will endure the praise of anybody besides themselves ; nay, they'll rather praise the wicked than the good ; the coward rather than the valiant ; the miserable than the generous ; the traitor than the loyal ; which makes wise men meddle as little with the affairs of the world as ever they can.

XII

I have observed, as well as former ages have done, that meritorious persons, for their noble actions, most commonly get envy and reproach, instead of praise and reward ; unless their fortunes be above envy, as Cæsar's and Alexander's were. But had these two worthies been as unfortunate as they were fortunate, they would have been as much vilified as they are glorified.

XIII

I have observed, that it is more easy to talk than to act; to forget than to remember; to punish than to reward; and more common to prefer flattery before truth, interest before justice, and present service before past.

XIV

I have observed, that many old proverbs are very true, and amongst the rest, this: ' It is better to be at the latter end of a feast than at the beginning of a fray '; for most commonly, those that are in the beginning of a fray get but little of the feast; and those that have undergone the greatest dangers have least of the spoils.

XV

I have observed, that favours of great princes make men often thought meritorious; whereas without them, they would be esteemed but as ordinary persons.

XVI

I observe, that in other kingdoms or countries, to be the chief governor of a province is not only a place of honour, but much profit; for they have a great revenue to themselves; whereas in England, the lieutenancy of a county is barely a title of honour, without profit; except it be the lieutenancy or government of the kingdom of Ireland; especially since the late Earl of Strafford enjoyed that dignity, who settled that kingdom very wisely both for militia and trade.

XVII

I have observed, that those that meddle least in wars, whether civil or foreign, are not only most safe and free from danger, but most secure from losses; and though heroic persons esteem fame before life, yet many there are, that think the wisest way is to be a spectator, rather than an actor, unless they be necessitated to it ; for it is better, say they, to sit on the stool of quiet, than in the chair of troublesome business.

NATURE'S PICTURES

DRAWN BY

FANCY'S PENCIL TO THE LIFE

Written by the thrice noble, illustrious, and excellent Princess, the Lady Marchioness of Newcastle

In this volume there are several feigned stories of natural descriptions, as comical, tragical, and tragi-comical, poetical, romancical, philosophical, and historical, both in prose and verse, some all verse, some all prose, some mixt, partly prose and partly verse. Also there are some morals, and some dialogues; but they are as the advantage loaves of bread to baker's dozen; and a true story at the latter end, wherein there is no feignings

1656

(The Life of the Duchess forms the Eleventh and last Book.)

BOOK XI

AN EPISTLE

I HAVE heard, that some should say my wit seemed as if it would overpower my brain, especially when it works upon philosophical opinions. I am obliged to them for judging my wit stronger than my brain : but I should be sorry that they should think my wit stronger than my reason : but I must tell them that my brain is stronger than my wit, and my reason as strong as the effeminate sex requires.

Again, I have heard some should say, that my writings are none of my own, because when some have visited me, though seldom I receive visits, they have not heard me speak of them, or repeat some of the chapters or verses ; but I believe, if they should desire the best orator to repeat his orations or sermons that he hath spoke *ex tempore*, he shall not do it although but an hour's discourse : for I believe Tully, who I have heard was an eloquent orator, yet could not repeat them over to his auditory. The same is in writers ; for I do believe Homer, as great and excellent poet as it is said he was, could not repeat his poems by heart, nor Virgil, nor Ovid, or any other ; nor Euclid repeat his demonstrations, numerations, and the like without book, nor Aristotle, who, I have heard, was a great philosopher, the explanations of his opinions by heart ; for I have heard that his memory failed in the writing, for that he hath sometimes contradicted himself ; and my Lord, who hath written hundreds of verses, songs, and themes, could not repeat three by heart ; and I have heard him say, that after he hath writ them, he doth so little remember any part in them, that when they have been a short time by, and then read them over, they are new to him. But he is not so forgetful of other things, for he hath an extraordinary memory for received courtesies, or to do any timely good or service, not only to friends, but to strangers. Also he hath an excellent memory concerning the general actions of and in the world. But certainly they that remember their own wit least, have the most of it ; for there is an old saying, and surely true, that the best wits have the worst memory, I mean wit-memory ; for great memories are standing ponds that are made with rain ; so that memory is nothing but the showers of other men's wits ; and those brains are muddy that have not running springs of their own, that issue out still fresh and new. Indeed, it's against nature for natural wits to remember ; for it is impossible that the brain should retain and create ; and we see in nature, death makes way for life ; for if there were no death there would be no new life or lives.

But say I were so witless I could repeat some of my works, I do think it would seem self-conceitedness to mention them ; but since that report, I have spoken more of them than otherwise I should have done, though truly I condemn myself ; for it is an indiscretion, although I was forced to that indiscretion, and I repent it both for the disfiguring of my works, by pulling out a piece here and a piece there, according as my memory could catch hold ; also for troubling, or rather vexing the hearers with such discourses as they delight not in.

Besides, it hath been a long and true observation, that every one had rather speak than listen to what another says ; insomuch as for the most part all mankind run from company to company, not to learn, but to talk, and like bells their tongues as the clappers keep a jangling noise all at once, without method or distinction.

But I hope my indiscretion in speaking of my works to my hearers is not beyond a pardon, for I have not spoke of them, nor parts in them, much nor often, nor to many, but to some particularly, as those I thought did understand poetry, or natural philosophy, or moral philosophy, though I fear not always according as their capacities lay. For I have observed, some understand commonwealths, customs, laws, or the like ; others, the distinguishments of passions, and understand nothing of law ; others, divinity, that understand nothing of temporal government, and so the like of many several studies ; and some may have a rational capacity to most sciences, yet conceive nothing of natural philosophy, as of the first matter, or innated matter, or motions, or figures, or

forms, or infinites, or spirits, or essences, or the like ; nay,
for the most part they conceive little further than an almanac
to know the time by, of which I am ignorant, for I understand
it not. And for poetry, most laugh at it as a ridiculous thing,
especially grave statists, severe moralists, zealous priesthood,
wrangling lawyers, covetous hoarders, or purloiners, or those
that have mechanic natures, and many more, which for the
most part account poetry a toy, and condemn it for a vanity,
an idle employment ; nor have they so much fancy of their
own, as to conceive the poetical fancies of others ; for if they
did, they must needs love poetry ; for poetry is so powerful,
and hath such an attractive beauty, that those that can but
view her perfectly, could not but be enamoured, her charms
do so force affection. But surely those that delight not in
poetry or music, have no divine souls nor harmonious thoughts.
But by those weak observations I have made, I perceive that
as most men have particular understandings, capacities, or
ingenuities, and not a general ; so in their discourses some
can speak eloquently, and not learnedly ; others learnedly
and not eloquently ; some wittily, and neither learned nor
eloquent ; and some will speak neither learnedly, eloquently,
wittily, or rationally. Likewise, some can speak well, but
'tis but for a time, some a longer and some a shorter time,
like several sized candles, are longer or shorter ere they come
to a snuff ; where sometimes some objects or conceits, unex-
pected objections or questions, or the like, do prove as a small
coal got into the tallow of their wit, which makes it bleer [1]
out sooner than otherwise it would do. Also some will speak
wisely upon some subjects, and foolishly upon others.

Likewise some will speak well as it were by chance ; others
in one discourse speak mixtly, now rational, then nonsensely,
at least weakly or obstructedly. But they are great masters
of speech that speak clearly, as I may say, untangled, which
can wind their words from off their tongue without a snarl [2]
or knot, and can keep even sense, like an even thread, or can
work that thread of sense into a flourishing discourse ; and
they have a quick wit that can play with, or on any subject,
which doubtless some can do of those things they never heard,
saw, or thought on, but just when they speak of it. And

[1] Probably 'blear', to make dim, used in the sense of to become dim.
[2] Halliwell gives 'snarle', a snare, and 'snarrel', a hard knot (Cumberland dialect).

some have great capacities, as may be perceived in their discourse : but yet their speech is like those that are lame, which limp and halt, although the ground whereon they go is even, smooth, and firm.   But some have such large capacities, elevated fancies, illuminated souls, and volubility of speech, that they can conceive, create, enlighten, and deliver with that abundance, curiosity, facility, and pleasure, as their conversible company is a heaven, where all worldly delights reside.

But to return to the ground of this *Epistle*.   I desire all my readers and acquaintance to believe, though my words run stumbling out of my mouth, and my pen draws roughly on my paper, yet my thoughts move regular in my brain ; for the several tracks or paths that contemplation hath made on my brain, which paths or tracks are the several ways my thoughts move in, are much smoother than the tongue in my mouth, from whence words flow, or the paper on which my pen writes ; for I have not spoke so much as I have writ, nor writ so much as I have thought.   For I must tell my readers, that nature, which is the best and curiousest worker, hath paved my brain smoother than custom hath oiled my tongue, or variety hath polished my senses, or art hath beaten the paper whereon I write ; for my fancy is quicker that the pen with which I write, insomuch as it is many times lost through the slowness of my hand, and yet I write so fast, as I stay not so long as to make perfect letters.

But if they will not believe my books are my own, let them search the author or authoress : but I am very confident that they will do like Drake, who went so far about, until he came to the place he first set out at.   But for the sake of after ages, which I hope will be more just to me than the present, I will write the true relation of my birth, breeding, and to this part of my life, not regarding carping tongues, or malicious censurers, for I despise them.

MARGARET NEWCASTLE.

A TRUE RELATION

OF MY

BIRTH, BREEDING AND LIFE

By Margaret, Duchess of Newcastle

My father was a gentleman, which title is grounded and given
by merit, not by princes ; and it is the act of time, not favour :
and though my father was not a peer of the realm, yet there
were few peers who had much greater estates, or lived more
noble therewith. Yet at that time great titles were to be
sold, and not at so high rates, but that his estate might have
easily purchased, and was pressed for to take ; but my father
did not esteem titles, unless they were gained by heroic actions,
and the kingdom being in a happy peace with all other nations,
and in itself being governed by a wise king, King James, there
was no employments for heroic spirits ; and towards the latter
end of Queen Elizabeth's reign, as soon as he came to man's
estate, he unfortunately killed one Mr. Brooks in a single duel.
For my father by the laws of honour could do no less than
call him to the field to question him for an injury he did him,
where their swords were to dispute, and one or both of their
lives to decide the argument, wherein my father had the
better ; and though my father by honour challenged him,
with valour fought him, and in justice killed him, yet he suffered more than any person of quality usually doth in cases of
honour ; for though the laws be rigorous, yet the present
princes most commonly are gracious in those misfortunes,
especially to the injured : but my father found it not, for his
exile was from the time of his misfortunes to Queen Elizabeth's
death. For the Lord Cobham being then a great man with
Queen Elizabeth, and this gentleman, Mr. Brooks, a kind of
a favourite, and as I take it brother to the then Lord Cobham,

which made Queen Elizabeth so severe, not to pardon him[1]. But King James of blessed memory graciously gave him his pardon, and leave to return home to his native country, wherein he lived happily, and died peaceably, leaving a wife and eight children, three sons, and five daughters, I being the youngest child he had, and an infant when he died.

As for my breeding, it was according to my birth, and the nature of my sex ; for my birth was not lost in my breeding. For as my sisters was or had been bred, so was I in plenty, or rather with superfluity. Likewise we were bred virtuously, modestly, civilly, honourably, and on honest principles. As for plenty, we had not only for necessity, conveniency, and decency, but for delight and pleasure to a superfluity ; it is true we did not riot, but we lived orderly ; for riot, even in kings' courts and princes' palaces, brings ruin without content or pleasure, when order in less fortunes shall live more plentifully and deliciously than princes that lives in a hurly-burly, as I may term it, in which they are seldom well served. For disorder obstructs ; besides, it doth disgust life, distract the appetites, and yield no true relish to the senses ; for pleasure, delight, peace, and felicity live in method and temperance.

As for our garments, my mother did not only delight to see us neat and cleanly, fine and gay, but rich and costly ; maintaining us to the height of her estate, but not beyond it. For we were so far from being in debt, before these wars, as we were rather beforehand with the world ; buying all with ready money, not on the score. For although after my father's death the estate was divided between my mother and her sons, paying such a sum of money for portions to her daughters, either at the day of their marriage, or when they should come to age ; yet by reason she and her children agreed with a mutual consent, all their affairs were managed so well, as she lived not in a much lower condition than when my father lived. 'Tis true, my mother might have increased her daughters' portions by a thrifty sparing, yet she chose to bestow it on our breeding, honest pleasures, and harmless delights, out of an opinion, that if she bred us with needy

---

[1] This was probably George Brooke, the brother of Lord Cobham, executed for his share in the plot called ' The Bye ', in 1603. I have not been able to find any mention of this duel.

necessity, it might chance to create in us sharking [1] qualities, mean thoughts, and base actions, which she knew my father, as well as herself, did abhor.   Likewise we were bred tenderly, for my mother naturally did strive, to please and delight her children, not to cross or torment them, terrifying them with threats, or lashing them with slavish whips ; but instead of threats, reason was used to persuade us, and instead of lashes, the deformities of vice was discovered, and the graces and virtues were presented unto us.   Also we were bred with respectful attendance, every one being severally waited upon, and all her servants in general used the same respect to her children (even those that were very young) as they did to herself ; for she suffered not her servants, either to be rude before us, or to domineer over us, which all vulgar servants are apt, and ofttimes which some have leave to do.   Likewise she never suffered the vulgar serving-men to be in the nursery among the nursemaids, lest their rude love-making might do unseemly actions, or speak unhandsome words in the presence of her children, knowing that youth is apt to take infection by ill examples, having not the reason of distinguishing good from bad.   Neither were we suffered to have any familiarity with the vulgar servants, or conversation : yet caused us to demean ourselves with an humble civility towards them, as they with a dutiful respect to us.   Not because they were servants were we so reserved ; for many noble persons are forced to serve through necessity ; but by reason the vulgar sort of servants are as ill-bred as meanly born, giving children ill examples and worse counsel [2].

As for tutors, although we had for all sorts of virtues [3], as singing, dancing, playing on music, reading, writing, working, and the like, yet we were not kept strictly thereto, they were

---

[1] Shark, to swindle, to trick dishonestly, to sponge on a person.

[2] The Duchess elsewhere describes the evils of familiarity with servants : ' Others through carelessness make their children fall into the same errors, not instructing them with noble and honourable principles, but suffering them to run about into every dirty office, where the young master must learn to drink and play at cards with the kitchen-boy, and learn to kiss his mother's dirty maid for a mess of cream.   The daughters are danced upon the knee of every clown and serving-man, and hear them talk scurrilous to their maids, which is their compliment of wooing ; and then dancing Sellinger's Round with them in Christmas time, and many other such things, which makes them become like unto like ; and their parents think no harm in it because they are young.'—The World's Olio, p. 79.

[3] Virtues, accomplishments.   According to Mr. Jenkins, in his reprint of this relation in The Cavalier and His Lady, in the copy of this book in the King's Library at the British Museum, the Duchess has with her own hand altered virtues into virtuosos. Accordingly he reads, ' As for tutors, although we had all sorts of virtuosos '.

rather for formality than benefit; for my mother cared not so much for our dancing and fiddling, singing and prating of several languages, as that we should be bred virtuously, modestly, civilly, honourably, and on honest principles.

As for my brothers, of which I had three, I know not how they were bred. First, they were bred when I was not capable to observe, or before I was born; likewise the breeding of men were after different manner of ways from those of women. But this I know, that they loved virtue, endeavoured merit, practised justice, and spoke truth; they were constantly loyal, and truly valiant. Two of my three brothers were excellent soldiers, and martial discipliners, being practised therein; for though they might have lived upon their own estates very honourably, yet they rather chose to serve in the wars under the States of Holland, than to live idly at home in peace: my brother, Sir Thomas Lucas [1], there having a troop of horse; my brother (the youngest) Sir Charles Lucas, serving therein. But he served the States not long, for after he had been at the siege and taking of some towns, he returned home again; and though he had the less experience, yet he was like to have proved the better soldier, if better could have been, for naturally he had a practical genius to the warlike arts, or arts in war, as natural poets have to poetry [2]. But his life was cut off before he could arrive to the true perfection thereof; yet he writ [3] *A Treatise*

---

[1] Knighted, April 14, 1628.

[2] Sir Charles Lucas, according to Clarendon (*Rebellion*, xi, 108), was held as good a commander of horse as the nation had. 'He had been bred in the Low Countries, and always amongst the horse, so that he had little conversation in that court, where great civility was practised and learned. He was very brave in his person, and in a day of battle a gallant man to look upon, and follow; but at all other times and places of a nature not to be lived with, of an ill understanding, of a rough and proud nature, which made him during the time of their being in Colchester more intolerable than the siege, or any fortune that threatened them; yet they all desired to accompany him in his death.' See also the note on his life in the Appendix.

[3] The Duchess wrote the following poem on her brother's death:

An Elegy upon the Death of my Brother.

Dear Brother,
    Thy idea in my mind doth lie,
And is entombed in my sad memory,
Where every day I to thy shrine do go,
And offer tears, which from my eyes do flow;
My heart the fire, whose flames are ever pure,
Shall on Love's altar last while life endure:
My sorrow incense strews of sighs fetched deep,
My thoughts keep watch o'er thy sweet spirit's sleep.
Dear blessed soul, though thou art gone, yet lives
Thy fame on earth, and man thee praises give:
But all's too small: for thy heroic mind
Was above all the praises of mankind.

          —*Poems*, p. 271, ed. 1664.

of the Arts in War, but by reason it was in characters, and the key thereof lost, we cannot as yet understand anything therein, at least not so as to divulge it. My other brother, the Lord Lucas [1], who was heir to my father's estate, and as it were the father to take care of us all, is not less valiant than they were, although his skill in the discipline of war was not so much, being not bred therein. Yet he had more skill in the use of the sword, and is more learned in other arts and sciences than they were, he being a great scholar, by reason he is given much to studious contemplation [2].

Their practice was, when they met together, to exercise themselves with fencing, wrestling, shooting, and such like exercises, for I observed they did seldom hawk or hunt, and very seldom or never dance, or play on music, saying it was too effeminate for masculine spirits. Neither had they skill, or did use to play, for aught I could hear, at cards or dice, or the like games, nor given to any vice, as I did know, unless to love a mistress were a crime, not that I knew any they had, but what report did say, and usually reports are false, at least exceed the truth.

As for the pastime of my sisters when they were in the country, it was to read, work, walk, and discourse with each other. For though two of my three brothers [3] were married

1 Sir John Lucas was created Baron Lucas of Shenfield by patent dated 3d May 20 Charles I (Collins, vii, 114). Clarendon gives an account of the manner in which he bought his peerage. John Ashburnham acted as broker. Clarendon, *Life* iii, 62, 63. Lucas was fined about £2,600 for his adherence to the King. *Calendar of the Committee for Compounding*, p. 1439.

2 John, Lord Lucas, is included in Walpole's *Royal and Noble Authors*, his title to inclusion being a speech in the House of Lords in 1671 against the burdens of taxation and the extravagance of the Government. It was printed, and burnt by the hands of the hangman. The speech is contained in *State Tracts*, vol. i, p. 454, and is also reprinted in Park's edition of Walpole, vol. iii, p. 119.

3 Sir Egerton Brydges gives the following pedigree : Sir Thomas Lucas of St. John's, near Colchester, married Mary, daughter of Sir John Fermor of Eston-Neston, in Northhamptonshire, by whom he had Thomas Lucas of St. John's, near Colchester, Esq., who by Elizabeth, daughter and co-heir of John Leighton of London, Gent., had three sons and five daughters, viz. :

1 John Lucas of St. John's, near Colchester, afterwards Lord Lucas, who married Anne, daughter of Sir Christopher Neville, Kt., younger brother of the Lord Abergavenny, by whom he had John, his son and heir, born about 1624.

2. Sir Thomas Lucas, a captain in London, who married a daughter of Sir John Byron Kt., by whom he had a son, Thomas.

3. Sir Charles Lucas.

4. Mary, wife of Sir Peter Killegrew, Kt.

5. Anne.

6. Elizabeth, wife of William Walter, Esq.

7. Catherine, wife of Sir Edmund Pye of London, Kt.

8. Margaret, afterwards Duchess of Newcastle.*

Arms.—Argent, a fess between six annulets, gules.

* Harl. MSS., 1541, f. 59.

(my brother the Lord Lucas to a virtuous and beautiful lady, daughter to Sir Christopher Nevil, son to the Lord Aber- gavenny; and my brother Sir Thomas Lucas to a virtuous lady of an ancient family, one Sir John Byron's daughter), likewise three of my four sisters (one married Sir Peter Kille- grew, the other Sir William Walter, the third Sir Edmund Pye [1], the fourth as yet unmarried), yet most of them lived with my mother, especially when she was at her country- house, living most commonly at London half the year, which is the metropolitan city of England. But when they were at London, they were dispersed into several houses of their own, yet for the most part they met every day, feasting each other like Job's children. But this unnatural war came like a whirlwind, which felled down their houses, where some in the wars were crushed to death, as my youngest brother Sir Charles Lucas, and my brother Sir Thomas Lucas. And though my brother Sir Thomas Lucas died not immediately of his wounds, yet a wound he received on his head in Ireland shortened his life [2].

But to rehearse their recreations. Their customs were in winter time to go sometimes to plays, or to ride in their coaches about the streets to see the concourse and recourse of people: and in the spring time to visit the Spring Garden, Hyde Park, and the like places [3]; and sometimes they would have music, and sup in barges upon the water. These harm- less recreations they would pass their time away with; for I observed they did seldom make visits, nor never went abroad with strangers in their company, but only themselves in a flock together, agreeing so well that there seemed but one mind amongst them. And not only my own brothers and sisters agreed so, but my brothers and sisters in law, and their children, although but young, had the like agreeable natures

[1] Of these three gentlemen, Sir William Walter of Sarsden, Oxfordshire, and Sir Ed- mund Pye of Leckhampstead, Bucks, took up arms for the King. Walter was fined £1430, and Pye £3065. Sir Peter Killegrew supported the Parliament.— *Calendar of the Proceedings of the Committee for Compounding*, pp. 1009, 1443, 3290.

[2] Sir Thomas Lucas left the Dutch service about 1638, and was given the command of a troop of horse in Ireland by Strafford (Strafford Letters, ii, 254 262). He fought under the command of Ormond throughout the Irish rebellion, and died about 1649. Carte, *Life of Ormond*, iii, 451, ed. 1851.

[3] A description of Hyde Park a few years later is quoted on p. 302. The same author thus describes Spring Garden : ' The manner is as the company returns (i.e. from Hyde Park), to alight at the Spring Garden, so called in order to the Park, as our Thuilleries is to the course : the inclosure not disagreeable for the solemness of the grove, the warbling of the birds, and as it opens into the spacious walks at St. James's.'—Evelyn's *Character of England*.

and affectionable dispositions. For to my best remembrance I do not know that ever they did fall out, or had any angry or unkind disputes. Likewise, I did observe that my sisters were so far from mingling themselves with any other company, that they had no familiar conversation or intimate acquaintance with the families to which each other were linked to by marriage, the family of the one being as great strangers to the rest of my brothers and sisters as the family of the other.

But sometime after this war began, I knew not how they lived. For though most of them were in Oxford, wherein the King was, yet after the Queen went from Oxford, and so out of England, I was parted from them. For when the Queen was in Oxford I had a great desire to be one of her maids of honour, hearing the Queen had not the same number she was used to have. Whereupon I wooed and won my mother to let me go ; for my mother, being fond of all her children, was desirous to please them, which made her consent to my request. But my brothers and sisters seemed not very well pleased, by reason I had never been from home, nor seldom out of their sight ; for though they knew I would not behave myself to their or my own dishonour, yet they thought I might to my disadvantage, being inexperienced in the world. Which indeed I did, for I was so bashful when I was out of my mother's, brothers', and sisters' sight, whose presence used to give me confidence—thinking I could not do amiss whilst any one of them were by, for I knew they would gently reform me if I did ; besides, I was ambitious they should approve of my actions and behaviour—that when I was gone from them, I was like one that had no foundation to stand, or guide to direct me, which made me afraid, lest I should wander with ignorance out of the ways of honour, so that I knew not how to behave myself. Besides, I had heard that the world was apt to lay aspersions even on the innocent, for which I durst neither look up with my eyes, nor speak, nor be any way sociable, insomuch as I was thought a natural fool. Indeed I had not much wit, yet I was not an idiot, my wit was according to my years ; and though I might have learnt more wit, and advanced my understanding by living in a Court, yet being dull, fearful, and bashful, I neither heeded what was said or practised, but just what belonged to my loyal duty, and my own honest reputation. And, indeed, I was so afraid

Y

to dishonour my friends and family by my indiscreet actions, that I rather chose to be accounted a fool than to be thought rude or wanton. In truth, my bashfulness and fears made me repent my going from home to see the world abroad, and much I did desire to return to my mother again, or to my sister Pye, with whom I often lived when she was in London, and loved with a supernatural affection. But my mother advised me there to stay, although I put her to more charges than if she had kept me at home, and the more, by reason she and my brothers were sequestered from their estates, and plundered of all their goods, yet she maintained me so, that I was in a condition rather to lend than to borrow, which courtiers usually are not, being always necessitated by reason of great expenses Courts put them to. But my mother said it would be a disgrace for me to return out of the Court so soon after I was placed; so I continued almost two years, until such time as I was married from thence. For my Lord the Marquis of Newcastle did approve of those bashful fears which many condemned, and would choose such a wife as he might bring to his own humours, and not such a one as was wedded to self-conceit, or one that had been tempered to the humours of another; for which he wooed me for his wife; and though I did dread marriage, and shunned men's company as much as I could, yet I could not, nor had not the power to refuse him, by reason my affections were fixed on him, and he was the only person I ever was in love with. Neither was I ashamed to own it, but gloried therein. For it was not amorous love (I never was infected therewith, it is a disease, or a passion, or both, I only know by relation, not by experience), neither could title, wealth, power, or person entice me to love. But my love was honest and honourable, being placed upon merit, which affection joyed at the fame of his worth, pleased with delight in his wit, proud of the respects he used to me, and triumphing in the affections he professed for me, which affections he hath confirmed to me by a deed of time, sealed by constancy, and assigned by an unalterable decree of his promise, which makes me happy in despite of Fortune's frowns [1]. For though misfortunes may and do oft dissolve base, wild, loose, and ungrounded affections, yet she hath no

---

[1] The letters of Margaret Lucas to the Marquis of Newcastle before their marriage are calendared in the *Report on the Duke of Portland's MSS.*, ii, 134-7. They deserve printing in full.

power of those that are united either by merit, justice, grati-
tude, duty, fidelity, or the like. And though my Lord hath
lost his estate, and banished out of his country for his loyalty
to his King and country, yet neither despised poverty, nor
pinching necessity could make him break the bonds of friendship, or weaken his loyal duty to his King or country.

But not only the family I am linked to is ruined, but the
family from which I sprung, by these unhappy wars. Which
ruin my mother lived to see, and then died, having lived a
widow many years ; for she never forgot my father so as to
marry again. Indeed, he remained so lively in her memory,
and her grief was so lasting, as she never mentioned his name,
though she spoke often of him, but love and grief caused tears
to flow, and tender sighs to rise, mourning in sad complaints.
She made her house her cloister, inclosing herself, as it were,
therein, for she seldom went abroad, unless to church. But
these unhappy wars forced her out, by reason she and her
children were loyal to the King ; for which they plundered
her and my brothers of all their goods, plate, jewels, money,
corn, cattle, and the like, cut down their woods, pulled down
their houses, and sequestered them from their lands and livings ;
but in such misfortunes my mother was of an heroic spirit,
in suffering patiently where there is no remedy, or to be industrious where she thought she could help. She was of a grave
behaviour, and had such a majestic grandeur, as it were continually hung about her, that it would strike a kind of an awe
to the beholders, and command respect from the rudest (I
mean the rudest of civilized people, I mean not such barbarous
people as plundered her, and used her cruelly, for they would
have pulled God out of heaven, had they had power, as they
did royalty out of his throne).[1] Also her beauty was beyond

---

[1] An account of the plunder of the house of Sir John Lucas at Colchester is given
in *Mercurius Rusticus*, No. 1 : ' On August 22, 1642, Sir John Lucas intended with some
horse and arms to begin his journey towards the north to wait upon the King.' This
was discovered to the leaders of the local parliamentarians by a treacherous servant,
and the roads were beset, and a guard set on his house. On his attempt to start the
town was raised, the volunteers and train-band assembled, and a crowd of 2000 people
broke into the house to search for arms and the suppressed garrison of cavaliers. ' The
people lay hands on Sir John Lucas, his lady, and sister, and carry them, attended with
swords, guns, and halberts to the common gaol. Last of all they bring forth his mother,
with the like or greater insolency, who, being faint and breathless, hardly obtained
leave to rest herself in a shop by the way ; yet this leave was no sooner obtained, but
the rest of that rude rabble threatened to pull down the house, unless they thrust her
out ; being by this means forced to depart from thence, a countryman (whom the alarm
had summoned to this work) espies her, and pressing with his horse through the crowd,
struck at her head with his sword so heartily, that if an halbert had not crossed the

the ruin of time, for she had a well-favoured loveliness in her
face, a pleasing sweetness in her countenance, and a well-
tempered complexion, as neither too red nor too pale,
even to her dying hour, although in years. And by her dying,
one might think death was enamoured with her, for he embraced her in a sleep, and so gently, as if he were afraid to hurt
her. Also she was an affectionate mother, breeding her children with a most industrious care, and tender love; and
having eight children, three sons and five daughters, there
was not any one crooked, or any ways deformed, neither were
they dwarfish, or of a giant-like stature, but every ways proportionable; likewise well-featured, clear complexions, brown
hairs (but some lighter than others), sound teeth, sweet
breaths, plain speeches, tunable voices (I mean not so much
to sing as in speaking, as not stuttering, nor wharling [1] in the
throat, or speaking through the nose, or hoarsely, unless they
had a cold, or squeakingly, which impediments many have):
neither were their voices of too low a strain, or too high,
but their notes and words were tunable and timely.
I hope this truth will not offend my readers, and lest they
should think I am a partial register, I dare not commend my
sisters, as to say they were handsome; although many would
say they were very handsome. But this I dare say, their
beauty, if any they had, was not so lasting as my mother's,

blow, both her sorrows and her journey had there found an end.' After this the house
was thoroughly plundered, deeds and papers destroyed, garden defaced, deer killed,
and cattle driven away. This was largely caused by a rumour that 200 armed men
were discovered in a vault at Sir John Lucas's, had killed nine men already, and were
issuing forth to destroy the town. ' And to show that their rage will know no bounds
and that nothing is so sacred and venerable which they dare not to violate, they break
into St. Giles's Church, open the vault where his (Sir John's) ancestors were buried, and
with pistols, swords, and halberts transfix the coffins of the dead.' Sir John was sent
a prisoner to London, committed to the Gatehouse, and after a short time released on
giving bail to appear on summons. His eight horses and his arms were employed for
the service of the Parliament. Parliament also published two *Declarations*, the one a
general prohibition to soldiers and others to break into and search the houses of persons
suspected of disaffection and popery (August 27), the other entitled *A Declaration concerning Abuses lately done by several Persons in the County of Essex.* —Husband's *Exact
Collection*, pp. 590, 592, 605. In this latter *Declaration* it is stated that the people, on
the order of the parliamentary commissioners, withdrew themselves peaceably, ' and
as they were required, did make restitution of plate, money, and many other goods '.
However, the Parliament's Commissioners did not come down till Thursday, and the
riot took place on Monday, and the worst feature of these outrages was the amount of
wanton destruction.

[1] Wharling—I can find no other use of the word. Halliwell explains ' wharling '
to mean ' an inability in any one to pronounce the letter R ' (*Dictionary of Archaic and
Provincial Words*). Shakespeare uses a somewhat similar word in *King Lear*, IV, vi
182-4:

" We came crying hither;
Thou knowest, the first time that we smell the air,
We wawl and cry."

Time making suddener ruin in their faces than in hers. Likewise my mother was a good mistress to her servants, taking care of her servants in their sickness, not sparing any cost she was able to bestow for their recovery : neither did she exact more from them in their health than what they with ease or rather like pastime could do. She would freely pardon a fault, and forget an injury, yet sometimes she would be angry ; but never with her children, the sight of them would pacify her ; neither would she be angry with others but when she had cause, as negligent or knavish servants, that would lavishly or unnecessarily waste, or subtly and thievishly steal . And though she would often complain that her family was too great for her weak management, and often pressed my brother to take it upon him, yet I observe she took a pleasure, and some little pride, in the governing thereof. She was very skilful in leases, and setting of lands, and court keeping, ordering of stewards, and the like affairs [1].   Also I observed that my mother nor brothers, before these wars, had never any lawsuits, but what an attorney despatched in a term with small cost, but if they had it was more than I knew of.   But, as I said, my mother lived to see the ruin of her children, in which was her ruin, and then died : my brother Sir Thomas Lucas soon after, my brother Sir Charles Lucas after him, being shot to death for his loyal service, for he was most constantly loyal and courageously active, indeed he had a superfluity of courage [2]. My eldest sister died some time before my mother, her death being, as I believe, hastened through grief of her only daughter, on which she doted, being very pretty, sweet natured, and had an extraordinary wit for her age. She dying of a consumption, my sister, her mother, died some half a year after of the same disease ; and though time is apt to waste remembrance as a consumptive body, or to wear it out like a garment into rags, or to moulder it into dust, yet I find the natural affections I have for my friends are beyond the length, strength, and power of time : for I shall lament the loss so long as I live, also the loss of my Lord's noble brother, which died not long after I returned from England, he being then sick of an ague, whose favours and my thankfulness ingratitude shall never disjoin.

[1] This refers to the management of manors and manorial courts. See Roger North's *Life of Lord Guilford*, pp. 34-6, ed. 1826.

[2] For contemporary accounts of the execution of Lucas see *Sir Charles Lucas his Last Speech*, printed for R. Smithurst, London, 1648, and *Clarke Papers*, ii, 31.

For I will build his monument of truth, though I cannot of marble, and hang my tears and scutcheons on his tomb.   He was nobly generous, wisely valiant, naturally civil, honestly kind, truly loving, virtuously temperate ; his promise was like a fixed decree, his words were destiny, his life was holy, his disposition mild, his behaviour courteous, his discourse pleasing ; he had a ready wit and a spacious knowledge, a settled judgment, a clear understanding, a rational insight ; he was learned in all arts and sciences, but especially in the mathematics, in which study he spent most part of his time ; and though his tongue preached not moral philosophy, yet his life taught it, indeed he was such a person, that he might have been a pattern for all mankind to take.   He loved my Lord his brother with a doting affection, as my Lord did him, for whose sake I suppose he was so nobly generous, carefully kind, and respectful to me ; for I dare not challenge his favours as to myself, having not merits to deserve them.   He was for a time the preserver of my life, for after I was married some two or three years, my Lord travelled out of France, from the city of Paris, in which city he resided the time he was there, so went into Holland, to a town called Rotterdam, in which place he stayed some six months.   From thence he returned to Brabant, unto the city of Antwerp, which city we passed through when we went into Holland, and in that city my Lord settled himself and family, choosing it for the most pleasantest and quietest place to retire himself and ruined fortunes in.   But after we had remained some time therein, we grew extremely necessitated, tradesmen being there not so rich as to trust my Lord for so much, or so long, as those of France ; yet they were so civil, kind, and charitable as to trust him for as much as they were able.   But at last necessity enforced me to return into England to seek for relief.   For I, hearing my Lord's estate, amongst the rest of many more estates, was to be sold, and that the wives of the owners should have no allowance therefrom, it gave me hopes I should receive a benefit thereby. So, being accompanied with my Lord's only brother, Sir Charles Cavendish (who was commanded to return, to live therein, or to lose his estate, which estate he was forced to buy with a great composition before he could enjoy any part thereof), so over I went. But when I came there I found their hearts as hard as my fortunes, and their natures as cruel as my miseries, for they sold all my Lord's estate, which was a very great one, and gave me not any part thereof, or any allowance thereout, which few or no other was so hardly dealt withal. Indeed, I did not stand as a beggar at the Parliament door, for I never was at the Parliament House, nor stood I ever at the door, as I do know, or can remember, I am sure, not as a petitioner. Neither did I haunt the committees, for I never was at any, as a petitioner, but one in my life, which was called Goldsmiths' Hall,[1] but I received neither gold nor silver from them, only an absolute refusal, I should have no share of my Lord's estate. For my brother, the Lord Lucas, did claim in my behalf such a part of my Lord's estate as wives had allowed them, but they told him that by reason I was married since my Lord was made a delinquent, I could have nothing, nor should have anything, he being the greatest traitor to the State, which was to be the most loyal subject to his King and country. But I whisperingly spoke to my brother to conduct me out of that ungentlemanly place, so without speaking to them one word good or bad, I returned to my lodgings, and as that committee was the first, so was it the last, I ever was at as a petitioner. 'Tis true I went sometimes to Drury House to inquire how the land was sold, but no other ways, although some reported I was at the Parliament House, and at this committee and at that committee, and what I should say, and how I was answered. But the customs of England

---

[1] The committee sitting at Goldsmiths' Hall was that for compounding with delinquents. ' Its object was to receive from delinquents themselves, either such against whom no information had been made, or such as were already under sequestration :
(1) A confession of their delinquency.
(2) A pledge of adherence to the present Government.
(3) A full account on oath of their possessions, real and personal.
Whereupon a legal report was made, and they were admitted to compound in proportions, according to their guilt ; half the estate was exacted from any delinquent Member of Parliament ; one-sixth from those who had taken part either in the former or latter war ; two-sixths or one-third from those who had been active in both wars, etc. Those who were in cities that surrendered on articles of war compounded according to the tenor of those articles '(Mrs. Greene's Preface to the *Calendar of Domestic State Papers*, 1649, p. ix.) A Calendar of the Proceedings of this Committee, filling five volumes, was published in 1889-92. The songs of the Cavaliers are naturally full of allusions to the committee :

Under the rose be it spoken, there's a damned committee,
Sits in Hell (Goldsmiths' Hall) in the middle of the city,
Only to sequester the poor Cavaliers,
The devil take their souls and the hangman their ears.

Another song says in allusion to the oaths :

They force us to take
Three oaths, but we'll make
A third, that we ne'er meant to keep 'em.

being changed as well as the laws, where women become
pleaders, attornies, petitioners, and the like, running about
with their several causes, complaining of their several griev-
ances, exclaiming against their several enemies, bragging of
their several favours they receive from the powerful, thus
trafficking with idle words bring in false reports and vain discourse.   For the truth is, our sex doth nothing but jostle for
the pre-eminence of words (I mean not for speaking well,
but speaking much) as they do for the pre-eminence of place,
words rushing against words, thwarting and crossing each
other, and pulling with reproaches, striving to throw each other
down with disgrace, thinking to advance themselves thereby.
But if our sex would but well consider, and rationally ponder,
they will perceive and find, that it is neither words nor place
that can advance them, but worth and merit.   Nor can words
or place disgrace them, but inconstancy and boldness : for
an honest heart, a noble soul, a chaste life, and a true speaking
tongue, is the throne, sceptre, crown, and footstool that advances them to an honourable renown.   I mean not noble,
virtuous, discreet, and worthy persons whom necessity did
enforce to submit, comply, and follow their own suits, but such
as had nothing to lose, but made it their trade to solicit.   But
I despairing, being positively denied at Goldsmiths' Hall (besides, I had a firm faith, or strong opinion, that the pains was
more than the gains), and being unpractised in public employments, unlearned in their uncouth ways, ignorant of the
humours and dispositions of those persons to whom I was to
address my suit, and not knowing where the power lay, and
being not a good flatterer, I did not trouble myself or petition
my enemies.   Besides I am naturally bashful, not that I am
ashamed of my mind or body, my birth or breeding, my
actions or fortunes, for my bashfulness is my nature, not for
any crime, and though I have strived and reasoned with myself, yet that which is inbred I find is difficult to root out.   But
I do not find that my bashfulness is concerned with the qualities
of the persons, but the number ; for were I to enter amongst
a company of Lazaruses, I should be as much out of countenance as if they were all Cæsars or Alexanders, Cleopatras or
Queen Didos.   Neither do I find my bashfulness riseth so often
in blushes, as contracts my spirits to a chill paleness.   But
the best of it is, most commonly it soon vanisheth away, and

many times before it can be perceived ; and the more foolish or unworthy I conceive the company to be, the worse I am, and the best remedy I ever found was, is to persuade myself that all those persons I meet are wise and virtuous. The reason I take to be is, that the wise and virtuous censure least, excuse most, praise best, esteem rightly, judge justly, behave themselves civilly, demean themselves respectfully, and speak modestly when fools or unworthy persons are apt to commit absurdities, as to be bold, rude, uncivil both in words and actions, forgetting or not well understanding themselves or the company they are with. And though I never met such sorts of ill-bred creatures, yet naturally I have such an aversion to such kind of people, as I am afraid to meet them, as children are afraid of spirits, or those that are afraid to see or meet devils ; which makes me think this natural defect in me, if it be a defect, is rather a fear than a bashfulness, but whatsoever it is, I find it troublesome, for it hath many times obstructed the passage of my speech, and perturbed my natural actions, forcing a constrainedness or unusual motions. However, since it is rather a fear of others than a bashful distrust of myself, I despair of a perfect cure, unless nature as well as human governments could be civilized and brought into a methodical order, ruling the words and actions with a supreme power of reason, and the authority of discretion : but a rude nature is worse than a brute nature by so much more as man is better than beast, but those that are of civil natures and gentle dispositions are as much nearer to celestial creatures, as those that are of rude or cruel are to devils. But in fine, after I had been in England a year and a half [1], in which time I gave some half a score visits, and went with my Lord's brother to hear music in one Mr. Lawes his house [2], three or four times, as also some three or four times

---

[1] Supply, to complete the sense, ' I resolved to return ', from p. 170.
[2] This was Henry Lawes, for his elder brother William was killed at the siege of Chester in October 1645. He composed the music for ' Comus,' and acted in it the parts of Thyrsis and the Attendant Spirit. Milton addressed to him on 9th February 1646 the well-known sonnet :

To my Friend, Mr. Henry Lawes.

Harry, whose tuneful and well-measured song
First taught our English music how to span
Words with just note and accent.
—Masson, *Life of Milton*, iii, 464.

Z

to Hyde Park with my sisters, to take the air [1], else I never
stirred out of my lodgings, unless to see my brothers and
sisters, nor seldom did I dress myself, as taking no delight
to adorn myself, since he I only desired to please was absent,
although report did dress me in a hundred several fashions.
'Tis true when I did dress myself I did endeavour to do it in
my best becoming, both in respect to myself and those I went
to visit, or chanced to meet.   But after I had been in England
a year and a half, part of which time I writ a book of poems [2],
and a little book called my *Philosophical Fancies* [3], to which
I have writ a large addition, since I returned out of England,
besides this book and one other.   As for my book entitled
The World's Olio, I writ most part of it before I went into
England, but being not of a merry, although not of a froward
or peevish disposition, became very melancholy, by reason I
was from my Lord, which made my mind so restless, as it did
break my sleep, and distemper my health, with which growing
impatient of a longer delay, I resolved to return, although
I was grieved to leave Sir Charles, my Lord's brother, he being
sick of an ague, of which sickness he died.   For though his ague

[1] In Evelyn's *Character of England*, 1651, Hyde Park is thus described :
' I did frequently in the spring accompany my Lord N. into a field near the town,
which they call Hyde Park ; the place not unpleasant, and which they use, as our Course ;
but with nothing that order, equipage, and splendour, being such an assembly of wretched
jades and hackney-coaches, as next a regiment of car-men there is nothing approaches
the resemblance.   This Park was (it seems) used by the late King and Nobility for the
freshness of the air, and the goodly prospect : but it is that which now (besides all other
excises) they pay for here in England, though it be free in all the world beside ; every
coach and horse which enters buying his mouthful, and permission of the publican who
has purchased it, for which the entrance is guarded with porters and long staves.'
[2] The book called *Poems and Fancies* was published in 1653, dedicated to Sir Charles
Cavendish, *The World's Olio*, in 1655.
[3] *Philosophical Fancies*, published in 1653, was afterwards expanded into *Philosophical Opinions*, which passed through two editions, 1655 and 1663.   In one of the Epistles
to the Reader in the edition of 1663, the Duchess writes : ' The ground of these my
philosophical and physical opinions was printed in the year 1653, to which in the year
1655 I made an addition, but after I returned with my noble Lord into England, I have
since recovered my former work, and finding it not so perfect, as I wish it had been, I
have employed part of my idle time to make it more intelligible for my readers.'
At the end of the same book she informs her readers, that it is her favourite work
(p. 457) :

> Of all my works this work which I have writ,
> My best beloved and greatest favourite,
> I look upon it with a pleasing eye.
> I pleasure take in its sweet company.
> I entertain it with a grave respect,
> And with my pen am ready to protect
> The life and safety of it 'gainst all those
> That will oppose it, or profess it foes :
> But I am sure there's none condemn it can,
> Unless some foolish and unlearned man,
> That hath no understanding, judgment, wit,
> For to perceive the reason that's in it.

was cured, his life was decayed, he being not of a strong constitution could not, as it did prove, recover his health, for the
dregs of his ague did put out the lamp of his life.   Yet Heaven
knows I did not think his life was so near to an end, for his
doctor had great hopes of his perfect recovery, and by reason
he was to go into the country for change of air, where I should
have been a trouble, rather than any way serviceable, besides
more charge the longer I stayed, for which I made the more
haste to return to my Lord, with whom I had rather be as a
poor beggar, than to be mistress of the world absented from
him, yet, Heaven hitherto hath kept us, and though Fortune
hath been cross, yet we do submit, and are both content with
what is, and cannot be mended, and are so prepared that the
worst of fortunes shall not afflict our minds, so as to make us
unhappy, howsoever it doth pinch our lives with poverty.
For, if tranquillity lives in an honest mind, the mind lives
in peace, although the body suffer.   But patience hath armed
us, and misery hath tried us, and finds us fortune-proof.   For
the truth is, my Lord is a person whose humour is neither
extravagantly merry nor unnecessarily sad, his mind is above
his fortune as his generosity is above his purse, his courage
above danger, his justice above bribes, his friendship above
self-interest, his truth too firm for falsehood, his temperance
beyond temptation.   His conversation is pleasing and affable,
his wit is quick, and his judgment is strong, distinguishing
clearly without clouds of mistakes, dissecting truth, so as it
justly admits not of disputes : his discourse is always new upon
the occasion, without troubling the hearers with old historical
relations, nor stuffed with useless sentences.   His behaviour
is manly without formality, and free without constraint, and
his mind hath the same freedom.   His nature is noble, and
his disposition sweet ; his loyalty is proved by his public service
for his King and country, by his often hazarding of his life, by
the loss of his estate, and the banishment of his person, by his
necessitated condition, and his constant and patient suffering.
But, howsoever our fortunes are, we are both content, spending our time harmlessly, for my Lord pleaseth himself with the
management of some few horses, and exercises himself with
the use of the sword ; which two arts he hath brought by his
studious thoughts, rational experience, and industrious practice, to an absolute perfection.   And though he hath taken

as much pains in those arts, both by study and practice, as chymists for the philosopher's-stone, yet he hath this advantage of them, that he hath found the right and the truth thereof and therein, which chymists never found in their art, and I believe never will. Also here creates himself with his pen, writing what his wit dictates to him, but I pass my time rather with scribbling than writing, with words than wit. Not that I speak much, because I am addicted to contemplation, unless I am with my Lord, yet then I rather attentively listen to what he says, than impertinently speak. Yet when I am writing any sad feigned stories, or serious humours, or melancholy passions, I am forced many times to express them with the tongue before I can write them with the pen, by reason those thoughts that are sad, serious, and melancholy are apt to contract, and to draw too much back, which oppression doth as it were overpower or smother the conception in the brain. But when some of those thoughts are sent out in words, they give the rest more liberty to place themselves in a more methodical order, marching more regularly with my pen on the ground of white paper ; but my letters seem rather as a ragged rout than a well-armed body, for the brain being quicker in creating than the hand in writing or the memory in retaining, many fancies are lost, by reason they ofttimes outrun the pen, where I, to keep speed in the race, write so fast as I stay not so long as to write my letters plain, insomuch as some have taken my hand-writing for some strange character, and being accustomed so to do, I cannot now write very plain, when I strive to write my best ; indeed, my ordinary handwriting is so bad as few can read it, so as to write it fair for the press ; but however, that little wit I have, it delights me to scribble it out, and disperse it about. For I being addicted from my childhood to contemplation rather than conversation, to solitariness rather than society, to melancholy rather than mirth, to write with the pen than to work with a needle, passing my time with harmless fancies, their company being pleasing, their conversation innocent (in which I take such pleasure as I neglect my health, for it is as great a grief to leave their society as a joy to be in their company), my only trouble is, lest my brain should grow barren, or that the root of my fancies should become insipid, withering into a dull stupidity for want of maturing subjects to write on. For I being of a lazy nature, and not of an active disposition, as some are that love to journey from town to town, from place to place, from house to house, delighting in variety of company, making still one where the greatest number is—likewise in playing at cards, or any other games, in which I neither have practised, nor have I any skill therein :—as for dancing, although it be a graceful art, and becometh unmarried persons well, yet for those that are married, it is too light an action, disagreeing with the gravity thereof—and for revelling, I am of too dull a nature to make one in a merry society—as for feasting, it would neither agree with my humour or constitution, for my diet is for the most part sparing, as a little boiled chicken, or the like, my drink most commonly water ; for though I have an indifferent good appetite, yet I do often fast, out of an opinion that [1] if I should eat much, and exercise little, which I do, only walking a slow pace in my chamber, whilst my thoughts run apace in my brain, so that the motions of my mind hinders the active exercises of my body ; for should I dance or run, or walk apace, I should dance my thoughts out of measure, run my fancies out of breath, and tread out the feet of my numbers. But because I would not bury myself quite from the sight of the world, I go sometimes abroad, seldom to visit, but only in my coach about the town, or about some of the streets, which we call here a tour, where all the chief of the town go to see and to be seen, likewise all strangers of what quality soever, as all great princes or queens that make any short stay.   For this town being a passage or thoroughfare to most parts, causeth many times persons of great quality to be here, though not as inhabitants, yet to lodge for some short time ; and all such, as I said, take a delight, or at least go to see the customs thereof, which most cities of note in Europe, for all I can hear, hath such like recreations for the effeminate sex, although for my part I had rather sit at home and write, or walk, as I said, in my chamber and contemplate ; but I hold necessary sometimes to appear abroad, besides I do find, that several objects do bring new materials for my thoughts and fancies to build upon.   Yet I must say this in the behalf of my thoughts, that I never found them idle ; for if the senses bring no work in, they will work of themselves, like silk-worms that spins out of their own bowels.   Neither can I say I think the time

---

[1] Supply ' I should injure myself ', or some phrase to that effect.

tedious, when I am alone, so I be near my Lord, and know he is well.

But now I have declared to my readers my birth, breeding, and actions, to this part of my life (I mean the material parts, for should I write every particular, as my childish sports and the like, it would be ridiculous and tedious) ; but I have been honourably born and nobly matched ; I have been bred to elevated thoughts, not to a dejected spirit, my life hath been ruled with honesty, attended by modesty, and directed by truth. But since I have writ in general thus far of my life, I think it fit I should speak something of my humour, particular practice and disposition.   As for my humour, I was from my childhood given to contemplation, being more taken or delighted with thoughts than in conversation with a society, insomuch as I would walk two or three hours, and never rest, in a musing, considering, contemplating manner, reasoning with myself of everything my senses did present.   But when I was in the company of my natural friends, I was very attentive of what they said or did ; but for strangers I regarded not much what they said, but many times I did observe their actions, where-upon my reason as judge, and my thoughts as accusers, or excusers, or approvers and commenders, did plead, or appeal to accuse, or complain thereto.   Also I never took delight in closets, or cabinets of toys, but in the variety of fine clothes, and such toys as only were to adorn my person.   Likewise I had a natural stupidity towards the learning of any other language than my native tongue, for I could sooner and with more facility understand the sense, than remember the words, and for want of such memory makes me so unlearned in foreign languages as I am [1].   As for my practice, I was never very active, by reason I was given so much to contemplation ; besides my brothers and sisters were for the most part serious and staid in their actions, not given to sport or play, nor dance about, whose company I keeping, made me so too.   But I observed, that although their actions were staid, yet they would be very merry amongst themselves, delighting in each other's company :   also they would in their discourse express the

---

[1] In the preface to her Philosophical Letters the Duchess says : 'The authors whose opinions I mention I have read, as I found them printed, in my native language, except Des Cartes, who being in Latin, I had some few places translated to me out of his works.' And again, in the same place : ' My error was I began to write so early, that I had not lived so long as to be able to read many authors.'

general actions of the world, judging, condemning, approving, commending, as they thought good, and with those that were innocently harmless, they would make themselves merry therewith.   As for my study of books it was little, yet I chose rather to read, than to employ my time in any other work, or practice, and when I read what I understood not, I would ask my brother, the Lord Lucas, he being learned, the sense or meaning thereof.   But my serious study could not be much, by reason I took great delight in attiring, fine dressing, and fashions especially such fashions as I did invent myself, not taking that pleasure in such fashions as was invented by others.   Also I did dislike any should follow my fashions, for I always took delight in a singularity, even in accoutrements of habits[1].   But whatsoever I was addicted to, either in fashion of clothes, contemplation of thoughts, actions of life, they were lawful, honest, honourable, and modest, of which I can avouch to the world with a great confidence, because it is a pure truth.   As for my disposition, it is more inclining to be melancholy than merry, but not crabbed or peevishly melancholy, but soft, melting, solitary, and contemplating melancholy.   And I am apt to weep rather than laugh, not that I do often either of them. Also I am tender natured, for it troubles my conscience to kill a fly, and the groans of a dying beast strike my soul.   Also where I place a particular affection, I love extraordinarily and constantly, yet not fondly, but soberly and observingly, not to hang about them as a trouble, but to wait upon them as a

---

[1] This is quite borne out by the remarks of Pepys and other contemporaries, and by her portraits.   For instance, Pepys on April 11, 1667, speaks of her coming to court, ' her footmen in velvet coats and herself in antique dress. . . .   There is as much expectation of her coming to court, so that people may see her, as if it were the Queen of Sheba.'   On April 26 he notes : ' Met my Lady Newcastle going with her coaches and footmen all in velvet ; herself (whom I never saw before), as I have heard her often described, for all the town talk is nowadays of her extravagances, with her velvet cap, her hair about her ears, many black patches because of pimples about her mouth, nakednecked, without anything about it, and a black just-au-corps.   She seemed to me a very comely woman ; but I hope to see more of her on May-day.'   On May-day, accordingly, Pepys went with Sir William Penn to the Park.   ' That which we and almost all went for, was to see my Lady Newcastle ; which we could not, she being followed and crowded upon by coaches all the way she went, that nobody could come near her only I could see she was in a large black coach, adorned in silver instead of gold, and so white curtains, and everything else black and white, herself in her cap.'   See also Pepys, May 8, 1667, and *Halton Correspondence*, i, 47.
Evelyn on April 18, 1667, ' went to make court to the Duke and Duchess of Newcastle at their house in Clerkenwell, being newly come out of the north.   They received me with great kindness, and I was much pleased with the extraordinary fanciful habit, garb, and discourse of the Duchess.'   On April 27 he saw her again, and remarks that her dress was ' very singular '.

servant ; but this affection will take no root, but where I
think or find merit, and have leave both from divine and moral
laws. Yet I find this passion so troublesome, as it is the only
torment of my life, for fear any evil misfortune or accident,
or sickness, or death, should come unto them, insomuch as I
am never freely at rest. Likewise I am grateful, for I never
received a courtesy—but I am impatient and troubled until
I can return it. Also I am chaste, both by nature, and education, insomuch as I do abhor an unchaste thought. Likewise, I am seldom angry, as my servants may witness for me,
for I rather choose to suffer some inconveniences than disturb
my thoughts, which makes me wink many times at their
faults ; but when I am angry, I am very angry, but yet it is
soon over, and I am easily pacified, if it be not such an injury
as may create a hate. Neither am I apt to be exceptious or
jealous, but if I have the least symptom of this passion, I
declare it to those it concerns, for I never let it lie smothering
in my breast to breed a malignant disease in the mind, which
might break out into extravagant passions, or railing speeches,
or indiscreet actions ; but I examine moderately, reason
soberly, and plead gently in my own behalf, through a desire
to keep those affections I had, or at least thought to have.
And truly I am so vain, as to be so self-conceited, or so naturally partial, to think my friends have as much reason to love
me as another, since none can love more sincerely than I, and
it were an injustice to prefer a fainter affection, or to esteem
the body more than the mind. Likewise I am neither spiteful,
envious, nor malicious. I repine not at the gifts that Nature
or Fortune bestows upon others, yet I am a great emulator ;
for, though I wish none worse than they are, yet it is lawful
for me to wish myself the best, and to do my honest endeavour
thereunto. For I think it no crime to wish myself the exactest
of Nature's works, my thread of life the longest, my chain of
destiny the strongest, my mind the peaceablest, my life the
pleasantest, my death the easiest, and the greatest saint in
heaven ; also to do my endeavour, so far as honour and
honesty doth allow of, to be the highest on Fortune's wheel
and to hold the wheel from turning, if I can. And if it be commendable to wish another's good, it were a sin not to wish my
own ; for as envy is a vice, so emulation is a virtue, but emulation is in the way to ambition, or indeed it is a noble ambition.

But I fear my ambition inclines to vain-glory, for I am very
ambitious ; yet 'tis neither for beauty, wit, titles, wealth, or
power, but as they are steps to raise me to Fame's tower, which
is to live by remembrance in after-ages.   Likewise I am that
the vulgar call proud, not out of self-conceit, or to slight or
condemn any, but scorning to do a base or mean act, and dis-
daining rude or unworthy persons ; insomuch, that if I should
find any that were rude, or too bold, I should be apt to be so
passionate, as to affront them, if I can, unless discretion should
get betwixt my passion and their boldness, which sometimes
perchance it might if discretion should crowd hard for place.
For though I am naturally bashful, yet in such a cause my
spirits would be all on fire.   Otherwise I am so well bred, as
to be civil to all persons, of all degrees, or qualities.   Likewise
I am so proud, or rather just to my Lord, as to abate nothing
of the quality of his wife, for if honour be the mark of merit,
and his master's royal favour, who will favour none but those
that have merit to deserve, it were a baseness for me to neglect
the ceremony thereof.   Also in some cases I am naturally
a coward, and in other cases very valiant.   As for example, if any
of my nearest friends were in danger I should never consider my
life in striving to help them, though I were sure to do them
no good, and would willingly, nay cheerfully, resign my life
for their sakes : likewise I should not spare my life, if honour
bids me die.   But in a danger where my friends, or my honour
is not concerned, or engaged, but only my life to be unprofit-
ably lost, I am the veriest coward in nature, as upon the sea,
or any dangerous places, or of thieves, or fire, or the like.
Nay the shooting of a gun, although but a pot-gun [1], will make
me start, and stop my hearing, much less have I courage to
discharge one ; or if a sword should be held against me, although but in jest, I am afraid.   Also as I am not covetous,
so I am not prodigal, but of the two I am inclining to be prodigal, yet I cannot say to a vain prodigality, because I imagine
it is to a profitable end ; for perceiving the world is given, or apt
to honour the outside more than the inside, worshipping show
more than substance ; and I am so vain (if it be a vanity) as to
endeavour to be worshipped, rather than not to be regarded.   Yet
I shall never be so prodigal as to impoverish my friends, or go
beyond the limits or facility of our estate.   And though I desire

---

[1] Pop-gun.

A A

to appear to the best advantage, whilst I live in the view of the
public world, yet I could most willingly exclude myself, so as
never to see the face of any creature but my Lord as long as I
live, inclosing myself like an anchorite, wearing a frieze gown,
tied with a cord about my waist.   But I hope my readers will
not think me vain for writing my life, since there have been
many that have done the like, as Cæsar, Ovid, and many more,
both men and women, and I know no reason I may not do it
as well as they : but I verily believe some censuring readers
will scornfully say, why hath this Lady writ her own life ?
since none cares to know whose daughter she was or whose
wife she is, or how she was bred, or what fortunes she had,
or how she lived, or what humour or disposition she was of.
I answer that it is true, that 'tis to no purpose to the readers,
but it is to the authoress, because I write it for my own sake,
not theirs.   Neither did I intend this piece for to delight, but
to divulge ; not to please the fancy, but to tell the truth, lest
after-ages should mistake, in not knowing I was daughter
to one Master Lucas of St. Johns, near Colchester, in Essex,
second wife to the Lord Marquis of Newcastle ; for my Lord
having had two wives, I might easily have been mistaken,
especially if I should die and my Lord marry again.

APPENDICES

APPENDICES

I

CORRESPONDENCE OF THE EARL OF NEWCASTLE
WITH STRAFFORD

A FEW letters between the Earl of Newcastle and Strafford have been printed by Dr. Knowler in the Strafford Papers.

Those from Strafford to Newcastle are five in number :

July 19, 1634, vol. i, p. 274 ; April 9, 1635, vol. i, p. 410 ; June 1, 1638, vol. ii, 210 ; December 10, 1638, vol. ii, 246 ; February 10, 163?, vol. ii, 281.

Those from Newcastle to Strafford are only two ; the first written under his earlier title of Mansfield.

The Lord Viscount Mansfield to Sir Thomas Wentworth, Bart.

NOBLE SIR,—I think myself much bound to you for your favours to me in my absence, and your kind letter with your good counsel, which I have taken, and writ my mind at full to my Lord Duke, and, I protest to God, no more sparing the old Cavalier or his nature than I would speak of him to you, nor mincing my desires or my nature, which is not to do courtesies for injuries. Mr. Endymion Porter, Mr. Richard Oliver, with Dr. More are my agents, and all with my own letters to my Lord Duke, but to let things stand as they were, which I hope is so reasonable a suit, since I am not repaired in the Keepership, that I shall not be denied. When that is done, I beseech you, sir, give this bearer Thomas Bamford leave to wait of you, with one Robin Butler to advise but how to make a ground to bring him into the Duchy, and have a suit of it, and then I make no doubt but to have the better of him. There is no man gladder than myself of your absolute liberty, and I hope now we shall not be long without a Parliament, which God grant. And so I rest affectionately, your most faithful kinsman and humble servant,

W. MANSFIELD.

WELBECK, *Jan.* 24, 1627

The Earl of Newcastle to the Lord Deputy

MY MOST HONOURED LORD,—I heartily congratulate your Lordship's safe arrival in Ireland, next I am to beg your pardon for not presenting my service to you by letter all this while; but in good faith, my Lord, the reason was, I daily heard you were going. I give your Lordship humble thanks for your noble and kind counsel; the truth is, my Lord, I have waited of the King the Scottish journey both diligently, and, as Sir Robert Swift said of my Lord of Carlisle, it was of no small charge unto me. I cannot find by the King but he seemed to be pleased with me very well, and never used me better or more graciously; the truth is, I have hurt my estate much with the hopes of it, and I have been put in hope long, and so long as I will labour no more in it, but let nature work and expect the issue at Welbeck; for I would be loth to be sick in mind, body, and purse, and when it is too late to repent, and my reward laughed at for my labour. It is better to give over in time with some loss than lose all, and mend what is to come, seeing what is past is not in my power to help. Besides, my Lord, if I obtained what I desire, it would be a more painful life, and since I am so much plunged in debt, it would help very well to undo me; for I know not how to get, neither know I any reason why the King should give me anything. Children come on apace, my Lord, and with this weight of debt that lies upon me, I know no diet better than a strict diet in the country, which, in time, may recover me of the prodigal disease. By your favour, my Lord, I cannot say I have recovered myself at Welbeck this summer, but run much more in debt than ever I did, but I hope hereafter I may. The truth is, my Lord, for my court business, your Lordship with your noble friends and mine have spoken so often to the King, and myself refreshed his memory in that particular, so that I mean not to move my friends any more to their so great trouble; but whatsoever pleases his Majesty, be fully contented, and look after some other little contentments within myself, which shall well serve me during my life, and if the King command me, I am at all times ready to serve him; if no commands, pray for him heartily. For, by my troth, my Lord, I know no man in the whole world more bound unto his Majesty than myself. For that point to try your Lordship's friends in my behalf, I humbly thank you for the motion, and I desire your Lordship to follow it. For the King's particular liking of my proper person, I think my Lord of Carlisle would do best, or what doth your Lordship think to his Lady, for further I would not willingly have it go; but I assure your Lordship I am most confident of the King's good opinion of me: and about my Lord Savile's business and mine, his Majesty pleased me extremely, being never moved by me or any friend in my behalf that I desired. My Lord Treasurer used me extreme well and extraordinary kindly; my Lord of Carlisle for your Lordship's sake, but the greatest news is my Lord of Holland courted me extremely; and so to conclude with this business, I intend to be quiet, and not press the King at all, but to leave his Majesty to his own time, and rest quietly here in the country; and this I assure your Lordship is my resolution and my full intention, and except it be to the purpose, their greatest friendship is to let me rest here. I humbly thank your Lordship for your noble favours to my old servant; for my groom, my Lord, I beseech you keep him, and I am sorry your Lordship will use such ceremony with me. For La Roche, I always told your Lordship my opinion of him, and, in good faith, he is no such horseman, neither for anything I ever saw, but got a great reputation with doing little: I would your Lordship had taken Porter, but I know not how he is disposed of. I assure your Lordship that horse you pleased to accept, I thought him the fittest horse in the world for that purpose, but your Lordship doth not write how you approve of him. My Lord, in a word, I desire no man's favour and love more than yours, or would be beholding to any man sooner ; for, I protest to God I honour and love you heartily, and I vow without any end or particular in the whole world ; your Lordship's favours to me are merely your own goodness, for I shall never be useful to you in any kind, which makes my obligation such that I must ever be faithfully,—Your Lordship's most humble servant,

W. NEWCASTLE.

WELBECK, *the 5th of August* 1633

II

NEWCASTLE AS GOVERNOR OF PRINCE CHARLES

Mr. Secretary Windebank to the Earl of Newcastle

MY LORD,—His Majesty having a purpose, according to the precedents of former times, to settle the government both of the person and family of the Prince in a way answerable to his state and years, and having deliberately advised upon some person of honour and trust to be near his Highness, and to be a chief director in so weighty a business, hath been pleased, in his gracious opinion of your Lordship, to make choice of you to be the only gentleman of his Bedchamber at this time, and hath commanded me to give you knowledge of this his princely resolution. And withal his Majesty's pleasure is, that you prepare yourself to come to the Court in diligence, and to attend his Majesty before the Sunday fortnight after Easter, which will be the eighth day of April. And lastly his Majesty hath expressly commanded me to let your Lordship know, that you have no particular obligation to any whatsoever in this business, but merely and entirely to the King's and Queen's Majesties alone ; who of their own mere and special grace and goodness have made this choice, and vouchsafed you this honour ; the countenance and increase whereof, and of much happiness with it, I wish to your Lordship, and so rest,— Your Lordship's humble and faithful servant,

FRAN. WINDEBANK.

At the COURT at WHITEHALL,
    19th *of March,* 1637

The Earl of Newcastle to Mr. Secretary Windebank

NOBLE SIR,—I beseech you to present me in the most humble manner in the world to his sacred Majesty, and to let his Majesty know I shall as cheerfully as diligently obey his Majesty's commands. Truly, the infinite favour, honour and trust his Majesty is pleased to heap on me in this princely employment, is beyond anything I can express. It was beyond hope of the most partial thoughts I had about me : neither is there anything in me left, but a thankful heart filled with diligence, and obedience to his sacred Majesty's will.

It is not the least favour of the King and Queen's Majesties to let me know my obligation : and I pray, sir, humbly inform their Majesties it is my greatest blessing that I owe myself to none but their sacred Majesties. God ever preserve them and theirs, and make me worthy of their Majesties' favours !

I have had but seldom the honour to receive letters from you ; but such as these you cannot write often. But truly I am very proud I received such happy news by your hand, which shall ever oblige me to be inviolably,—Sir, your most faithful and obliged servant,

W. Newcastle.

Welbeck, *the 21st of March,* 1637

(Clarendon State Papers, vol ii, p. 7)

With these letters should be read that of Strafford to the Earl of Newcastle, dated June 1, 1638, in which he gives him advice concerning the line of conduct to be followed in the Court (*Strafford Letters,* ii, 174).

The Earl of Newcastle's letter of instructions to Prince Charles for his studies, conduct and behaviour

[From a copy preserved with the Royal Letters in the Harleian MS., 6988, Art. 62. Printed by Ellis, *Original Letters,* ser. i, vol. iii, p. 288.]

May it please your Highness,—Since it pleased your most gracious father, his sacred Majesty, to think me worthy to be your Governor, I will justify his Majesty's choice ; for, what I may want in abilities I will make up with fidelity and duty to his Majesty, in diligence and service to you. Then for your education, sir, it is fit you should have some languages, though I confess I would rather have you study things than words, matter than language ; for seldom a critic in many languages hath time to study sense, for words ; and at best, he is, or can be, but a living dictionary. Besides, I would not have you too studious, for too much contemplation spoils action, and virtue consists in that. What you read, I would have it history, and the best chosen histories, that so you might compare the dead with the living ; for the same humours is now as was then ; there is no alteration but in names, and though you meet not with a Cæsar for Emperor of the whole world, yet he may have the same passions in him ; and you are not to compare fortunes so much as humours, wit, and judgment ; and thus you shall see the excellency and errors both of Kings and subjects ; and though you are young in years, yet living by your wading in all those times, be older in wisdom and judgment than Nature can afford any man to be without this help.

For the arts, I would have you know them so far as they are of use, and especially those that are most proper for war and use ; but whensoever you are too studious your contemplation will spoil your government, for you cannot be a good contemplative man and a good commonwealth's man ; therefore, take heed of too much book.

Beware of too much devotion for a King, for one may be a good man, but a bad King ; and how many will history represent to you that in seeming to gain the kingdom of heaven have lost their own ; and the old saying is, that short prayers pierce the heaven's gates ; but if you be not religious (and not only seem so, but be so), God will not prosper you ; and if you have no reverence to Him, why should your subjects have any to you. At the best, you are accounted, for your greatest honour. His servant, His deputy, His anointed, and you owe as much reverence and duty to Him as we owe to you ; and why, nay justly, may not He punish you for want of reverence and service to Him, if you fail in it, as well as you to punish us : but this subject I leave to the right reverend Father in God, Lord Bishop of Chichester, your worthy tutor : your tutor, sir, wherein you are most happy, since he hath no pedantry in him ; his learning he makes right use of, neither to trouble himself with it or his friends ; reads men as well as books ; and goes the next way to everything that he should, and that is what he would, for his will is governed by that law : the purity of his wit doth not spoil the serenity of his judgment ; travelled, which you shall perceive by his wisdom and fashion more than by his relations ; and in a word strives as much discreetly to hide the scholar in him, as other men's follies to show it ; and is a right gentleman, such a one as man should be.

But, sir, to fall back again to your reverence at prayers, so far as concerns reason and your advantage is my duty to tell you ; then I say, sir, were there no heaven or hell, you shall see the disadvantage for your government ; if you have no reverence at prayers, what will the people have, think you ? They go according to the example of the Princes ; if they have none, then they have no obedience to God ; there they will easily have none to your Highness ; no obedience, no subjects ; no subjects—then your power is off that side, and whether it be in one or more then that's King, and thus they will turn tables with you. Of the other side, if any be Bible mad, over much burned with fiery zeal, they may think it a service to God to destroy you and say the Spirit moved them and bring some example of a king with a hard name in the Old Testament. Thus one way you may have a civil war, the other a private treason ; and he that cares not for his own life is master of another man's.

For books thus much more : the greatest clerks are not the wisest men ; and the great troublers of the world, the greatest captains, were not the greatest scholars ; neither have I known bookworms great statesmen ; some have heretofore and some are now, but they study men more now than books, or else they would prove but silly statesmen. For a mere scholar, there is nothing so simple for this world. The reason is plain, for divinity teaches what we should be, not what we are ; so doth moral philosophy ; and many philosophical worlds' and Utopia's scholars have made and fancied to themselves such worlds as never was, is, or shall be ; and then I dare say if they govern themselves by those rules what men should be, or not what they are, they will miss the cushion very much.

But, sir, you are in your own disposition religious and not very apt to your book, so you need no great labour to persuade you from the one, or long discourses to dissuade from the other.

The things that I have discoursed to you most is to be courteous and civil to everybody ; set to, make difference of cabinges,[1] and, believe it.

---

1 So in the MS.—Ellis.

the putting off of your hat, and making a leg pleases more than reward or preservation, so much doth it take all kind of people. Then to speak well of everybody, and when you hear people speak ill of others reprehend them and seem to dislike it so much, as do not look of them so favourably for a few days after, and say something in favour of those that have been spoke against ; for you may say something of everybody to the best ; the other which is railing, scorn, and jeering, is fitter for porters, watermen, and carmen, than for gentlemen ; how much more then for a Prince, whose dislike is death, and kills any subject. Besides, you may be sure the parties will hear of it, and though they dare do nothing because they want power nor say nothing for fear of being troubled, yet believe it, sir, they are traitors in their hearts to you, and of your own making, and so are all their friends. Of the other side, to speak well of them will be told too, and that wins them as much ; the other loses them ; and this way you will get their hearts, and then you have all they have, and more you cannot have. And how easy a way is this to have the people. To lose your dignity and set by your state, I do not advise you to that, but the contrary : for what preserves you Kings more than ceremony. The cloth of estates, the distance people are with you, great officers, heralds, drums, trumpeters, rich coaches, rich furniture for horses, guards, marshal's men making room, disorders to be laboured by their staff of office, and cry ' now the King comes ' ; I know these maskers [1] the people sufficiently ; aye, even the wisest though he knew it and not accustomed to it, shall shake off his wisdom and shake for fear of it, for this is the mist is cast before us, and maskers the Commonwealth. Besides authority doth what it list, I mean power that's the stronger, though sometimes it shifts sides, therefore the King must know at what time to play the King, and when to qualify it, but never put it off ; for in all triumphs whatsoever or public showing yourself, you cannot put upon you too much king ; yet even there sometimes a hat or smile in the right place will advantage you, but at other times you may do more, and civil speeches to people and short doth much win of them : and certainly, sir, civility cannot unprince you, but much advantage you. To women you cannot be too civil, especially to great ones : what hurt were it to send them a dish from your table when they dine with some of your great lords, and to drink their health ? Certainly, sir, you cannot lose by courtesy. I mean not you should be so familiar as to bring you to contempt, for I mean you should keep yourself up Prince still, and in all your actions, but I would not have you so seared with majesty as to think you are not of mankind, nor suffer others or yourself to flatter you so much. The incommodities to·life and the sustaining of it, and the same things the meanest do, you must do the like or not live ; these things when you are pleased to think of them will persuade you that are of the lump of man, and mortal, and the more you repeat these thoughts the better Prince you will be, both to serve God and for distributive justice to your people ; for being a Prince you ought rather to give Almighty God thanks for the advantage-ground you have of other people, than to be proud. I mean not by repeating your mortality to have a death's head set always before you, or to cry every morning that you are mortal, for I would not have you fall into a divine melancholy, to be an anchorite or a capuchin, or with a philosophical discourse to be a Diogenes in your tub ;

[1] Here and four lines lower down I should suggest ' masters ' instead of ' maskers.'

but to temper yourself so by this means, as to be a brave, noble, and just King, and make your name immortal by your brave acts abroad and your unspotted justice at home, qualified by your well temper and mercy.'

In the Patent creating Newcastle a Duke, quoted in the *Life*, p. 180, King Charles II says : 'The great proofs of his wisdom and piety are sufficiently known to us from our younger years, and we shall always retain a sense of those good principles he instilled into us.'

III

NEWCASTLE'S MISSION TO HULL IN JANUARY, 1642

The following are the two letters mentioned in the note on p. 9 :

MAY IT PLEASE YOUR MOST SACRED MAJESTY,—I am here at Hull according to your Majesty's commands, but the town will not admit of me by no means, so I am very flat and out of countenance here, but will stay until I know your Majesty's further pleasure, which I hope I shall soon do. God preserve your Majesty,—Your Majesty's most faithful creature,

W. NEWCASTLE.

HULL, *the 15th of January* 1642

Sir,—My first address, in these parts, was to Sir Thomas Metham with his Majesty's directions, but I found him altogether incapable of any power to secure the Magazine or town of Hull, as being neither Deputy-Lieutenant or Colonel of the Trained-bands. When that hope was taken from me I conceived the best means I had was to prevail with the burgesses of the town, by themselves, to secure the place for his Majesty's service, and that work is very well brought to pass, for last night here arrived an express from Sir John Hotham, with an order from the Parliament for him to be Governor, and a power to draw in such forces as he thought fit, likewise a letter from him to the Magistrates for preparing lodging and billet for his regiments : his admission was quite denied, and a letter to the Parliament despatched with the hands of the chief burgesses to excuse themselves from receiving any garrison, they of the town being able to secure the place for his Majesty's service. This afternoon arrived here the Earl of Newcastle with his Majesty's commission for the Government, to which I shall (for my own part) be ever obedient, but I perceive not the townsmen be willing to receive him unto their command, but insist upon their own affections and readiness to serve his Majesty with all faithfulness. Now the means of present strength from Sir Thomas Metham or any near hand, being taken away, there is no mean for us but to assure the people of this town to his Majesty by holding off any other from the power of the place, and if ever his Majesty appear in person all will be absolutely at his disposing. When I received his Majesty's command, he told me his directions should be derived by (me from) you, and therefore I humbly beseech you to give him this account of me ; and I shall to my utmost power

labour nothing but his Majesty's service ; and shall ever be ready (as obliged) to express myself,—Your Honour's most humble and obedient servant,   WILL. LEGGE.
HULL, 14*th* *Jan.* 1642

(Endorsed as received on Jan. 18)

On January 21, 1642, Nicholas writes to Roe that the Earl of Newcastle is Governor of Kingston-upon-Hull, where the townsmen have manifested great affections to the King, and excused their not receiving Sir John Hotham, commanded to that charge by the Parliament. S. P. Dom. vol. 488, No. 80. The following are the entries in the Journals of the House of Lords referred to in the note on p. 18 :

The Earl was ordered, on January 20, to attend the House of Lords at once. The Earl was absent at a call of the House on February 9.

On February 14 it was moved ' That the Earl of Newcastle, being sent for to come and give his attendance on this House, hath daily attended this House, and now desires that he might have leave to go into the country for his health sake.' Hereupon the House ordered ' That the Earl of Newcastle shall deliver in his commission, granted to him under the King's manual, by which he was to have raised forces to go into the town of Hull, and to be Governor ; and that his Lordship be ready to attend this House when he shall have notice upon any occasion ' (*L. J.*, February 14, 1642).

The commission was delivered by the Earl on the afternoon of the same day. It is given in full in the Journals (p. 585).

The Earl was then excused attendance, and granted leave to go into the country.

IV

A NEW DISCOVERY OF HIDDEN SECRETS

In several letters, propositions, articles, and other writings concerning the Earl of Newcastle, Captain John Hotham, and many other malignant gentry of the northern counties. All lately found in Pomfret Castle ; the original whereof remain now in York, where they may be seen of any who desire it. With a declaration of the committee of Yorkshire and some observations thereupon to undeceive their deluded and oppressed countrymen.

LONDON, 1645

(Dated November 3d, by Thomason, E. 267 (2). British Museum
King's Pamphlets)

The Declaration is omitted.

It states that ' the letters are being examined by some of the committee appointed for that purpose, and the originals remain in safe hands to be seen by any man that shall desire it.'

My Lord,—It is the desire of us, and the most of the gentry of this country to crave assistance from your Lordship in this time of Mr. Hotham's infesting the country ; which favour we shall always acknowledge from your Lordship, and we are the bolder in this business, because we know it to be a great service to his Majesty, by the preservation of this country, and will be much to your honour, to preserve in peace and safety. my Lord,—Your Lordship's most humble servants,

SAVILE.	WILLIAM SAVILE.
HENRY SLINGSBY.	JOHN KEY.
FERDINAND LEIGH.	FRANCIS NEVILE.
JOHN GOODRICKE.	WILLIAM INGRAM.
GEORGE WENTWORTH.	THO. GOWER, VI. CO.
PETER MIDDLETON.	JOHN RAMSDEN.
JOHN MALLORY.	THO. INGRAM.
RICHARD HUTTON.	ROBERT ROCKELEY.

YORK, *September* 26, 1642

NOBLE GENTLEMEN,—I have received from you a letter of invitation by the hands of Sir Mar. Langdale, and Mr. Aldburgh, and shall (for the esteem and affection I bear in general to the country, being my native country, and in particular to many of you whom I have the honour to be known) be ready to contribute my best aid and assistance in that work, since it is likely to conduce to his Majesty's service, and peace and quiet of all his good subjects, and to conclude this agreement, I have sent you inclosed certain propositions which by way of articles should be drawn and signed and sealed by you, and as many more as you shall engage in that work, which I shall expect from you before I march. And so presenting my service to you all,—I remain your most faithful servant,

W. N.

NEWCASTLE, *September* 30, 1642

To the Right Honourable, and my noble friends the nobility and gentry now assembled at York for his Majesty's present service. Propositions in answer to your letter of invitation :

First, that I have all your consents and promises that the army be paid whilst they are in that county.

That an assessment be laid upon the country to enable you for that undertaking, and that if money be not gotten in time, that I may have free billet for the soldiers, for which billet you are to engage yourself to the quarters, and that the officers be paid according to his Majesty's present establishment, out of that assessment.

That there be some of the gentry of that county appointed as a committee, enabled by the rest of the gentry to agree and conclude of such further propositions as may happen to be necessary for this service, and not here mentioned, and to march along with the army, whose counsel and assistance from time to time I am resolved to use.

That I have assurance that all manner of provisions fit for an army be prepared and brought to the army the first day it enters.

That since this army was levied a purpose to guard her Majesty's person, that it shall not be held a breach of any engagement betwixt us if I retire with such numbers as I shall think fit for that service.

W. N.

My Lord,—We have received from your Lordship an answer to our letter of invitation, noble as yourself, which we hope shall make you the master of such a work of honour, as besides your great service it will be to his Majesty, shall both enable yourself farther and oblige us. We have signed and sent unto your Lordship, articles proportionable to your Lordship's desire, as we conceive, besides a particular power to those gentlemen now with you more fully to declare ourselves. My Lord, believe this, that we suffer here no distresses, but for our loyalty to the King, and your Lordship's favour to us will equally oblige both : therefore, good my Lord, make all possible speed to march hither, or to send some force before, lest a little delay make all our endeavours fruitless ; and in the general believe there is nothing in the power of us, or of this country, which shall not faithfully serve you ; and more you cannot expect from, my Lord, your most faithful and humble servants,

H. CUMBERLAND.	GEORGE WENTWORTH.
SAVILE.	CONYERS DARCY.
THOMAS GOWER, Vi. Co.	ROBERT STRICKLAND.
WILLIAM SAVILE.	WILLIAM WENTWORTH.
HENRY GRIFFITH.	INGRAM HOPTON.
HENRY SLINGSBY.	JOHN GOODRICKE.
EDWARD STANHOPE.	WILLIAM WENTWORTH.
JOHN KEY.	JOHN BATTY.
JOHN MALLORY.	RICHARD HUTTON.
FERDINANDO LEIGH.	FRANCES MONCKTON.
WILLIAM INGLEBY.	ROBERT ROCKLEY.
JOHN RAMSDEN.	W. THORNTON.

The answer of the nobility and gentry of Yorkshire assembled at York for his Majesty's service, to the propositions sent unto them by the Right Honourable the Earl of Newcastle.

1. That your Lordship shall have our consents and promises, the army which your Lordship shall bring with you into this country for the defence thereof shall be paid by this country.

2. There is an assessment of £8000 already laid upon this country, which shall be levied as soon as by your Lordship's assistance we are enabled to do it, and that till money be gotten in, your soldiers shall have free billet, for which we will engage ourselves to the quarters ; and for the payment of your officers for the army it is referred to the committee for this

county who have instructions and power to treat and conclude with your Lordship in that particular.

3. There shall be a committee of some of the gentry of the county appointed and enabled by the rest to agree, and conclude of such further propositions as may happen to be necessary for this service, not here mentioned, and to march along with your Lordship's army, whose counsel and assistance we desire your Lordship may use, the names of which committee we send your Lordship herewithal, who are appointed to attend you at Newcastle, and to march along with your army when you enter into the county.

4. That as soon as we have notice of your Lordship's march, we will use all possible means to bring to your army all such provisions as this country can afford.

5. We are tender of the safety of her Majesty's person, that we shall not only consent to your Lordship's performance of that service but will also contribute our utmost endeavours to assist your Lordship therein.

6. Lastly, we have appointed our committee to be, Sir Edward Osborne, Baronet, Sir Marmaduke Langdale, Knight, Francis Tindall and Richard Aldburgh, Esquires, and given them instructions and power to treat with your Lordship, and to conclude in such particulars as may further conduce to this service, or in these propositions admit a doubtful interpretation.

H. CUMBERLAND,
(and the rest signing before with the addition
of Walter Hawkesworth).

MY LORDS AND GENTLEMEN,—I am to give you many thanks for your favourable letter by Mr. Aldburgh, and the signing so far my desired articles, which had no other end than the better to enable me to serve you. And I beseech you to give me leave as I intend faithfully to serve you, so to deal clearly and freely with you, which I hold a duty ; the truth is, I am very sorry you pleased to leave out the article for the officers' pay, or coldly referred it to your committee, being the principal thing in all the articles, for you know the soldier is encouraged with nothing but money, or hopes of it, and truly last night when I was going to bed, there came colonels and lieutenant-colonels, and said they heard you had left it out, and for their parts that they must think that if you were so cautious not to grant it in paper before we came in, they doubted very much of it in money when they were there, and that the workman was worthy of his hire, and such like discontented words ; so the truth is, rather than not come cheerfully to serve you, I will not come at all, for I see beforehand I shall either disband with a mutiny, or fall of plundering without distinction, either of which would be destructive to me : and besides, I hold myself free, since my articles are not signed, for I never understood any of those articles to be referred to the committee, but such things as we could not remember, and the present occasion offered.   Could I pay them or his Majesty, you should not have such had an article, but since that cannot be, you will pardon me in telling you how I am capable to serve you, and how not, and so I rest in a huge disposition to be really your most faithful servant,   W. N.

NEWCASTLE, *October* 30, 1642

V

MISCELLANEOUS LETTERS RELATING TO THE CIVIL WAR IN YORKSHIRE

THE first of these letters was captured when Guilford Slingsby, to whom it was addressed, was defeated by Sir Hugh Cholmley at Guisborough on January 16, 1643 (Rushworth, III, ii, 125). Slingsby was severely wounded, and died a few days afterwards (Rushworth, *Trial of the Earl of Strafford*, 773). The letter was sent up to Parliament, and is now amongst the papers of the House of Lords, together with the instructions given to Slingsby which accompany it.

Sir,—I have received your letters this day, and return you thanks for the very good service you have done, and should be very glad to give you all the assistance you desire, and more, to prosecute your present levies, but I was informed that you had of your own levies 400 foot besides your troop of horse. And as the case stands I cannot furnish you with any more forces for the present. For these reasons, first, the forces of the Bishoprick were levied upon condition to remain in the country for the security thereof; and besides, they are appointed to guard the ammunition through their country, and if need be further; which I hope they will obey, for I hear Colonel Huddleston nor Colonel Clavering can either of them march for that convoy as was intended, and therefore I have appointed Sir Robert Strickland and his forces to wait upon that service, and I desire you will do so too, for I hear they have a design to surprise it if they can, and it deserves our best cares to secure it. When that service is done, I shall be ready to give you all the assistance I can. For the lady you mention use your own discretion towards her, for I have not been ever used to take ladies prisoners. For any goods or arms you shall take of disaffected persons or in their possession, keep them to your own use, the goods upon account for paying your soldiers (for we can get no money here to supply you) and the arms for arming your men, and though they be part of the Trained-band arms, yet being taken by you as a prize, they shall be accounted so. For your fortifying those castles you mention, I do not understand of what consequence it can be to you, except it be some one for your retreat and place of residence whilst you are levying your regiment. For the 500 arms you desire a warrant for, it will be very inconvenient to serve it upon their way, and therefore for it you must have a little patience. For the paying of your troop you propose one of three ways, but to resolve of which of them is to no end unless there was money to pay, but in that you shall have all the right that may best be, in time. Till then, as I told you before, you may make use of such moneys and goods you take of delinquents, or so much thereof as will serve you, for I perceive you meet with good store. And thus much for answer to your letters from,—Your very affectionate friend,   W. NEWCASTLE.

POMFRET, *8th Jan.* 1642.

(Papers of the House of Lords)

Instructions taken with Colonel Slingsby

The county (York) to be universally disarmed of all private arms, both of horse and foot, and those not borne in service to be brought into a magazine at York. The trained bands that rose with Hotham to be compelled to rise again, and serve in their persons, or every man to send an able-bodied man to serve for him. Considering her Majesty intends to commit her person into the protection of this county, a magazine is to be made at York to enable an army to subsist there in case of extremity or necessary retreat. All the gentry of Yorkshire to be unanimously moved to resort thither with their families and movables, as the contrary faction do daily to Hull, by which means the persons and estates of such as are not well affected will be secured, as such as refuse or decline it shall discover themselves, and every man's fortune and family being there engaged they will more actually move with a joint concurrence for the preservation of the place, which must be the retreat for the safety of the Queen's person, no other place being defensible and considerable to balance Hull. Those that decline this proposition are to understand that they must at their own peril undergo the plunder of the soldiers, if any fall out. The garrison in York shall be daily employed in making regular works upon the avenue and outworks, and encroachments upon the hills and other places commanding the town. No markets or fairs to be held in any place in the county except York. Some of the iron ordnance, sent over by the Queen to be sent for at the charge of the county to place upon the avenues and fortifications.

(From Report V of the *Historical MSS. Commission*, p. 69. For 'encroachments' in l. 21 we should most likely substitute ' intrenchments ')

Summons to Hull

When the news of the arrest of Sir John Hotham reached the Earl of Newcastle he wrote from Bowling Hall, near Bradford, where he was staying, after the capture of that town, the following letter to the Mayor of Hull :

Sir,—I hear there is some alteration in the government of the garrison of Hull, and because I have some prisoners there which I may have occasion to treat for, I desire to know in what condition it now stands, and whether I am to treat with his Majesty's loyal and faithful subjects or such as are in opposition to him, or neutrals, to that end that I may accordingly apply myself. So expecting your answer, I remain, your very affectionate friend to serve you,

W. NEWCASTLE.

BOWLING HALL, *4th July* 1643
To my very worthy friend, the Mayor
    of the town of Hull.

The Mayor answered :

RIGHT HONOURABLE,—It is true there is some alteration here of gover-

C C

nor, not government ; though the power of exchanging persons is not such as we assume for the present, nor know we any neutral or opposite here to his Majesty, all being, for aught we understand, as dutiful as ever, and as constant, and resolute to keep what we have hitherto defended for King and Parliament (God assisting), in confidence whereof we rest your Lordship's humbly devoted servants.

KINGSTON-UPON-HULL,
the 5th July 1643.

(Tanner MSS., lxii, 144, 151)

There is in the same collection a commission to Colonel Thomas Haggerston to be colonel of a regiment of 500 harquebusiers, April 14, 1643 (lxii. 51) ; and a warrant to arrest certain delinquents in Durham, dated 25th April 1643 (lxii, 80).

A Declaration and Summons sent by the Earl of Newcastle to the town of Manchester to lay down their arms, etc.

I presume you are not ignorant of the success it hath pleased Almighty God to give unto his Majesty's army under my command, and the great desire I have to avoid the effusion of Christian blood, which moves me before I proceed any further towards you, to make you an offer of his Majesty's grace and mercy. If you will submit yourselves, lay down your arms, so unjustly taken up in contempt of the laws of this kingdom, and immediately return to your due allegiance, his Majesty is graciously pleased to authorise me to receive you into his favour and protection, which I am as willing to do as to enforce your obedience. If you will refuse, I cannot but wonder, while you fight against the King and his authority, you should so boldly offer to profess yourselves for King and Parliament, and most ignominiously scandalise this army with the title of Papists, when we venture our lives and fortunes for the true Protestant religion established in this kingdom. Be no longer deceived, for the blood that shall be shed in this quarrel will assuredly fall on your own heads. I have no other ends in this but to let you see your error, if you please ; for my condition is such that I need not court you ; if not, let me receive your answers by this messenger, and you may expect to find little favour (if you force my nature), but such as is due to high contemners of his Majesty's grace and favour now offered to you by   W. NEWCASTLE.

BRADFORD, *5th July* 1643

Appended to this letter is the answer of Manchester, dated Rochdale, 7th July 1643. It ends :

Sir,—We are nothing dismayed at your force, but hope that God, who hath been our Protector hitherto, will so direct our just army that we shall be able to return the violence intended into their bosoms that shall assay the prosecution of it, which shall be the endeavour of his Majesty's most humble and obedient subjects.

In 'Certain Informations for Thursday, July 13' we are told that the Lancashire men 'have placed a garrison of 1200 men in Rochdale, and 500 more upon Blackstone Edge, to guard the passage into their country out of Yorkshire, and that they have sent away Colonel Goring and their other prisoners, but whither it was not known, yet is supposed to be Liverpool, to be conveyed thence by sea to London ; but it is now said they are brought to Nottingham.'

Letter to Lord Loftus, July 6, 1643

To Edward, Viscount Loftus of Ely, or the Commander-in-Chief at Middleham Castle

You cannot be ignorant of the good success it hath pleased Almighty God to give unto the army under my command. And that you may see the desire I have to avoid the effusion of more blood before I proceed any further, I have thought it my duty to God and the King to signify unto you that if you shall upon sight hereof submit yourselves, lay down your arms most unjustly taken up against your dread Sovereign, and immediately return to your due allegiance, his Majesty is graciously pleased to authorise me to receive you into his mercy and favour, which I shall as willingly do as to bring you to obedience by force if you shall refuse. And I cannot but wonder, whilst you fight against the King and his authority, you should so boldly presume to profess yourself for the King and Parliament. Be no longer deceived, for that blood that shall be shed in this quarrel will fall upon your own head. I have no other ends in this treaty but to let you see your error, if you please ; if not, let me receive your answer, and that without delay. And if you resolve to persist in your obstinacy, then I do hereby advise you to remove out of the castle all women and children, unto whom and all others well affected I do promise safe and free passage without any interruption. And then you may expect no other than what is due to so high a condemner of his Majesty's grace and favour offered. Given under my hand the sixth day of July 1643.

W. NEWCASTLE.

(*Ninth Report of the Historical MSS. Commission*, Part II, p. 317. From the Marquis of Drogheda's Papers.)

VI

A TRUE RELATION OF THE PASSAGES OF THE ARMY UNDER THE COMMAND OF HIS EXCELLENCY THE MARQUESS OF NEWCASTLE SINCE HIS COMING INTO DERBYSHIRE

(Printed at York by Stephen Bulkley, 1643)

Sir Thomas Fairfax and his forces being at Chesterfield, a part of our horse marched near unto them and beat in their scouts, and a troop of their horse, and showed themselves upon a hill within the view of the town a little before sunset, where they remained till it grew dark ; then the soldiers set the whins and gorse on fire upon that hill, which gave them such an alarm in the town, that Sir Thomas Fairfax presently called to horse, and about twelve o'clock in the night they quit both that town and a garrison they had in Sir Henry Humlock's house, and in great disorder away they fled to Nottingham without any stay, having lost many of their men, most of which are now our prisoners. About Broxtowe their men so straggled, that two parties met with one another in a lane, and conceiving they had met a party of ours, gave fire upon one another, and killed a lieutenant of their own. They passed to Nottingham extremely tired and wearied, and there remained three or four days ; from thence they went to Melton-Mowbray in Leicestershire, and stayed but a while there, not liking to remain long in one place. But we had no sooner possessed Chesterfield, before the rebels possessed themselves of a strong house at Alfreton and the church there, against which we sent two hundred musquetiers, who fell upon the church and took it by assault (without any loss on our part), and about twenty men in it, together with their arms ; whereupon the house and arms were surrendered with this condition, that they might march away to their own houses, making first protestation never again to bear arms against his Majesty.

About that time Colonel Dudley, Major-General of the Dragoons, was sent with a commanding party of horse and foot, into the Peak Country, where at the first, about Ashford, he encountered with at least five hundred foot and three troops of horse, which he charged home, and presently routed them ; some of them he killed, and took about twenty prisoners, but being late and growing dark the rest escaped, and in great disorder ran away to save themselves.

About the same time Commissary Windham going out with a party of horse and dragoons into Craven, was there encountered by some rebels, which he presently forced into a house (belonging to Sir William Savile) called Aireton Hall, where though he had some few men hurt, and himself shot through the shoulder (not without good hopes of recovery), yet continuing their assault, they took the house and sixty men in it (together with all their arms), whom now they have prisoners at the Earl of Cumberland's castle in Skipton.

Not long after this, about the twenty-seventh day of November, the Governor of Newark having intelligence from Belvoir that the committee of Leicester was at Melton raising money, with a guard of two or three troops of horse, and some dragoons (which town is sixteen miles distant from Newark), he drew forth about four troops of horse from thence, and having one from Belvoir to join with them, they marched away all night, and coming to Melton about break of day, they presently fell into the town, and without the loss of one man they took the committee (one Haslerig, Stanley and Hatcher), three troops of horse (every troop consisting of seventy), two troops of dragoons, and one company of foot, with all their commanders both horse and foot (except one Cornet), which are now prisoners at Belvoir Castle.

There comes news again from Colonel Dudley, who in the morning about three of the clock on the seven and twentieth day of this instant November marched out with all the horse and foot he had (excepting four companies of foot and two troops of horse, which he left to secure and attend the Commissioners of Array then sitting at Bakewell), and went towards the enemy's quarters about Hartington towards Staffordshire, with an intention to beat up those quarters ; but not coming so soon as to perform that intention, the rebels drew out a body of two thousand horse and foot (such as they were), and with a hideous noise, proclaimed the expectation they had of a sudden victory. But it pleased God otherwise to dispose of them ; for Colonel Dudley (leaving only a good reserve of foot and one troop of horse) charged the rebels with all the rest of his horse and foot in a full body at once, which was so home, that with his horse he beat quite through their rear of foot into the midst of their horse, and forced them to a disorderly retreat ; and not willing to give them time to recollect, he pursued and slew above one hundred of them upon the place, following the chase into Staffordshire near five miles together (almost to Leek), and doing sharp execution all the way. Then he drew up his horse in order, and made a stand, and sent back a messenger to know the success of the foot, who had by that time routed all the rebels' foot, only three hundred or thereabouts retreated into the church which they had prepared with strong baragadoes, but before this messenger came thither, the foot had forced one of the church doors, and taken and slain every man of them. They took ten officers, three colours of foot, and one of horse, and among others the brother of Colonel Ashenhurst.

About this time, upon the left hand, a body of three hundred horse appeared from Derby to join with the rebels, but they found that they came too late, and our horse, marching towards them, they fled away into Staffordshire.

And Colonel Dudley having then secured the prisoners, and given the soldiers the pillage of the field, marched again that night to Bakewell to his quarters there. In this whole action he knows not any one man slain on our part, and but five hurt, whereof not one officer but Lieutenant-Colonel Preston, and he not dangerously.

Upon the nine-and-twentieth day of November, so soon as the rebels who possessed Chatsworth House (the principal seat of the Earl of Devonshire), then under the command of Captain Stafford, heard of this news, though the place was very strong, and three hundred well provided to defend it, yet not adventuring either an assault or a summons, they quit their hold and are fled away.

VII

THE CAMPAIGN OF THE MARQUIS OF NEWCASTLE AGAINST THE SCOTS IN FEBRUARY, MARCH AND APRIL 1644

The best account of this campaign is that given by Rushworth III, ii, 612–16 ; it is a summary of the different news-letters published at the time, and seems to be derived entirely from writers favourable to the Parliamentary cause, and based mainly on letters from the Scottish camp. The object of this note is to collect some materials for the history of the campaign from Royalist sources. Some of the letters of the Marquis during the campaign are printed in Warburton's *Prince Rupert*. The long despatch which follows is from a copy amongst the Conway papers, now in the Record-office, and the extract from *Mercurius Aulicus* represents another despatch which has now disappeared.

Newcastle writes to Prince Rupert from York on January 28, 1644, telling him that his marching army amounted to only 5000 foot, and that his horse was not well armed, whilst the Scots numbered 14,000 and had advanced as far as Morpeth (Warburton, ii, 368). He concludes by regretting that he is to be left to fight the Scots unaided. A day or two later he set out for Newcastle ; the Scots appeared before that town and summoned it on February 3d, and the same day the Marquis arrived within its walls. Of the attack which followed, and the condition of their forces, Newcastle and King sent the following account to Charles.

A true and perfect representation of the state of your Majesty's army under our command and the condition we are in at this present

Your Majesty may be pleased to understand that the greatest part of this winter was necessarily spent in suppressing the rebellion in Derbyshire, which otherwise had grown to an irresistible head. And by the time we had reduced that county, and put in it a defensible posture, the disorders in Yorkshire, together with the rumour of the Scots' invasion, called us back into Yorkshire very much wearied and toiled, both horse and foot, where we had hopes to have refreshed and clothed our men, which were discouraged both for want of clothes and money. We remained there not above a fortnight, but the Scots had invaded the kingdom with a very great army, although the season of the year and a great snow at the very instant did persuade us that it was impossible for them to march. Yet not trusting to that, my Lord-Lieutenant-General hasted away with all expedition with such horse and foot as were quartered nearest to those parts, and, receiving intelligence of the Scots continuing their march, he hasted to Newcastle in his own person some days before his forces could possibly get thither; where truly he found the town in a very good posture, and that the mayor, who had charge of it, had performed his part in your Majesty's service very faithfully; and all the aldermen and best of the town well disposed for your service. And though our charge was very tedious, by reason of floods occasioned by the sudden thaw of the snow, yet I came thither the night before the Scots assaulted the town which was done with such a fury as if the gates had been promised to be set open to them; but they found it otherwise; for the truth is, the town soldiers gave them such an entertainment (few of our forces being then come into the town, and those extremely wearied in their march), as persuaded them to retire a mile from the town, where they have remained ever since quartered in strong bodies, and raising the whole country of Northumberland, which is totally lost, all turned to them, so that they daily increase their army, and are now striving to pass part of it over the river, so to environ us on every side, and cut off all provision from us. But we have hitherto made good the town and river, and shall do our best endeavour still to do so. But your Majesty may be pleased to know that the enemy's army consists of at least fourteen thousand foot and two thousand horse, and daily increase their numbers: and we cannot possibly draw into the field full five thousand foot and about three thousand horse: and besides, Sir Thomas Fairfax's success in Cheshire hath made him capable of drawing from Lancashire a very great force into the West Riding of Yorkshire, which he is ready to do. My Lord Fairfax hath sent forth of Hull into the East Riding two thousand foot and five hundred horse, all threatening to march towards us, which will make them a great body. And by this your Majesty may perceive where the seat of the war is likely to be.

The letter from which this is extracted is dated February 13 and signed by the two generals. They concluded by desiring the King's express commands ' whether we shall still continue in a defensive posture, and expect some assistance as well of force, as ammunition, from your Majesty, or whether upon this great inequality, we shall adventure to hazard the loss of the army, and so of all the north, by giving them battle ' (Warburton's *Prince Rupert*, ii, 481). This was followed by another letter of Newcastle's dated February 16, pointing out the advances of Sir Thomas Fairfax and his father in Yorkshire, and begging earnestly for aid. ' If your Majesty beat the Scots, your game is absolutely won; which can be no other way but by sending more forces, especially foot, and

either diverting Manchester, and those forces about Newark'
(Warburton, iii, 381).   The letter of March 9 gives an account of
the progress of the campaign from February 19 to March 8, including the three days' manœuvring and skirmishing near Sunderland
on the 6th, 7th, and 8th of March.   The skirmish near Corbridge
on February 19, is related at length in a letter from Edmund
Bowles to the younger Vane, which is printed in Terry's *Life of
Alexander Leslie*, p. 192.   Newcastle's own account of these incidents is headed ' A true relation of all the observable accidents and
passages that have happened in these parts since my last to your
Majesty and before the 9th of this month ; with the reason of
the impossibility of making good the river of Tyne against the
Scots ' :

SIR,—Thomas Riddell sent about 50 musketeers from Tynmouth Castle
to destroy some corn in the enemy's quarters, from whence they were drawn
out as he was informed.   But it seems his intelligence betrayed them to the
enemy, and about 45 of them were taken prisoners, who being carried to
Leslie he sent them to me as a token, and I returned him thanks for his
civility with this answer, that I hoped very shortly to repay that debt
with interest : which I did within a few days.   The 19th of February 1643
Sir Marmaduke Langdale fell upon their quarters at Corbridge in Northumberland, but the enemy having timely notice of his coming were drawn
into the field.   He thereupon sent some troops to second those that first
entered the towns, who charged the enemy, but the enemy with their
lancers forced them to retreat.   He sent more, but the enemy charged
them gallantly, but durst not pursue them because of our reserve.   At last
he rallied his forces and took about 200 foot with him and forced the
enemy to retreat.   He routed them totally and followed the chase three
miles, killed above 200, took above 150 prisoners, besides divers officers slain,
whereof one named Captain Haddon.   The prisoners Major Agnew, major
to the Lord Kirkcudbright, dangerously hurt, Archibald Magee his Quarter-
master, Haddon's Cornet Carr, grandchild to the Lord Roburgh.   There
was 15 of their troops of horse, whereof Leslie's life-guard was one, and 3
troops of dragooners, and that Leslie's son was their general, who is shot
through the shoulder.   There is 2 horse colours and a dragoon colour taken.
The same morning Colonel Dudley from his quarters about Prudhoe
marched over the river with some horse and dragoons and fell into a quarter
of the enemy's in Northumberland and slew and took all that was in it,
which was 55 prisoners, and gave such an alarm to four of their quarters
that they quit the same with disorder and some loss ; in which neither
had we suffered any loss at all had not Colonel Brandling been taken
prisoner by the unfortunate fall of his horse ; and Colonel Dudley, perceiving a greater force preparing to assault him, retreated, and in his
retreat took eight of the Scots prisoners, both horse and men, but they
took four of his dragoons, whose horse were so weak they could not pass
the river.   First, after I had made true inquisition of the passes over the
river Tyne, I found that there was so many fordable places betwixt New-
burn and Hexham, about twelve miles distant one from the other, that it was

impossible with my small number of foot to divide them so as to guard and make good every place, but to hazard the loss of them at any one place, and yet not do the work ; so I resolved of two evils to choose the less, and left them to their own wills : so they passed the river, and after some days' quartering upon the high moors which was beyond the river Derwent, so that I could by no means march to them, for the situation of these quarters gave them great advantage against our approaches, they marched thence, over the new bridge near Chester (le Street) to Sunderland, which pass our horses in respect of the inclosures could not hinder them nor charge them. Upon Wednesday the 6th of this instant March, at one o'clock afternoon, our first troops passed Newbridge and within a while after the enemy appeared with some horse ; when they advanced towards us with more than they first discovered, after some bullets had been exchanged and they appeared again with a greater body, we backed our party with my Lord Henry's regiment, Lieutenant-Colonel Scrimsher commanding them—being part of Colonel Dudley's brigade, with which he drew up after them—with whom also we sent some musketeers ; which caused the enemy that day to look upon us at a further distance, we judged they were about 500 horse when they appeared most, yet they continued most of that day in our sight, which satisfied us extremely in hopes the rest were not far off, yet far from troubling us except it were sometimes to make use of our perspectives.

The next morning, from the hill from whence the day before they viewed us, we discovered them, from whence setting ourselves in order we marched towards them, but they still upon our advance fell something obliquely from us on our right hand, bending towards Sunderland, placing their army upon a hill called ——, which was on the left hand of the town from the sea, there ranked themselves for their best advantage to display their own strength, and for their own security, upon which finding them thus backward to join, which truly we little expected, considering what great brags they had made, we resolved to march towards the town, either to possess ourselves of it or a piece of ground near unto it, which would have hindered them from coming back again to the town without fighting with us, upon which piece of ground they had left a good part of their horse and a strong party of their musketeers ; which they perceiving made them to draw down again to the same place with all the haste they could make, where again they possessed themselves before they could put over any troops. The convenient passage we could find to it being through some fields of furze and whin bushes, where we were to make our way with pioneers through three thick hedges with banks, two of which they had lined with musketeers, there also being a valley betwixt us and them, besides they had possessed themselves of a house, wherein as we guess they had put 200 musketeers and a drake, which flankered those hedges which were betwixt us, and from thence there ran a brook, with a great bank, down to the river Wear ; behind these places was this plain above-mentioned, where they stood in their best postures to receive us, having the sea behind them and on the left hand the town, the hill and inaccessible places, by which we must have fetched so great a compass about, that they would have been upon the same hill again to have received us that way. By this time the evening caused us to withdraw towards the higher ground, where being saluted with cold blasts and snow, our horses suffer-

D D

ance with hunger, that we seemed so far to become friends as in providing against those common enemies. The next morning both the armies drew up again into batalia, when with the continual snow that fell all that day, and by reason of the great fatigation of the horse it being the third day they had received little or no sustenance, it was thought by the consent of all the general officers not expedient that the army should suffer such extremity or for that time seek any further occasion to engage an enemy whom we found so hard to be provoked, who found from us I believe, contrary to their expectations, so much forwardness as they might plainly perceive we endeavoured what we could to fight with them, and were confident enough of our own strength could we have come unto them upon any indifferent terms of equality. And truly the forwardness of the soldiers was such as we would have been contented to have given them some advantages to boot rather than to have deferred it. But upon such disadvantages we had no manner of reason, being the ground would not permit us to draw up the fourth part of the army, by which we had been defeated of the advantage we had over them with our horse, and besides we should have been forced to have fought for that ground which afterwards we should have stood upon. We being now resolved to march off, and they having been so niggardly to afford us occasion to try what mettle each other was made of, in some measure to satisfy the great forwardness we found in our people, and also to give the enemy warning that they should not be too bold upon our retreat. For these reasons we sent off 120 horses to entertain them near their own leaguer, Sir Charles Lucas his major commanding them, where meeting with 200 of the enemy's, the first that charged them not passing 60 of this one regiment, notwithstanding the enemy was so placed before a hedge, where they had some dragooners as it seems, they were confident ours would not have come up unto them ; but when they saw that their muskets could not prevent the courage of our men, they turned their backs and leaped over their dragooners, affording our men the execution of them to a great body of theirs, in which chase our men killed some 40 of them, and had taken near 100 men, but they advanced so suddenly that we could bring off but 20 of them, of whom there were three English—one of them were handed (was hanged ?) immediately, having formerly served in our army : their lancers did seem to follow eagerly upon our men in their retreat in great numbers, but we had not passing six men hurt, whereof one died, and not any of the rest miscarried or are missing. In the meantime, we were drawing back our army, and the enemy, when they saw the greatest of our number to be marching, made a show as if they would have followed us : they therefore sent down about 600 horse and as many musketeers to try, as I suppose, our behaviour in our retreat, as also to requite us if they could, sending three bodies of horse into the field next the moor, by the side of which we passed, but still under the favour of their musketeers, which lined the hedges ; but we, being content to play with them at their own game, whilst we amused them by presenting some horse before them, our musketeers, which in the meantime stole down upon their flank towards their passage, gave them such a peal, that it made the passage which they retired over seem I believe a great deal straiter, and the time much longer than at their coming over, after which they were a great deal better satisfied with our retreat, and this was all we could do with the enemy. I must confess we brought our horse home very weary, which did us more harm than the enemy could have done, until they be again refreshed, which we make no doubt will be in a very short time. We could entreat the world to be content with further expectation.

A summary of this letter is given in *Mercurius Aulicus* for March 14, 1644. After the events narrated in the letter, Newcastle retired to Durham, and devoted himself to endeavouring to straiten the quarters of the Scots and cut off their provisions, in which he was very successful (Rushworth III, ii, 615). The Scots succeeded, however, in taking a fort at South Shields on March 20, and in surprising on the same day a detachment of Newcastle's horse at Chester le Street. On March 23 Newcastle marched from Durham to Hilton near Sunderland, and unsuccessfully endeavoured to bring on a general engagement. The skirmishes which took place on March 24 and 25 are narrated from a despatch of Newcastle's in *Mercurius Aulicus* for March 30.

'It being expressly certified from the noble Marquis of Newcastle that on Sunday last (March 24) he got the Scots out to West Bedwick near Hilton Castle in the Bishopric of Durham, where they sat fast upon Bedwick Hill : my Lord Marquis had often invited them to fight, with overtures of many advantageous opportunities, but could not possibly draw them out : on this hill four regiments of his Excellency's foot fell to work with six regiments of the rebels. The fight began about three in the afternoon (March 24) and continued from that time till night, and continued more or less till next morning, the rebels all this while being upon their own *Mickle Midding*, and there they lay all night ; next morning (being Monday) the Lord Marquis followed them till afternoon, and then they vanished instantly into their trenches and retirements in Sunderland. Then his Excellency (seeing no hope of getting them out) drew off towards his quarters, and they being sensible of so many provocations, came on his rear (which was 500 horse) with all the horse they had (for as yet they never looked the Lord Marquis in the face), but the rear (with the loss of some thirty men killed and taken) presently faced about, being seconded by that valiant knight, Sir Charles Lucas, with his brigade of horse, who fell on so gallantly that he forced all their horse (which is about 3,000) to hasten up the hill to their cannon, all the way doing sharp execution upon them so as their Lancers lay plentifully upon the ground (many others being taken and brought away prisoners) their cannon all that while playing upon the Lord Marquis his horse with so little success as is not easily imagined. In both these fights (on Sunday and Monday) they that speak least reckon a full 1000 Scots killed and taken which cost the Lord Marquis 240 of his common soldiers, scarce an officer being either killed or taken, though many of their leaders are certainly cut off. Their foot ran twice, and would not stand longer than their officers forced them on with the sword ; the Lord Marquis hath taken many of their arms, especially of their Scottish pistols. Next morning (Tuesday) his Excellency drew towards them again, faced them a long while, but they had too much of the two days before, and would by no means be entreated to show themselves.'— (*Mercurius Aulicus*, March 30, 1644).

On the 25th of March, after this unsuccessful attempt to bring on a battle, Newcastle wrote to congratulate Rupert on his successful relief of Newark and to urge again his own need of assistance. ' I must assure your Highness ', he says, ' that the Scots are as big again in foot as I am, and their horse, I doubt, much better than ours are, so that if your Highness do not please to come hither, and that very soon too, the great game of your uncle's will be endangered, if not lost ' (Warburton, ii, 397 ; see also 399). In his old quarters at Durham, Newcastle awaited the arrival of aid and continued his former tactics. The Scots established their headquarters at Easington, midway between Hartlepool and Durham, where they continued till the 8th of April, and then marched to Quarendon Hill, within two miles of Durham. On the 11th of April took place the defeat of Bellasis at Selby, and on the 13th Newcastle commenced his retreat to York. His next letter is dated from York, 18th April (Warburton, ii, 433) ; he says that Fairfax and the Scots are too strong for him, and ' have put themselves in such a posture as will soon ruin us, unless there be some speedy course taken to give us relief'. I have not been able to find any letter of Newcastle giving an account of the later part of the campaign, or the retreat to York.

VIII

EIGHT LETTERS WRITTEN BY THE MARQUIS OF NEWCASTLE DURING HIS EXILE

Of the following letters, the first was intercepted and published in a newspaper, and it is uncertain to whom it was written. The other seven were all written to Secretary Nicholas.

My Lord,—Your Lordship's Letter by Creswell is so nobly kind, friendly, and so wise counsel, as it is too big for my Pen, Inke, and Paper, only it hath made me all over thankfulnesse, and that is as much as I can either say or do. For my estate they are now selling of, it is against all the old tenents that I should be a Traytor and Rebell, and all my estate confiscate, and I to be hanged without mercy, and none will lend me two shillings here, but flye me, and know not how to put bread into my mouth, as if I was

the arrantest knave and Rogue in the World, I vow to God the ridiculous-
nesse of it makes me laugh heartily, like the Gentleman that had his ship
taken from him by our wise, just, and grave privy Councellors.   Againe
to passe the time away withall, my Lord Bishop of Derry, my Lady Oneale
and my selfe gravely sat in Councel, as wise and provident Parents to provide the best we could for our children, agreed upon a Match between
my son Harry and her daughter, and gravely articled, bought eighteen
pennyworth of Ribond for the wooing, the old Lady a lean Chicken in a
Pipkin for the Dinner, with three preserved Cherries, and 5 drops of Syrup
by them for the banquet.   One wiser than the rest asked how it should be
performed, which our wisdomes never thought of before, so when my estate
was examined, besides the Parliaments selling of it, That my debts were
so great with what was intailed upon my Son Charles as I could estate
nothing.   The old Lady was very angry at that, but I had more reason
than modesty, I examined her, having examined old Ladies in my time,
and found she had as little.   So the times have broke that grave intention,
yet the joynture and portion being alike one might think it might go on.
And so Harry is a lusty Batchelor begging homeward for England, but the
young lady truly is very deserving and vertuous.   [I am] one of the cast
Privy Councellors his Majesty left here behind : Every letter and book
of News we gravely deliver our opinions thereof, but first wipe our mouthes
formally with our handkerchers, spit with a grace, and hem aloud, and
then say little to the purpose : If our doubtful braines cannot resolve, then
we shake our heads and shrugge our shoulders with prudence, saying time
will produce more, but the Scots He say no more.   The sweet Duke of Yorks
Court is no more then was in Noah's Ark, 18 person with some beasts, and
these 18 persons are in 15 factions at least, to practice against you come to
White-hall, Ratcliffe like an Hermits staffe, and Doctor Killegrew, Dr.
Statesman great projects that comes to nothing, nor can come to anything,
they have hurryed the sweet Duke up and down, as I dare swear his High-
nesse is weary of them, but could not but laugh at Matchivell Deveeke, that
gravely broke his braine with thinking that there was something in it, some
whatchecalle, which is his by-word.   God blesse your Grace, and tell me
when I shall waite of you at White-hall : my Lord I am entirely

Your Lordship's most faithful
obliged Servant
W. NEWCASTLE.

ANTWERPE *the* 8 *of Feb.* 1650
    Pray burn this letter.

(*Several Proceedings in Parliament*, 18—25, *Sept.*, 1651.)

NOBLE SIR,—I desire you will be pleased to put his Majesty in mind
that he will be graciously pleased to renew those offices and places unto
me, that the King his father of blessed memory gave me, that others may
not possess them, his Majesty not knowing of it ; and those I have had
and desire to have are the following :

 1. Lord Lieutenant of the County of Nottingham.
 2. Lord Lieutenant of the Forest of Sherwood, which that worthy per-
      son the Earl of Clare hath had from the Parliament ever since my
      misfortune.

3. Then Custos Rotulorum of the County of Nottingham.

4. And Custos Rotulorum of the County of Northumberland.

Then if please God his Majesty come to his throne, which I make no doubt of, certainly all my land that the rebels have possessed themselves of I may lawfully take possession of without troubling his Majesty; but whereas my traitorous servant hath sold any land to any of those rebels, that I may have my land again, since it was but in trust, which the law will give me. But I speak of it only in this case, that any of the rebels that the King might give to any courtier or others, if they have any of my land I shall have great trouble with them, though justly they cannot possess it; and therefore I humbly desire his Majesty there may be an exception made in my particular and in acquainting his Majesty with these particulars you will oblige me very much,—Your most faithful servant,

W. NEWCASTLE.

ANTWERP, *the 15th of August* 1654
  To Sir Ed. NICHOLAS

(*Domestic State Papers.* Record Office.)

NOBLE SIR,—I received yours of the 22d, and give you many hearty thanks for the favour, for I assure you there could nothing rejoice me more in the whole world than the King and the Duke of York to be so kind, and my daily prayers shall be that it may ever continue. Now I will give you my intelligence. I hear my friend and neighbour, Sir Gervase Clifton, who at least is seventy years old, hath lately married, as I take it her name is the Lady Alice Hastings, sister I believe to the Lord Loughborough, with £1000 portion, Sir Gervase his second wife, so that off the next wife he comes eight, and then I believe the mark will be out of his mouth. I speak like an experienced horseman. This lady, I believe, is in years for a maid, and a pretty tough hen for this Lent without eggs. I am so tormented about my book of horsemanship as you cannot believe, with a hundred several trades, I think, and the printing will cost above £1300, which I could never have done but for my good friends Sir H. Cartwright and Mr. Loving; and I hope they shall lose nothing by it, and I am sure they hope the like. I hope this next summer I may be so happy as to see you, and believe me,—I am affectionately our most faithful servant,

W. NEWCASTLE.

ANTWERP, *the 15th of Feb.* 1656

(*Domestic State Papers.* Record Office).

NOBLE SIR,—I received the favour of yours of the 22d, and you have obliged me very much, not only by your own letter, but by sending that of Sir Henry Bennet. I beseech you put his Majesty in mind of his gracious promise to me, in giving Sir Henry Bennet thanks for his favours to me. I hope by your news that the Swede will go down. We have it here very confidently reported, that the peace between the two crowns is very far advanced (and truly I am not so wise as not to believe it, for all things considered, methinks it is very probable), and then I hope the King cannot fail of their aid. There are many noblemen, or at least lords, that are comed over to Paris it is true, but those lords that can take such sudden apprehensions of fears so far off, I doubt will hardly have the courage to help our gracious Master to his throne—woful people—and the next generation of lords they tell me are fools. It will be a brave Upper House ! Pray present my humble service to my Lord Chancellor. I have been indisposed this week, but I thank God I am much better now. And in all conditions I shall be entirely your most faithful servant,

W. NEWCASTLE.

ANTWERP, 23d *Jan.* 1659
I write with so much freedom to you that I pray burn this.
(*Egerton MSS.* British Museum.)

Newcastle to Nicholas

NOBLE SIR,—I thank you for your last and your favour to me in presenting my humble thanks to the King. I thank God I am for the time very much mended ; for age, I am in less than a year of you, and hope we may both live to see better times, for I will always hope the best. The Duke of Gloucester went away this morning, and the Earl of Norwich galloping along with him, as also my Lord Berkeley ; the young lady, Mrs. Hyde, her brother, and Doctor Morley went away this morning too. The noble Lord of Ormond and his company will be with you to-morrow. The Earl of Norwich within a few days will be with you too. I spoke with a young gentleman, one Mr. Smith, newly comed (coumde) out of England ; he thinks that Cromwell and the Parliament will agree, but I think he knows little. But I spoke with another, an elderly man and a stout, that served in my army, and he says they will fall to pieces, and that there will be great factions and divisions in England. The merchants have it here that certainly there will be no peace between the two crowns and that the treaty is absolutely broke ; others say that it is piecing again : they report confidently that some English ships have met with some Spanish ships and sunk them, but I do not believe it. Now if you can make anything out of all this you do very well, for I protest I cannot. Pray remember my service to Lord Chancellor and thank him for his favours, and so I rest constantly your most faithful servant,

W. NEWCASTLE.

ANTWERP, *the 2d of April* 1659
(*Egerton MSS.,* 536, f. 336.)

Newcastle to Nicholas

NOBLE SIR,—I now have two petitions to you—one to present this enclosed humbly to his Majesty, the next that you would favour me so much as to give me the most timely notice of the assurance of the peace between Spain and France. The reason is, the Burgomasters and Governors of this town desired me to let them know if I could the certainty of it. I told them that my King's principal secretary was my very noble friend, and I would write unto him ; thus, by your favour, I shall ingratiate myself very much to this town. Pardon me thus trespassing upon you and believe me, I am very constantly your most faithful servant,

W. NEWCASTLE.

ANTWERP, *the 18th of April* 1659
My service to my Lord Chancellor.
(*Egerton MSS.* British Museum.)

Newcastle to Nicholas

Noble Sir,—I received yours of the 30th last, and give you many thanks for the favour of your most excellent news. I am sure we cannot be worse than we are, and I hope in God that this peace may prove considerable for the advantage of our gracious King. But your son writ to Mr. Topp that the Lower House was divided and that the two houses could not agree, and that it was thought they would be dissolved—this may be considerable indeed. We have it here by some letters that the army stands upon terms of their own, that is considerable and to the purpose if it be so ; but we have so many lies here at Antwerp that we know not what to believe, for this morning the Lord Wentworth and Sir Cecil Howard came to me and told me that Major Wood told them that one of the Prince of Condé's followers told him that Sir Robert Welsh his son, and three or four more had a plot to kill my gracious Master, and they had no sooner said it but I received your letter dated yesterday, so then they saw there was no such thing : God ever preserve my gracious Master from all knaves, fools, and bloody rascals. My service to your younger son, with many thanks for his favours to me about Monsieur Juliane (?) ; though he hath not answered it I do not care, so that now he knows my mind, which is sufficient. It was about a truck for horses, and I would be loth to give a good horse for a jade ; and though there is none that is a piece of a horseman amongst them, riders or others, yet I assure you the greatest of them are horse coursers beyond any in Smithfield, and so they are in France, for it is two professions, a good horseman and a horse courser. I pretend to the first, but know nothing of the second, for I'll cozen nobody ; I only take care not to be cozened, which they find I can do reasonable well at that. Believe me it is not an easy thing to have a good horse nor a rare man in any quality.

Antwerp, May Day 1659

(Egerton MSS. British Museum.)

Newcastle to Nicholas

Noble Sir,—I received yours of the 12th, and give you many thanks for your excellent good news. We have it here that the Parliament is dissolved by Cromwell, but he was forced to it by the army who told him if he would not dissolve they would, and then they say they came to Cromwell and took away all the dishes of meat he had but one. Cromwell went presently to Hampton Court, and letters from the Venetian ambassador say that he believes by this time there is a guard set upon him. Fleetwood is made General of the Army, and Lambert Lieutenant-general, and this is the redcoats which I always said would do what they list. Some talks the Presbyterians begin to appear in divers parts of the kingdom, but I doubt that yet. Great confusions and alterations is daily looked for, and I hope in God it will produce excellent things for the King, for certainly Fleetwood and Lambert can never make their advantage and settlement so well as to serve the King. My service to my Lord Chancellor, and tell him that now I hope to wait on him to Westminster to see him take possession of the Chancery, and upon one of my horses of manage, which will be the quietest, safest, and surest he or any man can have. You see how my hopes transports me with the passion I have for my gracious Master. God send us a good meeting at Whitehall, and so I rest constantly your most faithful servant

W. NEWCASTLE.

ANTWERP *the* 13*th May* 1659
(*Egerton MSS.* British Museum.)

IX

TO THE TWO MOST FAMOUS UNIVERSITIES OF ENGLAND

MOST FAMOUSLY LEARNED,—I here present to you this philosophical work, not that I can hope wise schoolmen and industrious, laborious students should value it for any worth, but to receive it without scorn, for the good encouragement of our sex, lest in time we should grow irrational as idiots, by the dejectedness of our spirits, through the careless neglects and despisements of the masculine sex to the female, thinking it impossible we should have either learning or understanding, wit or judgment, as if we had not rational souls as well as men, and we out of a custom of dejectedness think so too, which makes us quit all industry towards profitable knowledge, being employed only in low and petty employments which take away not only our abilities towards arts, but higher capacities in speculations, so as we are become like worms that only live in the dull earth of ignorance, winding ourselves sometimes out by the help of some refreshing rain of good education, which seldom is given us, for we are kept like birds in cages, to hop up and down in our houses, not suffered to fly abroad to see the several changes of Fortune, and the various humours ordained and created by nature, and wanting the experience of nature, we must needs want the understanding and knowledge, and so consequently prudence and invention of men. Thus by an opinion, which I hope is but an erroneous one in men, we are shut out of all power and authority, by reason we are never employed either in civil or martial affairs, our counsels are despised and laughed at, the best of our actions are trodden down with scorn by the overweening conceit men have of themselves, and through a despisement of us.

But I, considering with myself that if a right judgment and a true understanding and a respectful civility live anywhere, it must be in learned universities, where nature is best known, where truth is oftenest found, where civility is most practised, and if I find not a resentment here, I am very confident I shall find it nowhere, neither shall I think I deserve it, if you approve not of me ; but if I deserve not praise, I am sure to receive so much courtship from your sage society as to bury me in silence, that thus I may

E E

have a quiet grave, since not worthy a famous memory, for to lie
entombed under the dust of an university will be honour enough
for me, and more than if I were worshipped by the vulgar as a
deity. Wherefore, if your wisdoms cannot give me the bays, let
your charity strew me with cypress ; and who knows but, after
my honourable burial, I may have a glorious resurrection in following ages, since time brings strange and unusual things to pass—
I mean unusual to men, though not in nature. And I hope this
action of mine is not unnatural, though unusual for a woman to
present a book to the university, nor impudent, for it is honest,
although it seem vainglorious. But if it be, I am to be pardoned,
since there is little difference between man and beast, but what
ambition and glory makes.

(Dedication by the Duchess of *Philosophical and Physical Opinions*,
1663.)

X

SIR CHARLES LUCAS

Sir Charles was the youngest son of Thomas Lucas, of St. John's,
Colchester. The Duchess gives an account of his youth in her
autobiography. He served, like most young soldiers of his time,
in the wars of the Low Countries. In the second Scotch war he
commanded a troop of horse (*Calendar of Domestic State Papers*,
1640–1, 318). He was knighted 27 July 1639. From the beginning
of the Civil War he served in the King's army. He was wounded
at the battle of Powick Bridge, September 22, 1642 (Warburton's
Prince Rupert, i, 409). He served under Prince Rupert also at
the capture of Cirencester, February 2d, 1643, and a contemporary
account notices his mercy in taking prisoners (*Bibliotheca Glouces-
trensis*, 170). On July 1, 1643, with three troops of his own regiment, he defeated Colonel Middleton with 400 horse and dragoons
at Padbury, taking 40 prisoners and killing above 100 of the enemy
(*Mercurius Aulicus*). In the autumn of the same year he served
for some months in Lincolnshire and Nottinghamshire, and commanded in an attack on Nottingham on January 16, 1644. The
committee, describing the attack in a letter to Gilbert Millington,
say that he 'reports himself General of this county and Lincolnshire' (*Memoirs of Colonel Hutchinson*, vol. i, pp. 298, 388). Immediately after this Lucas was ordered into Yorkshire. A remonstrance
of the committee of Newark complains that the recent capture
of Gainsborough and the Isle of Axholm 'have moved his Excellency the Lord Marquis of Newcastle to engarrison Doncaster now
in fortifying, and to command Sir Charles Lucas with his own regi-

ment, and the Lincolnshire horse, in all about 1400, to quarter
thereabouts for securing that fortification, which is like to be a
work of time, and so to procrastinate Sir Charles Lucas his coming
into these parts (whom we hoped to have been sent by your Majesty
for our immediate assistance) to the apparent hazard of this garrison
and these two counties' (Rushworth, III, ii, 305). From Doncaster, on February 2, 1644, Lucas wrote to Rupert a very interesting letter, thanking him for his recommendation to Lord Newcastle
(Warburton, ii, 370). He joined Newcastle in the north some
time before March 6th, and distinguished himself in the skirmish
at Hilton on March 25th (Rushworth, III, ii, 615-6). When the
Marquis was obliged to shut himself up in York, Lucas in command
of the horse was sent to quarter in Nottinghamshire and the Midland counties, and to take part in any attempts at the relief of the
besieged. He accordingly joined Rupert in his march to York,
and was one of the commanders of the left wing of the Prince's
horse at Marston, in which defeat he was taken prisoner, although
his division successfully routed that of Sir Thomas Fairfax, which
was its immediate opponent. Rupert as soon as possible negotiated
the exchange of Sir Charles, which probably took place in the
winter of 1644-5 (see letter in Warburton's *Prince Rupert*, iii, 38).
He was certainly released before March 1645, for in a letter of
March 5 Digby discusses the question of his appointment to the
government of Berkeley Castle (Warburton, iii, 66).

In July 1645 Lucas writes to Rupert from Berkeley complaining
of the inadequacy of the garrison, and the disaffection of his soldiers,
and of the people of the neighbouring country (*Hist. MSS. Rep.
ix*, pt. ii, p. 437). Berkeley Castle was stormed by Colonel Rainsborough on September 25, 1645 (Sprigge, *Anglia Rediviva*, p. 136,
ed. 1854). According to Sprigge it had endured nine days' siege,
but the capture of the church and outworks, and the planting of
cannon thereupon, forced the Governor to sound a parley and
treat. 'The castle was surrendered upon these articles: the
soldiers to march out without arms; the Governor, Sir Charles
Lucas, with three horses and arms and not above £50 in money;
every field officer with two horses, and but £5 in money; foot
captains with swords but no horse; the soldiers with not above
5s. apiece.' In the castle were taken provisions for six months.
Lucas had answered to the first summons 'that he would eat horse
flesh before he would yield, and man's flesh when that was done',
and returned an equally peremptory answer to the second summons.
The garrison marched out about 500 strong, but probably the disaffection before mentioned by Lucas still existed and contributed
to the surrender, and it is not likely that it had been increased in
numbers since he complained of its inadequacy to Rupert in July.

The table at the end of Sprigge's work seems to imply that forty of the garrison were killed and ninety taken prisoners during the siege. Before many weeks passed Lucas was again actively employed. In the diary of Richard Symonds for December 23, 1645, it is stated ' Lord Astley came to Worcester, being General of these four counties, Sir Charles Lucas with him, Lieutenant-general of the horse.' His career came to an end three months later with the defeat of Astley's army at Stow in the Wold in the following March. The name of Lucas is not mentioned in the list of prisoners given in many reports of the battle ; for instance, in the letter of Colonel Morgan to the speaker. This is explained by a circumstance mentioned by Vicars. ' Sir Charles Lucas, as was credibly reported, was also taken in the fight, but immediately after rescued by a party of fire-locks of the enemy, and on his rescue fled into the wood hard by for hoped safety ; but after the fight our forces searching the wood for stragglers found there the said Sir Charles Lucas ' (*Burning Bush*, 399). Thus Lucas became a prisoner, and it is presumed that he obtained his liberty by engaging himself to Fairfax not to serve again against the Parliament. The sole evidence for this fact, probable enough in itself, is in the letters exchanged between Fairfax and Lucas on June 19, 1648. Soon after the siege of Colchester began, Fairfax sent a letter to the besieged ' to acquaint them that Sir Charles Lucas had forfeited his parole, his honour and faith, being his prisoner upon parole, and therefore not capable of command or trust in martial affairs ' (Rushworth, IV, ii, 1160). To which Lucas replied : ' Sir, I wonder you should question me of any such engagement, since I purchased my freedom and estate at a high rate by a great sum of money, which I paid into Goldsmith's Hall, for which according to the ordinances of the two Houses I was to enjoy my freedom and estate. When I conceived myself in this condition, I sent a letter to your secretary, desiring him to advertise your Lordship that I had punctually performed my engagements as they stood in relation to your Lordship. Upon which I had notice from him that you accepted of my respects to you, which truly have never been wanting to your person. But, my Lord, besides my inclinations and duty to the service I am in at present, be pleased to examine whether the law of nature hath not instigated me to take my sword again into my hand, for when I was in peaceable manner in London, there was a price set upon me by the committee of Derby House, upon which I was constrained to retire myself into my own country, and to my native town, for refuge ' (*Fairfax Correspondence*, iii, 57).

In this letter Lucas admits that such an engagement as the one supposed to have been contracted after his capture at Stow had actually existed. At the same time he puts forward two pleas :

the first, that his engagement to Fairfax had been ended by his payment of a composition for his estates ; the second, that the action of the Parliament against him had justified him in taking up arms in self-defence. With regard to the first it may fairly be held that the personal obligation to Fairfax had been superseded and ended by the arrangement with the civil government ; from being a prisoner Lucas had become a citizen, and substituted for his former obligation to the commander-in-chief a new obligation to the civil power. In the list of compounders Sir Charles Lucas, knight, of Horsey, Essex, appears as having paid in part a fine fixed at £508, 10s. But the committee at Goldsmith's Hall, to which this composition was paid, exacted from delinquents an oath not to assist the King against the Parliament, ' nor any forces raised without the consent of the two Houses of Parliament in this cause or war ' (vide Husbands' *Collection of Ordinances*, fol., 1646, pp. 636, and 739). We know from his own petition that Lucas took this oath. The action of Sir Charles in taking up arms again in 1648 was a distinct breach of this engagement (*Calendar of the Committee for Compounding with Delinquents*, iii, 1821).

With reference to the second plea it may be stated that Lucas more than any other man was responsible, if Matthew Carter is to be trusted, for the refusal by the loyalists of Essex of the indemnity offered them by Parliament if they laid down their arms. (Passed in the House of Commons, June 5, 1648). Rushworth gives the following news from Essex under June 7 : ' That the Parliament's commissioners having published the indemnity at Bow to those that should lay down arms, Sir William Hicks and divers others of the gentlemen submitted, and the Lord Goring retreated back from thence. But Sir Charles Lucas, that eminent cavalier, is come into them, and keeps up the soldiers, making great promises to them ; and by his insinuations hath prevailed with the discontented party not to lay down arms.' It must be admitted that this circumstance, confirmed by the evidence of Rushworth and Carter, does not seem to bear out the statement of Sir Charles Lucas that he took up arms in self-defence. At the same time he expressly states that the committee of Derby House put a price upon his head, and till the truth or falsehood of that statement is ascertained a final judgment on this second plea is hardly possible.

For a detailed account of the siege the reader must be referred to Mr. G. F. Townshend's *Siege of Colchester*, to Mr. Markham's *Life of Fairfax*, and to the anonymous author of *The History and Antiquities of Colchester Castle* (Colchester, 1882). Carter's *True Relation of the Honourable though Unfortunate Expedition of Kent, Essex and Colchester*, together with the contemporary diurnals and the extracts in Rushworth, supply a full account of the incidents of the struggle. The pamphlet entitled *Colchester's Tears* charges Sir Charles Lucas with cruelty to the inhabitants of the town during the siege, but it deserves very little credit. However, Clarendon, in the extract quoted on p. 158, accuses Lucas of considerable harshness. But Rushworth quotes a letter saying ' the Lords Goring and Capel carry things very high and peremptorily, but Sir Charles Lucas more moderate ' (1181).

Colchester capitulated on August 27, 1648, and Lisle and Lucas were shot on August 28 by sentence of a court-martial. By the terms of the capitulation (quoted in the note to p. 49), the superior officers had rendered themselves to mercy, so this execution was not a breach of the terms of the capitulation. Fairfax gives two reasons for the execution : the first, 'satisfaction of military justice ' ; the second, ' avenge for the innocent blood they have caused to be spilt, and the trouble, damage, and mischief they have brought upon the town, this country, and the kingdom ' (Rushworth, vol. vii, p. 1243). The first of these reasons evidently refers to the breach of parole with which Fairfax charged Lucas. If the argument stated above holds good, this had been superseded by an engagement to the Parliament, and it would have been juster to leave the punishment of the breach of that engagement to the Parliament. The second reason given for the sentence, the punishment for raising a civil war (satisfaction of political justice, as it might be termed), is obviously a subject which should have been reserved for the judgment of a political authority like the Parliament rather than decided by a General, or a council of war. Parliament might have condemned Lucas, as it afterwards condemned Hamilton and Capel, and the justice of the sentence could hardly have been impeached, except by those who are prepared to hold that it is in no case just to impose the penalty of death on the leaders of a civil war. With reference to the personal share of Fairfax in this sentence, it may be pointed out that Clarendon says that ' the manner of taking the lives of these worthy men was generally imputed to Ireton, who swayed the General, and was upon all occasions of an unmerciful and bloody nature ' (*Rebellion*, xi, 109). In *Mercurius Pragmaticus* for October 3–10, 1648, the following statement is made : ' In (that) unworthy act it's said his Excellency had no hand, but only the council of war, by the special instigation of Ireton, Rainsborough, and Whalley.' An account of the death of Lucas is given in *Mercurius Pragmaticus* for August 29 to September 5, 1648. It will be seen that the conclusion here adopted differs from that arrived at in the note to p. 49, in granting that the composition might be fairly considered to put an end to the engagement of Sir Charles to Lord Fairfax.

A paper on *The Case of Lucas and Lisle*, by Mr. J. H. Round, is printed in vol. viii of The *Transactions of the Royal Historical Society*, new series. It gives the arguments against Fairfax.

XI

LORD NEWCASTLE'S ACCOUNT OF THE BATTLE OF ATHERTON MOOR

The original of the despatch in which Lord Newcastle announced his victory has not survived, but it appears to me to be contained in the following pamphlet. The pamphlet does not bear on its title the name of any place, but the device of an Oxford printer shows it to have been printed at Oxford. No author's name is attached to it, nor is there any signature ; but it is evidently an official relation, and the use of the first person (" I sent troops, etc.") shows it to have been written by the royalist commander-in-chief. Its style also rather resembles that of Newcastle's despatch on his campaign against the Scots, printed in Appendix vii. For these reasons I insert it here, but as being doubtful, have given it the last place in the Appendix.

An Express Relation of the Passages and Proceedings of his Majesty's Army, under the Command of his Excellence the Earl of New-castle, against the Rebels under the Command of the Lord Fairfax and his Adherents

[Printed in the year 1643.]

' We marched from Pomfret towards Bradford, and in our way thither we summoned Sir John Savile, commander of Howley, to deliver up that house, and lay down his arms so unjustly taken up, who returned an uncivil answer, and that he would keep it maugre our forces, whereupon we planted our cannon against that house, and environed it upon Wednesday the 21st of June in the after-noon, and next morning took it by assault, and in it the said com-mander-in-chief and all his officers and soldiers, about 245, some few whereof were slain, the rest taken prisoners ; where, by the unseasonableness of the weather, we were enforced to remain till Friday the 30th of June, from whence we marched early towards Bradford, and when we had marched two miles or thereabouts we found a great body of men, a greater number of foot than we, and almost all musketeers, and some twenty troops of horse, and had possessed a place called Adderton Moor, and taken the most ad-vantageous places thereof, and lined several hedges with musketeers, and played so fiercely upon us, and that before the whole body of our foot could be drawn up, and their horse likewise possessing a plain field and a great ditch betwixt us lined with musketeers, and keeping our horse in a ground full of pits, that for the space of two hours or thereabouts, we were forced to give ground, though very little ; but when our cannon was well placed, and our foot once drawn up, within half-an-hour we put their foot on the right wing of the battle to retire, and pursued them so hotly, that they presently were put into a disorderly retreat ; whereupon part of our horse fell upon that wing, and the cannon playing upon the body of their horse killed many and routed them, together with our horse charging at that time, so we pursued them, killing and taking them to Bradford town end, which was more than two miles, in which chase was slain (as is supposed) about 500 of the enemies, and about 1400 taken prisoners, amongst which many officers, together with three field pieces, and all their ammunition there, which was not much. We had many soldiers hurt, two colonels of horse slain, Heron and Howard, and some officers hurt, as Colonel Throckmorton, Colonel Carnaby, and Captain Maison, all recoverable, and not above twenty common soldiers slain.

'That night we came before Bradford, a strong town, and ill approaching to it, yet we made our approaches that night. The next day we had placed our cannon and made places of batteries very near the town and church, where they had two drakes upon the top of the steeple, and lined the steeple with woolpacks ; yet our cannon dismounted their drakes upon the top of the steeple, and battered the steeple so as none could stay on it, where they had many musketeers, and so we got both the ends of the town before Sunday night ; and in the night-time Sir Thomas Fairfax, governor of the town, his lady, Major Gifford, and Sir Henry Fowlis, escaped out of the town, and upon a moor was forced to charge with their party a party of our horse, where his lady and his cornet were taken prisoners, but he and the other two being well horsed escaped, though pursued very near Leeds, which was above five miles ; and that morning our men entered the town, took prisoners :

1. Colonel Malliver (Mauleverer ?).
2. Sergeant-Major Willshire.
3. Captain Mudd.
4. Captain Rogers.
5. Captain Bland.
6. Captain O'Neal.
7. Captain White.
8. Captain Smith.

9. Captain Dent.
10. Captain Stanley.
11. Captain Feure.
12. Lieutenant Popler.
13. Lieutenant Loveday.
14. Lieutenant Moore.
15. Lieutenant Sad.
    Sergeant Floyd.
    Sergeant Brabant.
    William Lowden and Nathaniel Goffe, gunners,

with all or most of the common soldiers, which are in number 300 or thereabouts, besides the enlarging of 200 prisoners of ours there, and taking of arms which are yet uncertain in number.

'That very day, within three hours after, came a captain of ours, who among divers other prisoners at Leeds, finding that my Lord Fairfax and his son were inclined to leave the town (as they did) attended with three or four troops of horse, 200 dragooners, and 300 foot, broke out of prison, possessed themselves of the magazine, took all the arms, which were 1500 at least, eight barrels of powder, and 12 pieces of ordnance, with a very great proportion of match and ball, and so kept the town till I sent forces into it, besides the enlarging of 700 prisoners there. The Lord Fairfax and his son marched towards Selby, in which march his 300 foot run away from him; and his forces left, being discovered by our forces at the garrison of Cawood were charged by them, and they fled into the town of Selby. Our forces being too weak for them were forced to retire; so my Lord, his son Sir Thomas, Major Gifford, Sir Henry Fowlis, and Sir Thomas Mauleverer, took a boat and passed themselves therein; and swimming their horses over the river, and as their men were passing over some of them were drowned with crowding the boats, and so they fled, we conceive, to Hull or to Nottingham, but to which is not certain.

'The same day news was brought us from Halifax, that all the forces were run from thence, and have taken with them all our prisoners that remained there, and so we are possessed of that town, as also of Denton House, my Lord Fairfax, his house, wherein there was a small garrison, two drakes, 200 men and arms.'

APPENDIX XII

THE DUKE OF NEWCASTLE'S RULES FOR HORSE RACING

' Being commanded by his Excellency the Lord Marquis of New-castle to publish the following articles for his new Course, I am first to inform you, that the work was begun so late, and is so great, viz. : the ploughing of five miles in length, and a considerable breadth, with the harrowing of it twice over, and sowing it with hay seed to sord (?) it, that there will be no firm riding on it before the last of July, when my Lord intends to give a cup of 5*l*., and the same he will do on the last of August and September, then ending the Course for this year.   But the next year (if God grant his Excellency life and health) he means to begin it on the last of April, continuing it on the last of each moneth till the last of Sep-tember inclusively, six months in all, giving each moneth a cup of 5*l*.

' THE ARTICLES

' 1. The horses are all to meet at Sparton-hill-top between eleven and twelve, where the riders are to be justly weighed, the weight ten stone downweight, by the weights (as they call them) of ' Aver-du-poyse ' : the horses are to be bridled, sadled, and shod.   After the riders are justly weighed by such a gentleman as shall be demed to be a just judge, not only of the riders weight, but also to judge who comes first to the stoup ; another gentleman must be appointed at the twelve-score-stoup, to judge what horse is rid out of distance, which is a maine businesse, and a third must be desired to see them start fair.

' 2. The horses must be led down from Sparton-hill to the start-ing-place ; and there must be three heats, the first heat to Sparton-hill, there to rub half an hour, and then the judge is to give them warning to get up and start ; but if in that half-hour they relieve their horses with anything but fair water, or if they ride out of distance, or the riders want weight, they must lose the cup ; only there is allowed two pound for wasting.   The second heat is to end where they begun last, and two gentlemen must be desired to see, not onely who comes first to the stoup, but at the twelve-score-stoup who rides out of distance, and who not : and 'twere well to have a flag at the ending stoup of each heat to be let down as soon as the first horse is past the stoup, for the Judges easier discern who rides within distance and who not : the riders must be weighed every heat, the relief is to be onely water, the rub but half an hour, and then the Judge is to bid them mount.

' 3. There being three heats he that wins the most heats wins the Cup, so he rides within distance, not otherwise, but that horse which is foremost the last heat ; this will make them ride for it. The stakes are ten shillings an horse, and to be put into the hands of the Judges who are to deliver them to the second horse.

' 4. He that wins the Cup saves his own stake, the second horse shall have all the rest.

' 5. It is to be considered that if any rider whip another rider, or his horse on the face, or pull back another's bridle, he shall lose the cup.

' 6. No bystander must ride in with the horses, to face, stop, or turn them over, or any way to hinder them, but must ride aloof from them.   If any such fault be committed, I must implore the gentry to help me in the legal punishing of the offenders.

' His Excellency saith, that, seeing he makes his Course only for the pleasure of the gentry, he hopes they will take in good part, he having no other end in it, except his Lordship's own contentment.   But his Excellency adds that he never yet knew any public thing that was not found fault with, and that everywhere there be many teachers, for if people did not find fault with everything, they would not be thought wise in anything : but his Lordship is very confident he shall find nothing of this humour amongst those noble persons whom herein he desires to serve.   And he commands me to tell you, that though this be not the Law of the Medes and Persians, yet he will alter nothing in it.   Every man may put in his horse, mare, or gelding at his pleasure, 'tis the Liberty of the Subject, and so his that sets up the Course.   When any man doth the like, he may make the Law what he pleases.   In the meantime his Lordship hopes this Course will please you all, since he has no other end in it.

' His Excellency further commands me to let you know, that his Course or heats continue no longer than his Lordship's good liking.

' Thus have I obeyed his Excellency's commands,

' Jo. ROLLESTON.'

26 May, 1662.   Given to me by Hen. Hall, the University Printer. A. Woode.'

(Bod. Lib., Wood 276A, 149.)

INDEX

G G

INDEX OF OBSOLETE WORDS AND PHRASES

www.ingramcontent.com/pod-product-compliance
Lightning Source LLC
Chambersburg PA
CBHW031345070726
47496CB00017B/1786